The
Time Engine

The
Time Engine

THE FOURTH BOOK OF THE MOONWORLDS SAGA

Sean McMullen

TOR®

A TOM DOHERTY ASSOCIATES BOOK

NEW YORK

THE TIME ENGINE

Map by Jennifer Hanover

A Tor Book
Published by Tom Doherty Associates, LLC
175 Fifth Avenue
New York, NY 10010

www.tor-forge.com

Tor® is a registered trademark of Tom Doherty Associates, LLC.

Library of Congress Cataloging-in-Publication Data

McMullen, Sean, 1948–
The time engine / Sean McMullen.—1st ed.
    p. cm.
"A Tom Doherty Associates book."
ISBN-13: 978-0-7653-1876-3
ISBN-10: 0-7653-1876-8
1. Time travel—Fiction. I. Title
PR9619.3.M3268 T56 2008
823'.914—dc22

                          2008020062

First Edition: July 2008

Printed in the United States of America

0 9 8 7 6 5 4 3 2 1

For Chris Lotts

Because without the people who work behind the scenes,
those of us in front of the scenes would not be there.

Those who make the worst use of their time are the first to complain of its shortness.

—JEAN DE LA BRUYÈRE

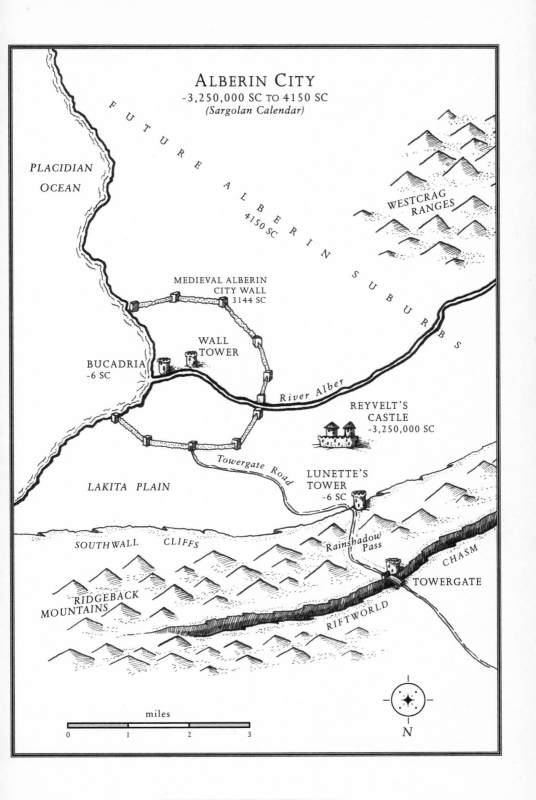

ALBERIN CITY
-3,250,000 SC TO 4150 SC
(Sargolan Calendar)

PLACIDIAN
OCEAN

F U T U R E   A L B E R I N   S U B U R B S

4150 SC

WESTCRAG
RANGES

MEDIEVAL ALBERIN
CITY WALL
3144 SC

WALL
TOWER

BUCADRIA
-6 SC

River Alber

REYVELT'S
CASTLE
-3,250,000 SC

Towergate Road

LAKITA PLAIN

LUNETTE'S
TOWER
-6 SC

SOUTHWALL   CLIFFS

Rainshadow
Pass

CHASM

RIDGEBACK
MOUNTAINS

TOWERGATE

RIFTWORLD

miles

0   1   2   3

N

The
Time Engine

PROLOGUE: PAST IMPERFECT

On the very last day of the year 3144 I vanished out of my life, such as it was. I admit that this does sound like death, but I am still alive. The problem is that I am now immortal.

✴　✴　✴

Upon that day I had just returned from a patrol in the West Quadrant, and was looking forward to having a quiet ale at the Mermaid's Slipper. As taverns go, it was an unlikely one for an inspector in the Wayfarer Constables to choose for relaxation, because more vice, danger, and criminal intent were enclosed between its four walls than any other alehouse on the continent. I walked through the door. The conversations faded to silence. I sat at a table. People in the immediate vicinity shrank away out of earshot, even to the extent of leaving the tables adjacent to mine empty. A wall of muscle with one eye and a meticulously shaven head swaggered over and stood before me.

"The usual, 'spector?"

"If you please, Craglin."

After three months of patrol, continually in the company of my squad, I was desperate for some time to myself. In the Mermaid's Slipper I was guaranteed that. I was known to be above corruption, so none of the regulars ever approached me with stolen merchandise or offers too good to refuse. Better still, none of the regulars wanted me to hear anything that they had to say to each other, so none even came near me. Nobody who knew me liked the place, so they never came with me. Even the lamplight girls avoided the place, so none would be sauntering up to me in search of work. By the time my ale arrived I had allowed my mind to go serenely blank.

"How is your wife, Craglin?" I asked as I paid.

"In t' stocks again, 'spector."

"Oh dear. Should I have a word with the magistrate?"

"Nah, couple more days won't do no 'arm t' baggage. I needs me sleep, don't ye know?"

"As you will."

"Good patrol, 'spector?"

"Worrisome. Electocratic agitators are in Hadraly. They want their king to stand for election. He wants to pursue them over our border and torture them to death, and is threatening war if we do not allow it."

"Aht, oligarchical reactionary monarchists got no place in t' future, that's as I sees it. What's it fer year's eve wi' yerself, 'spector?"

"I am to meet with my lady and her mother, apparently they have some surprise planned."

"Suppose I should be away ter stocks an' visit me lady come midnight, or I'll never hear t' matter's end."

Craglin left, and I settled down to enjoy some more peace. The other patrons had by now accepted that although I was a Wayfarer inspector with a field magistrate's crest, I had no interest in them. The buzz and rumble of conversation gradually returned to the room as money changed hands, winks and nods were exchanged, hands were waved, and ale was consumed.

It was the last day of the limbo year—in Greater Alberin, anyway. In 3144, by the old calendar, the kingdom of Greater Alberin had changed forever. First an invasion fleet had arrived from the moonworld Lupan, traveling in huge pottery cylinders. Their sorcerers had smashed our defenses and put our leaders to flight, but into the space left vacant stepped a former member of my Wayfarer squad, Riellen. That was the year's second big event, and it was of far greater consequence than the first. Riellen had preached electocracy, government by election. With this creed she not only managed to unite Greater Alberin, she had led the beaten, humbled kingdom out of its own ruins to defeat the otherworldly invaders. Now she was abroad, preaching electocracy to our neighbors.

Back in Alberin, at the scene of Riellen's first triumph, the calendar was to be changed in her honor. 3145 would become 1 YE, the first year of electocracy. We were currently in the last day of the year zero of the new calendar, the limbo year. Great celebrations were planned for the city, but all that was still four hours away, at midnight.

Throughout Greater Alberin there were celebrations to mark the first new year of a new era, because alone on the continent of Scalticar, we were ruled by an elected presidian. True, our presidian was a reformed undead fiend who had sworn off blood and come back to life, but when you consider that he had beaten a field of lawyers, accountants, priests, and nobles to win the job, we were very lucky to have him.

My thoughts drifted to the members of my squad and what they would be doing. Solonor, who was a gnome, was at some bawdy gnome show. Wallas, who was a talking cat, had tagged along. Lavenci was both the squad's forensic sorceress and my fiancé, but I would soon be with her again. Roval was more than a mere constable, but I could never learn what he really was. Greater Alberin was spreading electocracy to its neighbors, but officially Greater Alberin was doing nothing of the sort. Exports like that cause wars, after all, so Roval was hard at work in the shadows. Did Roval ever celebrate anything, I wondered?

The door of the taproom opened, and conversations were instantly replaced with astonished silence. A woman was standing in the doorway. I had been a patron of the tavern for some years, and apart from lamplight girls, the only woman I had ever seen in there was the former ship's figurehead that was bolted above the serving board. The newcomer was not dressed in anything specific, but darkness hung about her like robes and there was an ominous sparkling in her vicinity. She was carrying a large and corpulent black cat under one arm. The tapman grasped Craglin's arm, muttered something, and pointed to the new arrival. Craglin shook his head and took a step back. The tapman strode across the floor, put his hands on his hips, and barred her way.

The woman put out her hand and pushed against his chest. The front of his tunic caught fire. He turned and ran screaming from the taproom.

I had by now recognized the cat to be Constable Wallas, but although the woman was familiar, I could not quite place her. Her face had a very odd aspect to it, as if it were being seen through a smoked glass. After a glance about the taproom she walked straight over to my table and placed Wallas upon it. It was only now that I recognized her.

"Ah, should I make introductions?" asked Wallas as I stood and bowed.

"This is Lady Velander, a glass dragon," I responded.

"You are Inspector Danolarian, who commands Constable Wallas," she stated.

"Has Wallas managed to get himself into trouble again?" I asked.

"Wallas is relatively innocent. It is one of our number who is at fault."

Wallas, running foul of a glass dragon? It did not seem possible. True, he could be annoying, and back when he was a human courtier he had been quite obnoxious, but since being transformed into a cat he had more or less behaved himself. A glass dragon had been responsible for that transformation. It had been punishment for some transgression, but Wallas had not been near one since then.

"My life is in danger," said Wallas fearfully. "Another dragon creature, she almost caught me."

"I cannot stay long, you must help him," added Velander.

"Can someone please explain all this to me?" I asked.

"You are Constable Roval's commander," said Velander. "You must know that he was once in love with the sorceress Terikel."

"That I do."

"Terikel betrayed him with a number of other men. Did you know that?"

"Did anyone not know?" asked Wallas.

"It was not malice, or even passion, it was her way of getting things done. Important things. Had she been wiser she might have used other means, but that was her way. She thought Roval would never have to know, but he found out."

"I know, he spent his first two years in my squad in the company of the bottle," I replied. "During the Lupanian Invasion he came back from the edge, and he has been well ever since."

"But Terikel has not," said Velander. "The guilt from the pain she caused Roval drove her away from human company, and she was accepted as a neophyte glass dragon. Young glass dragons are well known for being unstable, and even dangerous, but we try to keep them to the wilderness, where they can do little harm. About a year ago Terikel left the support of the elders and our places of power in the mountains of southern Acrema. She began roaming the world of mortals, hunting down and slaying all of those who . . . who had taken the most fulsome delight of her company after she met Roval. One was eaten by sea creatures before she got to him, but others have been found with their chests torn open, as if by white-hot talons."

She placed her hand flat on the table, grew talons that shimmered with heat, then tore up a handful of smoking splinters from the surface. Wallas leaped up into my arms and sank his claws into my trail cloak.

"Only glass dragons can do that," Velander continued. "Terikel is quenching her guilt in blood. Your former commander, Captain Gilvray, was her latest victim. Before that a court minstrel named Selford died by her talons. We thought that Constable Andry Tennoner was the only survivor, and when he was taken to a place of safety, we thought Terikel's inner obsessions and fiends would be put to rest. It was not the case."

I took Wallas by the scruff of his neck and held him up to my face.

"You too?" I asked in disbelief.

"No, no, not at all," protested Wallas.

"It was a marginal transgression," explained Velander. "Terikel agreed to lie with Wallas because otherwise he would not—"

"But we never did!" interjected Wallas.

"Be that as it may, she did agree. To her that amounts to another betrayal of Roval, and the reek of that betrayal can only be washed away with blood."

"My blood," said Wallas apprehensively as I placed him back on the table.

"Is she nearby?" I asked.

"Is she ever!" exclaimed Wallas. "You never saw the like! Smoking pieces of black cat all over the rooftops."

"But you are unharmed."

"She attacked an event, a gathering of cats. It was a solemn occasion, a ceremony held on the eve of every new year."

"It is called the Sky Gymkhana," said Velander. "Naked female gnomes ride black tomcats across the roofs in the Wharfside quarter of Alberin, and male gnomes sponsor the cats. After the race there are unseemly activities, with the riders and sponsors paired up according to who finished in what place. This time the cats watch, and—"

"Is all this detail really necessary?" protested Wallas, staring down at the table.

"Fortunately for Wallas he is not the fastest cat on the rooftops."

"Well my rider was hardly the smallest gnome in Alberin!"

"Terikel struck at the end of the race, she did not realize that Wallas could have been so very far behind the tail end of the field. He arrived just as I did. Terikel fled when she saw me, but she knows that Wallas is still alive. Now I must go."

"Go?" I exclaimed. "But Terikel is still out there."

"That she is."

"But what about Wallas?"

"Yes, what about the cat?" Wallas added.

"There is nothing more that I can do here. Glass dragons have a certain empathy, and Terikel and I were very close as humans. Now she is radiating mania, and I do not have the experience to resist her influence. My mind tells me that she is insane, yet she is still my friend and . . . and somehow I too want to ease her pain by killing Wallas."

Wallas bounded up into my arms again.

"I am going," said Velander. "That is the only option open to me. The elders will hear my findings, and they will deal with Terikel."

"When?" cried Wallas.

"In their own time. Fortune be with you, Wallas. I have delivered you to the inspector, but I can do no more. Inspector, I know we meet again."

With those words she left. I looked around the taproom, and discovered that I was the only patron left. Craglin slowly emerged from behind the serving board. For some moments there was silence, then I heard the great whoosh of wings from somewhere outside. Velander, leaving. Velander, leaving as a glass dragon. Velander, showing anyone who was interested where she was leaving from. Suddenly I realized that she had been warning me about herself, as much as Terikel. "I want to ease her pain by killing Wallas," she had said. She had rescued

Wallas from Terikel, yet now she had shown Terikel where she had left him.

"Craglin, we are going," I called across the taproom. "If a very strange lady calls in, tell her what happened here, and that I have already fled with the talking cat."

"That's me," said Wallas.

At first I did not know where to go or what to do. Bundling Wallas into my pack, I hurried off into the narrow streets of Alberin. All about me crowds watched fire castings bursting in the sky above the city. The municipal sorcerers were putting on a show for the citizens, making sure everyone knew that they were as loyal and committed to electocracy as anyone else. The castings threw dancing, grotesque shadows, masking the approach of the shadow that I dreaded.

I saw her before she had managed to get too close. Whatever Terikel's powers and energies, I was better at the game of stealth. I was watching for any shape that lurked at the edge of my peripheral vision, but which dodged out of sight when I turned my head. Just such a shape was indeed there, close behind. It was a shape that glowed ever so slightly. Very quickly I established that Terikel gave me an extra margin of perhaps ten yards whenever I looked back to her.

A laneway loomed dark ahead of me. I glanced back to make Terikel dodge out of sight—and skipped sideways into the entrance. After nine paces into the blackness I leaped for the shape of a sign, caught it, and heaved myself straight up. From the sign I sprang across the laneway to the low roof opposite. Several slates smashed as I landed, but enough of them held to support my weight. I flattened myself out and lay still.

Down on the cobbles, a thin figure that sparkled dimly and crackled with badly masked energies tracked me to the door, then stopped. The light from her pale face actually lit up the sign, which declared the establishment to be the Sailor's Fancy. She knocked. A woman clad in enough lace to edge a medium-sized handkerchief opened the door, took one look at the glowing specter that was Terikel, and slammed the door shut. As I heard the rattle of the door's bolt from inside, on the outside I saw two hands whose fingers were tipped with white-hot talons burning into the timbers. Terikel began to tear smoking boards away, and fragments of burning door lit up the lane. From inside there were screams of outrage, then alarm.

Terikel entered, and almost immediately I heard the sounds of some sort of fight. A man was flung through a window whose shutters were closed. Normally this would have been impressive enough, but this man was in two pieces. Minimally clad women and men began hurrying out through the door; then a woman emerged wearing a black cat suit and carrying a feather duster. As she hurried off down the lane, Terikel emerged and ran after her. I suspect that the woman's life was saved by a real black cat that shot across their path. Terikel pursued the cat over a fence and vanished.

I crossed several roofs, then dropped back into another lane and sidled out into what turned out to be Lordworld Plaza. The first thing I noticed was the famous sundial, which was nightly converted to show the time by the lordworld's shadow. Next I saw the cowering shape of the woman in the cat suit with the feather duster. It was only now that I noticed that her breasts were protruding through a pair of holes.

"A constable!" she panted, springing up then clinging to my arm. "Back there, some sort of fiend!"

"It's hunting cats," I said as I hurried her back into the lane. "Get out of that costume if you want to live."

"But it's all I'm wearing."

"You can be alive and naked or dead and a cat, madame. Your choice."

"Danolarian!"

The voice came from deeper within the lane, and it had the dry, rustling sound of autumn leaves crackling underfoot. I turned to put myself between Terikel and the lamplight woman in the cat costume, but in her terror the woman flung her arms around me.

"Madame, really!" said Wallas, who was being squashed within my pack.

I twisted about, felt bare breasts, fur, and whiskers in the darkness, then wrenched the lamplight woman around and pushed her back into the plaza.

"Cat-lady, run!" I shouted after her.

Slowly I backed out into the plaza, my fencing ax held at high guard
and my Lupanian glass sword low at right point. Terikel followed, illuminated by the glow from the talons at the tips of her fingers.

"Wayfarer Constables, you are under arrest!" I shouted hopefully.

"Give me Wallas," Terikel snarled.

"Leave the lamplight woman, she is a bystander," I said as I retreated.

"I know Wallas is in your pack."

I began backing around the shadow clock. Terikel followed. It was
only a matter of time before she closed with me, and I already knew
how very fast, strong, and dangerous she was. I tried to think of my advantages, but could not come up with a single one. She suddenly lunged
for me and snatched for my ax, but I slashed down at her arm with my
glass sword. The blade bounced off, but she recoiled. There was an angry dark blue stain where the blade had struck.

I backed away under a flurry of slashes from Terikel's taloned hands,
but the ax kept her at distance while I cut at her with the sword. When
she finally seized my ax I let go at once. The wood of the handle smoked
in her hand, then broke at the middle. All that was stopping those talons
from ripping and burning through my chest was the glass sword, yet her
arms were now blotched with dark blue wheals, and she was favoring
her right over her left.

"Stand aside," Terikel crackled. "Just give me Wallas."

Wallas! In the heat of the moment I had forgotten that I was defending someone other than myself.

"Constable Wallas is of my Wayfarer squad, and under my protection," I said firmly, if not convincingly.

"I'll kill you to get to him."

"Try."

As I began backing away again I took off my cloak and draped it
about my left arm. It was not as good as an ax handle for parry work,
but it was better than trying to stop white-hot talons with bare flesh.
My glass sword was proof against whatever magic sheathed Terikel,
and was slowly cutting through that mesh of energies. I decided to target her neck, because whatever powers a neophyte glass dragon might
have, she would not get far without a head.

There was another flurry of slashes, but while a creature with hot talons for fingertips might be fearsome to behold, a man with three feet of blade has a much better reach. Again and again I struck at her neck as her talons tore smoking rents in the fabric of my cloak. Dark blue shadows appeared on her skin, and her forearms were soon black in places. Although nearly exhausted, I knew I was wearing her down. Amazingly, I was still without so much as a scratch.

"Inspector Danolarian?"

Both Terikel and I drew back and turned at the sound of my name. A spice pastry vendor had appeared, pushing a cart and enshrouded by a wide hat and baggy robes. A spice pastry vendor? I did not even like spice pastries.

"Get away, this thing isn't human!" I shouted, waving the glass sword in the direction of Terikel.

The distant figure raised a hand, and a thin, red line cut through the swirls of smoke in the plaza to center on Terikel's chest. It had no effect whatever. Terikel was turning back to face me when there was a sound like a huge rat having its tail trod upon. Almost immediately there was a massive flash of light from my opponent. At first I thought she had conjured a brilliance casting, but as I blinked the afterimages out of my eyes I saw that Terikel had been reduced to a glowing, smoking pile of ashes.

I turned back to the vendor just as the red line traced itself through the wisps of smoke between us, to center on my chest. My entire body flashed with such pain as you could never imagine, and that is all that I remember of being abducted into time.

✳ ✳ ✳

I was standing in near-darkness, apparently in a vast cavern. A river was flowing nearby, coming out of distant darkness and vanishing into darkness again. I knew it to be the river at the edge of life, for I had visited this place in dreams, long ago. I could see a white boat approaching a stone pier. It was garlanded with primroses, and was being poled along by a woman in a revealing red robe.

I had met the ferrygirl, I even knew her name. I made the reasonable assumption that I had been killed in Lordworld Plaza. The ferrygirl stepped from her boat onto the pier, but did not bother tying it up. Boats apparently behaved themselves in the afterlife, they did not drift away.

"Ferrygirl, Madame Jilli, alas I am your client," I said as she approached me.

"Oh no, this is but a social visit," she said, laughing, as she planted a kiss on my cheek.

"The thing that sent me here blasted a glass dragon in human form to ashes. How could I have survived that?"

"Terikel was more vulnerable to that weapon than you. She died, you were but stunned."

"Then why am I here?"

"Were you not listening? This is a social visit. My masters and mistresses, the gods of this moonworld, have a particular interest in you."

"Is this like my other dreams of this place?"

"None of those visits were dreams, Danolarian. Neither is this one."

Although the ferrygirl was showing as much leg and cleavage as I remembered from my other visits, her manner was quite different. Her sense of fun was gone, replaced by something that might have been concern. She did not have her picnic basket with her, and somehow that was the most ominous sign of all.

"We appear to still be alone," I said, glancing about.

"Oh, the others are on their way. Be warned, some of them are angry with you."

One does not look upon Romance, one just sees her light from behind, and sometimes one is favored by her hands upon one's shoulders. I saw the light, but I felt no hands. I was not in her favor.

"To die in defense of a lover is the very finest way to worship me," came her voice, silky yet cold. "You risked death in defense of a fat cat, Danolarian. That will never do."

"My apologies, but what else could I do?" I replied.

"Wallas is gross and obnoxious, he has never paid me tribute in his entire life. Fortune agrees with me. You have squandered her gifts, so you are out of favor with her, and she has a way of taking everything."

"You have lost everything," said a female voice some distance away in the darkness. "Very soon you shall learn of it."

"If Fortune overlooks anything, I shall take it," said a man walking out of the gloom in the distance. "I crush the weak and pull down the strong."

I recognized the grim face of Fate, and wondered what I had done to offend him. Fortune linked arms with him, and they stood sneering at me. I said nothing. They waited expectantly. When I remained silent, they began to fidget. Suddenly they winked out of view. The light of Romance now faded behind me, and I was left alone with the ferrygirl.

"Who else has a grudge to settle with me?" I asked.

"I have grudges against nobody," said the shape that was solidifying before us.

I had met Chance before, but was at a loss to know why he had any interest in me. I was not a gambler, and was not one to take risks for the sake of the thrill.

"If you have come to confiscate all that I have, you are a little late" was all that I could think to say.

"I am not like the others," said Chance. "In fact I have been known to help those with nothing. People with nothing bother me. They have nothing to lose, so they can do extreme things."

"You must know I am not one of your devotees, I am no gambler."

"Ah yes, but I am always in search of converts. Gamblers are the children of Fortune, they live in hope and die in poverty. The worship of Chance is nothing to do with taking risks."

"Are you proposing some bargain with me?" I asked suspiciously.

"Oh no, I merely came here to remind you that some gods do not lose their tempers and punish mortals out of spite. Keep your eyes open for the works of Chance, Danolarian. The good and the bad will be there in equal numbers."

When Chance had gone I looked to the ferrygirl, but she had turned away and was returning to her boat. I walked after her.

"Do not follow me, Danolarian, you are not dead yet," she said without turning.

"Please, what happens now?" I called.

"You endure the wrath of the gods, if you know what is good for you."

Part One

FUTURE TENSION

I awoke to find myself bound and gagged, with my hands trussed behind my back and digging into me very uncomfortably. I opened my eyes. There were two long bars of brilliant light above me. Turning my head away, I saw that I was in some manner of room, but nothing in it was familiar. It was filled with the strangest of machineries and engines, yet one fact was quite beyond dispute: the place was a mess. Sitting on the edge of what was either a bench or a bed was what I at first took for a boy; then I noticed the small breasts of a girl not far past puberty. Her hair was short, and cut in a strangely geometric style, as if a Palionese guardsman's helmet had been put on her head and all the hair still visible had been slashed away. She was smiling, but that did not seem like a very good sign, judging from the way she was rubbing her hands together.

"Inspector Danolarian, it's thirty generators, but at last I will be brought to justice," she declared in a very heavy accent; then she gave what was probably a curse in some unknown language.

She clenched her jaw, and the air hissed between her teeth as she drew breath.

"Inspector Danolarian, at last *I* shall bring *you* to justice!" she now shouted. "After thirty generations, that is, I *have*—no, I *shall* brought—bring—you to justice."

My impression was that she was presenting me with a very important speech, but that she had rehearsed and refined it somewhat too often. Princes at coronations, brides at weddings, criminals facing the noose, all have carefully rehearsed words, and most get a few of them wrong.

"Varria, is that you?" a male voice called in the distance.

"Yes!" my captor bellowed in reply.

"Don't you *yes* me, young woman! I want you out here in ten, and I mean seconds."

The girl stood, strode across the room, then loomed over me with her hands on her hips as she glared down.

"One sound, even so much as a thump against the floor, and you get a dose of *this* that will leave your nerves dead in a six-inch circle for the rest of your life."

She held up an oblong thing on a chain. It was about the size of a tinderbox striker, and I concluded that it was some utterly incomprehensible weapon. With that she walked out of the door, pulling it shut behind her.

For a moment I lay there, genuinely amazed and thoroughly alarmed. I was shocked not so much by my surroundings as by the fact that someone had tied me up yet left my boots on. In the Alberin of the limbo year nobody would tie anyone up without removing their boots. I rolled over, then got to my knees. Sitting back on my heels, I fumbled for the heel of my left boot, then twisted. It came free, and from within I took a sliver of razor-sharp obsidian. I prefer glass or flint for my heel blade, as boots do tend to get wet, and a rusted blade is of no use whatever. It was the work of moments to slice through the cords binding my wrists. With my hands free, I untied my legs and returned my heel blade to its proper place. Apparently people did not know about heel blades in wherever I was, and that was already to my advantage. As I sat rubbing the circulation back into my muscles I heard footsteps approaching outside.

I stood as a key rattled in the lock, and took up a position behind the door. Grasping the handle, I wrenched it open. My captor tried to hold on to the outer handle, and was pulled off-balance with her head forward. I now slammed the door back, and was rewarded with the heavy thump of wood striking skull.

As I again pulled the door open, I saw my young abductor lying against the opposite wall in the corridor outside. She was putting a hand to her forehead, and did not look to be at her most coherent. Glancing to and fro along the corridor, I saw stairs at one end and some manner of window at the other. *Stairs, people will come up them, window, glass, breaks easily, cuts skin, most buildings one floor high* flashed through my mind, then I put my hands on my head and my forearms over my face as I ran at the window and jumped.

With a very dramatic crash of shattering glass, I burst out into the night, prayed that I was only one floor up, and discovered that I was three floors up as I started falling. Almost immediately I encountered a tree, and began smashing down through the leaves and branches. I came to rest in a springy bush with prickly leaves. Somewhere above me a bell was ringing with unnatural rapidity. Dogs began barking, and brilliance castings came to life as I ran through garden beds. I came to a stone wall topped by iron pointwork, and taking the belt from my tunic I made a loop, snared an iron spike, then scrambled up over the wall and dropped to the street outside.

The street was something that nobody from the Alberin of 3144 could ever have imagined. There were white strips on either side, and the center was of black stone. Everything was smooth and without cobbles. There were gutters, but they were absolutely free of sewage. *Do these people not piss or drop turds,* I thought in wonder as I began walking away at burglar pace—which is fast but casual.

Intensely bright castings on poles illuminated everything as if it were near-daylight. I walked without looking back, keeping close to the walls. Huge carriages shot past on the black stone surface, driven along by invisible autons rather than horses, and equipped with lamp-castings that blazed brighter than the sun. I thought I was sure to be pursued and caught in moments, but those in the carriages ignored me.

As I reached a larger street, I slowed and turned. I had actually escaped from the Wall Tower building, which sat solid and dark amid a row of other buildings that seemed to be made largely of lights and glass.

A sign bolted to the wall on the corner declared this to be Chandler's Lane, and a sign below it read TOURIST WALK 17 and WALL TOWER— HISTORICAL SIGNIFICANCE GRADING B.

I kept walking. A walking man attracts a lot less attention than one who is running or loitering, after all. On the footway ahead of me I saw people, along with various other creatures. Some of those creatures were Lupanians. The deadly, near-invincible invaders from another moonworld were now just part of the crowd. A shop sign declared the goods on sale inside to be LUPAN RED FRIES, but none of the customers behind the enormous expanse of glass window were from Lupan. A Lupanian man with about a fortnight of beard growth was sitting against the shopfront with a sign that read HOAMLIS. Beside him was a cap containing a few silver coins.

As first I thought that I stood out, but the variety of weirdness in the clothing of that nightmare city meant that nobody gave a second glance to my Wayfarer Constable uniform of boots, drawstrings, and tunic, and even the charred slashes that Terikel's white-hot talons had put in my left sleeve drew no comment. Still, if the constables of this place were to be issued with a description of me, it would be a good idea to look a little different.

A glowing sign above a building declared 18 FIVEMONTH 1006 IS THE BEST DAY TO BUY A ZARVID. That was clearly a date, but 1006? *Is that a year,* I wondered. If it was a year, was it a thousand and six years from the one I was in about a quarter hour ago? If I was a thousand years in the future, rather than in some obscure part of hell, then this was quite possibly Alberin, I concluded.

"You look good, I'm depressed!"

The man addressing me was startlingly overweight, balding, and dressed in clothes that were wonderfully tailored, yet filthy. He was holding up some sort of daemon or auton that seemed little more than a single eye.

"You could be thin and rich if you but spent less silver on food," I advised as I walked on without breaking stride, confident that he could not keep up.

"I got your pix," he shouted after me. "I gonna sue 'cause you made me depressed by lookin' so good, an' insultin' me, an' not sayin' sorry . . ."

After nearly tripping over another Lupanian sitting on the footway and displaying a sign that declared ECONOMY VICTIM, I hurried on. Between LUPAN RED FRIES and the next street I was accosted and abused another half-dozen times for looking fit, looking fast, looking at someone, spare jingle, the good word on doomsday, and an offer of a good time with a Lupanian girl. From another shopfront that was just a huge expanse of glass and a door, a Dacostian woman dressed only in a folded handkerchief waved her four breasts at me and beckoned with her forefinger. The thought crossed my mind that a lamplight woman's bedchamber might afford a good place to hide for a half hour or so, then I was distracted as something cheeped on my left wrist. I saw that there was a loop of glowing material there, but it was not secured tightly and my wrists were slick with perspiration. It was the work of a moment to slip the thing off and drop it into the gutter.

A female voice erupted behind me.

"I saw that, I got your pix, I'm reportin' you for enviro-degradation atrocity."

A woman was waving one of the small eye-daemons at my back, and as I looked on she pointed the eye at the loop in the gutter, then waved it at me.

"I got evidence, this is a citizen's arrest," she declared.

Without warning we were bathed in light more intense than that of the sun at noontime. A booming voice from above told the two of us to throw down our weapons and lie on the ground with our hands above our heads or our right to sue for false arrest would be limited to five million electors. Needless to say, I turned and ran. There was the shrill squeak-sound of the strange weapon that had destroyed Terikel and stunned me, and I glanced back in time to see the woman collapse, still bathed in the intense light.

I knew that the constables in the sky above were sure to realize their mistake soon, and would be in pursuit of me. Desperate for somewhere to hide, I scanned the walls, shops, and signs. There were actually signs everywhere, and I could hardly believe that nobody had yet stolen them for firewood. One in particular caught my attention: BARGEYARDS HERITAGE BRIDGE 50 D. Where there was a bridge there would be water, and where there was water there was somewhere to hide. Fifty D turned out to be about thirty yards. Dodging the auton carriages that screeched and howled at me, I ran out onto the bridge in the middle of the nightmare Alberin that had not been there a quarter hour before. Vaulting the stone railing, I had a brief moment of serenity before hitting the water. Reasoning that my pursuers would be seeking me where I had dived, I used the light of their brilliance casting to swim underwater for the shelter of the bridge.

I surfaced again and saw that there was some sort of boat on the water, a large, oblong barge full of bright lights and people who sounded as if they were drunk. Shouts to the effect of "Man overboard!" echoed across the water to me, and I saw people throwing white, circular things into the water, while others hurled themselves into the river instead. From what I could tell, nobody seemed to be steering the barge, which was moving at quite a good pace in spite of having no oars, sail, or tow horse. It struck the central arch support of the bridge very solidly, cracked open, and began to take water.

∗　∗　∗

Keeping close to the stone wall that was now the bank of the river, and with my head just high enough above the surface so I might breathe, I moved with the current. The water smelled like a mixture of lamp oil, rancid vegetables, and rotten eggs, and it stung my eyes. I have never actually tasted sewage, but I imagine the taste of that river water must have been a good approximation. Beneath the next bridge, on a sandbank, I discovered a group of ragged people pointing to the commotion upstream. Bridge bears, we called them in my time. They were shambling beggars who lived beneath the city's one bridge—except that now there seemed to be a bridge every couple of hundred yards. Crawling up out of the water behind them, I huddled beside their little fire and squeezed water from my clothes. By the time I was noticed, I was no longer dripping.

"Ay stranger, what bring?" asked one who held a walking stick as if he knew how to hit with it.

I was in wet and unfashionable clothes, and had strange speech and a total lack of local knowledge. In my century were there people in my situation? To be sure, there were. They were generally press-ganged sailors who had taken the opportunity to escape a forced and unpaid voyage when their ship had docked in Alberin.

"Sailor," I replied, hoping that ships still existed, then added "from Gatria."

Gatria did not exist, but bridge bears were not known for their scholarship.

"Have coin?" asked the man with the stick.

I produced three silver reils. He took them, held them to the firelight, then called to someone.

"Sam t'Coiner, give say, on these."

A rank bundle of rags shambled out of the darkness, wheezing loudly with every step. When shown the coins he interspersed his wheezes with a whistle.

"First minting, Free Greater Alberin, 3144. See there, *Riellen Unites Us—3144* on rim. Very rare."

"Where lifted?" asked the man with the stick. "Which museum?"

I had no idea where any museum might be, but was fairly sure that I was supposed to have stolen the coins.

"Open window," I replied, and he nodded.

I soon learned that beggars were called treadfolk here, but they no longer had a guild. Instead they belonged to local gangs. I bought membership with the Scraps for a coin of Greater Free Alberin. This gained me a twisted nail on a string, which I was expected to wear around my neck. A little man named Pile was assigned to me as my mentor. Were he not human-sized, I would have thought him a rat who had been dropped into a cesspit once too often. My estimate was that I had so far spent an hour in this Alberin of the future, and I recalled that I had been fighting Terikel perhaps two hours before midnight. As I settled down for the night on the damp sand I was convinced that I was far too tensed to sleep amid so much weirdness, yet the sleep of absolute and bone-deep exhaustion came to me very easily.

The treadfolk were apparently the only people in the future who still retired and woke in time with sunset and sunrise. As the sun rose through a yellowish haze behind a mountain range of angular glass buildings, Pile and I set off for what he called the Uppers. The Uppers consisted of anywhere above the bridge. By now I had learned that they talked a form of Alberinese called Streetfox, a sort of rhythmic language where nearly all words were paired. It was strangely clear, concise, and easy to follow.

"You need, victim status," he explained as we walked. "Got accent, tha's good. You be, economy victim, from Gatria."

"Truly?"

"Tha's good, like that."

Pile took me to a tavern called Hurry Inn Takeaway. It served cooked food but no ale, and he explained that it was one to remember because it served treadfolk. I looked around as we waited in the queue. Mounted on a wall pedestal was a daemon with a single large eye and mouths to either side of it. The eye was the area of a dinner tray, and it was displaying small images that moved.

As far as I could tell, this was a distant descendant of the marketplace bulletin board, except that its bulletins spoke and moved. One bulletin was about the crash of a voidliner from Lupan, in which three hundred passengers and crew had died. There were images of a smoking hole about the size of a large village. The cause was mentioned as ceramic fatigue, whatever that was. Some electocracy named Zanon was invading its neighbor Ashkina in an act of self-declared self-defense, an action which had been condemned by a narrow majority in the Council of International Consensus of Electocracies. This bulletin was accompanied by images of what looked like glass dragons attacking a city with fire castings. The next bulletin declared that physicians had discovered that eating to excess and spending most of the day sitting down causes people to put on weight. After all this, some merchant-sponsored bulletins proclaimed the virtues of various low-cost foods and comfortable chairs.

It came our turn to be served. There was caffin drink on the menu board, along with various oddities that were apparently food. By my calculation, caffin's price had dropped by a factor of around ten thousand in the half-score of centuries since my time. I bought a waxpaper cup of caffin, along with a bread roll stuffed with four meatballs. It cost me nine silver coins, of the type that had a supposed likeness of Riellen but actually looked nothing like her. Pile and I sat on the stone steps of a deserted building to eat our meal. Several people said they would sue us for reasons that I found either unlikely or incomprehensible. Pile waved his twisted nail at them and chanted some sort of slogan. This caused them to hurry away.

I cannot say that I was feeling pleased with myself, but I was definitely happier for having escaped captivity, remained free, found shelter, joined a guild, and learned how to obtain food.

"What is to do now?" I asked as we finished breakfast.

"Going feefrees," replied Pile.

"Feefrees?"

"All stuff, what's free," he said, pointing across the street. "Like there."

The sign above a nearby building's entrance read FREE WHARFSIDE PUBLIC LIBRARY.

"A free library for the public?" I asked, baffled by the concept.

"That's yeah."

"But most of the public cannot read."

"Don't go, in libraries, to read."

"You don't?"

"Never do. Come on, we're fine, just say, self-improvement."

"Er, please explain further?"

"Read book, we stay, don't read, thrown out. Librarians like, self-improvers."

A library. I suddenly realized that at a single stroke I could learn all there was to know about the lunacy in which I was floundering. I washed my hands in the remains of a sweet-smelling but foul-tasting green drink that Pile had bought with breakfast. After all, librarians were probably still fussy about having their books soiled.

Pile walked into the library with so much confidence that one might have thought he owned the place. The word "public" apparently meant that anyone was able to enter, and we were certainly not challenged. I saw very few books, but rows of very bored-looking daemons sat on desks, some being interrogated by people. Pile sat down in a cubicle. I took the next cubicle. Pile soon began to doze.

I looked around, and noticed a young woman sitting beneath a sign that stated INFORMATION. I was in search of information, so this seemed a good place to start. I abandoned Pile to his dreams.

"The morning's greetings, ladyship, might I ask you about procedures in this free public library?"

She looked up at me and blinked. I was dressed for a very different Alberin, had been fighting a young glass dragon, had spent time in the river, and had slept on the riverbank. Quite possibly I smelled as bad as I looked, but I was well spoken, and this seemed to make all the difference.

"Er, so you know Alberinese?" she asked, noticing my heavy accent.

"It is not my first language, but I speak and read it, ladyship."

"What procedures do you want to know about?" she asked, writhing a little in her seat for some reason.

"All of them. Libraries are not like this in my homeland."

At this she stood up and gestured to another desk, where a daemon sat dozing.

"What did you want to read about?" she asked as she took me by the arm.

I recalled that there were plenty of signs about places of historical significance in the city, and guessed that this was the basis of some type of industry of scholarly pilgrimage. I improvised a new career for myself.

"Er, Alberin's history. I thought to learn about places of forgotten significance in the city, then take rich visitors there."

At these words she brightened even more.

"Oh, what a good idea. If only more people like, ah, well, with apologies, but like you could show such drive. What period did you have in mind?"

"The Lupanian Invasion, and the start of electocracy."

"Oh yes, yes! That is my favorite period. So exciting and romantic. You must have a good education, I just know it! Have you been to university? Where were you educated?"

"If I told you that, it would go badly for me," I said with some sincerity.

"Oh, a refugee intellectual, I knew it!"

One of the books that I was presented with had the text from my time alongside modern Alberinese, so I began to learn a lot about how the language had changed while I caught up on a thousand years of history.

✴ ✴ ✴

Three hours passed, and I discovered that I was dead. This should not have been surprising, given that it was well over a thousand years since my birth, but the date of my death had been the last day of the limbo year—when I had been abducted. I had died fighting a glass dragon named Terikel. A pile of ashes of roughly body shape was found near my Lupanian glass sword, and a lamplight girl in a cat suit had testified that I had died defending her from a glass dragon. The question of precisely what I was doing in the company of a lamplight girl in a cat suit was given an answer that seemed obvious to historians, yet was not in line with the facts as I knew them. The chronicle said that my fiancé, Lavenci, had been heartbroken by my crass and brutal betrayal of her, but did not mention how she felt about me being burned alive.

At this point Pile woke up and declared that it was time to go begging. I told him to go by himself, and that I would meet him outside the library when it closed. A small book with the title *Alberin for Refugees* filled in a lot of gaps in my background. The language was simple, there were pictures, and it dealt with the basics of surviving in the city's madness. *Electocratic Laws and Rights* left me astounded. You could literally be sued for picking your nose. Were you to murder someone, the penalty varied. A poor murderer could expect a month of street sweeping or trolling for rubbish beside the river. Were you a rich killer, you forfeited all of your property to the victim's family; then the city provided you with food and housing vouchers for the rest of your life. Apparently there was a thriving industry that involved killing relatives and blaming it on rich people.

Not surprisingly, a lot of effort went into concealing personal wealth. I glanced about the reading room. All the librarians wore signs declaring DOES NOT WORK FOR PAY OR ASSETS. A little more research revealed that librarians could be sued by people who learned unpleasant truths in library books. All of the books bore the warning label BOOKS MAY CONTAIN UNPLEASANT TRUTHS OR IDEAS in a half-dozen languages.

I moved on to books written to introduce children to things like modern locks and the cold sciences. The temptation to read broadly was almost overwhelming, but I forced myself to stay focused on a few key skills that I might need to survive. I learned that time travel was in theory possible, but depended on things that could not be made yet apparently existed. There was something called causative determinism that constrained time travelers, but by now my head was pounding with the onslaught of facts and ideas of the hours past. After glancing through a pamphlet about what were termed home security systems, I decided to read more history.

One of the books that I requested was very old, and I had to go to a special room to read it. This was because I had to read it through a display daemon, which showed me pictures of the pages. Because I had never used a display daemon before, the librarian woman assisted me again.

"Start with the Battle of Racewater Bridge," I began.

"Ah, a wonderfully heroic struggle," she said, sighing, her eyes brimming with admiration for the heroes of ages past.

"Stupid mistake," I mumbled, recalling what an appalling fiasco the battle had been.

"The greatest cavalry charge in the history of the world, a stupid mistake?"

I scanned the pages as she turned them. There was my name, correctly mentioned as one of the Journey Guard of Princess Senterri. The account was accurate from time to time.

"Forward, please, to the Lupanian Invasion."

Once again, the account in the book was a touch melodramatic but had something in common with the truth. I was cited as having captured an empty voidcraft from the Lupanians, and floated it down the River Alber to Alberin. It was also written that an Inquisition agent name Pelmore had tried to poison me and take credit for the voidcraft's capture. That was not entirely correct, but neither was it entirely a lie. Pelmore was said to have been executed. I was not mentioned again.

"Inspector Danolarian of the Wayfarer Constables," I said, looking up as the librarian closed the book. "How can I find out what happened to him after the invasion was defeated?"

She turned to a daemon, did something that I could not follow, and presently some lines of writing glowed on its eye.

"Which one?" she asked.

"Er, how many were there?"

"Danolarian was a common name, and there were two Inspector Danolarians in the earliest years of the electocracy. The first fought in the Lupanian Invasion, the second did nothing special. Its says here that Professor Higgory wrote a paper in 998 AE arguing that they were the same man, but that has been refuted by quite a long list of authorities."

When I had been in the Wayfarers, there had only been me, so I made the reasonable assumption that I was the first Inspector Danolarian.

"What do you know of the first?"

"I can tell you the general facts," she replied. "He was killed by the glass dragon Terikel. She was known for killing men who had slept with her when she was human, so this proves that he was one of her lovers."

"That seems like flimsy evidence," I said, flushed with annoyance. "He was not known to be a rake."

"I am afraid there is evidence to the contrary. After all, he died in the company of a biotherapy professional."

"I thought he died with a lamplight woman in a cat suit."

"Please, this library is a verbally correct language zone," she said with a wink, placing her hand on my thigh and giving it a squeeze.

Sheer, mind-numbing weirdness very nearly overwhelmed me. A strange woman of a thousand years in the future was making unsubtle advances upon me even though I was long dead. I had been walking through the streets of old Alberin with my fiancé and Wayfarer squad barely twenty-four hours earlier.

"What else can you tell me about his death?" I asked, trying to keep my mind focused.

"All that was ever found of Inspector Danolarian were ashes, but there is a very precise time and date for his death. One hour before midnight, on the eve of the new year, 3144, in Lordworld Plaza."

So, I was remembered as a rake, and I had deserved my death. There was also a very, very precise time and place recorded for my death. That was how my abductor had found me.

"Can your, your engine tell me what happened to Lavenci after Danolarian died?" I asked breathlessly.

"Lavenci . . . Lavenci . . . She married Laron, the first presidian of Alberin, in the year 1AE—3145 in the old calendar. It was on the very day of the first anniversary of the Lupanian Invasion. They had three children."

Again my entire world wobbled before my eyes. Lavenci, married to another man, a thousand years ago. She had waited all of a month and a half after I had supposedly died to marry Presidian Laron. Lavenci, of the snow-white hair that hung straight in gleaming cascades to her waist. In twenty-four hours of my time Lavenci had lived her life with Laron, raised a family with him, then died.

"Are you all right, sir?" asked the librarian, putting an arm around me.

I suddenly realized that I was sitting with my hands clasped over my head with tears in my eyes.

"Yes, yes, do not mind me."

"Do you have health insurance? I can call for—"

"No! Please, I just get emotional about romantic tales. I have other questions. What do you know of a man named Pelmore?"

"Another . . ." She lowered her voice and glanced at me conspiratorially. " 'Rogue' is the verbally incorrect term."

"Please go on, I am not offended."

"Professor Alsbrag says that the only real heroes of the Lupanian Invasion and electocratic revolution were women. Her latest research proves it, and she uses the examples of Danolarian and Pelmore extensively."

"Oh, indeed. What is Pelmore's story?"

"He fought against the Lupanian invaders in the Battle of Gatrov, but then he murdered someone. He was tried and executed only days later."

"I have heard that he slept with the sorceress Lavenci."

"Oh, possibly. Even the greatest of heroes can be so frail in matters of emotion."

"Please, tell me more of the story," I asked, hoping to bypass hours of research.

"Well, you must know about the great mother of electocracy, Riellen."

"Oh, of course."

"Well Riellen's early career was spent in the Wayfarer Constables. She was actually in Inspector Danolarian's squad, and there she became a rival for his affections with Lavenci. Many can't see why two such great women saw anything in a mere rogue like him, but then popular wisdom has it that many women like a bad boy." At this point she squeezed my hand, to hint that she might be susceptible to the occasional bad boy herself. I squeezed back to be polite. "When Lavenci had an affair with Pelmore, Riellen thought to expose her infidelity to Danolarian by casting a constancy glamour upon the couple."

That was definitely an embroidery of the truth, but I was not in a position to argue.

"I know a little of the old magic," I said. "I thought that the constancy glamour would prevent Lavenci from touching another man until seven years after Pelmore's death. You said that Laron and she were married long before seven years had passed."

"That was because Riellen was a great sorceress as well as a great leader and philosopher. She freed Lavenci from the glamour in an act of great forgiveness and generosity."

The history that I was hearing was thoroughly plausible, yet it was utterly false on so many levels. Frustrated by my inability to scream the truth to anyone who would listen, I merely nodded politely.

Returning to the general reading area, I read the middle chapters of a biography of Lavenci. Her first child was either quite premature or had been conceived a month or two before her wedding to Laron. Apparently I was not long lamented, but given the circumstances of my death that was not surprising. Laron had turned out to be good at winning elections, and had been reelected presidian of Greater Alberin three times. I read a selection of the love poetry that Lavenci had dedicated to him. The works were truly beautiful, but I recognized three that had originally been written for me!

I moved on to one of dozens of biographies of Riellen, and some lines that she had written as a very old woman caught my attention. *"All of you, my children, this I charge you with in return for the gift and blessing of electocracy. You will make scholarly study of the sorcery of time, and for generation upon generation you will not cease in your studies until a magical engine be wrought that can ply the river of time at the will of whosoever has a hand upon the steering pole. Then shall you sail back to the dark and terrible days of the Lupanian Invasion, and set right what I have done wrong. This must you do so that the curse upon Lady Lavenci might be lifted, and the greatest of heroes might live all at once with her in blissful happiness."*

I took the book across to the librarian who seemed to fancy me, and asked what it meant.

"This is a heavily allegorical passage," she explained. "The whole story is full of allegory, like Wallas the talking cat."

"Wallas?" I gasped. "An allegory?"

"Well, yes. Wallas is a mere literary convenience, someone for the hero to talk to when his thoughts need to be voiced."

I could hardly wait to tell Wallas that he had become an allegory.

"So, what does it really mean?" I asked.

"Well, after Riellen lifted the constancy glamour on Lavenci, she then ran straight to the arms of Danolarian."

"Some girls just love a bad boy."

"Allegorically speaking, yes. Professor Winstol has a very good theory on that passage, however. He thinks that Riellen is asking her distant descendants to come back through time and expose Danolarian for the rake that he was, so that Lavenci would leave him for Laron."

By now my head was spinning with paradoxes and contradictions, yet I persisted.

"But that is what happened, is it not? Danolarian died in the company of a lamplight woman in a cat suit."

"Ah, but Professor Winstol says that Danolarian was killed by some descendant of Riellen using a high-energy plasma domestic protection unit—hence the impression that the glass dragon Terikel killed him."

"I do not understand. Is this a fire weapon?"

"Of course! There are many weapons available today that could turn a body to ash," she said, smiling impishly and nudging me with her hip. "It could be that someone from this very century travels back through time and kills Danolarian."

You do not know the half of it, I thought as she spoke.

At this point I decided to break for lunch, for it was early in the afternoon. Besides, I had had more than enough history, and the creative modifications that historians had introduced into my life for the greater glory of their own reputations.

⋆   ⋆   ⋆

After a futile search for the shop where Pile and I had bought breakfast, I entered another food tavern, whose name was Food Grabbit and Run. I was ejected for being dirty and smelly. The next half-dozen food taverns did the same. All the guards and serving maids wore the sign DOES NOT WORK FOR PAY OR ASSETS, so threats to sue them gained me nothing. It was about now that a man standing beside a line of heavily loaded horseless wagons called me over.

"Ay, treadman, you look strong," he commented.

"It's true," I replied, immediately guessing what he had in mind.

"In a union?"

"The Scraps," I replied, tapping the nail amulet and hoping that was what he meant.

"But not a workers' union?"

"Er, no."

"Want to unload for spare coin? Slack-arsed tray gangers never showed, and I've got two hours to unload a whole fleet."

An hour of unloading the wagons that needed no horses to draw them earned me a handful of silver and a half-dozen green vouchers with *Bank of Greater Alberin, redeemable to the value of Five Electors* written on each. I was told that if I wanted to drift past any time, I could earn more money in that way. I asked where there might be a market, and my employer directed me to the BARGEYARDS GENUINE OLD-STYLE OPEN-AIR MARKET, which was a short walk away.

At a secondhand-goods stall I secured a shirt, trousers, jacket, and cloth pack, then made for a thing called a toilet block. It actually contained privies rather than toiletries, but it offered the privacy that I needed. Here I washed hastily in a basin, although several other patrons made images of me with their little artist daemon boxes and threatened to sue me for being offensive. Last of all came a weapon. This was a world in which even carrying a butter knife in public could have your

life's savings confiscated and given to the first person to declare themselves terrified and traumatized, so I had to improvise. Suddenly affect-
ing a limp, I bought a cane with a very nice fencing balance. Next I
chanced upon a barber's stall, and here I had my hair washed and my
beard trimmed to complete my transformation. All of my clothes from
medieval Alberin went into my pack.

As I returned to the library I was feeling quite heartened. I had em-
ployment, clean clothes, a weapon, and somewhere to learn about what
had happened to me. All of that optimism vanished as I approached the
building. Pile was outside, sitting on the steps and looking very uneasy.
The street seemed filled with people who were ambling along slowly, all
keeping a watch on the library steps while seeming to look elsewhere.
Having spent several years in the Wayfarer Constables, I could instantly
recognize my own kind, even a thousand years in the future.

It was now that I heard the *clack, clack, clack* of a woman's tower
heels behind me.

"Keep walking, pass library, turn corner, bad boy," said my librarian's voice behind me, although she was now speaking in Streetfox
style. "Cops called, want you. Inside, outside, they're waiting."

By now she was passing me. I could see her holding a remote speaking daemon to her ear and pretending to talk into it.

"Many thanks," I muttered without looking at her.

"Nice camo," she continued. "Back there, coffee caf, I waited. Good
luck, hang cool, bad boy. I'm Brieli, next time, we're dating, you're
paying, we're laying, bye now."

"Good fortune, ladyship,"

"You're cute, bad boy."

She turned and hurried up the library steps. I limped past without so
much as a glance at the building. Pile did not recognize me.

I was around a corner and considering whether or not to break into
a run when I heard another voice somewhere behind me.

"Turn into the park up ahead, Inspector, then sit down at the first vacant bench you find."

"Wallas?"

"Who else? Look smart now, I need your protection. The beggars eat
cats in this place."

Soon I was sitting on a bench with Wallas on my lap. He told me of how my body had somehow shielded him from my abductor's weapon, which was called a stuncast.

"Stuncast?" I asked.

"Yes. It casts stuns."

"Wallas, stun is a verb, not a noun. You cannot—"

"Inspector, instead of stunning a man with a club, there is an engine about the size of your thumb that lets you stun him from hundreds of feet away. They call it casting a stun, there's an end to the matter, and I am going to get on with my story."

Although not stunned, Wallas had been too terrified to move, so he had cowered in my pack as my abductor loaded me onto her spice pastry cart and trundled me through the streets to the Wall Tower building. Her time engine was hidden here, and I was loaded aboard. Wallas's account of our trip a thousand years into the future was very vague and confused, possibly because he was too frightened to look. Because my abductor had not been expecting anyone to be hiding in my pack, she had left it beside the time engine. Wallas had slipped out and hidden while she was looking elsewhere.

"I stayed in the house after you escaped," he explained. "They called the constables, and—"

"Wait, wait, just who are *they*?"

"The owners of that mansion that Wall Tower has become. The girl's uncle is one of them, I think. She told the constables that you burgled the place and tried to ravish her."

"Ravish, no. Lock her in the public stocks next to the rotten fruit and vegetable cart, tempting."

"The constables contacted them a few hours ago. A security daemon in the public library recognized your image from one painted by the guard daemon in the mansion. The girl is over at the library now, waiting to identify you. The messenger daemon said someone with piles is acting as bait, but I may have heard that part incorrectly. I ran after the wagon that took her to the library, then waited to warn you."

"You ran?"

"Yes I *ran*! No jokes, please."

"But those horseless wagons are very fast."

"The traffic was very heavy. Most of the time I only had to walk."

"You are a credit to the Wayfarer Constables, Wallas."

"Thank you, sir. I see that you have adapted fast and dressed well."

"I am a professional traveler. We are good at adapting."

"May I say that the cut of that jacket is far too bulky, though?"

"This jacket is about to grow a beer gut, Wallas, and that beer gut is you. Come along, in you get. Between us we should be able to find Wall Tower again."

Soon I was a somewhat overweight pedestrian, limping along with a cane. We crossed the bridge under which I had slept the night before, then followed a riverside promenade to the bridge where I had jumped into the water. I turned up the main road, going south.

"I caught one of the local mice, but I could not keep it down," said Wallas as I paused at a vaguely familiar building. "Dreadful taste. They feed on some sort of poison called convenient food, or so a local cat told me."

By now I was reading a brass plate bolted to the wall of a building.

"According to this plaque, this is the Lamplighter Inn, where Riellen wrote Greater Alberin's first electocratic constitution."

"She wrote it in the royal palace, after the regent fled during the Lupanian Invasion," protested Wallas.

"Indeed so."

"What is more, the Lamplighter had only a single level, if you don't count the attic doss rooms. This place is five floors high, built from milled sandstone, and about a hundred yards further back from the river than I recall."

"Time polishes grubby facts into gemstones, Constable Wallas."

"We must return to our own time, sir, this is an obscene world full of mad, degenerate people."

"I never thought I would hear you accuse anyone else of being degenerate, Wallas."

"But you must agree with me."

"Oh I do. It makes me ill to think that we spent our lives striving, fighting, and bleeding to build a better world, yet our descendants live in a farce like this."

"Speak for yourself, sir, I left no descendants."

"What about those two chambermaids in the Palion royal palace that you—"

"How did you learn about them?" wailed the bulge at my stomach.

"I am an inspector in the Wayfarer Constables, I know precisely how to question drunken men—and cats."

On the other side of the road a man wearing a highly stylized wig and black cape was walking along slowly, ringing a bell and calling "Lawsuits for shares! Forty per cent!" Pile had told me that such folk were itinerant lawyers.

"Lawsuits, now there's a riddle," said Wallas. "Everyone seems to be suing everyone else. I was wondering who does the work in this city?"

"One of the treadfolk I met under the bridge back there said everyone with any sense works for benefits. You can't be sued for benefits. Most possessions are owned by huge merchant houses that are protected by armies of lawyers."

✳   ✳   ✳

At Lupanian Epicure I bought something called a hamslab that was actually made of beef stock, bean extract, thickener, coal tar by-products, and breadcrumbs, according to the health warning label on the packet. I continued on south, sharing the nauseating thing with Wallas as I walked. We entered a better class of neighborhood, in which all the properties had high walls surrounding them. I recognized the mansion that Wall Tower had become.

There was a small shop nearby where the caffin drink was sold in ceramic cups, and one could sit down to drink it, just like a thousand years earlier. I also purchased a chocolate biscuit. Using the biscuit as a stylus, I began a chocolate sketch on a napkin.

"You are meant to eat those," said Wallas, poking his head from within my coat as I worked. "They are meant to taste very pleasant."

"Find me a charstick and you can have the biscuit."

"Never mind. Being a cat, I cannot taste sweet things."

"Really?"

"It is true. That's why I never bother with sweet wine."

"What about mead? You drink that."

"I like to savor the bouquet, and . . . Oh sir, I do want to go home!"

"I am working upon that."

"It all seems so hopeless."

"What in particular?"

"Getting back to our time."

"Maybe not, Wallas, never give up. What do you think of this?"

Wallas peered at my sketch.

"My word! That thing is the time engine."

"I have encountered it before, and even met myself," I said as I tapped the sketch. "The timefarer that I saw during the Lupanian Invasion did things with little levers on this lectern here. The machine vanished when she moved them. I suspect that they are like the reins of a horse, or the steering pole of a ship."

"I got a good look at the time engine," said Wallas eagerly. "I was left alone with it after the girl dragged you out to another room. There was indeed a lectern with slots, but I saw no levers."

"No levers . . . yet *I* saw levers. Perhaps the levers were keys, and could be removed. Lever-keys. Think, Wallas. Did you see her do anything with a key?"

"She had a key to a glass cabinet, but that was a very ordinary key."

"What did she do with it?"

"She opened it, then locked it again."

I thought over this, but could conclude nothing useful. Perhaps if I gained access to the room myself I could work something out.

"Direct my hand," I said as I turned the napkin over. "I want to draw the layout of the mansion of Wall Tower. Tell me what you saw of it."

✳   ✳   ✳

As the sun descended to the yellowish-purple horizon I extracted all the information I could from Wallas. His memory for floors and rooms was not at all bad, and he had explored the mansion quite thoroughly.

"There is a lock daemon on the outer gate, but it will open to the password *temporica*. The inner door, that to the mansion, is locked to a daemon that will open to *belcorian*."

"I cannot believe that you could have learned so much yet not been noticed, Wallas."

"Nobody thinks a cat is a threat, sir. They might have thought I was a friend of their house cat, Palladin. He's a very handsome lilac tabby, we get along very well, although, you know, he's been . . . how can I put this delicately? Neutered."

"The price of security, Constable Wallas."

"True, but he's quite bitter about it. Still, he showed none of that tomcat territoriality nonsense about me being in his house. Very decent of him."

"I can scarcely believe that the girl you describe could have designed and built the time engine," I said, randomly selecting one of the many paradoxes plaguing me. "Her ignorance of history rivals your ignorance of dieting."

"Now now, sir, no insults until we are back home."

"So, you used these passwords to get in and out, Wallas?"

"Oh no, there are special cat doors. They have a cat, remember? Palladin said they are called cat flaps. One cat flap leads into a big, empty room downstairs. It's to the left on your diagram. There is a second cat flap to access the inner house."

"A big and empty room?"

"Yes, I cannot think why it is not furnished. There are some sacks and oddments in it, I slept there last night in a very pleasant box. The main door to the outside is very large. Big enough to take a carriage."

"Perhaps it was a carriage house in times when horses were used for transport. Can this big door be opened by passwords?"

"No, there is some different auton or daemon that guards it."

"Then it is of no interest to us."

With the sun not long below the horizon I set off for the tower. Stopping before the gate, I said "temporica." The gate opened. A very polite voice bade me welcome, then told me that I was late and should hurry inside. The darkened garden looked familiar, even though I had paid it little attention when I had fled through it the night before. Looking to the top floor, I could see that a window had been boarded over. I said "belcorian" to the front door. It slid open. Now safely inside, I unbuttoned my coat and put Wallas on the floor.

"You are leading, Wallas," I ordered.

"I expect a bonus for this."

"You might even get a promotion."

The internal doors swung or slid open at our mere approach, and did not ask for passwords.

"Why do the doors have latches and handles even though guard daemons control them?" I asked.

"Palladin said there are heritage laws that force you to use old-fashioned fittings when you modernize old-fashioned buildings."

"Are you having a joke with me?"

"No! The security daemons can be put to sleep if you want to use the handle to open a door."

After ascending two floors by the stairs, we walked along a corridor with glowing panels in the ceiling. At the end of this was another door.

"The room beyond is a called a living room," said Wallas.

"So people live there?"

"No, they just sit there sometimes. Perhaps dead people are not allowed."

"Technically we probably *are* dead."

"Then we are not qualified to enter."

"Well we had better not tell anyone."

The door slid open. Before me were nine tall, heavily muscled, naked men, lounging before an open fire. What caused my mouth to hang silently open was not so much the fact that they were all pregnant as that their primary sexual attributes were being worn in teardrop-shaped jars around their necks.

"Hi, we're empathizing," said a blond man to the right of the fireplace. "I'm Olivarine, I'm into lifestyle."

"We're having a Wayfarer's theme tonight, that's our campfire," said a man lying stretched out on a rug with a gesture to the fireplace. He then tapped the container that held his penis and testicles. "I'm Breen."

"Wayfarer patrols were into empathy lifestyle, there's a new novel about it," said Olivarine.

About all that this group had in common with a Wayfarer patrol was the fact that they were on the same moonworld, but pointing that out would have achieved nothing. Introducing myself seemed to be the least suspicious thing that I might do, given that I was wearing clothes, anatomically intact, and certainly not pregnant. *Danolarian, not a good name in these times,* flashed through my mind. *Lariella, she was the other time traveler, and she was on my side.*

"My name is Darric," I managed, which was the first name that came to me. "I am a friend of Lariella."

"Ooh, her climax cutie, I'd wondered if she had one while I'm detached," said Breen.

"Nice rigout," said a swarthy man who looked as if he might be Vindician, "but the jacket is just too, too, bulko."

"I borrowed it from a bulko friend named Wallas."

"Super accent! Just too, too cute."

"I study Dawn Ages medieval languages, a little has rubbed off," I improvised as I scanned the room for a door that Wallas had spoken of.

"Lariella would just adore that," said Breen. "She likes her fantasies medieval."

"I believe that was what drew us together," I agreed as I sidled in the direction of the door leading to the next flight of stairs.

"You should see how she dresses me up, she has a thing about Wayfarer Constables, you know," continued Breen. "Actually, I have some pix."

"I'm Galvar, I'm into health," said the swarthy man as Breen snapped his fingers and called out some spellwords.

Until now I had not noticed a rather depressed-looking daemon on a pedestal in the corner. The lights dimmed of their own accord, and the daemon's single eye began to shine images onto the wall above the fireplace. The images were like those from the bulletin daemon in the food shop. For a moment I gaped in astonishment as images of Lariella and Breen cavorted and frolicked in a room filled with mirrors, cushions, rugs, and odd-looking straps that hung from the ceiling and supported things resembling fur-covered instruments of torture. Fear of not being believed prevents me from saying more, but if they were meant to be in the Wayfarer Constables then they were certainly not the Wayfarer Constables that I worked for.

It was as I stood dumbfounded by the images that the girl Varria arrived home from the library with three constables.

I turned as the door swished open behind me, then a familiar voice screamed "That's him!" I saw a hand raising a small black thing with a red light in the edge. Assuming that anything being pointed at me was sure to be a weapon, I slammed my walking stick down on the hand, knocking whatever it was across the floor.

My greatest mistake was underestimating the degree to which hand-to-hand combat had developed during the course of a thousand years. While I was good, I was in nothing like the same class as these constables of the future. I aimed a blow at the constable's head, but he made some elegant, sweeping motion with his arms and deflected my attack. I staggered with my own momentum, just as another constable leaped into the air and aimed a high kick at my head. His kick missed because I had lost my balance, and he too lost balance as he fell. As I recovered I struck out again with the walking stick, but the second constable ensnared it in his arms with an oddly elegant gesture, then wrenched it from my grip.

I was saved by a stampede of naked, pregnant men trying to escape the fighting. Rolling to the floor to avoid another kick, I found myself beside the fireplace. Here I seized a kindling ax and flung it at the third constable. He swerved to one side, collided with a pregnant man, and went down. The ax embedded itself in the wall. I snatched up a poker and ran back for the door through which I had entered. It slid open, admitting me, and as it closed again I thrust the poker into the wall, pinning the door shut. There was a crash as a constable collided with the door that could no longer open for him.

By now I had no idea where Wallas had gone and did not have the leisure to make inquiries, so I ran back down the stairs. Suddenly the rapidly ringing bell began to sound again, and I found that the door to the outside world would no longer open.

"Inspector, here!" called Wallas from beside a door with a flap-cat thing built into it, and this one did sweep aside as I approached. The room beyond was dimly lit by some small red and green lights on a box in one corner, and I could see that it was largely empty. Along one wall was a pile of brown boxes and crates.

"Wallas, what now?" I whispered.

"Think like a cat, hide in a box!" Wallas advised.

I had only just crawled into a box when the door swished open and lights blazed into life like a brilliance casting.

"Scanning for his GP tag," said a voice. "Registering . . . one life-form present."

"It's the fat cat."

"It registers three human-sized forms."

"Show me—clown! There are only two GP tags, you're picking up the cat."

"I have it set for forty-plus. A cat doesn't weigh forty-plus."

"I don't know, he's quite a size."

"We should check those boxes."

"If there's no GP tag there's no intruder!" snapped the first speaker impatiently. "There's nobody on this moonworld who doesn't have a GP tag, and there's only two GP tags in here. Come on, he must have got out before house security went to intrusion alert."

I lay unmoving and silent for a long time. The box was of some type of thick, stiff paper, and was actually quite comfortable.

"The constables have gone," Wallas reported, "but I heard them say that the mansion is being watched."

"Wallas, what is a GP tag?"

"A tag with GP written on it?"

"Whatever it is, every human on Verral has one except me."

"I'm human."

"All right, all right, every human not shaped like a cat has one. The point is, without one, we are invisible to their oracle daemons."

"But still highly visible to unaided eyes."

"Yes, but the people of this time do not seem to believe things to be real unless they see them on a daemon's eye."

"They're called screens."

"All right, a daemon's eye-screen. So, the mansion is being watched?"

"Apparently."

"By people using their eyes?"

"Perhaps."

"Well, no matter. We need to wait inside anyway."

"But for how long?"

"Until a woman named Lariella returns. She is married to one of the pregnant men upstairs, the one named Breen."

"I have not seen so much concentrated weirdness in one room since

I was guest speaker at the Fifty-Seventh Conference of Radical Eunuch Heralds!" exclaimed Wallas. "Did you notice that they were all totally hairless? Why, if I had not been there myself—"

"Later, later. What do you know about the doxy who abducted us, Varria?"

"She's Lariella and Breen's niece. I think she is staying here while she studies in one of Alberin's academies."

I had thought that I would have to wait for a rather long time for Lariella to return home, but for once Fortune was kind to me. There was a sudden whirring and rattling, then a whole wall of the room began folding up into the ceiling as light flooded in. I withdrew my head into the box.

"One of those auton carriages with no horses," said Wallas. "It's coming in here."

"We must be in the stables," I replied above the daemon's rumble. "Lie still, stay in the shadows."

The rumble stopped, and I heard the whirr of the wall unfolding back down from the ceiling. Footsteps clacked across the floor of the stables, the inner door swished open, then it closed again.

"Did you see who it was?" I asked Wallas.

"A woman, sir."

"What age?"

"Thirty, forty, fifty, they all look the same in this world and age. The lettering on the box she carried said LARIELLA CARVARAT and THIRTI-ETH WORLD CONFERENCE ON SPATIAL PHYSICS."

Lariella. That was the only word that meant anything to me, but it gave me a great deal of hope.

"Lariella, she built the time engine," I said, hoping that it was true.

"Is this good?" Wallas asked.

"Perhaps."

"Now what?"

"We wait here, Constable Wallas."

"Wait for what, Inspector?"

"Wait for the sounds of an argument."

✳ ✳ ✳

We did not have long to wait. As raised voices sounded somewhere above us, I crawled from my box, stretched, then left the stables and made for the stairs. As I climbed, I began to distinguish the words being shouted a lot more clearly.

"It might have been stolen!" declared an angry female voice.

"No bloody intruder could have stolen the time engine, it weighs a quarter of a ton!" retorted Varria's voice. "It wasn't my fault, I called the police."

"Just what do you *really* know about that burglary last night?" asked Breen.

"Nothing, nothing!" shouted Varria. "The time engine is still there, you just saw it yourself."

"Well I can tell you one thing for certain," said Lariella. "My stuncast has been fired three times, but it has not registered *any* shots with Central Correctness Headquarters."

"Impossible," said Breen. "An image of the target of every shot is automatically transmitted to Central Correctness."

"Well, look at the power levels. Three shots at maximum stun are on the counter, but no image was transmitted."

"Like Uncle Breen says, impossible," insisted Varria.

"No, *very* possible. All you have to do is go back in time and shoot it. If there is no Central Correctness Headquarters to receive the transmission, no image will be stored."

"The stuncast must have malfunctioned!"

"You played with my time engine, didn't you?"

"It isn't working yet, you said it yourself."

"It's complete, just not operational. I have some final tests to do, like automatic runs with mice to prove that it's safe to use. You *could* have used it if you were willing to take the risk."

"I didn't!"

"Who was that intruder?"

"A stranger. He tried to molest me. He hit me on the head."

"Breen found you with the stuncast in your hand."

"I just pointed it at him, but he hit me before I could fire. Then he ran for the window and jumped."

"So he hit you, then ran?"

"Yes."

"So he didn't try to molest you!"

"You're trying to confuse me!"

This seemed like a good time to introduce myself. Lariella was clearly the commander of the family group, and she was not sounding at all sympathetic to Varria. As I approached the door I dropped Wallas to the floor. The door slid open and I entered the room.

"Inspector Danolarian of the Wayfarer Constables," I announced to Lariella. "I have a complaint to make about the behavior of this girl, ladyship—"

In a most impressive display of speed and agility, Varria sprang at least ten feet across the room, snatched up the stuncast from the table, and pointed it at me. I cringed in anticipation of a blast of pain, but nothing happened. I could see her thumb working frantically.

"I removed the power source to check the number of shots fired, Varria, remember?" said Lariella.

"That man, he raped me, he stole the time engine, call the police—"

Varria was silenced as Lariella's hand slashed across her face. Everyone was silent for some moments.

"The report from Central Correctness says your GP chip registers your last sexual encounter at *five months ago*!" shouted Lariella, waving a glowing board covered in writing. "Duration . . . four minutes and thirty-one seconds. Moderate arousal, no orgasm, and the name of the partner was—Harliac Hasentov! Talk about desperate—"

"Aunt Lar, please!" squealed Varria.

"Well, what about the truth?"

Varria sank to a chair, folded her arms, and pouted.

"It was destiny!" she muttered. "I don't have to say any more."

Lariella now looked to me.

"I have a very bad feeling about what Varria has done to you, sir," she said, waving the glowing board again. "Do tell me your complaint. You say you are from some new police unit, the Wayfarer Constables?"

"Not so, ladyship, I am from a very old unit, the Wayfarer Constables. This girl abducted me from a thousand years ago, as far as I can tell."

"Don't listen to him, he's lying!" shouted Varria, her hands over her ears.

Lariella pointed some other odd device at me, then looked at her glowing board.

"Nothing," she said. "This man has no GP chip."

"But everyone has a GP chip," said Breen.

"Not someone who truly was born a thousand years ago," said Lariella.

"The little baggage abducted me as well," said Wallas as he sauntered forward, his tail held high.

After we spent a few minutes explaining the circumstances of our abduction, there was no more for Wallas and me to do but stand to one side and listen as Lariella and Breen screamed at their ashen-faced niece. The girl got some respite when Lariella contacted the constables outside with her messenger daemon, inviting them in. I was introduced to them as one of those men who slept with women while their husbands were pregnant. Wallas made a choking sound, then vomited on the carpet. The constables told Varria that she was in a lot of trouble, and would be compelled to pay for misuse of law-enforcement resources after a judicial hearing. After asking several times if I was sure that I did not want to commence a lawsuit against them, the constables left.

Very little of importance was said for some time, as our three hosts suddenly decided that they should be hospitable to us. They busied themselves with getting drinks and food for Wallas and myself, then as we had our meal we were shown family portraits, thousand-year-old manuscripts, and even little models of the time engine and the original Lupanian fighting tripods.

At last it was my turn, but I had nothing special to show. Facing the fireplace, sitting back in a chair that was built entirely of cushions, I gathered my thoughts. Wallas sat on the mantelpiece, more to be the center of attention than to be over the fire.

"It all happened during the great invasion from the moonworld Lupan, over a thousand years ago," I said, hoping that I was not sounding too pretentious. "I was in command of constables Wallas, Riellen, and Roval. We were in the river port of Gatrov, on leave. There my sweetheart, the sorceress Lavenci, was waiting for me."

"I can't believe it," exclaimed Lariella. "You commanded Riellen herself, the mother of electocracy."

"Oh do let him tell his story," said Breen.

"Strong words were exchanged between myself and Lariella, but it was a mere lover's quarrel," I continued. "Unknown to both of us, Riellen was also in love with me."

"Lies, lies," whispered Varria, but Lariella slapped her across the ear.

"During a town dance Riellen cast a glamour over Lavenci and a local yokel named Pelmore as they danced together. Pelmore was a river wharfer from the docks. Lavenci spent the night in his embrace."

"Lies! Lies! Lies!" shouted Varria, jumping to her feet with her fists balled. "Riellen was pure and noble, she would *never* have done that to Lavenci!"

"The veracity monitor on my Menial Lackey Organizer registers only truth," said Breen, holding up a little oblong daemon. "Danol—you don't mind being called Danol, do you?"

"Not at all."

"Danol, tell a lie."

"I am passionately in love with Varria—"

"MISTRUTH CLASS A!" bellowed the daemon. "DIRECT CONTRADICTION OF THE SUBJECT'S BELIEF OF THE TRUTH!"

"So sit down and shut up," said Lariella to Varria.

"Pelmore robbed, deserted, and dishonored Lavenci in the early hours of that morning," I continued once more. "The following day they both discovered that a constancy glamour was binding them together. Powerful magic prevented them from performing acts of dalliance with any other partner, and it was a type that persists seven years after either partner dies. Lavenci now hated Pelmore, of course, so there was no future for them as lovers."

"I register only truth," said Breen, holding up his little daemon.

"It was now that the first voidships from the moonworld Lupan began to drop out of the sky. Soon terrible fighting began, and amid the horrors and chaos of the Lupanian Invasion, Pelmore tried to poison Lavenci to free himself from the constancy glamour. Instead he killed a very brave militiaman, and very nearly killed me. Being ratified as a magistrate, I presided over a field trial in which Pelmore was found guilty of murder."

"But you should have declared an interest," said Varria.

"Why? Everyone knew I was very interested in having Pelmore hanged. Anyway, I convicted him of murder. Riellen's jealousy and treachery were also uncovered during Pelmore's trial, and through her spells she was technically guilty of ravishing both Lavenci and Pelmore, unlikely though it may sound."

"The veracity monitor registers all of that as true," said Breen. His eyes were wide with agitation.

"In spite of the enchantment that prevented us from touching each other, Lavenci and I made up our differences when we returned to Alberin," I explained, suddenly weary with the memories. "Here Riellen was sentenced to exile and Pelmore to death. A man with the general guise of Pelmore was executed in public, and Lavenci and I prepared for seven years of longing for each other but never touching."

I looked up. A tear was meandering down Breen's cheek, and Varria was sitting with her hands so tightly clenched together that her fingernails were drawing blood. Lariella was also sitting forward, a broad smile on her face and her mouth open.

"Now a very strange thing happened. Just before Alberin's final victory against the Lupanians and their tripod fighting engines, Constable Wallas reported that he had seen *me* here, in this tower, at the very time when I was elsewhere in the city."

"I did indeed," said Wallas from the mantelpiece. "In that year this tower was a mere storehouse, you see—although I must say you have done wonders with the renovation. I really like the contrast of the exposed bluestone and distressed beamwork with the velvet-sheened plaster and polished floorboards."

"Oh really?" said Breen, "I did all that—"

"MISTRUTH CLASS D: SUBJECT HAS INCORPORATED ELEMENTS OF TRUTH IN A FABRICATED SCENARIO," shouted the MLO daemon.

"Well a renovation company did the work, but the concept was mine, you stupid machine!"

"Please, I want to hear the inspector's story!" interjected Lariella, waving her hands for silence.

"At the word of Wallas I came to this very tower with the constables Andry, Costiger, and Essen. When we burst into a room on the floor above, a man with a stuncast like the one on the table brought us down. That man was myself."

"Your future self?" asked Lariella.

"Yes, and I was somehow revived earlier than the others."

"There's an option for that on the stuncast, I'll show you later. Go on."

"I saw that the real Pelmore was there, alive but bound tightly. It was then that I was introduced to yourself, ladyship."

"Oh, *ladyship,* I do love to be called that," squealed Lariella, pressing her hands to her cheeks.

"There was also, an—an engine, like that little model on the table. It was the size of a small cart."

"My time engine, it could have been nothing else," said Lariella.

"As I watched, you and my future self put Pelmore and Andry onto the time engine and vanished. Because Pelmore had ceased to exist without dying, the constancy glamour between Lavenci and he was thus broken, as I soon found out in the nicest way possible. Since then I have known that I would travel through time to help break the glamour between Lavenci and Pelmore. Now I find myself in the future, and it is not a pretty sight."

I had cast a glance at Varria when I said that. She made no response. She did not even mutter. Breen looked at the truth daemon, to make sure that it was still on duty. Apparently it was, and he almost seemed disappointed. Wallas twitched the tip of his tail. This was the language of his body, and what he was saying amounted to *I am pretending to be a cat who cannot talk and understands nothing.* It was Lariella who broke the silence.

"I really think you are owed so, so much apology, closure, compensation, and rehabilitation," she said, trying to look at ease by sitting back in her chair and draping a leg over an armrest. "I think the best thing would be to begin with some closure intimacy, and then—"

"Closure intimacy?" I interjected.

"Sex," explained Wallas.

I fought down an urge to leap for the nearest window and run very fast.

"I would like to hear your side of it, ladyship," I said hurriedly to distract her. "How did you come to build the time engine, and what did you think to do with it?"

Wallas, Breen, and Varria immediately looked a lot more at ease. Lariella frowned.

"There is little that you have not already heard," she said, running her hand along her thigh.

"I have heard it in slices. Now I would like to see the slices presented together."

The story of the time engine was clearly not foremost in her thoughts, and she had to stop and think. She reached across to a bookcase and drew out a very battered-looking tome, flicked through a few pages, then muttered some curses involving the lack of a search daemon.

"So, so romantic," Breen sighed, waving his MLO daemon. "And all true, too."

"I ought to know, I was there with him," said Wallas.

Finally Lariella seemed to find what she wanted in the book. She marked the place with a scrap of paper, then shut it.

"As you all know, this family is descended from the great mother of electocracy, Riellen," she declared. "When I was young I often wondered why none of us had been in politics for centuries. There were philosophers, physicists, mathematicians, engineers, and even sorcerers, but never a politician. It was as if Riellen had used up all our talent to lead for a thousand years. My thought was to break the mold, but then came the day that my father explained the secret family history to me. A thousand years ago Riellen had commanded her own son to study time, and to do the same with his children. They were to go on with studies of time until a time engine could be built that could travel back to the Lupanian Invasion of the year 3144. They were to change a small part of history."

"Did he mention me?" I asked, although I was fairly sure that I knew the answer already.

"No. My father and I only knew that a man named Pelmore Haftbrace was to be plucked out of 3144, in Alberin. He was to be taken far into the past and marooned there, that was known from family tradition. This was in order to break a constancy glamour between him and the sorceress Lavenci. The glamour was strong, and tightly fashioned, but it had been cast in a world where time engines did not exist. Thus it could cope with either of the partners being alive or dead, but not with one of them ceasing to exist without dying. Remove Pelmore into time, and Lavenci would be free to be intimate with Presidian Laron—er, as we thought, anyway. I did, of course, take up the challenge like all those before me, and after twenty-eight generations it was my honor to discover a means to travel back and forth through time. The trouble was that I knew nothing about your involvement, Danolarian."

"Your niece seems to have taken more of an interest in me."

"Varria's involvement . . . is complicated. My breakthrough took a long time to translate into a real engine, and when I turned fifty I was still unmarried. I told Varria the family's secret tradition, rather than letting it die. A year after that Breen and I developed an empathy contract, but by now the time engine was almost operational and Varria knew everything. Danolarian, I had no idea how obsessed she had become with Lavenci, and protecting her from you."

"So—so Pelmore was really a murderer?" asked Varria, who seemed to be struggling hard in a wasteland of shattered prejudices.

"As history's monsters go he was not among the worst, but he did rob Lavenci, poison me, and murder a militiaman," I replied, trying to remain impartial on a very sensitive subject. "What he did in bed with Lavenci . . . well, both of them were under an enchantment cast by Riellen."

"Riellen?" asked Lariella. "Are you positive?"

"Yes."

Breen tapped at the truth daemon, then held it to his ear and shook it. Apparently it felt that I was telling the truth, even though he did not.

"I should have abducted Pelmore instead, and brought him here to face justice!" Varria suddenly exclaimed.

"For what?" I asked. "Six months of intensive remedial counseling and a grief closure hugging ceremony with the descendants of his victims?"

"Does he get a slap on the wrist as well?" asked Wallas with a very unsettling cat sneer.

"Look, I know this is hard for you to accept," said Breen, "but standards of justice have evolved away from retribution to rehabilitation over the thousand years past."

"I find your idea of justice monstrous in the extreme," I said softly, staring at the coals in the fireplace. "Life savings confiscated for farting in public, yet murderers are let off with a stern warning as long as they say sorry."

"We value liberty," Varria retorted. "Riellen taught us to worship the right to be free to choose."

"Oh? So am I free to choose to punch someone in the face because he disagrees with me?" I asked.

"No, no, no, mediation counseling must be used," said Breen.

"If you are richer than I, might I choose to rob you?"

"Oh no, never!" Breen exclaimed. "You must be subjected to initiative enhancement therapy, in order to increase your desire for self-improvement. I have a practice in civil law, this is my stalking ground, so to speak. We have absolute freedom, as long as we observe all the limits."

"In other words, the freedom to choose is very, very narrow, even more so than in my century."

"You just don't understand," he said, sighing.

"Obviously not."

"Here are some chronicles about the invasion," said Lariella, who had been ignoring the banter about legal philosophy. "They were all written by people who were alive at the time. This is from *The Ballad of Burning Gatrov*:

Full fierce and furious came the Glasswalker,
All in his tripod with his spear of fire
But then Riellen commanded
'Stand firm!' and those of her ballista
Smote down the Glasswalker with oil of hellfire
Yet did other Glasswalkers rend this crew to ash
And leave Riellen dazed among the ruins."

"Actually Captain Danzar of the Gatrov militia was commanding that ballista, and I was calling the range," I explained.

"You were there?" gasped all three of my hosts together.

"I was there too!" exclaimed Wallas.

"MISTRUTH CLASS B: SUBJECT HAS SEVERELY DISTORTED A FACT."

"Well, I was hiding under the pier with Pelmore and Riellen."

The truth daemon stayed ominously silent.

"*Riellen* was *hiding* during a *fight*?" whispered Lariella.

"Do not be surprised," I commented. "Before electocracy it did not matter whether a king was at the head of his army or hiding in the palace cellars during a battle, the chroniclers would still say that he led army to victory. It is obviously the same for electocratic heroes as well."

Varria snatched the book from Lariella. Have you ever noticed that a reformed drunkard or lecher is always so much more fanatical than the rest of us about the suppression of vices in general and their own former vices in particular?

"They *lied* to us!" shrieked Varria as she flung her copy of *The Ballad of Burning Gatrov* across the room.

Nobody else moved a muscle as she snatched up a coal shovel, strode across to where the book lay on the floor, and proceeded to beat it severely. Next she tore a painting of Riellen in a heroic pose down from the wall and flung it to the floor.

"Filthy, scheming, deceitful little rapist!" she screamed as she jumped up and down on Riellen's portrait.

"Well, it looked nothing like her anyway," I said as I folded my arms and looked away to the fire.

"Political chroniclers are always superb liars," said Wallas. "They give a bad name to we bards who tell the truth."

"MISTRUTH CLASS B: SIXTY PERCENT DISTORTION OF GENERAL FACTS RELATING TO THE CONCEPT OF TRUTH."

"Oh shut up," muttered Wallas.

"Well put, for a literary allegory," I said smugly.

"If we could but visit the time of the scholar who wrote that about me, I would leave a mellow present in one of his slippers," responded Wallas.

By now Varria had taken out her remote speaking daemon, and was tapping at it furiously. She held it up to her ear.

"Hullo? Hullo? Greater Alberin Monarchist Revival Association? Yes? No! I want to become a member. Yes, I know it's eleven o'clock at night. I'll give you a credit string, and the name is Varria Seuderliv. Yes, we *are* the Seuderlivs directly descended from Riellen. A statement for the media? Try to stop me!"

Having become a financially verifiable monarchist, Varria now sank to the floor, burst into tears, and started screaming abuse about Riellen.

"I'll destroy her!" she shrieked. "I'll write the greatest history ever about the birth of electocracy and tell the truth this time."

"You?" scoffed Lariella. "You could not concentrate long enough to write a shopping list, let alone a history. Go away, do some lifestyling."

"Oh that was uncalled for!" said Breen, sounding hurt.

"I'll show you, I really will!" screamed Varria. "I'm free of the lies, I'm liberated."

"Thanks to people like you we have had a thousand years of people like the inspector being accused of eating babies and raping sheep," laughed Lariella. "You just like a good story, you care nothing for the truth."

Wallas jumped down from the mantelpiece and padded across to where Varria had been beating the book.

"I say, what page has the passage about the sheep?" he asked as he extended his claws and started delicately turning the pages of the battered volume.

Nobody answered.

"Well I think we should all have a nice coffee, or perhaps something stronger," said Breen as he got to his feet.

Varria continued to sit on the floor, weeping into her hands. Lariella came over to sit next to me, bringing her model of the time engine with her. She explained a few of the basics of its operation to me, emphasizing the more important aspects by touching me on the knee and thigh. I continually reminded myself that she was somewhere in advance of fifty, while I was not quite nineteen. Breen returned with a tray of drinks.

"There's nothing here about me!" called Wallas. "Nothing! This pack of lies has nothing about me."

"Welcome to the fellowship of maligned heroes" was my response.

Wallas turned around and squatted over the book.

"Your pardon, ladyship," said Wallas as he voided his bowels onto the open pages. "I have never done this indoors since being transformed into a cat, but this time I really must make an exception."

"I'll have it framed and hang it in my bedroom," said Varria.

"Oh really?" said Wallas, turning to admire his creation. "I suppose it does have a certain artistic flair."

"Coffee or Senderialvin Royal?" asked Breen.

"Senderialvin Royal!" exclaimed Wallas. "But that costs an emperor's ransom."

"Ninety-seven electors for a half pint is hardly cheap," said Breen. "I bought it at the ultramart last week, I should know."

"A thousand years have eroded more than the truth, Constable Wallas," I explained. "The treasures and luxuries of our time may now be bought like a loaf of bread."

✴ ✴ ✴

An hour later Wallas had rendered himself beastly drunk, thrown up yet again on the Vindician carpet, then passed out on Breen's lap. Varria had sealed the book with Wallas's artwork in a box for later framing, and Lariella had used some type of suction engine to clean up the broken glass from Riellen's portrait. After feeding the shredded, trampled painting of Riellen into the fire, Varria riffled through several books until she found a representation of the last pre-electocratic monarch of Alberin, Empress Wensomer. The empress was lying naked on a pile of red cushions and white furs, looking somewhat overweight and passably proud of it. The likeness was not at all bad. It was this that she pasted into the frame and hung on the wall.

"The revisionist chronicles state that you abused your position to seduce both Lavenci and Riellen," said Varria. "What else could I do but believe them?"

"I never laid a hand on Riellen, except to arrest her."

"You were said to have screwed every woman who served in your squad. Riellen was pregnant when she went into exile. I thought it was because of you. Causative determinism states that the past cannot be changed, but . . . but I hated you so much for defiling Riellen, I thought she was the greatest of heroes, I wanted you brought to justice. All the chronicles were clear that you died in Lordworld Plaza an hour before midnight on the last day of the limbo year, so . . . I took the time engine back to that time and waited. I was going to snatch you from the glass dragon that would have killed you, then bring you to justice."

"Are you all familiar with glass dragons?" I asked nobody in particular.

"They were very powerful sorcerers who become enmeshed in their own spells," said Breen. "They took on the form of natural dragons, except on a much larger scale. There have been none for six hundred years."

"Really?" I asked. "Why not?"

"They had no regard for electocratic processes," said Lariella.

"When weapons to disrupt their energies were developed, they were, ah, compelled to make way for electocracy."

"They were murdered by ambitious politicians trying to boost their voter base by means of cheap victories!" snapped the now arch-reactionary Varria. "Laron, that filthy lackey of Riellen who defiled your lady Lavenci, was the first to say that even glass dragons should vote and obey our laws."

Lariella and Breen squirmed. This was clearly a subject that was crammed with sensitivities. For a moment I sat speechless. The girl sounded almost exactly the same as Riellen, which made some sense because she was descended from her. If she had anything like the same drive as her distant ancestor, monarchical government was about to experience a massive revival.

"So why was the glass dragon trying to kill you?" asked Lariella.

"It's name was Terikel, and when she had been human she had been in dispute with Wallas—do not ask why. I was actually defending Wallas, two nights ago, in Lordworld Plaza. Two nights ago in my memories, anyway."

"This is terrible!" shouted Varria. "We must use the time engine, bring her here, introduce her to my therapist."

"Given your record so far with the time engine, I would advise against it," I warned.

"But—"

"Let the inspector continue," said Breen. "This is just too, too intense."

"I ran, with Wallas in my pack. A lamplight girl in a cat suit somehow got mixed up in the chase. I fought with Terikel in Lordworld Plaza, and I was holding ground against her when Varria arrived with the stuncast."

"I thought he was on the point of death!" protested Varria. "I thought to stun the dragon lady and take the inspector into time, to face proper justice. When I fired the stuncast at Terikel she—she caught fire and turned to ash. It was all so confusing."

"Glass dragons cannot sleep as we do, they lose control of the energies that give them their form. When you stunned Terikel, the energies that provide her dragon form were freed. Do continue."

"I fired at you, Inspector, then hid you on a cart that I had, er, stolen temporarily. As I was leaving a sex therapy professional in a cat suit arrived with some constables, pointed at the pile of ashes, and started screaming."

"Breen, are you sure your MLO is turned on?" called Lariella.

"Lie please, anyone?" called Breen.

"My head is not hurting at all," muttered Wallas.

"MISTRUTH CLASS A PLUS: OUTRIGHT LIE."

"More hangover spray?" asked Breen.

"You're such a treasure," replied Wallas, opening his mouth for another dose.

Varria apologized several times for ruining my life, pledged me her savings and future inheritance, and offered me a lifetime of grief amelioration by sexual therapy. Wallas snickered. Breen said that he had to feed the daemon that washed the dishes. Lariella squeezed my thigh and suggested that it was getting late.

"The rug in front of the fire looks more comfortable than any place I have slept recently," I began.

"Oh no no," exclaimed Lariella. "There are forty rooms in this tower, you have a choice of spares. Come with me."

The spare room that was put at my disposal was bigger than most cottages that I have had occasion to stay in. I reached out and felt the bed. It was harder than I had expected, yet strangely yielding.

"How does one command the lamp daemons to stop shining?" I asked as I turned.

Lariella had dropped every shred of her clothing to the floor, with the exception of her footware.

"Look I don't wish to insult you or anything," she declared without a trace of embarrassment or coyness, "but I would be more than happy to pop into bed with you, like as an interim gesture of reconciliation and all that."

"Interim?" I asked with no small degree of alarm.

"Oh yes. By law Varria must sleep with you to demonstrate that she has sincerely overcome her prejudices against you under the Perpetrator Anti-Bigotry Act of 987 AE."

I swallowed. Since Lavenci had kissed me goodbye, only two days earlier, I had traveled a thousand years and been in the close company of five women: a lamplight girl in a cat suit, a homicidal glass dragon, a megalomaniac teenager with a minimal grasp of history, a librarian with a fetish for men of unpleasant body odor, and now the wife of a pregnant lawyer in a pair of knee-high boots with tower heels. During those two days Lavenci had also lived out the rest of her life with another man, and had three children with him.

"Please . . . my values are a thousand years in the past and this is all very upsetting for me," I pleaded. "Are there no exemptions in your laws?"

"Ah, the Ethnic Sensibilities Exemption Amendment of 995," she said reluctantly.

"I am an ethnic, and my sensibilities have been severely strained of late," I insisted, stretching my talent for interpreting law to the very limit.

"But Varria needs a sense of closure for the crime she has committed."

"With no closure she will be all the more driven to write her chronicle."

"Well, I need closure for what my ancestor Riellen did to you a thousand years ago."

In my experience, there is no advantage to be gained by crossing any lady upon whose goodwill one's future depends. I tried weasel words instead.

"In my culture, it is bad manners to lie with someone you esteem on first acquaintance."

"Oh, Inspector, you *esteem* me!" Lariella squealed, wrapping her arms around me, then checking that I was in possession of all my teeth with her tongue. "I've never been esteemed before, what a thrill!"

Apparently that was enough to reassure her that she had saved face. She left. A moment later I was lying fully clothed on the bed, already in the deepest of black and dreamless oblivion.

⚹　⚹　⚹

The people of 1006 After Electocracy had absolutely no concept of modesty, privacy, or any other restraint concerned with nudity or reproductive activities. Around midmorning Wallas jumped onto my bed, started to tell me that an overdose of hangover mist had made him nauseous, then scampered out to be sick again. Breen arrived with a tray of breakfast. Once again, he was wearing his reproductive organs around his neck and nothing else. Lariella entered, not even wearing her boots this time, and holding an agenda of all the things she wanted to see when we traveled to the Alberin of my time. I had taken one mouthful of toast when Varria joined us, wearing not a stitch more than her aunt, and sat on the end of the bed with her autoscribe. Wallas now returned. He gave a hoarse meow, and Lariella lifted him onto the bed. Varria proceeded to read out the first few pages of her history, *Dawn of the Wayfarers*, from the eye of her autoscribe. I corrected several dozen factual errors, including that Pelmore was stunted, twisted, ugly, and impotent.

"He was tall, healthy, well muscled, and handsome in a rough, chunky sort of way."

"But he doesn't *deserve* to be like that!" she protested.

"Until last night *I* deserved to be ugly and twisted, as far as you were concerned. Tell the truth, and you will be all the more convincing because of it."

"Er, you said he lay with Lavenci for a whole night?"

"He did."

"But I can't have her defiled by such a monster in my book. It alienates reader sympathy."

"Read about how constancy glamours are established. He was definitely not impotent."

"Had he not performed the act with her at least once, they would not have been bound together," agreed Lariella.

"'Victim' seems to be a very popular word in these times," Wallas pointed out. "Play up the fact that Lavenci was Riellen's victim, and that Pelmore was just a pawn."

"But a very unpleasant pawn," said Breen.

"It really twists me to think that someone like her could invent such a fine thing as electocracy," said Lariella.

"I can help," said Wallas, frowning as only a hungover cat can. "I was there, after all. Did you know that Riellen, the inspector, and myself, er, what is that silly word you use in this century . . . oh yes, *workshopped* the idea on a barge, drifting down the River Alber?"

"Truly?" gasped Varria. "So she was an intellectual property thief as well!"

"We actually thought up the concept together, and it was the inspector who suggested the actual name electocracy. If you can give me some charm for this nausea, I shall tell you a lot more. I was once a bard, before I was reduced to a cat situation."

"Truly? A real bard of the Dawn Ages? Inspector, is it true?"

Wallas gave me a pleading look.

"He is from the Dawn Ages, and he did write a lot of what he sang," I said diplomatically. "If that is a Dawn Ages bard, then Wallas is one of those."

Varria called "Dictation start!" to her autoscribe, then hurried out with the machine under one arm and Wallas under the other. Lariella tried to participate in the first shower of my entire life. I came out to discover that Breen had cleaned my clothes. "Cleaned" is perhaps the wrong word. They were entirely purged of all stains and dirt, and had ceased to smell of anything whatsoever. Lariella slithered into what she called a gym suit, which had the effect of holding her breasts flat while emphasizing her muscles. Dressed in the clothes of my time, she might have been thought a man, and a very strong and fit man.

Wallas supervised as Breen worked some manner of tailor machine, and together they corrected the stylistic flaws in some period clothing that Lariella had been preparing for her trip back into time. I advised Lariella on what supplies and equipment to take, but she appeared to be disappointed with what she was hearing.

"Are you sure we need so very little to survive in ancient Alberin?" she kept asking.

"Attitude is what keeps one out of trouble, not stuncasts," I assured her.

"You mean I shouldn't take one?"

"We do take one, I saw myself use it."

Wallas padded across the table to where Varria was working with her autoscribe.

"So much to tell, so little time to tell it," he said before relating yet more of his life's story.

* * *

Because of the problems with Lariella's clothes, Varria's newly found desperation for true history, and Wallas's fondness for Senderialvin Royal, we stayed several days more in 1006 AE, which was 4150 as far as I was concerned. I did not venture outside the house. On the eighth night after my arrival Breen organized a type of revel called a party for his pregnancy support collective, their wives, and their wives' dalliance partners. Apparently Lariella's lack of a dalliance partner while Breen was pregnant was a source of embarrassment to him, so that this was his chance to show that there was another male in their house, point in my direction, nudge, and wink.

The sheer weirdness of the spectacle defied description, or even comprehension. Breen had hired what was known as a g-wizard, and this man was apparently a specialist in conjuring succubi and incubi. He provided other services as well, but these were far beyond my understanding. To my relief, Lariella insisted that I wear my Dawn Ages clothing, rather than nothing at all. After greeting the guests in a state of complete nudity, she spent the entire evening adding items of clothing until she was clothed like a man who would not attract undue attention in the Alberin of a thousand years earlier.

You may be familiar with those gatherings where you are new to a group: everyone wants to meet you, but nobody has much in common with you. At first the guests made a great fuss of me, but I had none of their small talk, so presently I was left to myself. I sat in one of the chairs that was made from cushions while trying not to think about anything at all. I do concede that I may have drunk too much wine. While I was of a mood to go to bed, my room was one of those in use by women trying out each other's dalliance partners. Wallas was more of a social success, once people got over the fact that he was a talking cat. Varria spent a lot of time in my vicinity, in a state of complete nudity and carrying her autoscribe.

"Is this typical of your time's courtship rituals?" I asked in a break between her questions about Riellen's shortcomings.

"Breen is one of the hedonista set, they really like getting into it."

"He seems to have little in common with Lariella," I replied, having not understood any of the previous sentence.

"I think Aunt Lari married him to try to get out of herself, you know? They were hyperdyned, and—"

"Hyperdyned?"

"Oh yeah, you wouldn't know. That's adding extra muscles, nerves, gland capacity, and discretionary control to their joyware."

"That still means nothing to me."

She pointed to her crotch, then to mine.

"They had this and that modified so they could do it whenever they like for as long as they like, and feel it ten times more intensely."

I swallowed, aware that I had not managed to hide my astonishment at all well.

"Er, and have you had this done too?"

"No, too dangerous. Hardly a week goes by without someone dying of giga-orgasmic shock."

"Are not the love poxes also a problem?"

"No, everyone has medichip implants."

"Ah, please translate?"

"Nobody can get sick anymore."

Varria left for her room, because her autoscribe was becoming confused by the background conversations. I found myself reading a collection of Lavenci's complete love poetry and letters, some of which had been written for me, but all of which now featured Laron's name. Having got over the initial shock of being jilted for someone else by a sweetheart long dead, I felt vaguely annoyed rather than distraught. I fell asleep.

Wallas was my next visitor. He woke me by jumping into my lap and presenting me with a thing about the size of a large rat that was a glowing green color, and looked like a cross between an octopus and a siege engine. He prodded it with his paw. It came to life! I leaped up from the chair, snatched a poker from beside the fireplace and beat the daemon until it stopped moving. Everyone laughed, then clapped.

"You have just beaten somebody's sex aid to death," announced Wallas.

I lifted the thing on the tip of the poker and peered at it.

"Sex aid?" I asked.

"It helps them do it more and feel it better."

"Wallas, these people have been modified by their physicians. Each one of them has the combined lust potential of a shipload of sailors after a voyage from Diomeda to Alberin against a headwind. Why would they need yet more help?"

"How should I know? They—they have been positively encouraging me to watch as they perform their antics. At first there was some novelty value, I do admit it, then it just became a bore. When do we go home?"

"We are not staying in these times through my choice, Constable Wallas."

"Constable Wallas," he said, sighing. "How pleasant to be reminded of who I am amid all this tasteless insanity. That name and rank are all that I have left to me."

Wallas departed, taking the mangled dalliance device with him. I flopped back into the chair, an arm over my eyes and my mind held studiously blank. A slight coolness indicated that someone was standing between me and the fire. Lowering my arm, I saw that the g-wizard was standing with his back to the hearth and staring at me with an expression of concern. He was clothed only in a posing pouch of orange fur shaped like a hamster with a silly grin.

"I think you would be happier if you shared it," he said tentatively.

"Shared what?"

"Your problem."

"This revel is a little more intense than I am used to."

"Oh is that all? I can give you the RLA of a good analyst."

"What are those things?"

My question was apparently about as fundamental as *what is a privy?* RLA turned out to be Resource Locater Address, and analysts were physicians of the mind.

"There is nothing wrong with my mind, it is perfectly well suited to the, er, place I come from," I said.

"So there are no parties like this in your homeland?" he asked.

"Absolutely not."

"Bor-ing. But you can be adapted."

"I do not wish to be adapted. Adapt me to be part of all this, and I will no longer be myself."

"But you could be so much more—Woo!"

The g-wizard suddenly doubled over in a spasm so violent that he spilled his drink. I heard laughter from across the room as he slowly straightened.

"They have incurred the wrath of the g-wizard," he said with a grin that was marginally sillier than that of the hamster on his posing pouch, tossing a little daemon like a stuncast into the air and catching it. "Little do they know that I hold the master caster."

"Should I know what that is?"

By way of reply he pressed the daemon. Every woman in the house shrieked and writhed simultaneously, and enough wine to fill two or three jars was spilled. Another lengthy explanation established that each of the dalliance stimulation devices that all the guests were by now wearing were controlled by tele-daemons, and could be started remotely. The tele-daemons had been handed out at random, so that nobody knew who was going to react when the things were made to work. The device that Wallas had presented me with was a museum piece by comparison.

Once the g-wizard had established that I was not willing to try any of his wares, he wandered off in search of someone else to amuse. Wallas returned. His fur was fluffed out with alarm.

"If I never witness another couple copulating as long as I live it will be too soon," he muttered as he sat on the armrest cushion of my chair.

"Don't tell me, you were sitting on one of those dalliance devices when it went off."

"Worse! Someone tried to use *me* as a dalliance device."

"I'm going back, Wallas," I declared, staring at the fire. "I can take no more of this. That fire and yourself are the only normal things in this room."

"Me, normal? The situation must be truly grave."

"Do you still want to come with me?"

"Silly question."

"But you are both welcome and safe here, Wallas. You are living better than even an emperor could in our time."

"This age is weird and tasteless."

"But it is not short on luxury. Why go back to life on patrol, cheap wine, and dried fish pieces?"

"To do more great deeds as a Dawn Age Hero, sir. What are luxuries and danger to being a true hero?"

"Tell the truth, Wallas."

Wallas tried to stare me down, failed, then turned away and licked his shoulder in embarrassment.

"Well?" I asked.

"I was telling the truth the first time, sir. This is a world gone mad and packed tight with weirdos. *Weirdo,* good word, is it not? A word invented by this world, for this world. *I* must be the only weirdo in the city."

"But the compensations—"

"The comforts and luxuries cannot make up for the company. Still, I am worried . . ."

Wallas sounding worried was subtly different from Wallas putting on a worried tone, but I had learned to tell that difference. This time he was genuinely worried.

"Worried?" I asked when he did not continue.

"There is no mention of you in the chronicles after the date of our abduction. Do you think you die, sir?"

"We all die, Wallas."

"Do you die unnecessarily early, sir?"

Within the entire moonworld, someone was genuinely worried about me. Admittedly it was a pretentious, egocentric ex-Sargolan Master of the Emperor's Music who had been shapeshifted into an overweight black cat working as a Wayfarer Constable, but even that was enough to cheer me just slightly.

"I know no more of my fate than you do, and that is the truth," I answered, trying to keep emotion out of my voice. "We can but do our best and hope that it will be good enough. Perhaps I become too unimportant to be mentioned in the chronicles, yet live long and well. I noticed that you are mentioned as a magistrate."

"Ah yes, I saw that too! I don't like it! Can you imagine it, me sitting up on a desk, and wearing a wig? Miscreants cowering in the dock? Miscreants that were my business associates? Miscreants willing to talk about my past to anyone who will listen?"

"I would give a florin to see that."

"Bastard—sir."

"Death penalty for accepting bribes."

"I know."

"Risk of assassination by disgruntled relatives of the executed."

"Perhaps it was some other Wallas," he said hopefully.

"The book just listed the names of Dawn Ages magistrates, it did not mention anyone in cat circumstances."

"What a relief."

"Perhaps you were transformed back into a human."

"But I like being a cat. It renders me special—no, no, *exclusive!*"

"Do you still wish to return with me?"

"Yes. I'll just decline any promotions."

"Then get along, Wallas, prepare to leave."

"How need a cat prepare to leave, sir?"

"A large breakfast and a trip to Palladin's sand tray, I should think. I shall have a word to Lariella next time she is between partners. The time engine works, we have the right clothing, I shall be her guide to Dawn Ages Alberin, I mean what else can be stopping us?"

Wallas sauntered off across the room, jumped up onto a table and proceeded to scoff down a plateload of marinated fish on little round pieces of toasted bread. I began to doze.

✴ ✴ ✴

I was quite surprised to find myself on the riverbank at the edge of life. I had thought that only people who were either dying or in extreme danger were drawn to the place. The previous time I had just been hit by the full force of Varria's stuncast, but where was the danger in Breen's party? Had the crumbed salmon fries fermented into something deadly? I recognized Chance in the half-light.

"So you have survived this future, Danolarian," he said genially. "Fortune is very annoyed about that, so beware."

"I recognized your gifts," I said, but it was just polite flattery.

"Very good, that pleases me. I hope you realize that. I am not to be depended upon, however. I scatter as many traps as gifts in the paths of mortals."

"What do you think of a future without Romance?" came a sad voice from a weak light behind me.

"You were cruel to me," I replied angrily. "You were too cruel to too many for too long."

"However cruel I may be, I am better than what is going on in the mansion."

"You cheated everyone, your gifts never last long," began Chance, but he was pushed aside by the next arrival.

"I cannot understand you!" snapped Temptation. "I am offering you so much in this future, yet you spurn everything."

"He is fated to lose everything and vanish from history," laughed Fate's voice from behind her.

"All that you offer are brainless bedmates," I replied. "Why should I find that attractive?"

"He has no spirit left, I have crushed him," said Fate.

"You can be outwitted," insisted Temptation, rounding on Fate.

"Try," said Fate smugly.

"I am the friend of all those cheated by Romance, Danolarian," announced Fortune as she made her entrance out of nothingness. "You are again in my favor, look out for my gifts."

"Fortune can be vindictive, I am impartial," said Chance, folding his arms and smiling. "I ask for no commitment, just belief."

"Even after a thousand years, you all still chase me like hounds after a fox," I cried. "Why do you bother?"

"We are gods, you could never understand," snickered Temptation.

"Go back, you are about to go on a journey," said Chance.

"I shall tempt you to outwit Fate," said Temptation, but I did not hear Fate's reply because the living room was coming back into focus around me.

✳   ✳   ✳

A human-shaped, semi-translucent thing sat down on the rug in front of the fireplace. It was male, and shaped with a musculature that was surreal, rather than merely improbable. Over its reproductive apparatus was a sort of prehensile tentacle which I tried very hard not to stare at. He looked at me as if I were expected to say something.

"I did not know that autons needed to rest," I managed.

"Oh I'm not resting, my cycle has run out."

"Your pardon?"

"I'm about to cease."

"You mean die?"

"I am not alive. You don't seem to have met an incubus before."

"True."

"I was cast fresh at the beginning of the party. Now I am old and jaded."

"Old? At four hours?"

"Have you any idea what I have been doing for those four hours?"

"Something extreme?"

"I have had to be eleven different forms—and act them out. Novelty is such a transient thing."

I was tempted to ask about specifics, but I decided that I probably did not want to know.

"How does it end?" I now asked. "Do you throw yourself into the fire or something?"

"No, I just fade. Thank you for speaking with me. It is our duty to cease alone, so the clients will not be depressed. I never thought I would have the honor of having a real conversation while I existed."

"How can there be unreal conversations?"

"I meant that you spoke to me as a person, and not just a function."

There was a slight crackling sound, then the incubus was gone. I looked at the clock picture on the wall, and saw that it was approaching midnight. I wondered whether I should try to be more sociable, then thought the better of it. There were five pregnant, naked men wearing their genitalia in jars between their breasts, two women who were naked except for tower heel boots and hamster-shaped sex aids, four incubi and succubi who looked as if they were awaiting permission to die, and a naked male dalliance partner who was asleep under a table. I cannot begin to describe how hard it is not to stare when one strikes up a conversation under such circumstances.

Varria reappeared from elsewhere in the building, carrying Wallas and my pack.

"You do come back, I know it," she said breathlessly as I stood up.

"Am I going somewhere?" I asked.

"We are going back to the Dawn Ages," said Wallas brightly. "Lariella means it to be a party trick, so don't tell anyone."

"You *must* come back, that *must* be why you vanish from history," continued Lariella. "You come back for me, I know it."

I was saved from having to reply by Breen, who came hurrying over waving one of those personal journal daemons. Even in the eight days that I had been in that future his breasts had grown alarmingly.

"Remember, I birth in two weeks," he said. "Do make sure Lariella comes back before then."

"And then you are all mine for closure!" declared Varria.

Wallas said something sarcastic in archaic Sargolan, but neither Breen nor Varria understood.

"Take lots of vidpix, said Breen, "and do bring something from Dawn Ages Alberin for the baby."

As I have said, Lariella had begun the evening naked, and had slowly been dressing as the hours passed. She now entered the room fully clothed as a Dawn Ages artisan and carrying a pack modeled on mine.

"Danolarian, have you been told?" she asked in a whisper.

"About leaving, here and now?"

"Yes, yes, are you ready? Is there anything you need to do, like visit the bathroom or say goodbyes?"

"When you are ready, so too am I."

"Good. Now remember, no hinting. I want this to be a complete surprise. Varria, go to the bedrooms, get everyone to gather here."

I put Wallas in my pack with just his head protruding, then stood beside the door to the stairs while Breen held up a glass jug and struck it with a spoon to get the attention of the guests. Eighteen guests, the g-wizard, nine succubi, and eight incubi ceased their conversations and fondling activities as they crowded around us.

"Empathenes, you might think that this gathering is the pre-birthing party for our little collective, but we also have a secret reason," Breen announced.

There was a rustle of eager whispers among the jaded guests. Their lives were an ongoing quest for novelty, and even though the novelties of the evening had my sensibilities screaming for mercy, it was nothing special for them. The door behind us slid open.

"I would like you all to come upstairs with us," said Lariella. "Take your time, there is more time in this house than you could ever guess."

I was weak-kneed with relief as we climbed the stairs. Very little of the Wall Tower building was as I remembered it, and it was not until I entered the room with the time engine that I realized where I was. The walls and floorboards were stark and rough-hewn: they had been preserved for a thousand years, rather than renovated and rendered tasteful. The only change was a large window in one wall, which was apparently where a loading bay had been added at some time in a more recent past than the one I knew. Apart from the time engine, the room was empty as we entered.

This was the first time that I had been given a chance to examine the time engine, and as the guests filed into the room behind us I tried to guess at its functions. Its dimensions were about those of a pony with short legs, and the legs were very similar to mechanical hoofs. In the place of a head was a lectern with four levers and some rows of little square windows. The body was long enough to seat three or four people, and there were running boards instead of stirrups. What really caught my attention were the four rings, roughly eight feet in diameter, that enclosed it. They were attached at no point, they merely floated in midair, enclosing the incomprehensible vessel-steed-machine-carriage. As I approached the time engine to look at the lectern I put my hand out—and it passed right through one of the rings.

The four levers were labeled ACTIVE, TEMPORAL, LATERAL, and VERTICAL. The TEMPORAL lever also had FORWARD and BACKWARD inscribed above and below, suggesting that it was the one that controlled motion through time. My overall impression was that it was a very complex mechanism that was quite easy to operate. Just as a large ship with a crew of hundreds might be guided by means of a single steering pole, so too was this vessel of time controlled simply.

I made up my mind to watch carefully as Lariella operated it. After slinging her pack over the backrest at the end of the saddle bench, she mounted this bench immediately behind the steering lectern, then invited me to sit behind her. From what I could hear of the whispers and giggles, most of those present thought it to be some manner of huge dalliance machine, and were anticipating a wildly novel performance by us.

"Just hold on to my waist and do not move," Lariella warned as she reached out and pulled the ACTIVE lever from OFF to ON.

"I may throw up," commented Wallas from the pack on my back.

"Friends, empathenes, as you all know, this family is descended from Riellen, the mother of electocracy herself," said Lariella as her hand reached out for the TEMPORAL lever. "Students of history among you may also know that Riellen charged her descendants with a mighty but mysterious task. It is now my pleasure to announce that after a thousand and six years, that task is finally nearing completion."

I detected tones of disappointment in the whispers and murmurs that followed her words. The general impression of the guests was that any task that had taken a thousand and six years was unlikely to have anything to do with sensual gratification or recreational activities involving genitalia.

"What I wish to do is announce a second party," Lariela continued. "That party will be in five days, and there you will be the first to see such sights as nobody on any moonworld has ever dreamed possible. Until then, think upon this."

Lariella pulled the TEMPORAL lever down, in the direction of BACK-WARD. The room instantly snapped into a grey, washed-out light, and I felt a wave a nausea grip me. Imagine that you are plunging headlong while staying in the same place, and you will have some idea of the sensation of time travel. The four circles of nothingness were spinning so fast that they formed a blurred sphere eight feet in diameter, and there was a very penetrating hum from somewhere in the body of the vessel. My host had positioned the time engine so that we faced the window, and through this I saw a day in that Alberin of the future brighten with dusk and fade with dawn in no more than a single minute. Lariella pulled the TEMPORAL lever back farther, and the pitch of the hum was raised as our speed through times already past was increased.

Part Two

PAST REPETITIVE

Through the window we saw the buildings of Alberin grow and collapse in reverse, at about the speed of a battle galley docking. Looking over Lariella's shoulder, I saw that the date was displayed in the square windows of the lectern. There was a flash of red as the city burned six hundred years into the past, then the decay and rise of the buildings continued on a smaller scale. At eight hundred years the window that had been our view out into the city suddenly reverted to an arrowslit, and thereafter we could see nothing but the flickering greyness of time travel, with the goods being stored in the room flashing in and out of existence.

For most of the time we said nothing, probably because we were overwhelmed by what we were seeing. Wallas had been awake for the journey into the future, but I had been unconscious and this was Lariella's first experience of her own invention. When the row of windows indicated that we were just a hundred years after my birth, Lariella moved the TEMPORAL lever to slow our progress into the past.

"Can you aim to stop in late afternoon, on the sixth day of Two-month, 3144 of the old calendar?" I asked.

"Oh yeah, no problem. It's a day before the first Lupanian attack on Alberin, right?"

"That is true. It is also the day before Pelmore vanishes from the dungeons."

"Don't we need more time to prepare?"

"More time to prepare is also more time to get into trouble. As I trust you to navigate this thing, please trust me to guide us safely through the Alberin of my time."

✳   ✳   ✳

Wall Tower was being used as a storehouse in the year 3144. When the individual storage rooms were not in use they were left unbarred, which was reasonable enough because they were empty.

The time engine came to rest with another lurch, but the room remained dim because little light was being admitted through the arrowslit window. After experiencing the disorientation of a journey through time, I now found that the very solidity of everything was unsettling as I got to the floor.

"Can I open my eyes now?" asked Wallas from within my pack.

"We are a year less a month earlier than when we set out," I replied.

"Old Alberin," said Lariella reverentially. "Alberin of the Dawn Ages."

Through the arrowslit I could see a cityscape of tiles, thatch, timber, and brick through a veil of hearth smoke. The only wagons visible were being pulled by horses, and there was not a pane of glass to be seen anywhere. I stared longingly out, like a sailor catching sight of a row of lamplight girls on a wharf after a long voyage.

"Is anything wrong?" asked Lariella as she took Wallas out of my backpack.

"No, nothing," I replied. "I was trying to estimate the time of day from the shadows. Two or three hours before sunset, I would say."

"According to our body clocks it is half an hour past midnight."

"There is no clock in my body."

"No no, a body clock is . . . oh never mind. What do we do now?"

"You stay here with Wallas and do nothing. I need to secure this room in my name."

I emerged onto what was now a timber walkway beside a central open space. Men were going about their business, carrying sacks and crates, and nobody paid me much attention. I was dressed as a Way-farer Constable, after all, so everyone was probably hoping that I was going to walk on past them and not stop to ask questions. I descended stairs that had not been there in Lariella's future, then went to the keeper's room and rapped on the door. The door opened. A man resembling a quarterstaff with a beer belly peered out.

"Aye?" he asked, not recognizing me, for he had only met me in the future.

"That room is splendid, I shall take it," I declared.

"Eh? What room?"

"Northwest corner, third floor. I have inspected it, and it's splendid. Is this enough for two weeks?"

I tipped enough silver into his hand to secure the room for a month.

"Aye, reckon this'll cover it. What's to go there?"

"My wife is soon to arrive on a deepwater trader, with many boxes of clothes from a trip to Sargol and Diomeda."

"Tell me 'bout it. Canna let mine near a market either."

"We have to keep her goods safe before they are shipped up the river to our estate at Gatrov."

"Gatrov, eh? Been hearin' strange tales 'bout Gatrov lately. Heard anythin' yerself?"

"Oh just some nonsense about it being burned by giant spiders from the moonworld Lupan."

"Oh, so ye reckon there's nothin' in all that?"

"Of course not."

I returned to the room where Lariella and Wallas were waiting with the time engine. Now that I knew how easy it was to operate, I had strong doubts about leaving it unguarded, even were there a lock on the door.

"Is there anything you can do to make the time engine immobile, ladyship?" I asked. "Remove the daemons that drive it along or some-such?"

"Oh, nothing easier, I just remove the drive keys."

As I watched, Lariella turned the ACTIVE lever a half rotation against the motion of a clock, pushed down upon it, then turned it another half rotation. She then withdrew the lever, revealing it to be something in the nature of a key. *Lever-keys,* I thought as she withdrew the other three in like fashion. *Amulets that both secure and operate the time engine.*

Lariella had a padlock that not only secured the door, but gave off some manner of aura that rendered people uneasy if they came too close. It was not enchantment, but it had the same effect. We set off into the streets of Alberin, and I was almost overwhelmed with relief to be home again, more or less. The keeper said that the warehouse was locked at sunset, but added that he lived on the premises if we needed access after dark and were willing to pay.

"I can't wait to visit my first tavern," said Lariella excitedly as we walked.

"You will not have to," I said, taking her arm and steering her to the right. "This is the Lamplighter, I need to hire some help here and stay the night."

The unimposing little building near the riverside seemed to fall short of Lariella's expectations.

"This? I mean I know that what we call the Lamplighter is a reconstruction, but this—this *shack* is . . ."

Words failed her, which was probably just as well. The tapman recognized me at once, and as soon as I took Wallas from my pack and placed him on the serving board a maid set a bowl of wine in front of him.

"So good to be home," said Wallas, sighing.

"The Lamplighter, I just can't believe that I'm here," said Lariella, now realizing that the reek of smoke, spilled and stale drink, burned pies, vomit, and unwashed bodies meant that this was not a sanitized reconstruction for the delight of tourists who would not be born for a thousand years.

"Remember, you are meant to be a man," I said sternly.

"Did I tell you I was once the cook here?" asked Wallas. "That was before my cat condition, of course."

"Need the back attic room, just tonight," I said softly to the tapman. "No questions. In days to come, make no mention of it unless I speak first."

"Right on, Inspector."

"Also need your handcart and cover. Tomorrow morning."

"What's to carry? Body or goods?"

"One body, alive, alive-oh."

"Alive is trouble. Why not just give 'im the big red grin and send 'im swimming?"

"Tempting, but I need him alive. Oh, and meet my friend Lars. He's got a talent for making people tell me things they'd prefer I didn't know."

"Say no more, lads. Lars, m'lord, feel welcome 'ere."

We ascended the stairs to the attic room, which contained four bunks and very little else. The one I selected had a vague reek about it if the window was not left open, but was otherwise fairly clean.

"Drunks sleep off the night's excesses in the attic rooms," I explained to Lariella as we returned downstairs. "The tapman is an old friend, and quite reliable."

"So we are staying here?"

"Just tonight."

"Magical!"

Lariella insisted on immediately drinking a pint and eating a pie in the Lamplighter's taproom, just to say she had done it. Three pints and two dances later she was making suggestions about what sorts of uses our two bodies might be put to in the attic room. Three dozen tunes, four dances, and nine pints later, I had to carry her upstairs to her bunk. On the other hand, this saved me from having to participate in genuine Dawn Ages courtship activities, which was a real issue for me. After all, I was in times when my sweetheart Lavenci was alive and still in love with me, and even though my earlier self was also in the city this made me feel as if I were hers again. Besides, I knew that Lariella had been massively enhanced in terms of being able to perform and enjoy the consummation of dalliance, so whatever I managed was sure to be a disappointment for her. Wallas spent the night curled up on her stomach, however, so in a sense she was not entirely without male company.

✳ ✳ ✳

The following morning Lariella was saved from a severe hangover by one of her philters from the future. She was, however, introduced to the unpleasant reality that folk of my time did not have showers, and neither did they bathe more often than every month at best. We began the day in the taproom, before dawn, with dried fruit, bread, and two pints of weak ale.

"I have not drunk anything without alcohol in it since arriving here," complained Lariella.

"Brewing renders water into ale, and thus safe from disease and bad humors," I replied. "It is the same with wine."

"Nobody drinks water," added Wallas. "Nobody who has ideas about staying alive, anyway."

"Curiously liberating, I suppose," she replied. "Do they have beer?"

"Not in quantity, hops are not grown in these parts. It is ale or nothing."

"What now?"

"We go to the palace."

"Oh, magical! Do we meet anyone royal?"

"Only if we want to get ourselves arrested. Greater Alberin is being ruled by a regent at the moment, and he is not a nice man. Pelmore is currently in the palace dungeons. My younger self has convicted him of murder, and is going to make sure that he is executed later today. We have to get Pelmore out of the dungeons before my younger self returns and meets me."

"Ah, so we'll fight our way in with the stuncast?"

"No, we shall sign the visitors' book, then write an entry in the prisoners' register stating that we have taken Pelmore out for preexecution processing."

"I—er, sorry?"

"Torture," translated Wallas.

"But the International Human Rights Consensus of 990—"

"Is nine hundred and ninety years in the future. I am one of Pelmore's victims, because he caused me to be poisoned. Thus I have the right to give him a damn good thrashing before he is hanged."

"But that's barbaric!"

"Inspector Barbarian at your service."

"I'm no barbarian," said Wallas haughtily. "Ale for breakfast, how very nauseating. I drink milk and wine."

"I will be able to remove Pelmore from the holding cells and take him to the persuasion chamber," I continued. "Lariella, you are to play the role of my contract torturer. Once Pelmore is out, we shall strike him over the head, bundle him onto the Lamplighter's cart, cover him with offal, and wheel him out of the refuse gate."

"Oh. Ah, but could we drop him with the stuncast?" said Lariella hopefully. "It is so much more humane, and there is no risk of concussion or brain damage."

"Very well, use your damn stuncast then."

* * *

Unlike anyone else in the city except Lariella and Wallas, I knew that a Lupanian attack on the city was only hours away as we wheeled the cart through the streets of Alberin in the early morning. I also knew that my earlier self was a mile or so across the city, having a very significant talk with Lavenci, so there was no risk of an embarrassing confrontation.

I was known to the guards at the palace, and at the front gate I told them that I was there to collect what was left of a prisoner who had died under torture. I was told politely but firmly that bodies were to be removed via the refuse gate, unless the body was that of a nobleman. A guard escorted us to the refuse gate. Here we were told that we could not have a pass issued to access the dungeons from the refuse gate, but could push our handcart through. Having pushed our cart through and proceeded to the kitchen vats, we loaded some pig organs and lengths of intestine into the cart. Wallas, who was riding in the tray of the cart, muttered a few protests. We then left the cart, returned to the front gate, and acquired our passes for the dungeons.

Our greatest advantage was that I had been in the dungeons two nights before—as a client, so to speak. I was now welcomed and even cheered by the guards. I produced a prisoner closure petition, which had been fabricated by Varria on her autoscribe a thousand years in the future, and which did not exist in these times. It incorporated a very good reproduction of the regent's signature from a display in the Electocratic Museum of Alberin.

"So wot's closure, then?" asked the warren guard as I explained all the words longer than four or five letters.

"It means I'm allowed to beat the shyte out of the bastard before he's hanged," I replied. "I'm a victim, you see, so I have the right to take out a bit of personal revenge."

"Closure, yeah, I likes that. I mean instead of bein' allowed to kick his head abaht the square once he's dead, you get to put the boot in while he can feel."

"You have it."

"Wot he do to you?"

"He tried to poison me. There was a lady involved."

"Say no more, m'lord. Arriolp!"

A large pile of muscles and hair that turned out to be a defrocked bridge troll unfolded itself into a standing position.

"Aye?"

"Fetch prisoner Pelmore Haftbrace."

Arriolp lumbered off with a ring of keys.

"So wot's the story on them spiders wot burned Gatrov, then?" the warren guard asked as we waited.

"Start running now," I replied softly.

"As bad as that?" he gasped, then he gave me a little push. "Yer just doin' a joke on me!"

"Afraid not. I helped kill one, that's why I'm a hero. It was pure luck."

"Reckon they'll come here?" he now asked, his eyes huge.

"Oh yes, maybe as early as today."

"Steamin' shyte!"

Pelmore looked strangely composed as I collected him, as if he knew something that I did not. The warren guard went out of his way to be helpful. Two nights before I had been a prisoner in his cells, but now I was not just free, I was a hero. I might even rise to become a noble, and if I did that, I might visit the dungeons to complain about the treatment during my single night there. Thus everyone wanted to be nice to me, in fact everyone could not do enough for me.

"Ya need a smithy," said the warren guard as I accepted Pelmore's tether from Arriolp.

"I already have a closure professional," I replied patting Lariella on the shoulder.

"Nah, you don't understand. Torturers might know how to *use* equipment, but do they know how to *maintain* it?"

"I'm sure my closure professional can cope," I began.

"Wot's a grumlin spike, then?" he asked Lariella.

"I specialize in handheld instruments," said Lariella, recovering well.

"Oh no you don't, I can see wot's to happen. You two will take one look at the intrusion rack and say 'Nothin's too good for our Pelmore!'"

"Intrusion rack?" gasped Pelmore.

We began to climb the steps out of the dungeons, the blacksmith tagging along with us. I had, however, prepared for any such difficulties by bringing money.

"Look, this man may declare some sensitive matters during procedures," I said to the blacksmith as we paused before the persuasion chamber's door.

"I rogered his sweetheart," said Pelmore smugly.

"See what I mean?" I responded.

"Rode her like a spirited palfrey," added Pelmore.

"People who hear what he shouts might well have to disappear," I warned.

"Really?" gasped the blacksmith.

"She loved every moment, that's what burns him," said Pelmore.

"Couldn't he wear a gag?"

"Oh no, it's important that I hear his screams," I insisted.

"I know the inquisitor general," said Pelmore smugly. "If anyone lays a hand on me, it will go badly for them."

"What say you put yourself out of earshot?" I suggested to the blacksmith as I slipped a few silver florins into his hand.

"I'll need a sign-off note for the hour," he said doubtfully.

"I'll give you one for the rest of the day."

The blacksmith hurried away, yet still Pelmore did not look unduly worried.

"The overseer of the persuasion chambers is with the inquisition," said Pelmore, inclining his head toward the door. "In there is the safest place for me in all of Alberin."

"Luckily we are not going in there," said Lariella sternly as she fired the stuncast at Pelmore.

Carrying Pelmore was no easy task, even though both Lariella and I were very strong. With a cloak over his shackles we got him through the kitchen, explaining that he was a courtier who had fainted with horror when I had told him about what the Lupanians had done during the battle for Gatrov. Once outside and alone, we sliced off most of his clothing, loaded him onto the handcart, then covered his torso with offal to make it look as if he had been drawn, but had died before we had managed to hang and quarter him.

"Now we should have no trouble getting him out of the refuse gate," I said, looking down at the mess that covered most of our prisoner.

"Do you think anyone will notice that he has two livers and five kidneys?" asked Lariella.

"I've never heard of a palace guard who has studied anatomy," said Wallas as I drew the tentcloth over the cart.

As we approached the refuse gate Lariella and I began some carefully rehearsed bickering.

"I told you that disemboweling would kill him," I snapped once we were within earshot of the guards.

"I've done it before, my clients have always lived at least four hours," insisted Lariella.

"There was a perfectly good rack available, but no, you had to use that damn boning knife."

"It's a family heirloom."

"Well it killed him!"

"Some people have no respect for tradition!"

We stopped before the guards, and I drew the tentcloth cover aside.

"I'm afraid there has been an embarrassing accident that needs to be disposed of," I said, untying my purse. "How much?"

Through a totally unexpected stroke of Fortune, one of the guards happened to cope badly with the sight of blood. He managed to run about ten feet before dropping to his knees and being noisily sick.

"So, got an embarrassment ter make vanish?" asked the other guard as I drew the tentcloth back over the body.

"How much do you usually charge?" I asked, displaying fifteen florins.

✳ ✳ ✳

Lariella was surprised to the point of being scandalized at how easy it had been to extract Pelmore from the dungeons.

"I know the system, as you people of the future would say," I tried to explain. "The guards knew me, and they thought that if I did anything funny I would soon be caught out."

"But you *will* be caught out!"

"Oh no, because I have seen the future. I know that the system will cease to exist in a few hours."

"I could hardly believe the sexophobic, verbally incorrect language that Pelmore used!" she snapped with considerable indignation. "It was such a gross abuse of the intimacy between him and a woman who had accorded him physically significant interactions."

"What do you suggest we should do?"

"He should be made to accept an empathy confrontation with Lavenci."

"I have a better idea. What say we exile him a few thousand years in the past, then sell him as a slave?"

"But slavery has been abolished under the International Human Rights Consensus of 990."

"Which will not exist for another thousand years, give or take. These are cruel times, ladyship. We have few dungeons, so death or exile are prescribed for everything that is not covered by a week in the stocks, a good flogging, or creative mutilation."

"Slavery is the closest thing to the prisons of your time," added Wallas.

"Taking Pelmore away into time is not just a way of breaking the constancy glamour between him and my truelove," I said firmly. "It is also his new sentence. Exile is a big advance on being dead."

By now we had reached the bottom of Palace Hill, and were on the fringes of the comfortingly crowded and chaotic streets of Wharfside. I tossed the offal covering Pelmore to some stray dogs, then replaced the cover of the cart.

"Ahead is the Metrologans' temple, but we are not going there," I explained. "A lady that I once protected has a house nearby. I happen to know that her house remains undamaged in the days ahead, so it is there that we shall go."

It is fair to say that Madame Dolvienne was startled to see me at her door.

"But Inspector, you just left," she said as Lariella and I bowed to her.

"Everything has changed," I explained. "I have a double playing my part, he was the one you have just been speaking with."

"A double? But he knew, well, everything about you."

"He is a very good double. This is Lariella. She is a woman in disguise."

"I—oh."

"She is a fugitive, and new to Alberin."

Having once been a fugitive herself, Dolvienne seemed to decide that sympathy was in order.

"Of course, if Danolarian has you in his care then welcome, madame," she declared sincerely, taking Lariella's arm.

"There is also a prisoner under the cloths on that handcart."

"A prisoner?"

"Yes. He must be hidden here too."

"So you want to keep him here, and not in the proper dungeons? Inspector Danolarian, this is just a house."

"It is only for a few days. There are people who would gladly see him walk free. Powerful people."

"I see. Well, keep him here, I suppose. I owe you so much, we have survived enough peril for many lifetimes."

"Aye, what other woman can say she fought in the Battle of Racewater Bridge?" I said, watching for Lariella's reaction out of the corner of my eye.

"Racewater Bridge?" gasped Lariella. "You are *the* Dolvienne?"

While Lariella deluged Dolvienne with questions, I wheeled Pelmore around to the stables. From here I carried him into the house, unseen by the neighbors. Dolvienne entered the room, Wallas in one hand and a bowl of wine in the other. Dragonfang, the large and indolent dog that Dolvienne kept for protection and company, looked up at Wallas, woofed once for the sake of form, then lowered its head to its paws and closed its eyes. Dolvienne set bowl and cat on the kitchen floor.

I sprawled on a bench for some moments, my mind blissfully blank. Lady Dolvienne's house had survived a thousand years from that day; I had even seen it in a tourist pamphlet of 1006 AE. Thus I knew it to be safe, but there was more than that. It was about to be what they called renovated in Lariella's time, and this would involve everything from rebinding the roof to ripping up and reseating the flagstones in the basement. This gave me hope for a little truth about my place in history finding its way into the distant future.

Going down into the cellar, I found some wine, oddments of furniture . . . and rolls of roofing lead. There were flagstones on the floor, and a few tools on shelves. In short, everything that I needed was there.

I was back in the parlor when Dolvienne presented Lariella for my inspection. The timefarer was now dressed in a most fetching green skirt, one meant to be worn with boots because it came down only to midcalf.

"I bought these just before the captain was murdered," said Dolvienne. "I have not had the heart to wear them since."

Dolvienne had a somewhat better curved figure than Lariella, but the timefarer filled the clothes well enough to be convincing. I said a few words about how alluring she looked, and she did not seem to know how to take them. Apparently complimenting women upon how well they looked was not verbally correct one thousand years in the future, even though spending ten minutes in bed together by way of greeting was considered to be good manners.

"Watch the public sundials, be sure not to linger too long at the market," I warned. "Be sure to be back here no later than two hours from now."

"But why?" asked Dolvienne.

"Trust me, ladyship, and ask no questions. Can you buy me ink, paper, and quills?"

"I have them already, they belonged to the captain. I have been unable to cast away anything that belonged to him, yet it is so sad to see his things go unused. Take them, with all my goodwill."

"My thanks, but just one more thing. Are there bows in the house?"

"There is the captain's."

"Then buy another, with a draw that you can use. Also, buy twelve dozen arrows, snaggleheads."

"*Twelve dozen?* But—"

"No questions, there is little time."

⚹ ⚹ ⚹

Once the women were gone, I began to write my version of the role of Inspector Danolarian Scryverin in the Lupanian Invasion. The words came easily after five years of keeping journal entries in the Wayfarers. More to the point, I already knew the story. After just a few lines I began to see everything through the eyes of the fictitious Wayfarer Constable Penwright.

This is the chronicle of Constable Penwright, a constable with the Wayfarers, one who served with Inspector Danolarian, Constable Riellen, Constable Roval, and the famous were-cat, Constable Wallas. As I write, it is the fifteenth day since the first of the voidships from Lupan began to fall, but this very day we did break the ranks of the Lupanians and defeat them forever. I am a boarder in the house of Lady Dolvienne, and although the folk of city are out and about, celebrating the downfall of the Lupanians, it is my intent to chronicle what I saw while it is fresh in my memory. While I did no more than cower behind the real heroes, I saw and heard everything that happened. My gift to the future is not a great feat of arms, the blessing of electocracy, or acts of clever magic. Alas, no acts of passion were mine to perform either, but I can write, and write I shall. My chronicle begins on the afternoon before the first of the voidships from Lupan descended from the sky, because on this very afternoon, electocracy was born. We were on a barge on the River Alber, floating downstream to the river port of Gatrov. For a time Constable Riellen practiced her skills of oratory upon some dozens of sheep that were the cargo of the barge. Presently a discussion began upon the theory of representation in government . . .

And so I wrote. True, I later wrote of events that happened a few days after I had seen myself disappear on the time engine, but I knew the future, so what did it matter? In a thousand years some artisan would find my chronicle, sealed within a lead pipe beneath a flagstone of Dolvienne's cellar. Then . . . I thought forward a thousand years, shuddered, then returned to my writing.

✳ ✳ ✳

Pelmore groaned, and I looked up from my chronicle. He seemed quite agitated to find himself in a house, as opposed to a cell, but this was only reasonable. A cell implied something official. A house suggested that someone, probably myself, had taken the law into his own hands. I had been writing for quite some time by then, and felt in need of a break. After standing up and stretching, I walked over and removed his gag.

"Now then Pelmore, before you speak let me introduce you to this little engine," I said as he drew breath, but before he could say anything. "You have already felt its touch, and you know that it really hurts. This slider here varies the intensity of the pain that it causes from merely *ouch* to such agony that you black out. This slider on the other side makes the beam narrow or broad, and this red circle on the top is the release that operates it. It may be discharged two thousand times before it ceases to operate, and it has only been used about a half dozen. Now then, will it be a scream for help followed by agony, or do you wish to speak quietly?"

"You'll never get away with this," muttered Pelmore.

"You think so? Watch me at work."

"I am an agent of the Inquisition Against Sorcery."

"You are a condemned murderer, and I am a field magistrate. Be nice to me, your sentence is at my discretion."

"You just want revenge. Lavenci chose me ahead of you."

"That was a love charm, put upon you two by Riellen."

"Wake up to yourself, Inspector! I know love charms, they don't work unless both partners already have a fancy for each other. I've paid plenty for them, they only work sometimes, when desire is present but being held down. Cast one upon a goodwife who is bored and inclined to adventure, and she will put aside vows of marriage and raise her skirts."

"Lavenci is mine now, nothing else—"

"Lavenci is bound to me by a constancy glamour, only I may pleasure her."

"From what I have heard, there was not much pleasure involved."

"She would not have told you the truth."

"I was outside in the stables, I heard all there was to hear."

"Lies."

"I was lying there, I saw you clamber from the window of Lavenci's room with all her possessions and clothes in a pack. You stumbled over my leg in the darkness, then kicked a pail, thinking it was me. Your pain gratified me, I am pleased to say."

They were the facts, so I had him. Pelmore floundered for words in the face of truth that did not support him, but the game was not yet over. Why did I let him do it? I should have kept him gagged, but I chose to stand and spar.

"Ah, so you did not see," he continued presently. "You did not see me astride her, my hands cupped over her mouth to stifle her moans and squeals of delight."

An image of a scene that may or may not have ever taken place flashed before me. I dismissed it, but it is not easy to remain impartial when matters like that are under discussion.

"I know why I'm here," he continued.

"Really?"

"I'm here because you don't want me killed. If I die, it will be seven years before the constancy glamour breaks down and you can touch your sorceress baggage. I'm safe."

"Not as safe as you think."

"I have my rights!"

"And I have power over you. That is something for you to worry about."

"I'm not worried."

"You should be. I have been doing some research, Pelmore. Those men and women who had constancy glamours imposed upon them in the past went to some ingenious lengths to sidle around the constraints. Women used sleeping philters, so that their lovers could at least have the delight of their slumbering bodies. With men it was harder, but again there were successes. Drink the juice of berries from a goadiar bush and what happens?"

"You get it up, but not for me. The constancy glamour vanquished even those effects."

"Some men tried following the juice with a sleeping philter. Would you believe that they were rendered fit for action, although asleep?"

"What good did that do them?"

"It provided some amusement for their ladies, but that is not my point. It proved that the glamour does not reside in the organs of delight, but in the mind. Smother the mind in sleep and you smother the glamour."

There was a very dangerous lesson in my words, but Pelmore was more intent on hurting me than looking to his own welfare. Not until it was too late, anyway. I returned to my writing. Pelmore brooded upon his single night in bed with my sweetheart.

"She likes to leave her clothes on at the first instance, did you know that?" he asked, but I kept writing. "She took her boots off because her feet were hot from the dancing, but then it was all tangled clothes and fumbling. The second time and thereafter, that is when she took her clothes off."

"I am aware of all that, Pelmore, Lavenci and I have no secrets from each other."

"Ah yes, but I have had what you will never have."

"Pubic lice?"

"I know women, Inspector Danolarian. She now feels guilt for taking pleasure with me. So many of Gatrov's girls will not play bull and cow with their lovers for memory of performing the act that way with me."

"I know from the divorce cases I have presided over that women often—"

"She will *never* want to leave her clothes on for you, Inspector, be sure of it. Kill me, wait seven years, then see. Oh she'll do it, but only if you beg her. I'll always be in bed with you two, Lavenci will delight in being naked with you, but should you do it clothed, she will be back in Gatrov, in an upstairs room of the Bargeman's Barrel, in bed with me while you lie alone in the stables."

Burning with malice, I paused in my writing and thought upon it. In what was currently the future, on the very few occasions that Lavenci and I had performed our dalliances clothed, it had always been at my suggestion. Perhaps Pelmore was right, we would never be rid of him . . . yet there was something else.

"I suppose I could kill you now and begin the experiment" was the best reply I could manage, for my mind was not focused upon clever retorts.

"I'll always be alive and between the two of you, Inspector—"

He stopped as I swept the table clear of papers, ink, quills, and blotting powder with my arm. I stood up, glaring down at Pelmore. He had suddenly become fearful, suspecting that he had pushed me too far. I tossed the stuncast in the air and caught it.

"The same lady that gave me this has . . . a ferry. It is a very special type of ferry, for instead of taking people to and fro across the River Alber, it carries people through time. I am not the Danolarian you think I am, Pelmore. I am from your future."

"Talk and boasts, that's only talk and boasts."

Defiance, he is showing defiance in the face of death, I thought. That was wrong, that was all wrong. The Pelmore that I remembered did not have such spirit as that, and people did not change so very much in a day or two. It was as if he were heightened or enhanced.

"In a few days Lavenci and I will begin sleeping together," I concluded.

"But the healer woman said that is not possible. Only seven years after the death of one partner bound by a constancy glamour may the other do all that with someone new."

"That is old magic, Pelmore, this is new magic."

I pointed the stuncast at him, moved the slider back to mere pain, and depressed the stud. He writhed and screamed most gratifyingly.

"The time engine is new magic too," I explained. "The constancy glamour is a spell that was devised before time engines were known. I know that I take you into the past, and that the trip through time breaks the glamour. Lavenci and my younger self will lie in each other's arms just six days from now. Once in the distant past, I shall be free to execute you with no consequences for Lavenci."

Pelmore should have cowered, but instead he laughed at me.

"She will never be free of her night with me," he said proudly.

Pelmore was not the sharpest ax in the armory, but he was not so stupid, brave, or even vindictive as to defy me like that. This is not quite Pelmore. Perhaps someone had enchanted him to goad me into killing him. Someone wanted me to be upset, to lash out. Without another word I pushed the slider all the way up, stunned Pelmore into silence, then went out into the street and walked up and down to calm my agitation. Pelmore had to live, no matter what my feelings.

✳   ✳   ✳

The ladies returned from the market after another hour, and not long after that the Lupanian fighting tripods strode out of the west and began attacking the city. There was little of the action visible from Dolvienne's house, but I knew that two of the tripods were out there. Both were made of glass spun into something lighter than wood yet as hard as metal. We went out into the street, where we saw flashes of light, clouds of smoke, and the towers of the palace crashing down one by one. Lariella swore that she caught sight of a glass dragon, but I saw nothing of it. All around us people stared, pointed, screamed, ran, or prayed, according to inclination.

I had seen it all before, and I knew that the Lupanians were defeated this time. Two glass dragons would destroy the pair of fighting tripods, but the cost would be the life of a glass dragon. At last it came, a truly massive flash of light followed by the loudest explosion that anyone in the city had ever heard. A glass dragon had died, taking two Lupanians with it. The fighting tripods took a day or two to spin out of melted sand, but the dragon that had died was at least centuries old. For our moonworld, it was a very costly victory.

For now the danger was past, however, so we returned inside.

"What is to be done?" Dolvienne asked fearfully.

"We must get some sleep, because there is a long and dangerous night to come."

Lariella had entirely different ideas about how to spend this particular night. She had lived her life under the delusion that Alberin's eighth night of Twomonth, 3144, had been one long orgy of drinking looted wine, absolutely unbridled sex, and liberating the property of the rich.

Naturally she was anxious to participate, and we found her trying on the female clothing bought in the market earlier that day.

"Something must be done about her," said Dolvienne as we began to unpack the weapons that had belonged to Captain Gilvray.

"I am tempted to say that this is the World Mother's way of weeding out the stupid ones" was my thought.

"We should still protect her from herself."

"Very well. I think I know a place."

There was a large mansion beside Kingshead Square that was not destined to be visited by marauding mobs in the night to come. It was all quite ironic, because a marauding mob had separated a king from his head in that very square a couple of centuries earlier. About three hundred people from the merchant classes would gather there, thinking to find security. They would drink their way through the host's wine collection, and by about the second hour after sunset an orgy on an absolutely epic scale would develop. Lariella would be unlikely to leave if I left her there.

"And what about my house?" asked Dolvienne.

"We shall have to defend it."

✳   ✳   ✳

At around sunset I escorted Lariella to the mansion overlooking Kingshead Square whose future I already knew. Fearful people were already gathering there, and they were mightily relieved to see a member of the Wayfarers arrive. The master of the house was a grain exporter named Catchwell.

"Look here, I can pay a substantial amount for protection," he assured me after I had introduced Lariella as a visitor from Acrema who needed shelter.

"No need, sir, this area has, shall we say, been marked for tranquillity," I replied.

"You mean, no harm will come to us?"

"On this night, no. Any mobs in search of victims such as yourself will be diverted. Tomorrow and thereafter, well that is a different matter. I suggest you drink your way through your wine cellar, but do it quietly. We may be at the end of the world."

"Really?"

"Really. Do what you like, sir, and there will be no consequences as long as you do not make undue noise."

With that I took my leave and returned to Dolvienne's house.

* * *

That night saw Alberin stumble, stagger, but not quite fall. While part of the population made ready to evacuate the city before more Lupanian fighting tripods returned to put it to the torch and eat whoever remained, the remainder saw fit to stage the largest and most destructive orgy in the history of the continent. Buildings were looted and burned, people were murdered at the whim of whatever armed, drunken churl happened to be passing, and there was debauchery on an unimaginable scale.

Dolvienne lived in a modest house, but it was on the edge of the more desirable areas of Alberin. Little by little the sounds of destruction and revelry came closer. Dolvienne turned out to be a better shot than I had realized, but then I had never seen her use a bow until then. She was a former handmaid to a princess, after all, and had done a lot of hunting in the royal game reserves of the Sargolan Empire.

The vanguard of a mob appeared at the end of the street, and from the shelter of her garden wall Dolvienne dropped one of the leaders at a range of about a hundred and fifty yards—and by torchlight too. As his outraged companions swarmed forward in some idiotic gesture of solidarity, the two of us poured snagglehead arrows into them as fast as we could set nock to string and draw. The snaggleheads meant that once they hit, the arrows did not come out, and because there was such a press, every arrow hit home. Thus even if the hit was not a kill, the reality of an arrow snagged in his flesh discouraged the victim in very short order. After no more than a dozen shafts each the spirit of the mob broke, and they retreated in search of a more compliant neighborhood.

"I count at least a dozen bodies lying on the cobbles," said Dolvienne, looking over our field of victory in Miral's green light.

"Fine shooting," I replied.

"But some are still moving."

"Good. I hope they are in agony."

"Inspector! They are in pain. Have you no compassion?"

"Have you been listening to Lariella?"

"Please! The sight of them moving is turning my stomach."

Venturing out into the street, I dispatched the wounded quickly and humanely, then dragged some of the bodies into neighboring streets. This gave the impression that a large militia was guarding the houses in this area, and that any disorganized mob would meet with highly organized resistance. We were not disturbed any further that night, but we slept in shifts and kept our bows to hand.

✳ ✳ ✳

The city was a much safer place in the light of the morning. I made a short tour of inspection in the immediate vicinity of the house as the sun rose, and found that the rioters and revelers of the night before were either asleep, dead, or awake and very sick. The more prudent citizens were making their way out of the city and heading for the mountains to the west as fast as the weight of their portable worldly goods would allow.

Upon arriving at Kingshead Square, I found the mansion littered with bodies. All were alive, but those who were awake were seriously interested in dying to escape the consequences of what they had done the night before. Lariella, who had been a major feature of the night's entertainment, had dosed herself with the miracle philters and pills of her own century, and so was suffering from just lack of sleep when I found her among the unclothed and mostly comatose revelers. I was appalled to find her purse with the time engine's four lever-keys lying on a pile of discarded clothing.

"You really should have stayed, it was the most uplifting night," she said as she dressed in a selection of clothes that I had gathered from the floor.

"I think you have had quite enough uplifting for now."

"It would have helped you get over the loss of Lavenci."

"I shall deal with my grief in my own way, thank you."

"What *did* you do last night, anyway."

"Actually Dolvienne and I fought off attacks by gangs of drunken looters. We killed about a dozen."

"Killed?" she gasped, suddenly putting her hands to her mouth. "You mean, ah . . ."

"Rendered them from a state of being alive and riotous, to being dead and well behaved."

"But, but you should have called the authorities."

"*I* am the authorities. Come along, we must be getting home."

Lariella had spent the night within one of the finest mansions in Alberin, enjoying what might as well have been a costume dalliance revel in her own century. The facilities had been a little quaint as far as she was concerned, but that had all been part of the fun. To her it had seemed as if nobody had been hurt at all in Alberin, but the bodies in the streets soon jolted her into reality. Flies, birds, and the occasional dog were beginning to take an interest in the corpses, but the surviving citizens of Alberin were ignoring them. In Lariella's time death was tidied away and sponged clean very quickly, it was something that people saw in a sanitized state on their Daemon Vision Devices as part of dinnertime entertainment. When they had to be stepped over or walked around, corpses ceased to be entertainment.

"Look, er, when will the city authorities remove the dead to the grievery?" Lariella asked as we walked.

"The city authorities fled yesterday, after the attack," I replied.

"But how will the next of kin be located?"

"Those next of kin who are still alive are concentrating on how to put as much distance between themselves and the city as possible before the Lupanian fighting tripods come back."

Lariella and I knew that the city came to no real harm, so it was like being in a vast stage play whose story we already knew. Nevertheless, the bodies were real, and for the first time since I had met her Lariella was silent for more than a quarter hour. I drew a pail of water from a public well so that she might wash. This caused her some distress, for she seemed to think that a hot shower was a nicer way to freshen up. The fact that there was not a single shower on the face of the moonworld somehow came as a shock to her.

Back at Dolvienne's cottage yet more realities of living in the past began to sink in for Lariella. These included having to wash clothes by hand, sharing those clothes with fleas, cleaning teeth with a cloth, the reason for a box of dried grass in the privy, and the fact that the privy consisted of a beam of wood over a deep hole.

I unpacked my quills, ink, and paper, trimmed a quill to my satisfaction, then returned to my account of what would happen that day.

The sheer numbers of the citizens fleeing Alberin soon overwhelmed the militiamen, Wayfarer Constables, and guardsmen who had stayed to do their duty rather than fleeing with the regent the day before. The line of citizens soon became a torrent of despair. The weak fell, to be trampled underfoot, and outlaws gathered in the distance to strike at the refugees at their leisure. It was now, when all hope was gone, and even the Wayfarers and militiamen began to quarrel among themselves, that Constable Riellen stood upon a broken and discarded wagon by the roadside, raised her ax to the sky in defiance of the Lupanians, and cried "Brothers! Sisters! People of Alberin! Why are you fleeing? Are you going to let the alien imperialist tyrants take Alberin without a fight?"

What seemed like hours passed, for writing has a way of accelerating the passing of time as surely as any time engine.

"Danolarian?"

I looked up to see Dolvienne standing before me with a tray containing a length of preserved sausage, an apple, and a mug of tea.

"The day's compliments, ladyship. Is all safe in the neighborhood?"

"Yes, but it is Lariella who concerns me. She actually wants to go out and see the sights!"

"She is a type of pilgrim, she finds Alberin exotic and romantic."

"Romantic? A city full of vandalized buildings, dead bodies, and hangovers?"

"Yes. As I said, she comes from a sheltered place."

"But it is not safe to leave the house. Can anything be done? Can you speak with her?"

I folded my arms and tried to think clearly, staring absently down at the chronicle that I was writing. Without even realizing that I was doing it, I began to read aloud what I had just written:

"It was now, when all hope was gone, and even the Wayfarers and militiamen began to quarrel among themselves, that Constable Riellen stood upon a broken and discarded wagon by the roadside . . ."

"Your pardon?"

"There is column of people fleeing west from the city," I said without looking up from the paper. "Take Lariella, join them, but stop at a broken cart about a half mile from the gates, on your left. You cannot miss it, there is only one such cart."

"Flee the city? But you said—"

"Just go as far as the cart. Wait there, and you will hear a speech. It is a very good speech, the most inspiring speech you will ever hear. It is a speech that changes the entire moonworld."

"But the danger is too great."

"We three survive this day, Dolvienne, in fact I know that you live to be old."

"You—you speak of what is to come. Can you see the future? Are you an oracle?"

"I have been . . . told about some great events to come."

"But if you saw the future, why did we fight last night? Did we have to shoot down any of those rioters? You knew we would live."

"I know only of great events, not the fate of individuals like us. Go now, take Lariella. Last night she played a silly game of orgy with rich, terrified people. Today, let her see courage at its very best. One more word, however."

"Yes?"

"When you see me out there, at the broken cart, do not speak to me."

"Why not?"

"Because I will still be here."

*   *   *

Dolvienne and Lariella left, and I took the opportunity to fabricate a lead pipe that would hold my manuscript. On the outside of the tube I inscribed the words THE DAWN OF ELECTOCRACY BY WAYFARER CONSTABLE PENWRIGHT. After raising a flagstone in the basement and digging out a space large enough to hold my pipe, I returned to my chronicle of what was about to happen. Again time speeded up as page after page became covered in writing. I had reached the part where Riellen had led most of Alberin's citizens back into the city and was setting up an interim administration to oversee the first election in the moonworld's history when I realized that a very large number of voices were chanting in the distance.

Ri-el-len,
Unites us,
We'll never be defeated!

Nearly a year earlier I had started that chant, giving the citizens of Alberin something to rally behind as Riellen led them back into the city to set up an electocracy and fight the invincible invaders from the moonworld Lupan. I was out there now, one of Riellen's warriors, and was soon to be a founding member of her Revolutionary Interim Council Electoral Advisors of Greater Alberin. A thousand years in the future scholars would still be arguing about the peculiar grammar of Riellen's ludicrously long name, but the truth was that the scribe had been having trouble keeping up with Riellen's declarations and had omitted an "of." I set the matter straight in my chronicle, thereby ruining many academics' reputations some time in the next millennium.

"Er, Inspector?" said Wallas as I wrote the story of a man who did not exist.

"I do hold that rank."

"Pelmore's sawdust needs changing, and he has not been fed for six hours."

"From the heroic to the repulsive," I sighed as I stood and stretched.

Pelmore was sullen and subdued as I assembled a fresh pail of sawdust, some bread and cheese, and a mug of dinner ale. Unfortunately he had to be ungagged in order to be fed.

"My head itches," he muttered as I cleaned up beneath him.

"Good," I replied.

"You need me alive."

"So I do, but I do not need you ungagged."

"No! No! I'll not be mmff . . ."

"Most sensible thing you ever said."

Even as I tied the cloth in place the thought returned that Pelmore seemed very anxious to goad and humiliate me. He was a man in my power, and what was more I was also a man legally entitled to execute or exile him, with torture and mutilation as a possible option. Why did he want to talk? Where did he get the courage and malice to boast about what he had done with Lavenci? At one level I wanted to ask him, but at another I wanted to keep my suspicions within the privacy of my mind.

✳   ✳   ✳

It was evening when Lariella and Dolvienne returned from watching history being made, and Lariella's attitude had been transformed. Gone was the sense of play from the night before, and even the horror of seeing so many dead bodies in the morning. Instead, she now had a pair of hands that had helped to lay the foundations of electocracy itself. She had been one of the first to march with Riellen, the very mother of electocracy, on the day that electocracy had been born.

"I helped smash the throne!" shouted Lariella as she rushed into the cottage. "I was there! Costiger himself lent me his ax. He actually spoke to me, he said 'There ya go, ladyship!' He was such a gentleman. Can you imagine it?"

"We heard Riellen's speech!" cried Dolvienne, who was also bright with emotion. "It was so—so moving and inspiring."

"I got it all on my vid," added Lariella waving the little daemon at me. "I got you, er, that is, your double, leading the chant."

Lariella dashed off to the other room to rummage in her pack. Dolvienne stared at me, her hands on her hips.

"Danolarian, just which Danolarian are you?" she asked. "Who is Lariella? Where did all her strange daemons and autons come from? Is she the oracle who told you the future?"

"After a fashion, yes," I replied. "She is a powerful sorceress, but a little eccentric, and from a very sheltered place."

"She showed me how to use her image daemon. It seemed more like a machine than something magical, I—"

"Oh and we met Lavenci!" cried Lariella, dashing back into the room.

My head snapped around. Lavenci had never told me that.

"We were back in the city, eating at the Lamplighter. She just walked in, just like that. She was looking for you. Dolvienne introduced us, she said I was a long-lost cousin. I told Lavenci how much I loved that song she wrote for you, 'The Banks of the Alber,' and then, oh Inspector, you will never guess!"

"She sang it for you?"

"Yes, yes, yes, and I vidded the entire song!"

I was not so churlish as to seem bored by what Lariella and Dolvienne had just experienced. Dolvienne had been in mourning for her murdered husband for quite some time, so she was probably ready for a chance at some cheer. Lariella was one of those people whose mood could swing very widely and with great speed. Now she was suddenly a warrior of electocracy, fighting to change our moonworld for the better and knowing that her side would win.

Dolvienne opened a bottle of her late husband's wine, then another, then yet another. At some very late hour, by which time we had had five viewings of Lariella's image daemon showing Riellen's speech, Lavenci singing "The Banks of the Alber," and Lariella helping to chop up the imperial throne, we carried Dolvienne to bed. Lariella did not have a good night's sleep in mind for us, but she passed out on the way to the bedchamber. This was because I had swapped her tablets that proofed her against alcohol with sugar balls. As I heaved her onto the bed my hand encountered her purse.

During the orgy of the night before Lariella had cast that same purse aside onto a pile of discarded clothing, and it was merely Fortune's whim that some greedy servant had not stolen it. Was she to be entrusted with the lever-keys? I knew that she still had them some days later, when we took Pelmore away into time, yet what might happen after that? People in the habit of discarding clothing for newly met admirers were liable to have that clothing ransacked during the night. I removed the lever-keys from her purse, then stole from the room.

✳   ✳   ✳

Although I dearly wanted to get some proper sleep, I set off into the darkness. After walking about a mile, I rapped at a door.

"Wayfarer Inspector, in the name of Riellen, open up."

The shutter of a peephole slid aside.

"Electocratic business, four keys to duplicate," I whispered into the square of blackness.

"Lordworld's rings, ye really be a Wayfarer Constable!" a voice exclaimed.

"This is secret business!" I hissed. "Let me in, we must talk."

The shutter slid back, there was the sound of rummaging from behind the door, and finally the bolt rattled back. The small, ratty-looking man who beckoned for me to enter was fully dressed, because people who do most of their work at night do tend to be fully dressed when roused at that sort of hour. He held his thumblamp up to my face.

"Oi, you're the Wayfarer Inspector what was with Miss Riellen when she gave that speech," he said.

"And you are Filewright, who does hurried duplications of keys without questions."

"That I was, but after that speech of Miss Riellen, I'se sworn to be a warrior or electocracy."

"Good, because I am indeed calling upon you to serve the Greater Alberin in the name of electocracy."

"Ya want me ter fight?" he asked, reaching for a fencing ax on a rack.

"No, just look here." I held out the lever-keys to Lariella's time engine. "These are the keys to a Lupanian weapon. How soon to make a second set, and how much?"

Filewright shrank back for a moment, then tentatively pointed at the lever-keys.

"Are they safe? Like they won't shoot a death beam at me or nothin', will they?"

"They are what unlocks the weapon, not the weapon itself."

"But if ya got the weapon, why make a second set?"

"We have two weapons, but only one set of lever-keys."

"Ah, should have said so. Give here, then."

I tipped the lever-keys into his hand. He held an enlargement glass up to them.

"In steel, like these is, maybe two days. In brass, before dawn."

"Brass it is."

"Brass may not work, like."

"The Lupanians are sure to attack again, Filewright. It might be as soon as tomorrow, so we must take our chances with brass. How much?"

"For the glorious, down-with-the-monarchist, electocratic revolution, I work for free," he said jubilantly. "I saw ya with Miss Riellen, Inspector. I was so proud ter be from Alberin, an' like I can't wait ter get them Lupanian bastards!"

"At least take some silver to cover materials."

"Nah, couldn't."

I seized him by the wrist and slapped four silver florins into his hand.

"It is the duty of every citizen to accept fair payment!" I said firmly. "You must maintain your workshop, in case the electocratic revolution needs you for other work."

"Er, like what?"

"Making crossbow releases and arrowheads. We may need you to make those."

"Yeah?"

"Yes."

"Oi, never thought I'd be ruled by someone what forced me to take money."

"Welcome to the age of electocracy, Brother Filewright."

True to his word, Filewright had the lever-keys finished before first light began to glow on the eastern horizon. After hurrying back to Dolvienne's house, I found that Lariella was still asleep. Thus I had no trouble returning the steel keys to her purse, and my own brass keys went into the false heel of a boot. Finally I stretched out on the kitchen floor beside Dragonfang to snatch a few hours' sleep.

✳   ✳   ✳

It was around midmorning when I awoke. I went to Lariella and shook her awake, but she was severely hungover and did little more than insist that she wanted to die. I settled down to continue writing my chronicle, and did not break from the work until early evening. Lariella awoke about sunset, ate dinner, threw it up, and returned to bed. During this night I slept at the table, alternately dozing, then returning to my chronicle. Although I had another four days in the Alberin of 3144, there was much writing still to do. I had to chronicle events that would happen in the days after I left.

✳   ✳   ✳

The following morning I was much the worse for lack of sleep, but Lariella was once again insufferably cheerful and bursting with energy. She was also intent on fighting in the next battle against the Lupanians.

"I thought you had moral objections to fighting and killing," I reminded her.

"Well, I would not actually kill anyone."

"Have you ever been in a battle?"

"Er, yes."

"When?"

"Um, it was actually a football riot—but a lot of people were hurt. I helped with the first aid, I have medical training."

As before, I knew where the safe areas were for the hours ahead. We were ahead of schedule as far as preparing for the trip into the past was concerned, and if the truth be known we could have put Pelmore onto the time engine within that very hour and broken the constancy glamour between him and Lavenci. The problem with that plan was that we were in heroic times, and Lariella was determined to experience them. I was also determined that a complete and truthful version of my part in history should be left to future generations, and my chronicle was still days from completion.

"Dolvienne, you must know the Sea Wharf area," I said, waving vaguely in the direction of east.

"Yes, Inspector, it is the eastern edge of Wharfside, where the biggest deepwater traders tie up and unload."

"And do you know a tavern called the Mermaid's Slipper?"

"That filthy place?" she exclaimed. "I would not enter it for a stocking full of sapphires!"

"You do not have to. All I want you to do is take Lariella to the area of the Sea Wharf near that tavern. There will be a battle nearby, and the

services of healers will definitely be needed. There will be many suffering from burns."

"Ah, so we should take a pack of bandages and oils?"

"I think two packs would be even better."

✳   ✳   ✳

With the two ladies gone, I returned to my writing after feeding Pelmore. I made the mistake of not gagging him.

"I have been tied up for three days," he said sullenly.

"True, and it gives me great satisfaction to see you bound," I replied.

"I'm losing the feeling in my hands and feet."

"You only have to last another four days."

"Can't I just be free to lie on the floor or something? I'll swear not to
escape."

I reminded myself that if he lost the use of his legs we would have to
carry him back to Wall Tower, or borrow the Lamplighter's cart again.

"Very well then, you can stretch out unbound," I decided. "Here,
drink this."

"What is it?"

"A philter that relieves cramp."

Pelmore took the little phial from me and drained it. A distant ulula-
tion announced the beginning of the battle with the Lupanian tripods.

"I know that sound!" gasped Pelmore.

"A Lupanian battle tripod's call," I said calmly.

"We have to run."

"We stay here, it is safe."

"I'm not staying . . ."

Pelmore took just one step, then very hurriedly sat down on the rug.
He put his hands to his head.

"What was that muck you gave me?" he cried.

"A somnolent."

"A what?"

"A sleeping philter."

"You lied, you said it was to relieve cramp."

"It will. You will be very relaxed, once asleep."

* * *

With Pelmore free but fast asleep on the rug, I returned again to my chronicle. Outside the cottage I heard gongs, trumpets, and shouting as the city rallied itself against the Lupanian battle tripods. I wrote of what was still to happen, aware that my younger self had a good view and was watching the battle even as I wrote.

"Danolarian."

I whirled, stood, and drew my fencing ax all in one movement, sending my stool flying in the process. Standing in the doorway was a young woman. Her outline was blurred, in fact most of her was so indistinct that I was not entirely sure whether she was wearing robes at all.

"Do you know who I am?" she asked.

"You are Lady Velander," I responded, slowly lowering my ax. "You were once a Metrologan priestess, but you are now a neophyte glass dragon."

"Good, you remember me, that makes things easier."

I blinked and shrank back as she entered. She looked human, yet I knew what she was. What she was would not fit within the cottage if expanded to its true size.

"Danolarian, there are two of you," said the woman's image that was the current shape of the creature.

"This me is from the future," I began, feeling self-conscious about just how ridiculous I must have sounded.

Velander looked down at Pelmore.

"He must not hear what I have to say," she said. "What can be done?"

"He has drunk a little somnolent. So very restful."

"So he cannot wake?"

"No."

"Then sit, we must talk."

Velander did not sit. In her dragon form her body was the size of a small ship, with wings that could easily span the Alber River. Her human shape seemed to be a strain for her to maintain.

"I mourn for the loss of your wingmate," I said sincerely. "Alberin would have fallen had not those two glass dragons flown here to stop the Lupanian fighting towers."

"They did not come here to fight the Lupanians," replied Velander.

"They did not?"

"One might say that the Lupanians just got in the way."

Aware that I was speaking with a glass dragon, I thought carefully about what she had said, and chose my words in the hope that I was not violating protocols that I did not even know to exist.

"So they were here for an even more important reason than the Lupanians?" I asked.

"Yes," she replied. "There is something seriously wrong in Greater Alberin."

As a Wayfarer Inspector I knew that there were a great many things wrong in Greater Alberin, but none of them seemed in the same class as the Lupanian Invasion.

"Is it like Silverdeath, the etheric machine that destroyed the entire continent of Torea?"

"No, worse than Silverdeath."

Worse? My head spun and my vision blurred for a moment. Worse than something that could destroy a continent?

"Do you know what it is?" I asked.

"A disturbance, that is all that we understand about it. There is something in this world that does not belong here."

"Ah, with all due respect, have you heard of the Lupanians? They come from the moonworld Lupan. *They* do not belong here."

"There is something else, Inspector. Our guess is that it is defending itself from the Lupanians. It is hitting back with Riellen, Lavenci, and even you."

"But what is it?"

"A change in reality, more than that I cannot describe. Glass dragons have senses that you do not. The Lupanians interrupted something, some plan, some great endeavor. It involves an ether machine. It also involves you."

"Me?"

"Oh yes. Have you noticed how in five years this moonworld has seen three major threats to its very existence? The ether machine Silverdeath destroyed a continent. Next came Dragonwall, which almost wiped out civilization everywhere. Now there are the Lupanians. We do not know why."

"Do you know of the time engine?"

"Yes, I have entered your room in Wall Tower and examined it."

"What? How? The door was locked."

"It still is. I am a glass dragon, I ignore locks."

"What did you find?"

"Something so very big that it did not notice me."

"You are speaking in riddles. Can you describe it?"

"No, it is too strange. Danolarian, I thought to come here because I wanted you to know what I have just said. Knowledge is power, words are weapons, and you are in need of both. Your destiny is bound to the time engine, but be aware that it is not just an engine."

With these words she began to turn away, but I jumped up and went after her.

"Please, wait," I called. "There is another matter."

"The neophyte glass dragon, Terikel," she said without prompting.

"Yes, yes, the one who is mad."

"We prefer to say transcendent," said Velander, turning again with the grace of a swan on water.

"She was once Roval's lover, but some odd lust drove her to betray him with several other men."

"I know, betrayal has a strong allure for her. The fault is not hers."

"That is little comfort to those she betrayed," I said sternly. "Roval's mind snapped when he found out. Now she is trying to repent by murdering all of those who lay with her after Roval entered her life."

"Sad, but true. Our neophytes usually rise above such petty concerns, but alas, not Terikel."

"Andry is the only man left."

"And I have been keeping her apart from him, it has not been easy. We had hoped that she would outgrow such behavior, but she is spiraling deeper and deeper into the abyss of grief and guilt."

"I intend to take Andry into the past," I explained, hoping that I was not revealing too much to her. "There he will live out his life as normally as anyone does, and die before she is born. She can never reach him there. Can you tell her that?"

"I shall, but it will make no difference, she will look for others. Men who she fancied and would have taken to herself if they had but asked, men who asked but were driven off by circumstance, even men who she fancied within her heart alone."

"But some of those men would not have even known her to exist."

"I know. She could wipe out the entire world to quench her guilt, then rage against the emptiness because her guilt remains. I have been charged with either seeing her through these difficult years or killing her. She was once my friend, but if she continues to kill I shall have to do what I would rather not. I must go now. Is there anything else?"

"Yes—no. Well, yes. Just something silly."

"I fancy something silly. Ask."

"Wallas, how did he became a cat?"

"Wallas was given, shall we say, a trick question by a very wise and powerful glass dragon."

"So . . . his answer was less than satisfactory?"

"Oh no, he was sure to give the answer that he deserved to give. Thus it was appropriate that he became a cat. There are words of release, but they may do him no good."

"May?"

"Yes. Speak them, and he may remain a cat if he has not changed within himself. When he deserves to become a man again, he will indeed change."

"So should I bring him before you for a test speaking every so often?"

"No, I shall tell you the words and you may speak them as often as you wish."

"Really?"

"Yes, but from what I have seen of Wallas, he still faces quite a long sentence in the shape of a cat."

"After three years of being his commander, I tend to agree."

Velander left without a goodbye, but that was her way. I returned to my writing, but felt too distracted to be productive. Pelmore lay on his back, snoring. I got up and rolled him over. The snoring stopped, but now there were echoing explosions from the direction of the harbor. That would be the Lupanians suffering their greatest defeat thus far, I knew it from my memories. The wooden battle galleys *Megazoid* and *Gigazoid* had been destroyed, yet had taken three tripod towers with them.

It was the turning point of the invasion, the Lupanians would be desperate from now on. All of that went into my chronicle, yet my innermost thoughts remained just thoughts. What had Velander meant when she said the time engine was something very big, and that it was aware of me? Was it a creature rather than a vehicle? A ferry was a vehicle, but a horse was a creature. Both were transport. Was the time engine a type of horse? If so, had Lariella found it rather than built it?

Lariella and Dolvienne did not come home that evening, but they did send a runner to tell me that they were all right. Many hundreds of rowers and sailors who had survived the fighting between the two war galleys and the Lupanian towers had been burned terribly. Anyone who knew anything about treating burns was very much in demand, and the two ladies of the house were just such people. I continued to write. Around sunset, when Pelmore finally awoke, I marched him and Dragonfang around the nearby streets for some fresh air and exercise. My prisoner was sullen, yet the fool had never learned to keep a bridle upon his tongue. Once he had been exercised, evacuated, washed, fed, and tied up for the night, I returned to my chronicle.

"So how much longer does this go on?" Pelmore asked.

"Two days, and a half," I said without looking up. "I have a chronicle to finish."

"What then?"

"The time engine on which we shall travel will take us into the past, where I shall leave you."

"The past?"

"The past. You will go into exile, Pelmore. Remember, I am your executioner, so I am charged with executing your sentence. I have chosen exile instead of death."

"Bastard."

"Pelmore, I am not just a bastard, I am a selfish bastard. I think you deserve death, but I am going to take you into exile for one reason, and for one reason only. I *have* to do it. I want you alive when I take you back into time. Taking you into time will break the constancy glamour between you and my sweetheart, Lavenci."

"Yes, you can't afford to kill me, so—"

"Not another word! You have to be alive in two days and a half, when I load you onto the time engine. After that, your fate depends on my mood. Now shut up, I have work to do."

✴ ✴ ✴

The ladies came home the following morning. Dolvienne was no stranger to warfare and merely looked very tired, but Lariella was quite traumatized. Both had the scent of burnt meat about them, and because the public baths had closed for the war effort, they spent two hours fetching water from the neighborhood well and scrubbing each other. Once Dolvienne had finally gone to bed, Lariella came to sit on a trunk beside the table where I was writing. She said nothing for a time, she just stared at the image device without activating it.

"Those ships, the *Megazoid* and the *Gigazoid,* I never knew," she said at last.

"Knew what?" I asked, looking up from my chronicle.

"I never knew what really happened. The histories say that they charged the Lupanian tripod towers that were wading in the harbor, and that they got close enough to topple them under the cover of smoke from the burning city. It was nothing like that! Those two ships, those wooden galleys, they were only armed with catapults, yet—yet they charged the Lupanians across half a mile of water in clear air and bright sunlight. It was catapults against laser cannons, yet they beat them. They were set afire, they were in flames from stem to stern, yet they held the charge and rammed them. It was the finest, it was the bravest, most noble thing I've ever seen. Oh Inspector, I know it's not the verbally correct thing to say, but I was so, so moved."

"Did you save many survivors?"

"Yes, yes, but too many were burned. I had my medical kit with me, but everything ran out within the first half hour. There were hundreds, and all we had were oils and bandages. I think we did some good, but they kept dying. All through the night, they died, one after another. I was even dispensing hangover pills to ease the pain of the most seriously burned."

"You have a good heart."

Again she did not speak. Instead she commanded her image daemon to show scenes from the battle on the harbor. I returned to my writing, and reviewed what was still to go. I had covered the election of Laron as presidian in two days' time, then the final battle with the Lupanians two days after that. All that I needed to do now was chronicle how Greater Alberin healed its wounds and fought off the attempts by neighboring kingdoms to overthrow electocracy and restore the empire's regent.

"Inspector?"

I looked up. Lariella was attaching her stuncast to a chain of Zurlanian gold around her neck. It made quite an attractive pendant.

"Yes."

"Is Pelmore sedated or just asleep?" she asked, noting that he was stretched out on the rug and unbound.

"I have given him a sleeping philter, if that is what you mean."

"When will he wake?"

"When I empty a mug of cold water over his head. Don't worry, he knows he is to travel into time with us, to break the constancy glamour between him and Lavenci. He will get his potency back, while going into time-exile for murdering Captain Danzar. He will cooperate."

"It was not a fair conviction, you know."

"It was too! *I* convicted him."

"But when he committed his crimes he was influenced by Riellen's glamours and enchantments, it was not truly his fault. He was traumatised—"

"Ladyship, a lot of people were traumatized by the battle on the harbor yesterday, including yourself. Are they out and about, murdering?"

"You are being too extreme."

"Murder is about as extreme as you can get. In my experience. Once someone gets away with one violent crime, the floodgates are open to commit more. They become confident, you see. For the protection of other folk, I *should* execute Pelmore once he has been taken away to some other time. Perhaps I shall."

Lariella clearly disliked that line of reasoning, but she seemed to have no reply. As I wrote on I decided to truncate the part about the battles to overthrow electocracy. They were already more or less accurately documented, and I had already set the history right about myself, Lavenci, Riellen, and Pelmore.

"Do we have the privacy to talk about some intimate matters?" asked Lariella, again breaking my train of thought.

"Pelmore is asleep on the rug, Dolvienne is asleep in her bedchamber, and Wallas is sunning himself on the roof and probably asleep too. That is about as private as it gets in a cottage such as this."

"Dolvienne and I have been talking. Captain Gilvray, her husband, died last month."

"That he did. It was very sad."

"You have been lost to your lady, the sorceress Lavenci, for about the same number of days."

"True, in terms of days I have lived through."

"I think you and Dolvienne would be very good for each other."

I buried my face in my hands and rubbed for a moment. *Is there no end to the woman's insensitivity?* I wondered.

"Ladyship, the problems of the moonworld's many peoples are not going to be solved by everyone flinging off their clothing and leaping into bed with each other," I began.

"No, please, hear me out. She said you have known each other for three years. You were in the personal guard of Princess Senterri when she was a handmaid of the princess. She said you even kissed her."

"That was a long time ago, we were little more than children. She later married Captain Gilvray, my commander, and there was true love between them. I was only her, ah, little fluffy thing."

"I think you mean bit of fluff, and no, you were not. The captain was noble, brave, and worthy, and he had also been injured and betrayed. Women often marry such men because they think it is their duty. It is called nobility syndrome in my time, therapists are always citing it in divorce cases. I know all about things like that, I've been in therapy since I was five years old."

"You are starting to lose me."

"Dolvienne likes you, and she is sad, lonely, and confused. We all know that you vanish from the history books a year from now, perhaps you even die. Danolarian, she wants to be more to you than a teenage sweetheart. Two days from now you vanish from her life, and she is taking it as badly as her husband's death."

"Ladyship, I do admit she is my oldest surviving friend, yet circumstances are hardly appropriate for that sort of courtship. This is a small cottage, and I am shy about any sort of intimacy within earshot of Pelmore and Wallas, let alone yourself."

"Inspector, you said that Pelmore is not going to run away, that he is probably even looking forward to traveling through time and getting his potency back."

"Repulsive prospect though it is, but yes."

"Why don't I take Pelmore and Wallas to some inn near Wall Tower for the next two days? You and Dolvienne deserve some time together."

"Who said we were even interested in—"

"Again, hear me out! Would it not be better for you and Dolvienne to have at least had the chance to be something to each other? Whether or not you decide to consummate, why spend the rest of your life wondering?"

What could I say? I had stayed away from Lavenci out of a sense of duty. Her affection belonged to my younger self, I was already lost to her. Might the physicians of the mind be right? Lariella had built the time engine, after all, so she was no fool. Perhaps there was a lot of truth in what she was saying.

Just then I was feeling very much in need of foundations and roots in my life. I had known Essen and Costiger almost as long as Dolvienne, but they were casual friends at best. Aside from them, there was only Roval and . . . Wallas. No, there was too little for me to cling to, and I seemed doomed never to stop wandering. *Perhaps I should at least talk to Dolvienne,* I decided.

"There is an inn called the White Charger about a hundred yards west of Wall Tower, at the corner of Nobby Point Lane and Pokingham Crescent," I said, "but I feel nervous about you being alone with Pelmore."

"What can he do to me? I have the stuncast, I know weaponless self-defense, and he will not get his potency back if something happens to me. He is actually the best possible bodyguard that I could have. Anyway, we will have Wallas as a chaperone."

"For what it is worth, which is not very much. Very well then, ladyship, what will you be doing?"

"Today I'll be doing the markets, Pelmore can carry things. Tomorrow is the big election, the first electocratic election in the history of the moonworld. I can't wait to vote."

"Pelmore is a condemned criminal, he will be recognized."

"An eyepatch and some bandages will be good camo."

"Camo?"

"Camouflage."

"Camouflage?"

"Disguise. There are plenty of bandaged men in Alberin just now. Don't worry, I think of everything."

I woke Pelmore with a half pint of water to the face, then fetched Wallas down from the stable roof. With the three of them gone, the cottage seemed strangely quiet and free of tension. I found myself becoming drowsy, now that I was not on alert for misbehavior of one sort or another. In a flurry of impatience I summarized the conclusion of the electocracy wars and signed my pseudonym at the end of my chronicle. I do not even remember putting my head down on the table for a moment's rest.

I awoke with Dolvienne shaking my shoulder, and opened my eyes to twilight. There was the scent of roasting meat on the air, and something was bubbling in the kitchen.

"Inspector, can I interest you in dinner?" she asked.

"I—I—yes. That is, I need to explain about Lariella, Pelmore, and Wallas. They—"

"Lariella left a note on the slate, I know they have gone to stay at an inn for the next two days. You will be able to finish your chronicle in peace."

I shook my head and looked about at the reedpaper pages of my chronicle, then started to gather them together.

"Actually it is finished. I thought to bury it in your basement, sealed in a lead pipe."

"But nobody will ever find it."

"A thousand years from now your house will be, er, 'restored' is a good enough word, I think. When the flagstones are dug up, the pipe will be found."

"If you say so. Will you be long? The evening meal is nearly ready."

"A quarter hour, no more."

When I returned from the little basement, I found that Dolvienne had tidied the place and laid mugs and trenchers on the table. It was apparent that both of us knew why we had been left alone, yet that subject did its best to stay out of the conversation. The meat was succulent, the beets firm yet juicy, and the pastries sweet. All that I can say about the wine is that it seemed to be far too easy to swallow. We were into the second jar before the conversation moved beyond banalities.

"Is it wise to have Pelmore free?" Dolvienne asked as she filled my mug yet again..

"It is in his interests to cooperate with us. He knows we can break the constancy glamour on his gronnic, and that he will go into exile alive and functional."

"Exile where?"

"Far, far away. Too far to ever return."

"I have known courtiers like him in the imperial palace in Palion," said Dolvienne doubtfully. "They always know precisely what they can get away with, and they always do just that."

"Pelmore is no fool. This is a battlefield where everyone can have a victory if they but work together."

I tossed a bone to Dragonfang, who thumped his tail, weighed the effort of getting up against the prospect of the bone, then decided that the bone was worth it.

"Danolarian, may I ask of the future?" Dolvienne asked as I nervously nibbled a crumb of trencher.

"I know only a little of it. I may not be much help."

"It is what you have not said that concerns me. You have very cleverly kept us all busy with one thing and another, yet never said a word about yourself. I live to be old, Lariella and Pelmore vanish, Wallas serves in the Wayfarers again, but what about you?"

"I do not know," I confessed.

"You mean you die?" she asked, her eyes wide.

"Lavenci marries Laron in a year, so I must vanish from her life. I do not have much interest in her now, knowing of her long and happy life with him."

Dolvienne reached out across the table and squeezed my hand. The thrill was like the touch of a magical casting.

"Always everyone else, never the inspector," she said. "Do you too vanish out of Alberin forever? Do you live?"

"Staying alive is high on my list of things to do, ladyship."

"Do you remember our days in the palace, in Palion? Me a handmaid of Princess Senterri, and you one of her guardsmen?"

"We kissed. You seemed annoyed."

"At first I was annoyed because I thought you were being too forward. Then I was annoyed because you were not being forward enough."

"You are somewhat daunting when annoyed."

"I am not annoyed now. What else do you remember, Guardsman Danolarian?"

"I remember that you were younger than I."

"Is that important?"

"Yes. Every woman of any significance in my life has been older than me. You were younger, that gave you extra allure."

"Why did you not say as much?"

"You seemed annoyed with me."

"Oh, I do apologize. I longed for yet another kiss, I thought you very dashing. In my daydream fancies I thought you a prince in disguise, come to court Princess Senterri in secret, yet allured by me instead."

"A fine thing to learn now," I sighed. "In two days this me vanishes forever, yet only now I learn the memories of your heart."

We sat holding hands across the table for quite some time, looking into each other's eyes and no longer drinking. Our knees began to rub. In my experience, rubbing knees means very significant interest between two people.

"Perhaps you do return, but change your name and marry me," whispered Dolvienne.

"Well, in a year or so I shall be short of a date."

"What date is that?"

"It is a misuse of the word, a folly that folk will use in the future. It means to court a lady by taking her to the playhouse, tavern, dance, or some such courtship activity on a prearranged day."

"Oh. So if I say the twelfth day of Twomonth in the year 3144, what would you do?"

"That is today. Is it suitable?"

"Yes. What sort of courtship activity do you have in mind?"

"You are uncannily forward, ladyship. You must have been talking to Lariella."

"Oh yes, and she said she would talk to you. She thought we two should go to some inn and have two nights and a day together. Instead I awoke to find you here and everyone else gone."

"Circumstances changed. Look, I—I can't help but feel awkward, even guilty. It seems too soon, too hasty, too . . . indecent."

Without letting go of my hand Dolvienne got up, walked around the table, and sat next to me, pressing her hip against mine. I reminded myself that Lavenci was lost to me.

"Lariella explained all about how love is sometimes duty in disguise. She said that the mind physicians of her homeland discovered that people like me can think they are in love with someone because they are good and noble, but all along they really love someone like you. I . . . must admit that the captain is never far from my thoughts, but if masters of the cold sciences have proved that I am deluding myself, I suppose they must be right."

Again, there it was, a strange little voice cheeping that something was wrong. This was not the Dolvienne that I knew, yet this was a very pleasant Dolvienne.

"I feel as if I have known you for a very long time," I said, even though the opposite was true.

"But you have," she giggled.

"I mean as in the hour past, yet . . . yet I feel as if all this is too hasty, somehow wrong."

"I may never see you again after two days," she replied. "Why spend a lifetime regretting two days squandered?"

We retired to her bedroom, then spent the entire night awake because we had both slept during the day. We then proceeded to sleep for much of the day that followed, during which Alberin had its first election, and Laron became the very first presidian. In the evening Dolvienne and I went to a tavern where neither of us were known, and there had a pleasant meal and even danced a few sets. After that we walked along the short fragment of the old city wall that still survived, and was now a promenade for lovers. Miral had risen in the east, and the lordworld's green light made the city seem like some strange and exotic place that was almost too romantic to bear . . . yet this was not Dolvienne. Dolvienne had a certain edge, a need for something or someone to be dedicated to. This woman was reasonable, affectionate, and understanding, and that made no sense. Again we returned to her house, fed Dragonfang, and retired to bed.

✴   ✴   ✴

It was around noon the following day that we finally arose and dressed. Perhaps we were reluctant to get up because we might never see each other again after this day, let alone share a bed. As we ate lunch, we chatted about trivial matters and exchanged affectionate pleasantries. This was some ideal woman; she was perfectly even in her temper, and one could not help but be put at ease by her, but Dolvienne she was not.

"If you return, will you still want to see me?" she asked.

"*When* I return, I shall see nobody else but you."

"Perhaps you change your name and marry me, Danolarian. Perhaps the fiend that tore the captain apart with white-hot claws also hunts you, and you change your name to elude it."

"The fiend dies, a year from now. I survive."

"Oh. I—I hardly know what to say. Who was it? What was it?"

"When I return, I shall tell you. For now, there is only so much strangeness that a person may cope with in one week. We might go back to Sargol, and even live in Palion. Princess Senterri's brother now rules there and they hate each other, so you would have a welcome. I know he wants to set up the Sargolan Imperial Wayfarers on the Alberin model, so I could get a transfer and—"

I was interrupted by a loud and plaintive meowing at the front door. When I opened it, Wallas shot in, frantically glanced to and fro as if looking for something, then scrambled across the floor and hid behind Dragonfang. The dog raised his head, woofed at nothing in particular, then went back to sleep.

"There is obviously a problem, Constable Wallas," I said, assuming the role of an inspector in the Wayfarers at once.

"They stuffed me into a sack, then they took it!" cried Wallas. "It was not my fault, the baggage must have been planning it all along. I was two days in that filthy sack. I only escaped because the door was open and the tower watchman came in. He untied the sack, he was looking for loot, and that's when I got out. I ran straight here, Inspector, I swear it. Two days I've been starved and thirsting—do you have some chilled mead, or perhaps a nice dry white wine?"

"Ladyship, if you please?" I said as I picked Wallas up. "Now then, what has been taken, and from where?"

"The time engine, sir. She never went to the White Charger, she took us to Wall Tower, and the room with the time engine. Before I knew it, she snatched me up, bundled me into a sack, and dumped me onto the floor. I heard her telling Pelmore to get onto the time engine behind her, then there was a sharp bang and a swirl of wind. Two days and nights I've been in the sack, too frightened to meow. They drown cats when then put them in sacks, did you know that? Sacks have very bad cultural symbolism for cats."

"She took Pelmore away on the time engine?" I asked, unable to believe what I was hearing.

"Yes, yes. Just smell the cat pee on me. I was two days in a sack and—that reminds me, can I get down, call of the World Mother, you know."

While Wallas dashed outside for a bowel movement, Dolvienne laid out a bowl of water and some dried fish pieces on the table. I fetched my ax and thrust it into my belt.

"What is the time engine?" Dolvienne asked.

"A vessel for traveling through time."

"But time just happens, you can't travel it like a road."

"People talk about life's journey, do they not? That is through time. The time engine lets you take that journey faster, or even in reverse."

"I . . . ah . . ."

The concept of time travel is not easily mastered, and I did not have time to give Dolvienne a tutorial.

"Ladyship, what sort of tracker is Dragonfang?" I asked, looking down at the dog.

"He is quite a good tracker, and you are meant to call me darling or Dolvi, Inspector—oh!"

In spite of the circumstances we hugged each other and laughed for a moment, then Wallas returned and jumped onto the table.

"Lariella, I should have known," I said as Dolvienne put on her walking boots and I strapped a collar and lead on Dragonfang. "For her century even a slap on the wrist and a week sweeping up dog turds on the streets is an inhumanly severe sentence for murder. She's taken him into time to escape me . . . yet this is all not as I remember it."

"What is your need for Dragonfang?" Dolvienne asked.

"Even a short trip through time should break the constancy glamour between Lariella and Pelmore. Wallas was left in a sack, and she would not let him die."

"I should hope not," said Wallas with his mouth full.

"So she will be back. I know we leave for the past on this very day, later in the afternoon. Myself, Lariella, Pelmore, and Andry will be on the time engine, I remember that. Wallas, you are probably in a pack."

"Second-class travel for cats, blatant discrimination."

"My feeling is that Lariella returns about now, hides Pelmore in another storage room, then when we arrive she says that the constancy glamour is broken, and that Pelmore has fled. I intend to have Dragonfang sniff out Pelmore's hiding place. He will *not* get away with murder."

✳   ✳   ✳

Dragonfang was not at all happy about a walk during his daylight sleeping hours, but it was clear that neither Dolvienne nor myself was in a mood for nonsense. The tower's watchman was a little sheepish when he caught sight of Wallas.

"I, er, the pussy cat were meowin', so I went in yer room an' let 'im out o' that sack," the man explained.

"I was doing nothing of the sort," said Wallas from my arms.

The watchman stared at Wallas, then backed away into his room and slammed the door. As we began to climb the stairs we heard the sound of a jar being smashed.

We reached the third floor, then proceeded along the landing. The lock was hanging unused on the latch, but the door was shut. As I put my hand to the door to push it open, Dolvienne put her hand on my arm. From beyond the door was a muffled squealing, barely audible above the sound of workmen loading and unloading on the lower floors. Putting Wallas down, I drew my ax and held it club form, just behind the metal blade.

I pushed the door open with my foot, and was confronted with Lariella bent over on the floor with her skirts around her ears. I was also presented with a second viewing of Pelmore's bare buttocks. He whirled and stood, the knife that he had been holding against her throat slashing out for me, but the handle of my ax gave a very satisfying crack as it struck his wrist. The knife fell. I thrust the butt of my ax into his abdomen. With a rasping wheeze, he collapsed to the floor, and with no sense of fair play whatsoever I belted him over the head.

Pelmore had stuffed the sack that had contained Wallas into Lar-iella's mouth and bound her wrists with its cord before forcing his at-tentions on her. Dolvienne drew the sack out at once, but Lariella could only gasp for breath as her wrists were untied. The time engine was standing where we had left it. Wallas entered.

"I say, is it safe in here?" he asked.

"Pelmore has just discovered that even someone as free with her fa-vors as Lariella has standards," I explained.

"My word!"

"He, he . . . just grabbed me," Lariella panted. "Soon as we stopped. We did a two-day jump, just to break the glamour."

"But I thought you had combat skills from the future," said Dolvi-enne.

"They are only transmitted . . . through the chip implant . . . within me," she said slowly. "If Central Correctness considers me . . . in danger . . . it transmits skills to defend myself . . . to my chip."

Dolvienne and I stared at each other blankly.

"I think that means she can't fight because she is in the past," ven-tured Wallas.

"More or less, yes," said Lariella miserably. "Then . . . oh man, then . . ."

"He insisted on a practical demonstration of his restored potency?" asked Wallas.

"I would have been happy to have closure sex therapy with him, but he just grabbed me and shoved that filthy sack soaked in cat pee into my mouth."

Wallas turned to lick his shoulder. Pelmore groaned and stirred. Lar-iella got to her feet and kicked him in the stomach.

"Are you all right?" I asked.

"Yes, yes, it was just his—his attitude. I have never been in—in the *power* of someone else before. I need to interface with my chip for ther-apy."

"That engine inside you?" I asked.

"Yes, please, I just need somewhere safe and quiet so I can be cycled through my victim, anger, and closure moods."

"Will it work? We are in the past."

"I . . . oh. No."

I snatched up Pelmore's trews and tossed them to him.

"Put those on," I ordered.

Pelmore drew on his trews and tied them while still lying down. Now I picked up the length of cord and bound his wrists. Lariella clapped as I pulled the reeking sack over his head then hauled him to his knees.

"I am taking him out for an hour or so," I said as I put my ax back in my belt. "Dolvi, can you stay here and keep people away?"

"Oh yes, I can do that."

"And can Dragonfang be ordered to bite?"

"Take him, Fang!" cried Dolvienne, pointing to Pelmore, and Dragonfang sprang into action, sinking his teeth into Pelmore's buttocks.

"Most impressive," I said as Pelmore ran straight into a wall while trying to escape. "How do you call him off?"

"Fang, heel!"

Dragonfang released Pelmore and returned to Dolvienne's side.

"Be warned, Pelmore," I said as I hauled him back to his feet. "Any nonsense at all and I set the dog upon you."

"I normally don't approve of dogs, but that was splendid!" exclaimed Wallas. "Can I come along to call orders to him, just in case Pelmore tries to escape?"

Thus it was that we left Wall Tower. If anyone thought it odd to see a cat riding a large tracker hound and a Wayfarer inspector escorting a man with a sack over his head, they said nothing. After all, it was the time of the Lupanian Invasion, and there were exceptional sights to be seen at every turn.

I stopped at an artisan's shopfront, above which hung a plaque consisting of a wooden dagger and two pinecones nailed to an oak board. The name below this was Horvis the Chop. I had expected Horvis to be a slight, serious little man, as is so often the way with Alberin's physicians. They have no strength to maim as warriors, so instead they heal. This man was built like a blacksmith. Dragonfang woofed, then cowered away in fear. To my surprise Horvis ignored me, bent over, and smiled at the dog.

"Ah, Dragon-with-fang, how are faring?" he asked genially. "Who is pussycat on back?"

"You know each other?" asked Wallas.

"Yes, two years since business meeting—" Horvis suddenly straightened and looked to me. "Cat, he can speaking Alberinese."

"Well you try to order a decent white wine by saying meow," said Wallas.

"Special breed, they can speak," I explained.

"What breed is?"

"Er, a Sargolan Imperial Wallas."

"Ooh, I like that," declared Wallas.

"I have a client for you," I said, indicating Pelmore. "How much for no questions?"

"Ah, five silver ones."

"How many more florins for not entering this job in your register and forgetting that it ever happened?"

"Big haggle, not need. Nine?"

"Nine, then. Take this man, enhance his value."

"Ah, no, no, no, no, Horvis is not doing enhancings. Horvis is doing art."

"Very well, take this man and transform him into one of your artworks. Please, proceed."

"Who is this man, where am I?" asked Pelmore from within the sack.

"What option, great and wise lordship?" Horvis asked me. "There is empty purse, clean field, and all those between."

"Why not clean field?" I decided. "It is harvest time, after all."

"Furrow or fallow?" Horvis asked.

"Oh . . . you are the artist," I said, placing a hand on Horvis's shoulder. "I leave it to you."

"Oh great lordship, you are being too kind," cried Horvis, taking my hand in his, dropping to his knees and bowing. "Too many clients, ah, they think they know what they want, but they having no understand of art."

We entered, except for Dragonfang, who apparently remembered what went on inside the shop and could not be persuaded to come inside under any circumstances. Wallas jumped onto a shelf and watched intently as Horvis untied Pelmore's wrists, then strapped him spreadeagled to a table. I left. Wallas had an interest in the unspeakable in all its forms and shapes, but I did not.

"I am removing sack," came Horvis's voice as I reached the door. "You drink this, have big relax."

"Who are you?" called Pelmore, now sounding thoroughly alarmed.

"My friend, think of me as artist," replied Horvis as I sank to the doorstep beside Dragonfang.

"What are those knives, bottles, and needles?" Pelmore shouted from inside. "Get me out of here! There's nothing wrong with me!"

Dragonfang whined and cowered against me. I am not normally one who feels much empathy for dogs one way or another, but I put an arm around the hound and gave him a reassuring hug.

"Think upon this not with distressing," said Horvis cheerily. "Is security of working until life's end. Have testimonials of satisfied clients. Now, take this."

"What is it?"

"Special philter, mortenvoice. Deaden tongue, many hours, prevent screaming."

"What? No, never!"

"Come on, just a taste."

"Oh World Mother!" Pelmore screamed. "Gods of Miral, save me! Get away, get awrgrff . . ."

Pelmore said nothing else coherent, but there was the sound of a lot more struggling because he was very strong. Horvis was a lot stronger, however, and it was his vocation to deal with difficult patients. Time passed, and Dragonfang and I dozed together in the sun. It was so seldom that I did not have something urgent to do that I actually felt lost to be at a loose end.

"There there, my friend, it's always worse when you know what you will be missing."

I opened my eyes to find a Racitalian merchant patting Dragonfang's head. He pressed a copper into my hand then hurried away. Next a matronly-looking woman stopped, put her hands on her knees, and looked into Dragonfang's eyes.

"I know it's a loss, but you will live longer for it," she said.

"It will seem longer, anyway," said the man behind her, who appeared to be her husband.

By the time the latch clacked behind me and Horvis pulled the door open, Dragonfang had been given a chocolate and honey pastry, half of a beef and groundnut roll, five coppers, and a lot of reassuring words and pats. Wallas dashed out of the shop and bounded onto my lap, his fur fluffed out to its fullest extent.

"Words cannot describe what I just witnessed," the cat rasped.

Dragonfang gave his face a sympathetic lick, possibly fearing the worst.

"Is Pelmore all right?" I asked.

"Yes," replied Wallas. "Most of him, anyway."

"Nice pussy, very interested," said Horvis.

"Tracker cat," I said, tapping my nose then making running movements with my fingers. "Highly intelligent."

"Ah, clever pussy!" said Horvis, who was apparently one of those people who assumed that the world contains a lot of very strange but nevertheless normal things. "You come, see. Work of art."

I found Pelmore still spread-eagled on the table, a tranquillity casting still sparkling about his groin. Sawdust had been spread beneath him to absorb the mess. Upon his face was an expression of absolute horror, and between his legs were some neat stitches and . . . nothing much else. Closer examination revealed that he had been made to look convincingly female to the casual glance.

I suppose that I am a bit self-righteous, and for that reason I seldom feel guilt. On this occasion, however, I most certainly felt remorse in the extreme. It was possibly what Lariella described as a male thing. Pelmore tried to say something to me, but his tongue appeared to be outside of his control. *The mortenvoice,* I thought.

"Puss, puss, puss?" called Horvis from out in the street.

"No thank you, diet and all that," replied Wallas.

"Nice doggy, these are for you," said Horvis.

A sharp, intense cramp stabbed at the area just behind my scrotum. The look in Pelmore's eyes almost made me doubt the ethics of what I had just commissioned Horvis to do. He came back inside and began washing his hands in a pail.

"That man just made me the most indescribably gross offer imaginable," muttered Wallas from the doorway.

Dragonfang managed to overcome his fears and entered the shop. He looked expectantly up at Horvis and thumped his tail.

"Big sorry, all gone," said Horvis.

"Confirms my worse suspicions about dogs," said Wallas.

"What you think?" Horvis asked me, looking a little anxious.

"Quality work, the finest I have ever seen," I replied as I reached for my purse.

"No, no, not work. Art."

"I was told you are a man of skill and honor."

"Pah! Honor for warriors, myself am *artist*!"

I took great care not to touch his hand as I counted out nine silver florins, then I added a tenth.

"For art," I explained.

"No, not, is not just art, is *pleasure*."

"Is he in pain?" asked Wallas, entering the shop again.

"There is a tranquillity casting about his groin," I explained. "It will cloak the pain for a day or so, but he has been aware of everything that has happened. Horvis, how soon can he be walking?"

"Walking now, problems are none. Myself artist, not butcher."

It would be fair to say that Pelmore waddled rather than walked as we returned to Wall Tower, but at least I did not have to carry him.

✷ ✷ ✷

At the tower I gave Pelmore into Lariella's care after extracting a promise that she would not do anything too horrible to him. I also bid goodbye to Dolvienne, while Wallas had an oddly emotional farewell with Dragonfang.

"I know you're a dog, old chap, but I do know how you must have felt," said Wallas as he rubbed against Dragonfang while the dog licked his ears.

Now alone, I went in search of myself. I knew that I found myself, of course, for my younger self had to see me vanish into time with Pelmore, and thus learn that the constancy glamour on Lavenci was broken. Finding myself was not hard, for I knew where I had been training Alberin's defenders for the next day's battle with the Lupanians.

I watched from back within the crowd as I drilled my recruits in the basic arts of standing in a line and continuing to fight while those all about were dying. I noticed the earlier instance of Wallas catch sight of me, which was my intention. I then set off for Wall Tower, for I wanted Wallas to follow me there.

"They are on the way," I announced as I entered the storage room.

Pelmore was cowering in a corner, curled up as small as he was able to make himself. Wallas was sitting on the bench of the time engine.

"How is Pelmore?" I asked.

"Not suffering enough," muttered Lariella.

"Wallas? What did she do to him?"

"She left him alone after the first few kicks," said Wallas. "I explained that the mortenvoice stops him crying out in pain."

"It's very annoying, I wanted screams," said Lariella.

"Well try to leave him alive until we take him away into time."

We settled down to wait for me to arrive. I had seen myself, and I wanted to know who I was. It was necessary for my younger self to see the time engine and all of us together. He had to know that Pelmore was taken away into time, he had to know that the moonworld had been sponged clean of Pelmore without Pelmore dying. I was intelligent; I would conclude that it would break the constancy glamour.

I was on the way with Costiger, Essen, and Andry, but I already knew what I did to myself. Wallas hid in my pack, which explained why my younger self had no memory of him being there.

"Are you sure about what happens next?" asked Lariella.

"I have told you everything I remember," I assured her, holding up her stuncast.

"Then it will happen that way, causality commands it."

"I cannot understand this causality law. Why can things that have happened never change?"

"Because time works that way, Danolarian. You saw Pelmore taken away on the time engine, so you know that the constancy glamour was broken. It has already happened, so it will always be that way."

"So why do we bother doing anything—"

The door burst open, and Costiger stumbled into the room. I fired the stuncast, and he fell to the floor. My earlier self was next through the door.

"Wayfarer Constables!" my younger self shouted. "Throw down your weapons and raise your hands!"

I fired the stuncast just as my earlier self fired his cavalry crossbow. Essen and Andry followed my younger self into the room, but I dropped them with no more damage or injury.

"He hit the time engine!" exclaimed Lariella angrily.

"The bolt did no real damage," I assured her.

"It pierced the cowling of the temporal displacement amplifier."

"I remember you taking it off and repairing something."

"How can that be? Your younger self is unconscious."

"I revive myself. This stud with the green jewel inset within it, I believe."

I watched my earlier self awake after a touch of the invisible magic from the stuncast. Andry, Costiger, and Essen remained lying on the floor. Presently I saw myself realize that Pelmore was sitting in a corner, bound and gagged, then notice Lariella. She was carefully removing the crossbow bolt from the mechanism of crystal, glass tubes, and precious metals. Finally, I noticed that I was myself.

"Ah, good, I remember reviving about now," I said. "Behave yourself, Danolarian. I know you do because I remember it, but one never knows with this time business."

"Causality," muttered Lariella.

My words had been different from what I remembered. Not strikingly different, in fact most people would not have noticed, but I was an inspector and field magistrate and I took note of all words. I had not intended to speak different words, I just let them come out as they would. They had come out a little differently. Perhaps my inner self had wanted to make a little test of my circumstances. I remembered saying *waking up,* but now I had said *reviving,* and there was more. Causality had been broken. The past *could* be changed.

"Who are you, and why are you rescuing Pelmore?" my earlier self asked.

" 'Rescuing' is such a strong word," I replied, putting thoughts of causality aside for contemplation later.

"Moving to more appropriate confinement," snapped Lariella, who was still understandably angry with him.

"Just as soon as we're in Bucadria I am going to remove his head," I insisted.

"Well I think we should perform a small but humane operation and sell him in the Wharfside slave market," said Lariella, confirming to me that Wallas had kept our secret. "We don't have the death penalty where I come from."

"I'll wager castration is not in the register of penalties either," I responded, smug in the knowledge that the sentence had already been carried out.

"True, but abduction is also against the law, and we did just that a few days ago. Death is so final, and anyway, is it not more cruel to have Pelmore condemned to watch others doing it for the rest of his life, while all he can do is stand guard, and serve tea and cakes?"

"Er, who are you?" my earlier self asked.

"This is Lariella, I believe you already know Pelmore, and of course, I am you."

"My friends," my earlier self asked. "Are they dead?"

"They each got a direct hit from this stuncast, and will be asleep for another quarter hour. You have been revived deliberately."

"Will someone tell me what is going on?" my earlier self demanded.

"Your crossbow bolt nicked the mercury regulator for the temporal displacement amplifier!" Lariella suddenly exclaimed.

"Er, what does that mean?"

"I thought you said that the bolt did no real damage," said Lariella, ignoring my earlier self.

"I remember the machine working after the shot," I retorted.

"Well at least two pounds of mercury have leaked out and run down between the floorboards. I suppose I can seal the tube with beeswax and bleed some mercury off from the quantum bypass reserve."

Lariella began the work. I kept the stuncast trained on my earlier self as she worked.

"Lariella is descended from Riellen," I said as the silence began to gather tension. "Twenty-eight generations, is it not, Lari?"

"That's right, we have kept the family tradition of doing this alive for over a thousand years."

"I would still like to know what is going on," my earlier self insisted.

"I don't tell you, but you catch on," I assured him.

"Time to go," said Lariella, standing up and turning to face us with her hands on her hips.

"Go?" my earlier self. "Where?"

"Actually, it's when," I explained.

Lariella hunkered down again and fished her image daemon out of a box.

"My recording of Lavenci first singing 'The Banks of the Alber,' " she said as she clipped it to her belt. "It's just so romantic, I just can't wait to play it for my friend Darriencel. She's descended from you and Lavenci."

My earlier self did not know quite how to take that. Neither did I. Was Lavenci pregnant with our child when I was abducted? I handed the weapon to Lariella, then walked over to the very anxious Pelmore and untied his feet.

"On your feet, Pelmore, we are about to terminate your existence," I declared.

The words could easily have been chosen with more care, but I was in a mood to make him suffer. In spite of still having his hands tied behind his back, Pelmore struggled and kicked as I forced him across the room. Even though I was trying to restrain him, he managed to kick the time engine a couple of times. This was not a wise move, given Lariella's mood. She struck Pelmore over the head with the handle of Costiger's ax.

"Now look what you've done!" I exclaimed. "He's out to it, I'll have to carry him."

"Where?" my earlier self asked again.

"We're going to sell him in the Wharfside slave market," I replied.

"White eunuchs were worth a lot in Wharfside," added Lariella.

She began to strip off her clothing, revealing the purple skintight garment that covered her from her neck to her wrists and ankles. I noticed the belt with her image daemon fall to the floor, and without thinking I reached out and removed the device from the belt.

That had not happened. I had spoken words that had not been spoken when my younger self had witnessed that scene. What had happened in the past? Lariella had left a pile of ordinary clothing on the floor, and mixed up with that pile had been what I now knew to be a guide to the historic sites of Old Alberin from her own time. I had not seen myself take the image daemon from her belt, yet it had not been there when I had examined the clothing, yet she had removed the belt with the image daemon on it, yet the image daemon had not been on it . . .

An inspector does not show his emotions when on duty, and I hoped that my face betrayed nothing of what I was thinking. I noticed that my earlier self was goggling at Lariella in her tunic of the future that made her look purple, yet naked. Had I been so preoccupied with staring at her that I had not noticed myself remove the image daemon from her discarded belt? That was not likely. My future self had been holding a weapon, and no matter what alluring sights were on display, I would always have taken note of any move by someone pointing a weapon at me.

Was this a play without a playhouse? Did I have an audience? Remembering the script, such as I knew it, I hoisted Pelmore onto the time engine.

"At last, after a thousand years, Riellen's mistake will be put right," said Lariella. "When my daughter is born next month, she will not have the burden of a thousand-year-old obligation to follow."

"You're eight months pregnant?" my earlier self exclaimed.

"No, my husband is. Now then, just one more mistake to correct."

On that cue I helped Lariella lift Andry from the floor. We hoisted him onto the time engine and I propped him behind Pelmore.

"Leave him, he's done nothing," my earlier self pleaded.

I shook my head.

"Remember Wallas's gossip?" I asked. "I am afraid Andry lay one night with Learned Terikel, who is now a young glass dragon. She is no longer entirely human, and she is atoning for her infidelities to Roval by killing all her other surviving bedmates. Gilvray and that musician were two of them, the rest died from unrelated causes. Andry is the only other one, so he is in danger of having his heart ripped out. We shall take him into the past, and in a few moments he will be centuries dead."

For a moment I considered explaining that Andry's wife had died that morning, then I decided that it was too blatant a violation of causality. I knew that such a violation could take place, and that was

enough for now. I was the magistrate and something was on trial. I was
not sure what, but the feeling of a trial was definitely there. Wallas and
his relationship with Terikel was yet another complication in my younger
self's future, but meantime he would enjoy a few months of delight with
Lavenci.

"I have arranged money and protection for his wife and family," I
concluded. "They have to stay here."

"Causality," said Lariella. "It's too hard to explain."

My earlier self tried to get up, but his legs were still not entirely under control. I noticed that Velander had appeared in the doorway behind him.

"Terikel . . . will never believe," he said.

"She will when I tell her," said Velander. "Thank you for taking
Andry to safety. My loyalty lives, even though love has died."

Lariella and I climbed onto the time engine and seated ourselves. It
was somewhat cramped, what with the two extra passengers.

"Ready, Danol?" asked Lariella.

"When you will, ladyship. Goodbye, Lady Velander, goodbye, young
self. Oh, and Danolarian, take my—and your—advice, and try to be a
bit romantic with Lavenci tonight. Tomorrow you will both be too
tired, because—"

The time engine got under way with the usual sickening lurch.

"—because you will have just won a great battle," I concluded, but I
already knew that my words of reassurance were not heard by my earlier self.

Part Three

PAST IMPLAUSIBLE

The time engine was about the length of a pony, so that with four people astride it, the saddle bench was very crowded.

"Take us at a slow pace, stop two centuries into the past," I said to Lariella.

"Only two hundred years?" she asked.

"It is far enough, but not too far."

We stopped. Now the room within Wall Tower was dusty and neglected. Nearby a drunken voice was singing something incomprehensible in what sounded to me like a very affected accent. I eased Andry down off the time engine and laid him out as if he had fallen and sprawled on the floorboards. I took care not to leave any footprints in the dust.

"Now we go," I said.

"But we should revive him and—"

"No! We go now!"

"A note, he at least deserves a note," insisted Lariella. "We have silver florins to spare, and—"

"Absolutely not! This must look to Andry like some terrible accident that threw him back through time. Pull back on the Temporal lever, do it now!"

The comforting greyness of time travel enfolded us again, and my stomach slowly started to unclench.

"Andry deserved better," began Lariella as we traveled.

"I gave Andry the best," I whispered. "His wife was seeing another man."

"Oh good, was he a dalliance partner or a therapy professional?" she asked with not a trace of concern in her voice.

"You do not understand, do you? We folk of the past get very sensitive about that sort of thing. People lie, murder, even start wars over an act that you future people perform as easily as handing out drinks at a panty."

"Party."

"Whatever. Andry's wife bedding another man is as serious as, as . . ." I struggled for a moment, trying to think of anything that the folk of the future might get emotional about. "As you throwing Breen's detachment pendant on the fire."

"Oh. Well that would be bad manners, but we could always have new ones grown."

In the future there were no limits to bad behavior, and the laws prohibited wrongs that were meaningless. I shook my head.

"What could Andry expect?" I continued, giving up. "He married a pretty, hot-blooded young wench, then left her at home with a young family while he traveled on constabulary work, or spent evenings playing tunes in the taverns."

"But that happens all the time in my century. I had to undergo neglect counseling in all five of my previous marriages."

"We take that sort of thing more seriously."

"How did you find out?"

I unslung my pack and drew out Wallas.

"Tell her," I said, holding him on my lap as the centuries drifted by.

"The inspector sent me on a mission with a message for Andry," said Wallas. "Naturally I proceeded with stealth, being a cat and a Wayfarer Constable, and besides, I like to suddenly appear and announce myself. It startles people so, especially if they are up to something. I fancy myself as sort of benign genie, except of course I cannot grant three wishes if caught—"

"You are trying to avoid the unpalatable truth, Wallas."

"I do have a sensitive palate, sir."

"Wallas!" I shouted, holding him out near the edge of what Lariella called the time statis bubble by his tail.

"Please! No theatrics."

I put him back on my lap.

"Well?"

"When I arrived at the house, the lie-down wagon was in the street."

"Lie-down wagon?" asked Lariella.

"The wagons are a service run by widows and grandmothers. Every second day one will call at a street. They amuse the children and tend the babies for a couple of hours while mothers go to market or just lie down for a rest. I found Andry's wife lying down in company."

"Where is the harm in that?" asked Lariella in complete innocence.

In some ways this woman is more alien than the Lupanian invaders, I thought, but I knew that I could not say it.

"Trust me, ladyship, for us it is jammed solid with harm," said Wallas. "Anyway, I hung about and listened, as is my way. In their pillow talk the woman said that Andry had not been astride her, even though it was now four weeks since she had given birth. You know, she then gave her guest a very curious compliment which must give heart to all men of magnificent girth, she said—"

"That's enough, Wallas," I said sharply. "Ladyship, in your free public library of the future I read a history of some common heroes who died in the Lupanian attacks on Alberin. It said that Andry and his wife died when their house burned on the day that we left. I wager that Terikel arrived, and found two shapes tumbling and giggling under the bedcovers in the gloom of the bedchamber. She slaughtered them together, thinking the man to be Andry. Their children were outside, with the lie-down wagon. They survived."

"I see," said Lariella.

"The children were brought up in the palace, and both prospered. Terikel probably never realized her mistake."

"I—you mean she thinks he is dead? We did not have to hide him in the past?"

"Yes and no. We are hiding him from the truth. Is it worse for him to know he was betrayed in 3144, or to think of his wife as faithful while he is marooned in 2944? He is young and has many skills, he can start a new life. The Wayfarer Constables were founded around the time that we left him, he may even play a part in their formation."

"All of this only strengthens the case for sexual liberation and tolerance being taught to children before puberty, as part of a national curriculum," said Lariella firmly. "I mean I understand why Andry had to be protected from all that, but it was his own attitudes that you were protecting him from."

At this point Pelmore groaned. I turned to see him shaking his head. He glared at me.

"So, Pelmore, you are now supremely well qualified to guard the wives of the rich and jealous," said Wallas. "Good enough for tomcats, good enough for men."

"What do you mean?" exclaimed Lariella, twisting about in the saddle to face us.

"Er, I . . . sorry, Inspector," said Wallas.

"I, ah, took Pelmore to a physician for, er, enhancement therapy," I explained, yielding to the inevitable.

"I think he was more of a vet," said Wallas. "Anyway, he removed Pelmore's ravishing engine."

Lariella gasped loudly and put a hand to her mouth. I had forgotten how quickly her moods could swing. Her anger was gone, and I suspected that it had been replaced by sympathy.

"I am a field magistrate, that is an appropriate penalty for what he did to you," I said firmly.

"Er yes, yes, I see," said Lariella, struggling with yet more realities that were beyond her experience. "I mean, in my time that sort of thing happens when a man is to become pregnant. Where is the pendant?"

"Pendant?" I asked.

"The detachment pendant, where his, well, organs are kept for reattachment."

I tried to speak, but the words would not come.

"Wallas, please explain" was all that I could manage.

"The detachment pendant's name is Dragonfang," said Wallas bluntly.

Lariella fainted, and I had to lunge forward to stop her toppling from the time engine's saddle.

"We have to stop this thing," I said to Wallas as I held her upright and looked in bewilderment at the controls. "Wallas, make some suggestions."

"You could try pulling the Active lever back."

"That could be like jumping from a galloping horse."

"Well what about the Temporal lever? Try moving it from Backward to Rest."

Very, very slowly, I eased the key to the REST setting. Color and bright daylight returned to our surroundings, and a puff of breeze drove pleasantly warm air across us. The time engine was standing in a field surrounded by a lot of very nervous-looking sheep. A man whom I took to be their shepherd was running away in considerable haste.

I got off the time engine and drew Lariella after me. Wallas jumped from my shoulder to the grass. After some minutes, Lariella revived and sat up.

"What year is this?" she asked listlessly.

I went across to the time engine and looked at the little windows in the lectern. The ACTIVE lever-key was still engaged, so they were displaying their numbers. There was a negative number for the years. I did a quick calculation in my head.

"The year 850 by the old calendar of the Etheorens," I announced.

"Beyond the limbo year of the old calendar, at the end of the Placidian Empire," said Wallas. "Alberin was called Bucadria then. The name is from the Imperial Vindician words '*bucad*' for market and '*ria*' for slave," I replied. "It was changed to Alberin around 1590 in our calendar. The new name was from the Old Scaltic word for port, '*albeer*,' and '*ryn*' for fast-running thief, thus port of fast-running thieves."

I looked around. A dozen or so sheep stared at us with bland, blank eyes. The city was just a village in this year, but there were a dozen deepwater traders and one war galley in the harbor, and I could see a timber bridge across the river. The ships had odd, cross-shaped rigging, and I had never seen the like. The place was obviously an important trading center, but apart from the fortress and market it was very little else.

"Pelmore, we must take him to a clinic," Lariella suddenly babbled as she got to her feet. "Call the authorities, a trauma counseling unit, his legal representatives, and, and, and . . ."

Her voice trailed away as the reality of our situation hit home.

"This is what you call a frontier trading port," I pointed out. "None of the things you wish to call, including the far-speaking daemons to call them, will exist for, er . . ."

"Four thousand years," said Wallas.

"Thank you. You could try shouting for the constables, but you will only get myself and Wallas."

"I can't believe this!" exclaimed Lariella. "Pelmore is a living, breathing person. How could you possibly do that to him?"

"It was his sentence, for what he did to you. I am a field magistrate, my job is to try, judge, and sentence people."

"This is monstrous!" cried Lariella. "*Why* did you commit such a crime?"

"It was not a crime! I am a field magistrate, and Pelmore was under a discretionary sentence for what he did to you. This is the past, ladyship. Being locked in cells is for the rich and highborn. For all the others, floggings, the stocks, and exile provide an incentive not to reoffend, while amputation and the gallows provide certainty for the incorrigibles."

"Think of it as career security," added Wallas.

Lariella took several deep breaths at precise intervals. It appeared to be some manner of composure exercise.

"Decent of you, not killing him," she said in a remote, neutral voice, as if her mind were hard at work elsewhere. "So, what happens to Pelmore now? What else is his sentence to be?"

"The worst is over," I said, as much to reassure myself as her. "In this year, three thousand years before my own time, this place is a colony of Vindic. Scalticarian men were very much in demand in the Vindician homeland. Their white skins, muscular bodies, and great height were greatly prized."

"I'm sure Pelmore will find that a comfort."

"Their skins were particularly sought after, because they blended in with the white marble of the Vindician palaces," explained Wallas. "Vindicians were greatly concerned with matters of art and decor."

"Pelmore the fashion statement?" asked Lariella.

"It is a very light sentence," I pointed out.

"He will never be free!" insisted Lariella.

"He will certainly never offend again."

"Are you sure this was not an act of revenge?"

"Pelmore murdered a man, he nearly murdered me, he tried to murder Lavenci, and he even gave you some rather unwelcome attention of a highly personal nature."

"Circumstances tempted him."

"Circumstances tempted *me* to murder your niece for what she did to me, yet she was still alive when last I saw her, ladyship. Temptation is not a crime. Surrendering to temptation is where evil lies."

"What about forgiveness? Can you not find it in your heart to forgive him?"

"No! Forgiveness without punishment is an incentive to offend again."

"Had he not slept with Lavenci, what would his sentence have been?"

"The very same. Death or exile."

"You cannot be serious. You would take a life?"

"I have taken dozens of lives. Wake up with yourself, or whatever it is that you future people say."

"Stern acts bring stern retribution, even when done in the name of justice," warned Lariella.

"Given the lack of *any* stern retribution in your times, ladyship, I wonder what qualifies you to say as much."

"We have less crime—"

"Only because nearly everything is allowed or excused! Murder is not murder to you if a copy of the victim's body can be grown from whatever is left after the crime—I read it in your free library. Take that little trick away and your murder rate is a thousand times that of Dawn Ages Alberin. What would your sentence be for Pelmore? A stern talking-to? A slap on the hand? A closure confrontation with the victim?"

"Confiscation of his assets—"

"His assets were burned when Gatrov was destroyed by the Lupanian fighting tripods."

Although it was obvious that I was not going to be swayed, it was equally obvious that Lariella was not convinced. Pelmore said nothing, which should have warned me, yet in my pride I felt so very much the master of the situation.

"What do we do now?" asked Lariella, inclining her head toward Pelmore.

"Push him off the time engine and leave. He is a eunuch, that makes him very valuable as a slave. He will have—what is the expression of your future? Security of lifestyle?"

"But he will be a slave!"

"Living out the next forty or fifty years standing guard over Vindician palace orgies is not among the worst of history's occupations."

"Look, I've been thinking."

"That always worries me."

"Why not take Pelmore back to my century?"

"Absolutely not! Within half a day Varria will be down at the hypermarket buying him a new set of balls and gronnic. Pelmore must go into exile, not paradise. *This* is exile."

"Sir, might I make a comment?" asked Wallas.

"If it's the one about the eunuch who said no, Wallas, I've already heard it."

"Actually, I was wondering if that silvery fluid was meant to be leaking from the bottom of the time engine."

Lariella gasped, then dropped to her hands and knees and stared into the mechanism, her eyes wide with alarm. Suddenly I no longer felt master of the situation.

"Your crossbow bolt hit the mercury regulator for the temporal displacement amplifier," she said, reaching in and prodding at something. "Yet . . . yet I can see my repairs, and they are holding. We could not move through time at all without that unit working."

"Pelmore kicked the time engine twice before you struck him senseless," I pointed out.

"He must have broken a tube near the temporal motion pump . . . which is under the reserve tank."

"Is that serious?"

"It is if we lose all the mercury," said Lariella as she stood again.

"So we are in danger?"

"Repairs will be tricky. The time engine is well armored on the outside, yet the mechanisms within are incredibly delicate."

In an instant I developed an entirely new attitude to the time engine, and found myself stepping back a pace lest even breathing on the thing should damage it.

"Ladyship, are you initiated in the arts of repair?" Wallas asked.

"I designed and built the entire engine, but many of the raw materials were just bought over the counter in my century. I don't know how to make mercury."

"I know the method for refining mercury out of certain soils," I said.

"You do?"

"Mercury clocks were once the standard in Greater Alberin, before the reciprocating beam balance was invented, and many toys still use mercury. Those who refine it do tend to die young, however, and as a Wayfarer inspector I have investigated three such deaths. That involved having the process explained to me."

"Well, that's reassuring, but it should not be necessary," said Lariella. "No more mercury will leak out unless the time engine is in motion, and if I can find beeswax or resin for repairs, the remainder should be all that we need."

"Ladyship, can we travel a few days further back?" I asked, taking her by the arm and pointing to the east. "People on horses are coming this way, probably guardsmen or militia. The shepherd must have told them that strange people on a horseless chariot are trying to steal his sheep."

"But why should we flee?"

"Because they are probably on their way to kill us."

"Why do you always think the worst of everyone?"

"Because I am usually right! If we just— No!"

Out of the corner of my eye I had seen Pelmore lean forward along the saddle of the time engine, his hands still bound behind his back. He grasped the lever-key marked TEMPORAL in his teeth, and the time engine vanished with a loud bang and a puff of breeze.

✳ ✳ ✳

For a short time even Lariella had nothing to say.

"I should have told you, never, never leave the Active key engaged when you get off," she said numbly.

"If there is a next time, I shall know."

"I'm so, so sorry," whispered Lariella, pressing herself against me as the riders fanned out to encircle us.

"Can Pelmore return to our time?"

"I doubt it. The time engine will stop when the last of the mercury in the reserve tank runs out, and there could not have been much left."

"So we are marooned here, with no way back other than living for a very long time."

"I can't tell you how sorry I am, Danolarian."

In very short order we were surrounded by warriors dressed in helmets, sandals, leather straps, and nothing much else.

"Vindic warriors," said Wallas. "They liked to have it all on display."

"Invincible in battle, except during the winter," I added.

The warriors barked questions at us, but they were speaking too fast and I had only ever seen the archaic form of their language in books. I did catch several references to Pelmore, however, and a quite terrible truth suddenly hit me.

"Pelmore traveled into the past," I explained to Lariella. "These men are expecting us."

✳   ✳   ✳

All of our weapons and devices, even my ax, were in a rack on the time engine. At first the naked warriors circled us warily, but upon seeing that we intended to do no more than raise our hands, they began prodding at us with their spears. When that produced no reaction, they began shouting at each other.

"Who are these people?" hissed Lariella. "What are they saying?"

"I am only catching occasional words," I replied.

"The conversation is in a very archaic form of Vindician, one used for holy texts," said Wallas. "Of course I was never one for holy texts, but I had something of them beaten into me by my tutors when I was a boy. Most of the talk involves who had the honor of subduing the mighty time wizards in a bloody and near-fought battle."

"Time wizards?" gasped Lariella. "Bloody battle?"

"I think they mean us," I replied.

"They are also highly offended that Lariella is wearing what they call a naked robe."

"Do they mean my skintight jumpsuit?"

"Yes."

"I can take it off—"

"No!" warned Wallas. "In these times men went about naked and women were heavily robed. They also think the inspector is something of a pervert for wearing clothes."

"For the sake of cultural sensitivity you should—" began Lariella.

"No!" I snapped. "What else, Wallas?"

"We appear to have been expected. Governor Barratier's men are in charge, and they are in favor of taking us to the castle. Prince Halverin commands the guardsmen of the empress, however, and he is all for putting us straight onto a ship."

The spectacle of a talking cat had impressed the spearmen, who now all but ignored Lariella and me. Wallas was ringed by some two dozen spear points, then was seized and thrust into a type of saddle sack. Lariella and I had our hands bound.

I visualized the field, perhaps half a dozen years into the past. Pelmore appearing astride a crippled time engine that had finally run out of mercury. Pelmore boasting that he was a wizard from the future. Pelmore being understood by nobody. Pelmore using the stuncast on people and demanding that they make him their leader. Pelmore's horror when the ether magic powering the stuncast became exhausted. Pelmore learning the language with the aid of red-hot needles under his toenails. Pelmore screaming that the time engine would allow anyone who commanded it to rule the world. Pelmore screaming that we would suddenly appear in the year 850 of the Etheorens, and that we could repair the thing.

All these people had to do was wait for the year when those who could repair the time engine would appear. It was little wonder that the Vindician guardsmen came so quickly when alerted by the shepherd.

We were not far from the port when three or four dozen men dressed in rancid sheepskin kilts blocked the way and started shouting in an old form of Alberinese. I managed to follow about three words in every five. They seemed to think that they should be given the honor of fighting for the right to fight the time wizards—us. They were flanked by a group of riders wearing green and purple dye, and shouting about battle, blood, honor, and where they should sit at the victory feast. Someone in our group blew a trumpet, and yet more naked riders began streaming out of the gates of the fortified village.

Soon about five hundred men had gathered, and were arguing about who should have custody of us, who had the right to fight for custody of us, who had the right to fight us then carry our heads away on long spears, and several other options that I would rather not think about. The riders from the port were allied with Governor Barratier, and a heated exchange now took place between them and the prince. The conclusion seemed to be that the governor could have Lariella, while Wallas and I were to be marched down to the riverbank and ferried out to a deepwater trader bound for Vindic. Prince Halverin seemed unhappy about this, but most of his men were away hunting, so he was at a disadvantage.

Lariella was covered in a saddle blanket for the sake of public decency, then hoisted onto a horse. Her threats that she would summon the constables, her lawyer, and the Electocratic Rights Commissioner had no impact whatsoever on anyone. As the riders bore her away, Wallas and I were taken to the riverbank through an increasingly large and hostile crowd of horsemen. It was by now past sunset, but the lordworld was not yet in the sky. I felt wretchedly helpless, because this was so far into the past that all my knowledge of the future to come was of no use. Besides, Pelmore might have had years to establish any number of lies about me.

"Listen to me!" I called to the horsemen. "We must be kept together if you want the time engine repaired—"

That was as much as I managed before I was struck over the head from behind.

It came as no surprise that I found myself on the dark riverbank. At first I could see only the ferrygirl.

"In the hours to come I shall be very close, Danolarian," Madame Jilli warned. "Mind what you do and who you trust."

Fate strode out of the gloom, and he had a very cocky look about him.

"Try to cheat Fate, and worse will always happen," he said, laughing. "See what little Miss Revenge got for you? She always charges such a high price for such a small return."

"My services are free," said Chance as he arrived. "You just have to recognize my gifts and avoid my pitfalls."

A bright glow from behind me announced the arrival of Romance.

"I am pleased that you made good use of my gifts, Danolarian," she said, "but mind that you do not spurn me again. Revenge and I are sisters, you know."

"You are close to me, Danolarian," warned the ferrygirl again, but this time she winked. "Mind that you remain my friend, and do not become my client."

The ferrygirl? My friend? Only now did a quite obvious thought come to me. I had met Madame Jilli when she was alive, thousands of years in the future. How could she be here, in the past? Her words seemed some type of warning, yet why would the ferrygirl warn me about death? Was she trying to put me on my guard against something else?

"Is there another time engine?" I asked suddenly, staring squarely at Fate. "How do you know all that happens to me in the future?"

I might not gamble, but I do like games of bluff and strategy. The ferrygirl had given me a clue. Now I wanted everyone to see me take the wrong conclusion.

"We are gods, we know the future," replied Fate smoothly.

"Ah yes, silly of me to forget. Might I ask why you take such an interest in my deeds if you already know—"

"Our reasons for doing anything are no concern of yours!" snapped Fate sharply. "Return to your life, your insolence will be punished."

Do they know that I have won this flurry of moves? I wondered. Powers of prophecy could not have brought the ferrygirl back through time. All was not as it seemed, but I had to be careful. I was a field magistrate alone, with no squad of Wayfarer Constables to back me up. I might discover the truth and expose the guilty, I could even pass sentence, but nobody but me would be punished unless I gathered allies behind me.

I suspected that I had caused some discomfort by the way that the gods deserted the riverbank in considerable haste.

"You remain close, Madame Jilli," I said to the ferrygirl. "Is that a bad sign?"

"It is indeed, Danolarian, but as your wench from the future would say, you are a survivor. Until your next social visit, fare well and prosper."

✴   ✴   ✴

I awoke with my head feeling like a melon that had been dropped onto flagstones. I was in complete darkness, but whatever I was chained to was rocking gently, and there was a strong reek of tar and bilgewater.

"Where am I?" I asked the darkness, suspecting that any answer would involve a ship.

"We have been taken aboard the largest of the deepwater traders in the harbor," replied the voice of Wallas. "The shipmaster was told to stay at anchor until Prince Halverin had convinced the governor to put Lariella aboard the vessel as well. Apparently the empress herself wants us alive."

"Why was I hit?" I asked.

"Someone thought you were speaking a magical incantation."

So, these people were liable to kill anyone who did anything that they did not like—speaking out of turn, for example. Attempts to negotiate were clearly not going to get me anywhere. That left escape.

"Wallas, what can you see with your cat's eyes?"

"We are in a hold belowdecks. You are chained to a wooden beam, and I'm in a birdcage. So humiliating for a cat. Promise you won't tell anyone?"

"Are there any weapons in here?"

"No, only some mallets, chisels, and the like in a rack, but they are yards out of your reach."

At the back of my mind was something that Velander had once told me: Wallas could be released to his original form with his truename and words of unbinding. Wallas released to his full potential was Wallas restored to a fairly large and overweight man. Even the transformation process would burst him out of the wicker cage that now held him. I was chained to the hull of the ship . . . yet this was ancient iron, and it was both thin and relatively soft. A mallet and chisel could free me.

Would Wallas transform at all when I spoke the words? I wondered. He might not yet be worthy of becoming a man again, but there was one way of finding out.

"We could swim ashore if we were to get out of here," I suggested.

"I can't swim, sir, two yards would have me drowned."

"But I can swim. I can get us both ashore."

"You are forgetting the dozens of crewmen between us and the side of the ship."

"No I am not."

Were Wallas a human again, none of the crew would expect the transformation, and we could cross the deck and slip over the side in the darkness. Escape was ours. All I needed were five words. One was the truename of Wallas, which I knew to be Milvarios from my service in the Sargolan court of the distant future. The others were the words of release, and these were the common names of the sorceress and three glass dragons that he had offended in some grubby incident in his past. He merely had to hear them spoken together.

Suddenly matters were taken out of my hands. There were shouts from the deck above, then the very distinctive sound of four or five dozen oars creaking and splashing in unison. The words "war galley" had no sooner entered my mind than there was a colossal impact and the deepwater trader lurched over so far that I was thrown against the hull. Water began to stream in as the sounds of fighting commenced above. I had to get a mallet and chisel immediately or learn to breathe water. For that I needed Wallas in human form.

"We're rammed!" yowled Wallas. "I'll drown!"

"Wallas?"

"Aye?"

"Brace yourself."

"Please, not another sailor joke."

"Milvarios, Judge, Examiner, Teacher, Terikel!"

It is fair to say that nobody really had a clear picture of what happened next, and even I did not guess at the truth for some time. I heard the wicker cage burst, then a presence began to fill the hold. There was a deep rumbling and creaking as I crawled into a corner and tried to make myself as small as possible. Flames billowed above me, and I heard a terrible roaring mingled with shrieks and cries from the deck above. Timbers were creaking, splintering, and snapping, water began to pour in all around me, and then the deepwater trader burst apart.

As chance would have it, one of the timbers that snapped was that very beam that I was chained to. Finding myself in clear water, I began swimming. By the time I got over my panic enough to look back, I was able to see that the deepwater trader had sunk, and that the war galley was on fire from stem to stern. I called for Wallas, but there was no answer.

✦   ✦   ✦

Midnight found me crawling ashore at the edge of the Lakita Plain, which was north of the River Alber. I was dragging a length of chain and iron band after me and shivering with the cold. In the distance I could hear gongs and trumpets sounding in the port, and I guessed that the fires that had consumed the war galley had not just been visible, they had been quite a spectacle. Most likely the governor had ordered the war galley to attack the deepwater trader, take possession of Wallas and myself, and convey us to the fortress. Whatever I had done to Wallas had changed all that.

I now made my way a little inland, because Miral was rising in the east, and I was fairly sure that local people would be making their way to the shore to check for loot and kill any survivors who might have a claim upon it. In the shadows of a sandstone outcrop I began grinding the shackles from my wrists. As I suspected, steel had not yet been invented, and even iron did not seem to be available in quantity. This iron was both thin and soft, and in the six or so hours that Miral took to climb to its zenith I had removed the shackle from my right wrist and was a goodly way through the metal on my left. By now there were several dozen people on the beach, and some of them were warriors on horseback.

I was still wearing my tunic, trews, and even my original Wayfarer boots. After six hours of exertion I was also relatively dry, so that I no longer looked like a shipwreck survivor. The east began to glow with first light, meaning that the dawn was less than an hour distant. Soon I would be visible, and that was bad. Already I could see and hear the scavengers who had come to the beach in search of loot being killed by warriors shouting challenges to the mighty wizard from the future.

Minute by minute more warriors were arriving. To me it seemed like a good idea to arm myself as a warrior, not because I could fight my way out of any attempt to recapture me, so much as to resemble those who were hunting me. Using my shackle chain, a round rock, and a short, stout stick, I improvised a chain mace. True, it would have earned me no praise with Alberin's Guild of Armorers, but that guild was a long way in the future and my weapon looked convincing at a distance. I decided to remove my tunic, reasoning that being naked from the waist up would help me blend in better. The long lacing cord of my tunic and three apple-sized rocks provided me with a tanglestar.

With dawn came the realization that well in excess of a thousand naked horsemen were on the shores of the Lakita Plain. The warriors and their mounts had crossed the timber bridge over the Alber River around first light, and more were arriving all the time. As the sun cleared the horizon I saw a wagon and several horses approaching, and even at the distance of a quarter mile I could see that the time engine was on the wagon.

At first I thought I had been discovered, as the group with the wagon came straight for me. I soon realized that I was standing beside the only rocky outcrop for about half a mile in any direction, and apparently someone wanted a vantage. As people began to gather around the outcrop I allowed myself to be crowded away and out of sight. Someone began a speech in Vindician, but there were a half-dozen translators shouting his words in other languages. I managed to decipher that we were being addressed by Governor Barratier, and that he was in search of a time wizard—me. I was, apparently, one of two time wizards whose arrival had been predicted by the prophet Pelmore. It was around now that I realized that my grasp of the local languages had improved considerably. *Suspicious,* I thought, without knowing why. I was comprehending the words with a skill that should have taken months to learn.

"The man who delivers this wizard Danolarian to me shall be granted equal status as a warlord of time," declared the governor. "Danolarian knows the secret of repairing the time chariot. He is quite harmless to warriors such as ourselves, however, and must not, repeat *not,* be killed."

"The time wizard sank a war galley and a deepwater trader in the harbor last night!" called a naked horseman who was probably someone important.

"Aye, he's a mighty wizard, and mighty wizards gotta be killed!" called someone behind me.

"Lots of honor for killing mighty wizards!" cried someone farther away.

"Under no circumstances must the man Danolarian be killed!" insisted the governor. "Anyone who kills Danolarian will answer to the empress of the Vindic Empire."

All the while I was making my way farther and farther away from the outcrop on which the governor was standing. My estimate was that at least three thousand horsemen were present by now, with more arriving all the time. I saw Alterrian mountain ponies ridden by highland lancers wearing sheepskin slings, Dorcian riders wearing only mutton fat and soot, Terrisian lancers dressed in blue, red, and orange dye, Vindician cavalry wearing brass helmets and suntans, and Fralland nomads looking positively overdressed in loincloths and headbands.

A scant half mile ahead of me, the Northwall Cliffs rose from the Lakita Plain. For most of their length the cliffs were sheer, but in a few places there were washaways that were merely extreme slopes rather than sheer rock faces. Pretending to look at the ground very carefully, and so hoping to be taken for a tracker, I made my way north from the gathering of horsemen that encircled the governor.

The problem with looking like a tracker and walking purposefully is that people who know little about tracking think that you know something that they do not. Perhaps I should have tried to look more doubtful and scratched my head occasionally. Instead I made straight for a washaway in the cliffs as if I were following a definite trail.

I managed to get quite some way unchallenged, because the first half-dozen warriors following me at least kept their distance and let me get on with it. Suddenly a horseman from another group rode out in an arc to cut me off, while his four companions lingered behind to confront those who were already following me. I was now a mere four hundred yards from the base of the cliffs.

"Ho there, what manner of degenerate rideth not a horse?" might have been the gist of the man's challenge.

"I am tracking the time wizard, who walked this way last night," I called back.

"The time wizard is a mighty warrior, and the mighty ride, not walk," he replied smugly.

"The man I follow was walking, he was too mighty for a horse" was the best I could do in the circumstances.

"You rideth not, you are no . . ." I am still not sure what his last words meant, but they were along the lines of *warrior with huge muscles who is proud to display his penis because its size renders his enemies dismayed.* "You weareth clothes, only slaves do so, thus you are my slave."

Later I was told that by claiming me as a nonriding slave, this man was trying to take possession of the time wizard that I was meant to be tracking. I was meant to reply that although the time wizard that I was tracking was indeed mighty, he was not sufficiently mighty to ride a horse. That was later. At that moment I did not have access to what Lariella would have called a cultural liaison interpreter.

Perhaps *"Piss off, smelly pervert who hath never known the delight of women"* was not the most diplomatic of replies that I could have managed, but then I was feeling a little short of patience. The Dorcian howled incoherently with outrage, then charged, his lance lowered. I had been untying my tanglestar, and they do not take long to set whirling. My cast ensnared the forelegs of his horse, and it went straight down, landing the Dorcian at my feet. One blow to the head from my chain mace sent him to the halls of his forefathers for an eternity of feasting, fighting, and singing about feasting and fighting.

The quite marvelous thing about warriors of honor is that they place great value on individual combat. As I salvaged a knife, shield, and string of coins and seashells from the man I had just brought down, the others began a loud exchange about which of them should have the honor of killing me and avenging the honor of their brother warrior *with huge muscles who is proud to display . . .* and so on. I began to retreat for the Northwall Cliffs again, and amazingly the horsemen seemed in no great hurry to follow. Apparently they thought that no honorable warrior would go where a horse could not be ridden, so I was obviously trying to get the cliffs to my back before my next fight.

The sound of hoofs at the gallop told me that the argument had been resolved, and the lucky challenger chosen. I stopped and turned, but this time I had no tanglestar. The shield was half my height, however, and solidly fashioned from crossed planks bound with resin. Standing tall, I held the shield up and began to whirl the chain mace, hoping that the rider would think it another tanglestar and break off. Apparently stupidity and a reluctance to learn from the disasters of others was high on the list of criteria for becoming a Dorcian warrior, because he rode on regardless. At the last moment I dropped to kneel behind the shield and lashed out blindly with my chain mace. His lance thudded into my shield and snapped, and an instant later the rock on the end of my chain mace struck the muzzle of his horse. As far as I could tell, the horse attempted to buck at full gallop, and the Dorcian went down. Unlike his predecessor, however, this one was quickly on his feet, with his shield up and his ax held high.

Any warrior who has spent a lifetime fighting is going to be a dangerous opponent, and to be approached very warily. On the other hand, any warrior encountering a new weapon for the very first time is going to have no experience at all with its dangers. The Dorcian held his ax back, then dropped his shoulder as if about to strike for my leg before punching the blow upward for my head. I was very nearly taken in by the feint, but managed to parry my shield upward with the barest of margins to spare. The blade of the ax actually touched my hair as my shield was forced back by the blow, but by now my chain mace was swinging in a somewhat clumsy overhead strike. The midpoint of the chain struck the top of his shield. This would have been enough to stop an ax, but the stone on the end of the chain kept swinging over the edge of the shield. Unluckily for me, the stone had come loose with what was only its third blow. Unluckily for the Dorcian, the stone had struck him squarely on the crown of the head before coming loose.

Snatching up the fallen Dorcian's ax and knife, I ran on for the cliffs. By now a considerable number of horsemen had noticed that some sort of genuine fight was in progress, and were cantering over to see if they could join in. Alarmed that they might have competition for the glory of capturing me, the nine remaining Dorcians charged. I was only two hundred yards from the cliffs now, and already among the boulders that had fallen from the heights over the decades and centuries. Two Dorcians tried to bracket me as I ducked behind a boulder, but ended up colliding with each other. As they began shouting at each other about shoddy horsemanship and honor, I flung a knife in the direction of the third as he slowed to see where I had gone. Not being an expert in knife throwing, I missed him, but I did hit his horse in the hindquarters. It bucked, throwing him. He tried to get up but collapsed immediately, most likely with a broken leg.

Leaving the fallen Dorcian screaming something about perverts who would dare to mistreat an enemy's horse, I scrambled up the washaway in the cliff. The slope was steep, but I made good progress. It was only at this point that the remaining warriors realized that I was escaping and rode after me. My first, horrified thought was that their wretched horses knew mountaineering, for they traveled a long way up the slope. I was preparing to defend myself again as the lead rider plus horse reached the point on the increasingly steep slope where their combined center of gravity moved from between the animal's fore and hind legs to somewhere to the rear of its hind legs. It toppled backward, then crashed down on the riders who were following.

I have related the details of my fight with the eleven Dorcians in some detail so that the reader may better appreciate what happened next. In a fight, a hundred feet vertically can be worth more for one's safety than a mile horizontally, yet one can hear shouted conversations among one's enemies with no problems at all. Several dozen riders from various clans and nomad nations arrived at the base of the cliff, and the Dorcian survivors now attempted to give an account of their defeat.

"Mighty wizard!" and "Defeated us with magic!" featured prominently in the explanation, along with "Three yards tall!" and "Flung our horses about like newly born puppies." My favorite was "Muscles like giant barrels of mead!" but then I always have been a little vain.

I was out of sight by the time all this began, but I did take the time to roll a few of the more precariously balanced boulders in the washaway down as I climbed, hoping to discourage pursuit. From what I could hear, this gave weight to the story that I was a giant which even eleven mighty Dorcian warriors could not match.

I was about two hundred feet up when I heard someone pleading for everyone to ride for the Towergate road to cut off my escape, but this just led to arguments about who had the right to face me in single combat. I heard something about "You Metrians, your fathers rode cows and your mothers lay in the long grass with . . ." Yet again, it was a word that was not in usage by the time whoever wrote the classics of North Scalticar were alive. Inarticulate shouts of outrage and the clang and thud of weapons replaced the arguments.

When I reached the top of the cliff, I found myself looking down upon a pitched battle between several dozen factions totaling about five thousand horsemen. It was only a matter of time before some group broke clear and set off for the Towergate road, but for them that was three times farther than I had to travel to reach safety.

The path at the top of the cliff was actually a long, gentle, and relatively straight walk of about three miles to the Towergate road. I started off at a run, and at the junction I came upon a shepherd taking a flock of two or three dozen sheep to Bucadria. The man spoke no language that I knew, but with a lot of pointing and waving I soon exchanged the first Dorcian's gold and seashell necklace for a reeking wolfskin jacket, six uncured wolfskins, a quiver of competently made hunting arrows tipped with rock crystal, and a bow with a draw of about seventy pounds. Several hundred yards farther on I hid the shield and my tunic, then shaved off my beard with the nomad warrior's knife. Having rubbed dirt onto my face, I was now indistinguishable from any other mountain hunter.

My plan was to go straight to the village of Towergate, where I would pretend to be a hunter from the mountains while I got my thoughts in order and made plans that involved more than merely staying alive and free. Towergate was a mile farther, and I must have covered the distance in no more than one eighth part of an hour.

Although Towergate was about seven miles from the port of Bucadria, the road was one that was only traveled by trappers, shepherds, and occasional donkey caravans. The village was no more than a few cottages huddled around an inn, and a scatter of farms. It only existed because of a bridge across a deep ravine, this being the only way north into the Ridgeback Mountains. Straddling the road immediately before the bridge was a stone tower, built as a defense against invasion from the north. This was because the folk of the Ridgeback Mountains wore clothes, did not ride horses, and were passably deadly archers at up to a couple of hundred yards. All mountain traders had to leave their clothing and weapons at Towergate if they wanted to travel down onto the plain where the naked horsemen ruled. Most chose to trade their wares in the village's market, and not go near the river's flood-plain or anyone on a horse.

A scout from the governor's party warned the villagers that he was on the way, so they had time to prepare. I had been selling the wolf-skins in the market and generally trying to pass as a local when the over-guard of the tower noticed the bow that I carried and pressed me into the village militia to fill out the numbers. Including myself, the militia had four bowmen, six spearmen, and five others armed with just axes and wickerwork shields. The governor and his people were riding at a canter as they approached the tower, with the cart bearing the time engine bouncing along behind them. He gave a signal to stop when he noticed that the militia was drawn up for inspection beside the road.

I counted forty-seven in Governor Barratier's party. Most of them were dressed as royal Vindician lancers, that is to say they wore plumed helmets and suntans. To my relief, the time engine seemed undamaged. Sitting on the bench beside the driver was Lariella, and she was looking very fearful indeed. She was now fully clothed, which was a sign of being either female, a slave, or a very questionable male. There was a pale band of sparkle around her neck. One of the Vindicians carried a lance bearing the head of the shepherd from whom I had bought my bow and wolfskins earlier that morning.

From the state of the riders, I guessed that they had taken the worst of it in the battle on the Lakita Plain, because they were bloodied and hunched over with fatigue. Two of them wore helmets with violet plumes. Violet was the color that signified magic for Vindicians, so they were certainly sorcerers. They were flanking the governor, and even the guardsmen deferred to them. The governor looked as lean and fit as the best of the warriors who rode with him, which was only to be expected. There can be no pretension when you wear no clothes.

Overguard Morian, who was a stonemason, wore our only helmet. One of the Vindician guardsmen rode ahead to inspect the tower as the governor gave us his attention.

"Your name, Overguard?" the governor demanded of Morian in the Merchanteer common language. His voice was hoarse and soft, as if he had been shouting too much.

"Overguard Morian Audinva, Your Supremacy!" our overguard babbled eagerly.

The governor surveyed the boys, men, and dotards of the militia, then gave a nod of approval. The women, who had scrambled to gather flowers to wear in their hair and robes, got a smile and a wave. I heard squeals of delight and embarrassment from behind me; then the governor turned back to Morian.

"Five centivars of nomad cavalry are pursuing me," said the governor.

Morian glanced at his fingers to confirm what five might be, although the concept of a centivar was quite beyond him.

"Five centivars, Overguard Morian," the governor continued. "It is not a large force, but they cut me off, and they outnumber my guardsmen. If they are stopped here, I will gain time to rejoin my army. It is very, very important that my enemies be stopped here."

"Yes, Your Supremacy," replied Morian with a stupid grin. The issue was so simple that even he could grasp it.

"Brave lad, you are braver than the ignorant nomads who turned against me in the battle on Lakita Plain this morning. You may well be the salvation of . . . of a most important treasure. The empress herself will call for you to sail to distant Vindic, there to be rewarded."

"Yes, Your Supremacy!" responded Morian breathlessly, probably understanding only the words 'empress' and 'rewarded.'

"I am pursing a very important man," the governor said gravely, like an artisan explaining some important technique to a very slow apprentice. He gestured to the head of the shepherd. "That shepherd was found just near Rainshadow Pass. He was carrying goods from the man I pursue, so for assisting my enemy I struck his head off. Now I ask you good people: has anyone seen a wizard passing through here?"

Fortunately Morian was rather thick, and took the words literally. As far as he was concerned, I was not wearing a wizard's plumes and had not actually passed through the village, thus I was not the man the governor was chasing. Quite probably the unfortunate shepherd had only spoken some obscure dialect, and had not been able to tell the governor that he had sold me the bow and wolfskin jacket in return for the Dorcian's gold. As it was, Lariella was the only person in the governor's group who knew me by sight.

"Ah, more'n a hand's fingers o' men traveled northly over t' bridge this morn, but not two hand's fingers," said one of the militiamen. "I wus guardin' and collectin' t' copper fer toll."

"That's between five and ten," translated Morian.

"Were any riding?" asked the governor.

"All wuz walkin'."

At this point the Vindician warrior returned from the tower, which was just as well because Morian seemed in real danger of bursting with sheer pride.

"That stone tower straddles the road, and guards the bridge that crosses the ravine," reported the warrior. "It has stout doors on both sides, and the walls are sheer to the battlements. This is definitely the only way across, and nobody can cross without passing through the tower."

"Could the village militia hold the tower against attack from this side?" asked the governor.

"It is designed to repel attacks from the north, by mountain folk, not be defended against attack from here."

"I repeat, could the tower be held by the village militia?"

The Vindician warrior stared at us for the space of four or five breaths. It was not so much that he was assessing us as that he was going through the motions of looking in our direction and being seen to take us seriously. A moment's glance was all that he really needed. We were already dead. The real issue was whether we could delay their pursuers a little before being swept aside.

"The tower is stout, and garrisoned properly it could hold out for months," he replied diplomatically.

"Then get my guardsmen to the other side and tell Arrin-sez and Melitovel to stand ready," said the Vindician governor. "I shall follow in a moment. Regisor, to me."

The guardsman looked to the southeast as he turned his horse, and I glanced around too. There was dust, and in such quantities that only thousands of horses could have raised.

"The nomads are coming, Your Supremacy," the guardsman warned. "You do not have much time."

Lariella caught my attention for a moment. She spoke with her eyes, and her eyes seemed to say *We are both doomed.*

The governor stared at the dust cloud, nodded, then gestured that the others should move on. He turned back to us as his retinue made for the bridge. The smallest, most scrawny horseman that I had as yet seen now joined us. He had a guild crest of gold plate around his neck.

"What do you think, Regisor?" the governor asked. "Fifteen against five centivars."

"That's bravery, Your Supremacy," said Regisor.

Slowly, and with the stiffness of someone who had spent the entire night awake and all morning in the saddle, most of it fighting, the governor dismounted. With Regisor hurrying along beside him and holding out a black sash, he approached us. At a prompt from Regisor, Morian knelt. The governor touched a finger to the black sash that Regisor was holding.

"By the powers invested in my supremacy, I award to you, Overguard Morian Audinva of Towergate, the Black Sash of Valor and declare you Baron Morian of Towergate," Governor Barratier announced as Regisor hung the black cloth embroidered with silver stars on Morian's neck.

Regisor now hissed at the rest of us to kneel, and we did so. The clerk rummaged in a pouch, produced more black sashes, and draped them on his arm. The governor touched a finger to each.

"To all members of your militia who stand here, I also award the Black Sash of Valor," he continued. "All of you are now kavelars and nobles, and will receive an estate, a pension, and a bonus."

Regisor hurried along the line of kneeling men, hanging a black sash upon the neck of each. At a word from the governor, we stood.

"Regisor, record the names of my loyal new kavelars," said the governor as he got back into the saddle.

We called out our names as Regisor paused before us with a slate folder and chalk.

"Darrik, Bane of Wolves," I declared when my turn came.

Alone of all the men there, I could read a little Vindician, so I could see what Regisor was actually writing. Morian had been recorded as Baron Pigfarter, and I was recorded as Kavelar Muttonhead. Towergate was Cesspit Bridge. At the edge of my vision I suddenly noticed that the governor was staring at me.

"Your face is shaved clean," he observed. "Who was your father?"

"Dunno, Supremacy!" I replied smartly.

"What about your mother?"

"Dunno, Supremacy!"

"Well, what is your earliest memory?"

"Huntin' wolfs, Supremacy."

My accent was thick, and different from that of Lariella, so it cloaked me well. It could not cloak my face, however. The governor turned to Morian.

"This hunter is oddly well groomed. Is this usual in the Ridgeback Mountains?"

"It's markey day, he's probably here from the uplands in search of a wife. Hard life, though, no girl would—"

That explanation was enough to blunt the governor's interest in me.

"Have you heard of a man named Danolarian?" he asked Morian.

"Aht, never heard t'name, Supremacy," replied Morian.

"Anyone else?"

The rest of us shrugged, glanced to each other, then shook our heads.

"I must find the man Danolarian, I have a bargain for him: his services for the life of his . . . his woman."

"We'll be sure to tell this Danolarian if he happens by," said Morian, "but if he's on this road then he may be one o' those less than ten and more than five folk what crossed the bridge already. The village Porion's said to be longways north by donkey caravan. Er, like, longways more is port of Falgat, on Strait of Dismay."

"You seem unsure of this," commented the governor.

"Truth is, never been more than a day's trek from Towergate. Only been to Bucadria twice, like."

"Regisor?"

Regisor drew a scroll from his robes and glanced at it for a moment.

"Porion is a village with one inn, nine cottages, and a rope and timber bridge over a very deep river," he announced. "After that there's Port Falgat. It's a halfmonth by caravan."

"That is six days riding at haste. Why would Danolarian go there?"

"Perhaps he had nowhere else to flee," suggested Regisor.

"We must catch him, if he brings the bridge of Porion down . . . Are you done with the names, Regisor?"

"Yes, Your Supremacy."

"Then join the others. Baron Morian, you *must* hold this tower. Hold it for a week, then I shall send an army to raise the siege."

"Yes, Your Supremacy."

We militiamen remained in line until the governor's horse was across the bridge, then Morian spoke to the village elders. They were full of that inane optimism that one sees in the very most ignorant and ill-informed of people. Several of the girls settled themselves on a low stone wall, and began sharing a cut of goat's cheese. I hurried over to them.

"You can't stay here!" I cried, trying to wave them away.

"Aye we can," drawled one with flaxen curls. "Morian said so. Morian's a baron now."

"We's gonna watch the fight," added the plump wench beside her.

"We's gonna see them five Metrians killed by our lads. Never seen a Metrian killed."

"Never even seen a Metrian, truth is," said the second girl, laughing.

By now several more villagers had wandered over to listen. I had already learned that apart from passing donkey caravans, and the midsummer fertility rites that had taken up most of the week just past, there was little public entertainment in Towergate. This was the way to the mountains, where people used bows and arrows, so that the hordes of horsemen who lived to the south never bothered with the Towergate road. Any villager walking to Bucadria risked being taken as a slave by anyone who happened to be riding by, so they seldom went to Bucadria. Only donkey caravans traveled from the Ridgeback Mountains to the port, because people riding donkeys were considered to be honorary free men. Thus although Towergate was just seven miles from the port, it might as well have been seven hundred.

"A Metrian centivar is not a single warrior!" I shouted, abandoning my backhills accent. "Each centivar is a *thousand* cavalrymen, and there are five of them."

"Aht, not so much, I'd reckon," said an elder.

"You don't even know what a thousand is," I replied, on the verge of giving up. I pointed out across the meadow that stretched away to the edge of the ravine, and which was blanketed with tiny red flowers at that time of year. "You see those red flowers?"

"Aye, they's midsummer kisses," giggled a girl coyly.

"Five thousand is more than all of those flowers."

There was a collective gasp as the reality of what was bearing down upon Towergate suddenly struck home.

"There ain't that many folk in all the world," said the elder.

"You are not only wrong, you are about to find out the hard way."

With that I turned upon my heel and strode for the tower. Again I thought upon the subject of language. The languages of the past had been impossibly thick and difficult to comprehend at first, yet within one day of arriving in this very distant period I could understand most sentences clearly and speak coherently in reply. This was too good to be true. I had studied Alberinese as a child, yet it had taken me many months to learn to speak it clearly when I had found myself living in the place. Some enchantment was at work here; all was not as it seemed.

Morian had ordered the gates of the tower closed and barred, and I was the last of the militiamen admitted before the bar was dropped into place. Being an archer, I was sent up the steps to the battlements at once. To the southwest I could see a torrent of riders streaming through Rainshadow Pass, then fanning out to more or less follow the road. A few sensible villagers were already running for the hills with packs on their backs, and others were banging on the tower's gates and calling for sanctuary, but the rest were still sitting about near the road, hoping for a good view of the action.

Morian stationed our six spearmen on the stone steps built against the inner wall of the tower, with the axmen behind them. We archers were up on the battlements, ready with our arrows, a sheepskin of meadowseed oil, and a dozen sheepskins of water. It was a sensible disposition, in terms of keeping us alive for an extra quarter hour.

Looking down at the bridge, I saw the governor's two sorcerers kneeling at the edge, their hands on the timber planks. Violet, jagged-looking things that seemed alive yet were made of fire were spreading out from their fingers, and wherever they went the castings were digging into the wood and flinging out splinters like dogs digging in a garden. The flying splinters left thin arcs of smoke in the still air, and I could see that the structure was already sagging. Abruptly the left beam snapped, the bridge buckled, then the second beam began to splinter. With one final splintery snap, the remains of the bridge plunged into the ravine.

The sorcerers had to be helped back to their feet, such was the effort of creating those castings. The governor favored us with a wave, then set off into the meadowlands between the mountains with Lariella, the time engine, and all that remained of his entourage. Now we returned to the other side of the tower, and were in time to see the advance guard of the pursuers streaming through the village. There were more horsemen than any of the militiamen had seen in their entire lives, with the exception of myself, and most were clothed only in dye, tattoos, or sheep fat and soot.

"Now there's a clever man!" cried Morian, trying to look upon a bright side that did not exist.

"Where?" I asked.

"Why, the governor."

"If he's so clever, why was his army shattered?"

"He explained, like, he got cut off. It wasn't fair."

"We can do no more, we must surrender."

"He honored us, we've gotta give him time."

I recognized the vanguard of the enemy as Metrian kavelars. They made straight for the tower.

"At my word . . . shoot!" cried Morian.

The arrows flew. Two riders fell, but the others seemed not to even notice that they were under attack. They just kept milling around at the base of the tower, shouting, and waving their axes. Some even banged on the gates with their axes and lance butts, and demanded that we open up. Seven riders had been shot by the time the Metrians began pointing up at us. I had been aiming my arrows at the ground, but now the riders were packed so heavily that it was impossible to shoot without hitting a horse or rider.

"Surrender the tower, we can do no more!" I called to Morian above the noise from below.

"No, no, we can't betray the governor."

"You just want to die fighting for him, you stupid yokel."

"The governor depends on us."

"You don't care whether it does any good or not."

"He's gave us the Black Valor Sash."

"Aye, and I'll wager he'll award it to every village idiot who gives him a cheery wave between here and Falgat. He's using honors to cover his retreat."

With that I tore the black sash from my neck and flung it into the ravine.

"You're a coward!" cried Morian in astonishment, as if unable to believe that anyone could cast such an honor away.

"And you're an idiot."

For a moment Morian seemed to consider attacking me, but then I was one quarter of his four archers and thus of great value, given the circumstances.

"Shut up and shoot at the enemy!" he ordered.

Back in the village, a swarm of nomads from the Dorcian Plains had arrived and noticed that the tower was offering resistance. They were, however, unable to get close enough to be shot at, owing to the press of Metrians. Some chieftain now concluded that anyone not on a horse was an enemy. Elders, women, children, all were set upon and butchered. Within the time it takes to draw a dozen breaths, thirty or so heads appeared on spears. This made the conflict more personal for the three other archers, and they increased their rate of fire.

Gradually the cavalry commanders seemed to comprehend that people on top of the fifty-foot-high tower were shooting at them. Although they began to pull their men back, others pressed forward, apparently eager to die gloriously. Someone thought to tear button grass thatch from the roofs of the village, pile it against the gates, and set it afire. Morian now emptied a sheepskin of water into the stonework guttering, which channeled it down onto the flames. Finally the chieftans and commanders persuaded their cavalrymen to withdraw out of bowshot and dismount.

"Stopped 'em!" shouted Morian, and the others cheered too. "We held the tower! Victory is ours!"

"Metrians advancing again!" I warned. "Shields locked."

My first thought was that more thatch was being brought up to burn through the gate while the shields fended off the arrows and water, but the situation was a lot worse. The shield roof reached the gates, and almost immediately I saw violet streamers of fire spreading up the timbers of the gates and even shredding some of the closest shields. Although Morian poured skin after skin of water down into the stone channels and onto the gates, the castings were some type of fire that could not be quenched.

It was now that the Dorcian nomads charged, apparently on their own initiative. Both the Metrians holding the shields and the sorcerers were crushed and trampled, while those who managed to flee were cut down by the Dorcians—for not being mounted, as far as I could tell. Fortunately for the attackers, the gates had by now been so weakened that they collapsed as the horsemen pressed against them.

The design of the tower was primitive in the extreme. The center was open to the sky, with only stone steps ascending the inner walls up to the battlements. Three or four nomads tried to ride their battle ponies up the steps, only to be toppled down onto their own people by our spearmen. Those who dismounted to begin the climb were more of a challenge because they had lances and were very good with them. Our spearmen were forced upward, while we archers hardly made a difference no matter how many we killed. By now I too was shooting to kill, having seen what had happened to the villagers.

Metrians with javelins entered the tower. Apparently the javelin was the only projectile weapon that was considered honorable. It needed no mechanical aid to be launched, and somehow that made all the difference if you were a naked, barking-mad horseman concerned about honor. Two of our militia archers fell to javelins, leaving just four of us to continue the fight. It was now that Morian deployed the last of his defenses. Holding a torch in one hand and squeezing a sheepskin of meadowseed oil under his opposite arm, he sent a torrent of flame down past our men and onto the steps. Being totally unused to siege warfare, and being stark naked, the Dorcians broke, many leaping from the steps in flames.

Glancing down at the shadow from a crenellation, I estimated that we had held the tower for less than a quarter hour.

"They've had enough!" panted Morian.

"You're out of oil, and there's only four of us left!" I shouted back.

"The governor expects—"

"We surrender now!" I shouted.

It was true, we had bought some respect from the enemy, and the horsemen were probably taking a few moments to plan a more coordinated attack to wipe us out. What the Metrian commanders did not know was that just four of us remained alive. I knew it, however, and my agenda did not involve defending the tower. I wanted to stay free, find the means to make mercury, then contact the governor. The lever-keys to operate the time engine had been removed, I had seen that. The governor would think it immobilized, and would trust Lariella and me to be alone with it while we did our repairs. We could escape, it would actually be easy.

In the meantime I had to stay alive, but Morian was doing his best to get me killed in the name of stupidity. He had two militiamen backing him, but I was desperate. Odds of three to one are not to be faced casually, but are not actually impossible.

"I command here," said Morian, who apparently expected that those words would settle the argument.

"I am taking command," I replied.

Being the strongest man in the village, Morian had never once had his authority questioned. For a moment he was quite literally lost for words. The two youths on the stairs looked fearfully up at us.

"You're, er, betrayin' the governor," said one of them.

"Look upon this as a palace rebellion," I replied, advancing on Morian with my ax held at guard. "Not much of a palace, admittedly, but let us make do."

Faced with mutiny, Morian swung his ax but I parried his blow down into the flagstones. A brief exchange of blows established that although he was a lot stronger than me, he had probably built his ax technique upon bluster, intimidation, and hitting very hard. He had certainly never encountered an opponent with superior skills, and was caught quite unprepared when I did the unheard-of by stepping into his attack. I was close enough to smell the onion grass on his breath as I hooked my heel into the back of his knee. We crashed to the stone walkway, and the back of his head slammed into the flagstones. He was saved from being stunned by the helmet that he wore. I knew that strong, heavy men preferred to grapple and roll when on the ground, and thus it was that I pulled clear as Morian rolled. He rolled straight over the edge of the walkway.

There was an echoing cry that was truncated by a thud like a sack of wet sand being dropped. I looked over the edge to see Morian lying in a pool of burning oil. He was not moving. The two youths regarded me from the stairs, their mouths hanging open. I had beaten Morian. Nobody else in the village had ever beaten Morian. More to the point, Morian was dead.

"What are your names?" I demanded.

"Narrian."

"Hastil."

"Do you wish to live?" I asked, and they both nodded. "Take off those black sashes and give them here."

After casting their black sashes into the ravine, I descended the steps to the floor of the tower. Amid the flames and reek of burning flesh I salvaged a Metrian battle pennant from among the dead. Returning to the battlements, I called Narrian and Hastil to me.

"Let me do the talking," I said. "I'll say we are enemies of the governor, and that we scaled the tower from the river side and killed the remaining defenders. Now, repeat what I just said."

After a several frantic rehearsals they got the story established well enough to repeat back to me. It was now that I waved the Metrian pennant above the battlements. After some moments that lingered almost beyond enduring, the besiegers finally noticed that their pennant was flying above the tower. As the cheering began I felt an odd mixture of pride and guilt known only to traitors who are responsible for great victories.

"Give your arrows to me, but put your bows with the corpses," I said as we descended the stairs, "the nomads seem very touchy about archers."

"But why keep your own bow and arrows?" Hastil asked.

"It is part of my disguise."

What I had said was true, but I had another motive as well. Being the only man among five thousand who could kill over a distance of two hundred yards might be an advantage in the hours and days ahead.

✳ ✳ ✳

Oddly enough, we three were largely ignored by the lancers who swarmed into the tower and began to put out the fires and drag away the dead. I watched as a man with the guild plate of a master artisan first inspected the tower and bridge, then stood looking out across the ravine. When he turned back he was frowning. Two nobles now rode into the tower. One a sorceress, all resplendent in purple robes, and with an eagle perched on the rollpack behind her saddle. The other was a kavelar wearing blue plumes in his helmet, and from his cuts, scratches, and bruises I deduced that he was the type who actually led his men into battle, rather than calling encouragement from the rear.

"How long to rebuild the bridge?" asked the prince-kavelar, his arms folded as he surveyed the scene.

"The governor's lancermages used the very same woodbane castings to destroy the bridge as those of Ladymage Lunette used to shred the gates. Using the northern doors of the tower and roofing beams from the village houses we could build a bridge wide and strong enough to take one horse at a time."

"But the horsemen have already begun to burn the village houses," said the prince.

"Well I suggest you stop them," replied the artisan.

Without another word the prince rode from the tower. Silence descended. The sorceress looked down at me. I hoped that she did not remember me from the siege, but I had been at the top of the tower with the other archers. She did not seem unduly hostile.

"So, you are the spy who took the tower," she declared at last. "Who are you?"

"Darrik," I replied, fairly sure that here was someone important.

"I am Lunette, ladymage to Prince Halverin, who has just left in search of unburned timber. This is Kesleir, an artisan guildmaster."

"Who commands you?" asked Kesleir, now that introductions were out of the way.

"I may not speak openly, lordship."

There was a dangerous silence, but I knew what I was doing. Defy someone important, and you establish that you are either a fool with an interest in painful suicide, or that you are working for someone with even greater authority.

"Well then, Darrik, you did splendid work, taking the tower as you did," said Lunette.

"Thank you, ladymage."

"Tell me, what did you see of the governor?"

"He rode past with forty-six companions."

"What manner of warriors were they?"

"Most were lancers, and they had a cart with a strange daemon statue on its tray. A woman also rode on the cart. I heard the governor mention the sorcerers Arrin-sez and Melitovel by name, and his clerk was Regisor."

By now I had the undivided attention of the sorceress and the guildmaster.

"No yokel hunter could know to make observations like that," said the artisan, giving me a subtle smile.

"We have already established that he is no yokel," replied the sorceress.

Lunette dismounted, walked over to the base of the drawbridge, and tore up a handful of wood. It was without strength, as if it had been rotting for decades. Now she walked to the remains of the gates, reached out, and crushed a chunk of the remaining wood to powder.

"The castings of the governor's sorcerers are inferior to those of ours," she said, displaying a handful of splinters beside a handful of dust. "This is significant, because Arrin-sez and Melitovel are highly adept at the casting arts. Within a thousand miles I am probably their only peer, yet look at the evidence in my two hands. They have done too much, and too quickly."

"So, they are weak and tired," said Kesleir with a shrug. "That will do us no good unless we can catch them."

At this point the prince returned and reported that the fires in the village were out. Kesleir and the artisans in his own entourage got to work at once, dismantling the doors in the northern arch of the tower and binding them to charred roofing beams from the village. Lunette and I stood watching while Kesleir and his men worked, and Prince Halverin shouted at various mounted leaders about who had the right to be first over the bridge once it was complete.

Once again, everyone seemed to be developing a good grasp of Vindician, and even I could understand everything! I felt like pointing it out to someone, yet I also had the impression that staying quiet about it gave me an advantage. Was it a function of time travel? Did the language of the times slowly permeate into one's head over the course of a day or two? It did not seem likely.

Lunette sauntered over to stand beside me. In some respects she vaguely reminded me of Empress Wensomer, in the same way that a hawk might vaguely remind one of a chicken.

"You are a very observant man, Darrik," she said casually. "Tell me more of what you saw on the governor's cart."

"I noticed that the woman on the cart with the governor's daemon statue had an afterlife tether on her neck," I now mentioned.

"It was cast by the governor," said Lunette. "If he is killed, it will contract and choke her, dragging her into the realm of Death with him. The empress also has them about the genitals of her guardsmen. It is an extra incentive for them to look to her welfare. Do you want to know what the thing on the cart really is?"

"Er, a magical statue?"

"It is a chariot for traveling through time, but it is damaged. The woman on the cart is the artisan who built it, so she must be saved. Understand? Only she can repair it."

"Ah, aye."

"Prince Halverin wants to kill the governor as soon as he is within reach of his ax. Some matter of the governor stealing the time chariot, abducting the lady wizard, sinking the prince's deepwater trader, plotting to conquer the world, and saying that his father rode a cow. Kill the governor and the woman dies. She *must* be saved."

"Can I help?" I asked.

"I can transfer the afterlife tether to myself. I have no plans to die soon, so the prince could do whatever he wished to the governor."

"You and I can take the wizards, and they will be with the governor," I suggested. "I can try to bring down the governor before the prince arrives, then you can do your enchantments."

"Wizards can turn metal blades and arrowheads aside," she warned.

"My arrows are tipped with rock crystal."

"So, you have fought wizards before."

"Yes."

"And still you live. Impressive."

I was giving myself away, but that was my intention. As a guide or spy I was just a minion, but as myself I was no less a treasure than Lariella.

"Are you Danolarian?" Lunette suddenly asked.

"I can guarantee you an audience with him, ladymage. What do you want?"

"What our governor, the Vindician empress, Prince Halverin, and two or three dozen local warlords seek: mastery of the time chariot out there on the cart. Unlike them, however, I want the time chariot for my empress."

By now I had pieced together some fragments of the picture. Pelmore had arrived some years in the past, and his claims about the time engine and such devices as the stuncast and image daemon would have had quite an impact. He would have told them that he had abandoned us in the year 850 of their calendar, and that we knew how to repair the time engine. *Where is he,* I wondered? Wallas was dead, although I was not at all sure how. Perhaps the spell compressing his corpulent human body into his corpulent cat body had bound up substantial energies, and those had probably been released in an uncontrolled manner when I had spoken the words of release. Strangely enough, this made me very sad. As a human he had been obnoxious, yet as a cat I was quite happy to accept him for what he was.

Lunette was an unknown, yet I doubted that she could do anything to surprise me. Were she not loyal to the empress of Vindic, she would want mastery of the time engine. Only those two possibilities existed as far as she was concerned. Soon Lariella would be bound to her with an afterlife tether . . . yet traveling away into time had broken the constancy glamour between my former sweetheart and Pelmore. Might it not break the afterlife tether were Lariella to travel into time?

"Mastery of the time engine for the empress," I replied, trying to sound a little crushed. "Very well."

"How do I know that you and Ladymage Lariella will not flee into time on the, ah, time engine, as you call it?"

"Because you will hold an afterlife tether bound to her."

Lunette considered this, and it seemed to make sense to her, because she nodded, then smiled in a sly sort of way.

"You are sure to have some tricks that I know nothing of," she said slowly, as if she wanted to be sure that I comprehended, "yet remember that I have a good many tricks as well."

"Agreed, ladymage."

"Well then, what need I tell the prince?"

"Just suggest that I be taken along once a bridge has been improvised," I said with a courtly bow.

Less than an hour after the horsemen had arrived in the village, the frame of a rudimentary bridge was beginning to span the ravine. The prince and I stood talking as we watched the progress.

"I may be a fool for trusting you," Halverin said as we stood waiting with our mounts, "but Lunette trusts you and I trust Lunette."

"Sound reasoning, Your Highness."

"You say you know the country to the north, and that also counts for a lot. The barbarian pigs who follow my vanguard have slaughtered all the other locals who could have been guides." He turned and pointed back into the village. "See that row of heads on pikes outside the inn?"

"That I do."

"The one on the extreme left belongs to my captain of intelligence."

Clearly Halverin was not only a man who expected results, he could be very scratchy about failure.

"Er, so he was not sufficiently intelligent?"

"Correct. The man was meant to have known all that there is to know about the time engine, he has had the seven years since Pelmore arrived to study it. He said that the woman was a mere plaything of the time wizard. Lunette discovered that she was really the sorceress who designed it. He also said that the time engine had been sent to the empress, along with the toys that came with it and the eunuch Pelmore. It seems that the governor had had a mockup built from sea dragon ivory, gold, crystals, and brass. That was what had been sent to the empress, but the original no longer functioned, so who could tell the difference?

The governor's thought was to become emperor of all times, as well as all the world. Should he catch Danolarian, he could still do it."

"So hard to tell who one may trust, Highness," I said, truthfully enough.

"The empress trusts me because I am already prince of the largest kingdom within her empire. When my dotard father dies, I shall be king. The empress will marry me then, and our son will be emperor. You see? My blood shall rule the empire anyway. That is why she trusts me."

I knew that we had strayed onto sensitive subjects, so I decided to remain silent.

"What of the road ahead?" he now asked.

"For the governor the road is passable all the way to the sea, but at Porion there is a rope and slat bridge over a chasm. If he destroys that in his wake, you will not be able to follow."

"Damn him!" hissed the prince. "If he has caught Danolarian by then, all is lost. Does he have a guide? You mentioned no guide in the governor's retinue."

"I saw no guide, but Regisor had a map," I replied.

"A map?"

"It is a scroll describing the road in pictures and words. It is like a guide, except that you cannot kill it for being wrong."

The prince gave me a long, hard glare.

"Do you wish to discover how good the view is from the top of a lance?" he asked.

"I am more than I seem, Highness," I said, determined to establish my own authority. "I am doing you the courtesy of letting you know that."

"I . . . do believe we understand each other, time wizard," said the prince, then he stalked off to test the surface of the improvised bridge.

Prince Halverin was actually smiling as he returned to us, and he announced to his waiting riders that the new bridge over the chasm was almost ready to take one horse at a time.

"The governor will die by my own hand, and I shall ride back across this bridge with his head on my lance," he announced. "Stop him, wound him, but do not kill him."

Lunette was with her eagle, which had just returned from a flight over the road to the north. She had its head between her hands and was pressing her thumbs against its eyelids.

"I see him!" she called. "All is here, in Starlien's memories. Four dozen riders and a cart."

"Distance, speed?" barked the prince.

"Fifteen miles, but very slow."

"The cart is slowing them down," said Halverin. "Guide, how many other paths branch from the road ahead?"

"For two score miles, just one," I said at once.

"He tells the truth, from what the eagle has seen," said Lunette.

"How is the bridge?" called the prince to Kesleir.

"We can begin leading horses across now."

"Then do so. Darrik, you will ride with my vanguard, as our guide."

* * *

The prince was in a hurry to catch the rebellious governor, and so it was that only eleven of us set off along the limestone pebble track while other horses were being walked over. We rode in single file and spaced well apart for fear of trip-ropes. The horsemen hated the limestone pebble surface, as their mounts tired very quickly. Suddenly we caught sight of a score or so men on the road ahead.

"You there, I am Prince Halverin, and these are my Deathstalker lancers," the prince called to the group. "They are so named because even Death fears being stalked by them. Do you surrender?"

Having met Death, I was fairly sure that she would not give a toss about his naked warriors. In any case the prince's question was quite academic, for the answer was beyond doubt. The fight was short and sharp, and our lancers soon had the enemy vanquished for no casualties at all.

"Kesleir, inspect them, make sure the governor is not among their number," said Halverin to his captain as we approached.

"Do not bother," said Lunette, but the prince chose to ignore her.

"Highness, the governor is not among these people, living or dead," called Kesleir.

"Then mount up, we can still catch him."

Another quarter mile down the road was a junction, and it was here that the wheels of the cart were no more to be seen. Worse, the two groups of horses diverged.

"Guide, what have you to say?" asked the prince as I dismounted.

"The cart is being driven ahead of one group, so that the horses will trample and obscure its tracks," I concluded. "The ground is poor for tracking, but I see freshly disturbed pebbles in two directions."

"That must have been why he abandoned that group we just swept aside," said the prince. "Were I him . . . I would send his clerk ahead leading the twenty spare horses, while the cart and his remaining men go the other way."

"He seemed to think that Danolarian would be going directly north," I suggested. "That is what he was saying in Towergate."

"Maybe so, but if Danolarian took this turn to the west, that is where the governor will go now."

"He went north," said Lunette.

The prince was not used to even taking advice from women, let alone following their orders. She was aware of this, and seemed of a mind to make him sweat. He looked to me. I shrugged. He stared down one road, then the other. Neither held any clues. He looked back to Lunette.

"Well?" he asked in a tone that he probably reserved for condemning people to a painful death.

"Starlien has been asked to follow the group with the cart," she replied, inclining her head to the north.

Immediately all eyes turned north, and sure enough there was a dark speck circling slowly on the air currents.

"Do you know this path?" the prince asked me, as if reluctant to admit in front of his Deathstalkers that he would take a woman's advice.

"It leads to Alterrian eventually, but it is only a path for sheep, goats, and herdsmen."

"Alterrian is loyal to the empress, although the governor's treason is not yet known to them there. My force would be halved if I were to go after both groups, everything is a gamble. Tell me, are there any bridges to the west?"

"No, Your Highness."

"Then he went north! He will be thinking to bring down the bridge, so that none may pursue him."

It was not much of a reason, but the prince was a man whose agenda was not to take orders from any woman in front of his guardsmen, even when that woman had just told him a barefaced fact. He now had another reason to follow her advice, so we went north.

✳   ✳   ✳

When we finally caught sight of the governor's squad, there was no finesse in our attack. We merely rode at a gallop and bore down on them, and they lost ground to us very rapidly. At last, after so much flight, the governor wheeled his guardsmen and charged us. We closed and engaged. Lunette fought the governor's lancermages while Kesleir and the Deathstalkers clashed with the guardsmen some distance away. The prince and I stayed with the sorceress, shadowing her as etheric castings crackled and flashed around us. Suddenly I saw that the governor was with neither his sorcerers nor the kavelars.

"That rider beside the cart," called the prince, pointing. "He is the governor."

"I can bring him down," I replied.

"No, you stay with Lunette."

He rode off, leaving me with nothing but the hope that the governor was the better fighter if Lariella was to be saved. The lancermages flanked Lunette, dividing her attention as they closed. From ballads, however, I knew that their archaic enchantments were powerful but cumbersome. Choosing the sorcerer who looked less steady, I selected an arrow with a bodkin head made from a sliver of rock crystal, took aim, and shot. The man was very, very good, and actually managed to fling a casting up—but it was of the type that only turns aside metal arrowheads. The arrow struck him in the throat, but he did not fall. I charged, my ax held high. I remembered swinging for his chest, then there was an immense blast that I felt and saw, but somehow did not hear.

As I shook my head to clear it, I discovered that I was lying on the pebbles of the road and holding only the charred stump of my ax handle. Lunette gestured to a smoking mess that was her own opponent.

My horse was already quite distant, and fleeing at a gallop. The governor and Halverin were still at each other, ax against ax. Lariella was beside the kavelar who was driving the cart. She was unarmed and helpless, merely watching to see what her fate would be. I called to Lunette and waved in the governor's direction.

"I can't fight the prince, what can I do?" I asked.

"Secure the time vessel, I'll deal with them."

Probably realizing that all was lost, the governor shouted to the man on the cart to destroy the time engine. He stood up on the seat, raised his war ax above his head—and a sudden blast splattered everything above his navel over a very wide area, including Lunette and myself. Velander's words returned to me from what seemed a very long time ago. The time engine was very big, and was aware. Apparently it could also defend itself. I had put a crossbow bolt into it by accident, and Pelmore's kicks were probably also accidents, but had any of that damage been deliberate . . .

"I didn't do that!" exclaimed Lunette in astonishment.

The governor had also turned to stare at the cart, where a pair of legs and very little else was standing on the driver's bench beside Lariella. Prince Halverin took the opportunity to cut under the governor's guard and bury his ax in his ribs. The horse harnessed to the cart bolted, and the legs toppled. Lariella had never driven a cart in her life, and anyway the reins had fallen.

"Highness, the cart!" shouted Lunette as she dismounted.

As Halverin rode off in pursuit of the cart, Lunette knelt beside the fallen governor and put her hands about his throat as if to strangle him. Roiling threads like glowing blue snakes boiled out between her fingers and crawled up her arms. I dropped to my knees beside them.

"Tell me what to do," I asked the sorceress.

"Draw your dagger, cut the great artery between his hearts."

"But—"

"Do it now!"

I have never been one for futile arguments. I had to trust her because I had no alternative. I plunged the blade of my dagger into the wound made by Halverin's ax, then jerked it upward, severing the great transverse artery between his right and left hearts. He did not take another breath. I removed the dagger and wiped it as Lunette fought the energies around his neck. Slowly the energies dissolved into her skin, and she withdrew her hands. Halverin returned driving the cart, with Lariella beside him. For some reason I expected that she would be clinging to him, but she seemed strangely composed.

"How is your breathing, wench?" Lunette asked, looking up at the timefarer.

"I am able to breathe," Lariella replied slowly, as if not really believing it. "A sorcerer told me that I would die if the governor did."

"You are obviously alive and safe," said Lunette as she stood. "I took possession of the tether casting before he died."

"By my ax?" demanded Halverin.

"Oh yes."

"You must know that the danger is not yet over," said the prince, addressing us all. "Behind us are five thousand nightmares held together by daisy chains."

"I saw, back at Towergate," I said.

"Danolarian, who are these people?" asked Lariella in an oddly casual manner. "I—"

I raised a finger to my lips, but my name had been spoken, so it was already too late.

"So, it really is true," said Lunette. "Best not to let anyone else know that, do you not think so, Your Highness?"

"Of course, too many barbarians want the honor of killing them," suggested Halverin, putting a protective arm around Lariella's shoulders.

"Then we had best keep temptation out of their path," said Lunette.

Kesleir and five Deathstalker lancers were approaching as Halverin got down from the cart. He raised a bloodied ax for everyone to see.

"All here, bear witness that I slew the governor of Bucadria, capital of the Alberland Colony, and struck off his head," he shouted. "Lady-mage, move aside."

Lunette stepped back as the prince swung his ax. The blade came down on the neck of the corpse. Halverin was very strong, and needed just a single blow to sever the governor's head.

Suddenly there was a great stillness, then the victors cheered. The governor was gone, and Lariella and the time engine were in the prince's hands. For the guardsmen there was the matter of catching the mysterious wizard Danolarian and his talking cat, but Lunette and Halverin knew better.

Leaving Kesleir and the lancers to guard Lariella and the cart with the time engine, Halverin, Lunette, and myself now rode north for Porion. We reached the village early in midafternoon, to find the bridge down, the houses abandoned and burning, and a couple of hundred mountain archers on the other side of the river shouting defiance at us.

"Word of what happened at Towergate must have got here ahead of us," said Halverin. "How did they find out so fast?"

"A messenger bird with a piece of string on its leg," I explained. "In my day the code in the string was: one knot Wayfarer inspector coming, hide the contraband; two knots, rich caravan approaching, lay in supplies and raise prices; three knots, invasion, run for your lives."

"Well, all the better. People will think the elusive Danolarian warned this village to burn the bridge before crossing."

"Why did we come here?" I asked. "Both of you know that I am Danolarian, and that there is nobody on the road ahead to pursue."

"So you know nothing of strategy, time wizard?" sighed Halverin. "If people think that we do not yet have all the people to master the time engine, they will go after Danolarian, thinking to use him as a bargaining token. If they see that we have both time wizards and their time vessel, they will attack *us*. Better to let them think that Danolarian is on his way north, to Falgat."

"What will you do now?"

"Send Kesleir back to Bucadria, where he will take a deepwater trader to sail around to Falgat to cut Danolarian off. Nomad chieftains will try to get to Falgat by other mountain paths when they see me still trying to catch him."

With that we turned back. By the time we got back to the cart Halverin's other lancers had reached it and were standing guard, but they were not the only riders who had crossed the makeshift bridge at Towergate.

My stomach turned as I saw what had happened on that mountain road as we returned to Towergate. Hundreds more kavelars had crossed the river, and these were now riding about in search of anyone they might kill. Travelers and surviving guardsmen were ridden down, killed and decapitated by nobles and barbarians desperate for a fragment of the glory of this battle. Even hersdmen bringing sheep to market from the mountain pastures were slaughtered. With genuine followers of the governor and innocent bystanders beginning to run out, the victors began killing each other, for one head on the end of a lance is much the same as another. Lariella and Halverin rode on the cart, while Lunette and myself rode beside them. The cart became a moving sanctuary, because the prince had declared it to be his prize of war, and thus it was the safest refuge north of Towergate.

"So, you are a time wizard too, Danolarian," Lunette said as we traveled slowly along amid the lengthening shadows of late afternoon, watching the princes, warlords, and chieftains displaying severed heads to each other.

"I prefer to be called Darrik."

"Sensible of you."

"Are we to be taken to the empress?" I asked.

"The empress is not fit to rule time itself," said Lunette, and Halverin nodded. "Enough said."

This was interesting. Yet another faction of those working for the empress were mutineers.

"And you are fit to do so?" I asked.

"I am an explorer, not a ruler. Is that not right, Your Highness?"

"Absolutely true, ladymage," agreed Halverin.

"I wish to travel, observe wonders, and learn. Nothing more."

I was clearly meant to be reassured by her words. I was not reassured in the slightest, but I gave the answer that was expected of me.

"I too am an explorer, ladymage. Most likely we have a lot in common."

"The eunuch Pelmore told the empress that you are a ruthless slave trader and a coldhearted killer."

"I am a servant of my . . ." Thoughts of explaining electocracy, presidians, constitutions, or even the rule of law wandered into my mind, shook their heads, and wandered out again. "Of my king. Pelmore killed a hero, and was sentenced to exile. For him, this century is exile."

"Pelmore said that you gelded him."

"That is a lie."

"Indeed?"

"I paid a physician to do it."

Lunette snickered. "Why?"

"I am not trained to—"

"I mean why exile a man in the past yet keep his pleasure baubles in his own century?"

"To ensure that his exile is not a pleasant one," I said tersely, not willing to discuss Pelmore, Lavenci, Riellen, Laron, and other people and complications beyond counting.

"Do you wish to expand upon that?" she asked.

"Only if you wish to hear lies."

"A good answer, I like that. I was given the task of assessing Pelmore's devices and tales when he was brought to the imperial palace, half a world away."

"Where is Pelmore now?" I asked.

"He is still there, telling tales of the future centuries. I now know most of them to be lies, yet those who listen are entertained, so no harm done."

Pelmore, living in luxury. The thought was very annoying, so I sought to change the subject.

"How can you know that there is little truth in Pelmore's stories and claims?" I asked. "You have not yet spoken of the future with Lariella here, or with me."

"Ah, but there is Wallas."

"Wallas!" I gasped. "He's alive?"

"So, you *do* know him. Yes, he is quite an animal."

A vision passed through my head: Wallas paddling ashore after the shipwreck, meowing pathetically for hot, spiced mead and marinated fish pieces, preferably with the bones removed.

"Wallas told me that Pelmore spent a night with your truelove."

"He was not lying. Not that time, anyway."

"So, Pelmore's gelding was revenge."

"I do not wish to discuss the matter further."

"I can arrange for Pelmore to die horribly."

The offer was tempting, but by now I had become suspicious of such offers. Whatever I did to Pelmore came back to haunt me, and I was thoroughly sick of having him in my life. Revenge was a god of balance: as much as one hurt, so much would one be hurt in turn. If I accepted

Lunette's offer to have him killed, it was sure to rebound upon me in some manner. *Best to leave him alone,* I decided.

"His sentence was exile, and he is in exile."

"But he is your enemy, and he is prospering."

"Fortune has chosen that he should prosper in luxury. One must not anger Fortune, so as far as I am concerned, there's an end to it."

"As you will."

✳   ✳   ✳

By the time we got back to Towergate the bridge had been made wide enough to take the cart. That night there was a great gathering of kings, princes, clan chiefs, and warlords in the remains of the village, at which the heads of over nine hundred of the governor's supposed guardsmen were displayed on lances. After all, who looks at all closely at severed heads on the end of nine-foot lances in the twilight, by the dim glow of the dung and grass thatch fires? The heads of at least thirty sheep were among the trophies, the claim being that they were shapeshifted guardsmen.

Unseemly behavior was a feature of the celebrations. More leaders died in duels that night than in the morning's battle on the Lakita Plain. Naturally the slave bards began composing epics of how their masters had died in the final battle with the governor. The two surviving village militiamen boasted that they had destroyed the bridge and fought the governor's army until Prince Halverin arrived. Like all the other liars out and about that night, they were believed, honored, and rewarded—initially, at any rate.

It was still early when Lunette approached me. Lariella and I had taken refuge in the burned-out, roofless shell of one of the cottages, mainly because it put us out of sight of several thousand drunken, naked horsemen. All three moonworlds were near their zenith and very bright, although the lordworld had not yet risen.

"As I entered I put a mild terror casting on this ruin," said Lunette. "It will give unease to anyone nearby and prompt them to go elsewhere."

"Should we stay here until the nomads leave?" I asked.

"No, it is effective only until daylight, the casting depends on darkness and shadows for its cues. At dawn the unease turns to suspicion. Never fear, I have another means that will be ready before then."

"Then all is well?" Lariella asked, probably not really believing that anything could be well for us under the circumstances.

The light of the moonworlds showed that Lunette was not smiling.

"Lariella, you are, of course, aware that we are the only two women within five miles who still have their heads attached. You may also know that what little discipline that exists here is breaking down. Halverin thinks that I can keep the time vessel and ladymage safe. This I can do, but not without help."

"Defeating the governor was probably all that held the nomads behind Prince Halverin," I agreed.

"Quite so, which makes it very dangerous for us. Many have set off to catch Danolarian at Falgat, but some warlords are planning to seize the time chariot and Lariella. They are too stupid to know what it really is, they think it is a means of flying to the feasting halls of the spirits of their ancestors without dying."

Nothing and nobody is left to protect us, I concluded in an instant.

"How do you know all this?" I asked, words catching up with my fears.

"A little bird told me."

"Actually it was me," said Halverin as he stepped through the doorway that lacked a door.

Lariella hurried across to him at once, and they embraced. To me it seemed quite out of character for her, and it made me wonder what had happened to her in the day that we had spent apart. Something within her seemed . . . not so much broken as transformed. She seemed to glow, she seemed hungry for the prince, there was now a strange depth to her that had not been there before. Had she learned to love? Had she risen above the barren poking and grunting that was stupidly referred to as making love in her century? Halverin had defeated the governor to save her, so Halverin was her hero. It all made sense, yet somehow my mind was clouded with doubts.

"How did you avoid my terror casting?" asked Lunette, looking merely annoyed with Halverin rather than actually angry.

"I felt some terror, but I ignored it."

"But surely others could do that too," I pointed out.

"Danolarian, should you see a beautiful woman trying to entice you into a dark alleyway in the dead of night, what would you do?"

"Cross the street, walk faster, and give serious thought to running."

"Most of the men out there would smile, wave their purse, and walk straight in. You and I have more sense. I suspect that you could walk through a terror casting as easily as I just have, my friend. We see through guile: I through yours and you through mine. That is a good arrangement."

It was a warning, but it did not concern me as yet. Halverin leaned against the wall with Lariella in his arms. There was still annoyance on Lunette's face, but she was one of those people who said nothing if she had no suitable retort.

"Highness, what else have you found out?" I asked.

"There are five warlords from the Dorican plains with a tradition of celebrating victory by imposing their personal attentions upon the women of the vanquished before burning them alive. No such women are to hand, but apparently Lariella and Lunette are to be made honorary courtesans of the governor. We cannot stay here."

"I have a clifftop tower four miles from here, overlooking the Lakita Plain and the port of Bucadria," said Lunette. "We could make a dash for it."

"No chance. The road there is jammed solid with naked, drunken nomads looking for an excuse to challenge anyone to a fight."

Reaching down into the front of her robes, Lunette drew out a small, black thing about the size of a grape. It was like a tiny patch of black smoke that somehow held a globular form.

"Have you ever seen one of these?" Lunette asked.

I shook my head. She closed her fingers over it, then squeezed. I felt the oddest sensation, as if an arrow had just streaked past my head, missing by a hairsbreadth.

"Help is on the way," she announced. "All that we need do is get clear of here so that my helper can distinguish us from the others."

"Three of us are wearing clothes," I pointed out. "Surely that is enough?"

"It is too hard to explain. When the help arrives, we must be where it is clear and we can be seen. Highness, what do you say?"

"I have noticed that there are no horsemen on the other side of the ravine," said Halverin.

"There is a guarded bridge to cross," I said at once. "Once we are over it, every one of the horsemen here will be after us. They are all better riders than me or Lariella."

"Put your mind to it!" insisted Lunette. "I have already signaled for help, we must be in the open in a half hour. What I shall do will draw a great deal of attention, it is *vital* that no horsemen are nearby."

"So, we must cross the bridge, then you ride away north with Lariella?" I asked.

"Yes."

"I can arrange that."

"How?"

"Probably by getting myself killed. Prince Halverin, would you like to get yourself killed in the defense of two ladies?"

"An honorable death guarantees enhanced delights in the afterlife."

"I shall take that as yes."

"I'll fetch my Deathstalker guards, they are guarding the time engine."

"Best not to," I warned. "Too much force on show and we would not even get over the bridge. We need to draw no more attention to ourselves than needs be until we are well on our way. Your Highness, can you use a bow?"

"No!" he exclaimed, greatly affronted. "Men of honor use only the javelin."

"Well could you just go out and collect a half-dozen quivers of arrows for me?"

"Arrows? In a camp full of nomad horsemen who despise bowmen? Have you not noticed the sneers that have been cast your way all day?"

"I thought it was because I was wearing trews and boots."

"Women wear robes and perverts use bows. Well, some perverts wear robes, too."

I had to remind myself that I was clothed from the waist down and carrying a bow. It was probably a wonder that I was not already taking in the scene from the top of a lance.

"Just go find four horses, if you please," I said, sighing. "Collect a few javelins, too."

"Ladymage?" asked Halverin, sneering at me.

"Do it," said Lunette firmly.

Interesting, I thought at once. *A prince who defers to a sorceress. That means either a a weak prince . . . or a very, very powerful sorceress.*

* * *

Halverin slipped away into the darkness after taking his leave of Lariella. I began to string my bow.

"Your pardon, ladies, the resident pervert needs to do something obscene to keep us all alive," I said as I tried the draw. Lunette smiled at me.

"Take no offense, Halverin is a tolerant and honorable soul in his own way."

"What about the time engine?" I asked, trying to stay focused on strategic as well as tactical escape.

"It will have to stay here, but only for a short time."

"What do you mean? What is your plan?"

"Just get us safely across the bridge, Danolarian. After that it is *I* who will be defending *you.*"

Halverin returned with the horses as I was speaking. He said they were half-lights, bred specifically for chases in near darkness. He also had six javelins.

"Inspector, may we know your plan now?" Lunette asked.

"The bridge is not heavily guarded, and there are no guards on the other side of the river. We can storm across."

"That is true," agreed Halverin.

"Good, good. Then our only problem is that this side is swarming with naked, drunken, heavily armed oafs who did not get a chance to fight today. Highness, you and I must make a stand at the other side of the bridge. One archer can hold it as long as he has arrows."

"What?" he exclaimed. "Fight beside an *archer*?"

"Very well, you may flee with the ladies," I said smoothly. "I shall stay and fight to the death, alone."

These words had much the same effect upon Halverin as a very hard kick to the testicles. He hunched over a little, then took several deep breaths.

"There is nothing that I would not do in defense of the ladies," he muttered. "I shall fight."

"Hold the bridge until there is a great light from the north, then ride in that direction," said Lunette.

"Ladymage, how far?" asked Halverin.

"One mile," said Lunette.

"And then?"

"Keep riding until you are rescued."

"What? Is that all?"

"That is the best I have to offer."

With Halverin apparently in charge of us, we were left alone as we rode through the encampment for the improvised bridge. I found my-self next to Lunette, with Lariella and Halverin riding in front.

"We are nearly at the bridge," I said. "When will we know when you are safely away, or do we merely fight to the death?"

"Have you not been listening? Hold the bridge until there is a flash of light from the north."

"We shall be looking the other way if we are fighting."

"Trust me, you will notice the light."

"Very well. Then we ride for where the light blazes out?"

"Yes. Are you sure you can hold the bridge against all comers?"

"No, the bridge has been made wide enough to take the cart, which means it can take two riders abreast. I can shoot down one at a time, but not two."

"Perhaps the prince can engage any who get past you. I am sure he would love to die in defense of Lariella."

"Why does every man here want to die fighting? Has nobody heard of staying alive and enjoying the spoils of victory?"

"You are very obviously from another age, Danolarian."

"Besides, is not Halverin supposed to be something special to the empress?"

"The empress would spurn him with contempt if she thought that he was not constantly astride other women. He has to prove his manhood, do you not understand? She has a spy close to him who keeps a tally, so that—"

"All right, all right, I think I understand. The more that things change, the more we never get anywhere."

✳ ✳ ✳

The horsemen of Dorcia who were meant to be guarding the bridge were gathered around a fire beside the tower, playing at dice and not in a mood to be disturbed.

"Notice, a good time is being had by the glorious victors," commented Lunette.

Although the improvised bridge was under guard, the way was physically clear as we approached. One of the Dorcian guards climbed unsteadily to his feet, strode across to stand in our path, then waved his ax.

"At'sen! At'sen!" he called.

"Lensi, id sa'bin Halverin!" Halverin called back in a different language, stressing his name.

"Halverin!" the nomad exclaimed, enraged, and with his companions cheering him on. "Pist! Pist!"

"What are they saying?" I asked Lunette.

"Several warlords are now claiming that Halverin had robbed them of the credit for killing the governor, and this man is evidently a vassal of one of them."

The nomad began brandishing his ax, and he approached us in a step-feint form that was spoiled by his lurching, drunken gait.

"Brilliance casting?" asked Lunette.

"No thank you, they attract the wrong sorts of people," I replied as I raised my bow from the shadow of my horse and shot the nomad down.

✳ ✳ ✳

A brilliance casting would have alerted the entire encampment that something of importance was happening at the bridge. This way, the cries of outrage from the other guards were lost amid the general babble of the encampment as we urged our horses through the tower and out onto the decking of the bridge.

"Lariella, stay with Lunette whatever happens," I said as I dismounted, in case she had any ideas of heroically staying with Halverin.

To my dismay Lunette now dismounted, ran back onto the bridge and dropped to her knees. Halverin seized the reins of Lariella's horse as she tried to follow her. Tendrils of blue light spread out from Lunette's fingers, and burning splinters were flung through the air. Lunette ran back to her horse.

"I had time to cast no more than the weakest of woodbane spells," she said as she paused, panting. "It will not bring down the bridge for some time, but the horsemen do not know that. Now help me into the saddle."

The two women rode off into the darkness to the north, while I tied my horse behind the shelter of the ornamental stone arch that marked the northern end of the bridge.

"Man in clothing, is the woman Lariella dear to you?" Halverin asked tentatively.

"Dear no, costly yes."

"I mean are your hearts entwined?"

"Absolutely not."

"Really?" he asked in genuine surprise.

"Yes!"

"So she is, ah, whole of hearts?"

"Your Highness, I cannot believe this! We are facing an army of four thousand insane horsemen who have only stopped killing each other because they have an excuse to kill us, we are unlikely to live long enough to need another piss, yet you want to know if Lariella is free for courtship activities?"

"A man who wears clothing could not understand."

"Enough! There are riders coming."

The guards on duty were apparently anxious for others not to hog their glory, for they had raised no general alarm. Instead they mounted up and set out across the bridge in pursuit of us. One by one I shot them down. Riderless horses clattered past us into the darkness; then more riders appeared. I shot down another five before the sheer numbers storming over exceeded my rate of fire, then Halverin dropped another with a javelin and engaged two others with his battle-ax.

"Any signs of a bright light?" I shouted, trying to discern what was happening at the other end of the causeway.

When there was no answer I turned, saw Halverin bracketed by two riders, and shot the one on his left. Both Halverin and his opponent screamed in outrage, then returned to their battle-ax duel. The outcome was settled when the Dorcian's horse lost its footing at the edge of the chasm and plunged into the darkness.

"You filthy wretch!" screamed Halverin, pointing to the man lying on the ground and featuring an arrow in his chest. "His spirit will be reborn as that of a woman because he died by an arrow."

I began to appreciate how the governor had felt when he had passed this way just a half day earlier, then suddenly hope blazed up in me. Sure enough, there was a large group building up on the other side, but they seemed nervous about attacking. The woodbane casting was still eating away at the bridge, but its light was so weak that the nomads could not have noticed it from where they were. Why were they hesitating? Perhaps it was me.

"Are you saying that those idiots on the other side are fearful of crossing because of the disgrace of being shot with an arrow?" I called to Halverin.

"Yes!"

I sent an arrow right over the ravine to give the horsemen some incentive to withdraw further, but suddenly a group broke away and charged for us. As I drew out another arrow my fingers told me that only three were left—and abruptly the decking of the eastern side of the bridge gave way beneath the lead rider. Lunette's woodbane casting had not been strong enough to bring the bridge down, but it had still been able to do some damage. Two more riders plunged into the gap before those behind reined in, and I shot down the lead man who had crossed on the other side. Halverin engaged the rider behind him, I shot another on the bridge, then those behind retreated again.

Now a great light blazed out behind us, a brilliance casting that only a sorceress with Lunette's power could have conjured.

"Our cue to flee!" I cried to Halverin, then I shot down the man he was fighting.

"Don't shoot honorable horsemen, you filthy degenerate!" Halverin shouted as I mounted my horse.

"If I see any honorable ones I'll leave them to you!" I retorted as I turned my horse to the north.

✳   ✳   ✳

The three moonworlds gave just enough light to show the way on the pebble path. When I looked back I could see a depressingly large number of torches assembling at the base of the bridge. They had light, and had heard us riding away. Now they would be after us. They were all better riders than me, and Lunette said that many were renowned for being able to track game in the winter half-light of the far south.

"Riders behind," called Halverin.

"How many?"

"Hard to tell in the darkness, but it looks like all of them."

"So turning to fight is not an option?"

"Only if you like the view from the end of a lance."

Soon I could hear war cries and cheers. I was looking ahead when there was an almighty blast of red light and heat from behind. I turned in time to see Halverin outlined against an inferno of burning men and horses, a pair of wings with a span greater than most castles are broad, and an enormous set of talons sweeping toward me.

I probably shrieked with terror as I was seized, and I definitely remember screaming as I was drawn up into the starlit blackness. A huge, oval patch of glowing pebbles and burning pasture shrank as we ascended. I continued to scream about as often as I could draw breath.

"Don't carry on, it's only a glass dragon," Halverin called.

"*Only* a glass dragon?" I replied. "It's got me in its claws."

"They're too proud to let folk ride on their backs. Be at ease, he'll not bite."

"Much," rumbled a deep voice somewhere above us.

"You could have warned me!" I protested.

"Do you think anyone thought to warn *me*?" he shouted back.

We were by now so high that I could see the lordworld's disk rising in the east. Snow-enshrouded peaks, glaciers, and meltwater streams were visible in the distance as chill winds tore past us. I was too confused to fully comprehend what was happening until we were actually coming down near a clifftop tower that had become a ruin by my century. Lariella was waiting at its base as we were set down, and for a long moment she and Halverin hugged each other—in his case probably as much for warmth as for comfort and reassurance.

Lunette appeared from a door in the tower, now wearing furs.

"Ask no questions, you are safe," she said, then pointed upward.

Looking to the top of the tower, I saw an enormous shape that might have been taken for a spire in the darkness.

"I was happy as a cat," rumbled a voice so deep that I fancied the very ground beneath my feet was shuddering.

I caught the word "Wallas?" while it was still in my windpipe, strangled it, and cast it back down into my lungs.

"You have my word that I shall somehow find the means to change you back!" called Lunette.

"Brought low by a woman," muttered the enormous shape. "Actually it was several women over a number of years. You are a woman. I am not sure I should trust you. My own commander did this to me, and he is a man. Not sure that I can trust anyone."

"Great and lordly Wallas," shouted Lunette, "we still have to snatch the time vessel."

"Rescuing women, rescuing men, rescuing time engines," muttered the glass dragon. "Very well. Where is it?"

"Take me in your talons, I shall guide you. Prince Halverin, go inside, drop the stone door."

"Aye, ladymage."

Wallas spread his wings and dropped to snatch up Lunette, raising a great swirl of dust. With another great flap he was in the air again, and soon we could see nothing of them at all.

"How did he become a cat?" asked Halverin as we approached a very narrow door in the base of the tower.

"Some incompetent sorceress named Wensomer shapeshifted him," I said with malicious satisfaction. "He was once a courtier."

"And then?"

"There was an unfortunate accident, and I have no more to say on the matter," I said sullenly. "Best not to call me Danolarian in front of Wallas. Calling me inspector would not be a good idea either."

The door at the base of the tower was all of two feet wide, and was certainly not wide enough to take the time engine.

"Why do you not have a larger door at the level of the ground?" I asked.

"Behind and above this little door is a slab of rock two yards thick," said Halverin. "Were the tower to be attacked, it can be dropped in an instant, forming a door that no battering ram could ever crack, and no woodbane enchantment could shred. There is a crane at the summit. It is a door that can only be used with the cooperation of those within. Watch now."

He called to some guardsmen, who ran off to fetch yet more guardsmen. Presently a dozen guardsmen were straining at two thick wooden levers, and there was a grinding sound like that from a badly seated millstone. Suddenly there was the crash of something so heavy that it literally bounced me into the air. I looked into the doorway. It had become a wall of solid rock.

✴   ✴   ✴

Halverin and I were keeping watch from the top of the tower when Wallas returned with Lunette and the time engine in his claws. He hovered, his wings raising a blast of wind like a storm front, then set his passenger and cargo down on the wooden decking at the summit. Lunette bowed to him as he perched on the crenellations and sat hunched over, his wings folded.

"Great and powerful Wallas, I thank—"

That was as far as she got. Wallas suddenly howled, wrapped his wings even more tightly about himself, and made a rasping noise like a battle galley grinding onto a reef.

"I can't believe I ate those filthy, rancid Dorcian horsemen!" Wallas cried out to the night. "I mean as a cat I was happy with just a plump, grain-fed mouse and a bowl of chilled mead. Now—now I'm going to be sick!"

Without another word he spread his wings and cast himself out into the blackness.

"The pig, he ate two before snatching the cart with the time engine," said Lunette.

There was a huge gout of flame away to the east as Wallas threw up.

"Is your life usually as interesting as this?" Halverin asked me.

I watched as Wallas circled the tower, then landed on a mountain about half a mile to the north. By the light of the lordworld, I watched as he folded his wings, extended a hind leg into the air like a cat, and began licking himself.

"Why are there no guards on the battlements?" I asked. "The road to

Towergate passes close to this tower, we might well be under siege soon."

"Very soon there will be nothing and nobody on the road," Lunette replied. "Pardon me, if you will."

The sorceress breathed tangles of etheric energies into her hands, just as Lavenci and all the folk of the magical arts did in my century. I knew well enough to look away as she flung the ball into the air, and moments later a brilliance casting blazed out for Wallas's attention. As he returned I slipped back into a shadow. His wings again raised a gale as he landed uncomfortably close to us.

"My apologies," he said in a hoarse voice. "Vomited all over Lakita Plain, then had to lick my arse to take the taste away."

Might that be how Mount Dragon's End got its name? I wondered, while resisting the temptation to snigger. *So much for the legend of a dragon being slain there.*

"Lord Wallas, your prowess in battle will be sung of in ballads as long as there are bards to sing," said Lunette.

"*I* was once a bard," replied Wallas. "Nearly starved. What is my next task?"

"Lord Wallas, in your generosity you have done more than I could ever have hoped."

"Good, good, but see here, ladyship, I am not a real glass dragon so I do not have to be humored or flattered. What do you need done?"

"Fly back to Rainshadow Pass, snatch boulders and drop them. Cause landslides, block the pass to those naked, drunken idiots on the other side."

"Drop rocks? How very lower-class."

"Lord Wallas, this is very important!" pleaded Lunette.

"Oh very well."

We all wished Wallas good fortune, then he glided off into the darkness.

✴ ✴ ✴

Luntette's servants were quick to improvise a meal for us, and it was only now that I realized that I had eaten nothing and drunk only stream water since arriving in this time. In the distance we could hear the rumble of

Wallas dropping boulders into Rainshadow Pass. Once we had eaten, the exhausted Lariella began talking about how pleasant it was to throw off the bonds of things called sociopolitical conformity and verbal correctness and allow herself to be rescued by warriors. Halverin volunteered to see her to one of the bedchambers.

"Remember the curfew," called Lunette after them.

"Curfew?" I asked.

"Within my tower we sleep alone, in our own beds, in our own chambers."

"For reasons of morality?"

"No, out of curfew you may sleep where you will, with whoever you fancy. In curfew, you sleep alone with the chamber door barred from both sides."

"May I ask why?"

"Because of my guards."

I was still too keyed up to sleep, and thus it was that I soon found myself at the top of the tower with Lunette, watching the guardsmen lowering the time engine into a hatchway in the decking. This was done by means of a very primitive treadmill crane, in which one guardsman walked while the others pulled at guide ropes, called orders, made suggestions, or stood and watched. All were, of course, shivering with the night's chill, being stark naked apart from their helmets.

"Below this are the chambers where I practice the arts of my calling," said Lunette. "Your time engine will be safe there."

"This is such a sophisticated and luxurious tower for such a primitive land," I said as the time engine descended out of sight. "Who had it built?"

"Oh I did," said Lunette. "We knew that you and your companions would appear in this year, but Pelmore did not know the day, or even the month. Prince Halverin and I could hardly be expected to live in the governor's pathetic fortress while we waited, so I had this tower built. Kesleir designed it and supervised the building."

"The prince must be very wealthy."

"Oh yes, he is a favorite of the empress."

"Not to mention a certain female time wizard?"

"So it seems."

Lunette was also rich and powerful, there was no doubt of that. The tower was a very comfortable residence, yet was impregnable to anything but a large and well-organized army with lots of siege engines. The local nomad horsemen thought siege warfare was for women, slaves, and perverts, so the tower was of no interest to them. After the ropes were withdrawn from the hatchway and the cover replaced, Lunette suggested that we go down into her chambers. Here a maidservant appeared with a jar and goblets on a tray. The drink resembled nothing more than honey-flavored tar, but it had a considerable kick.

"Just how much of a favorite is Halverin with the empress?" I asked Lunette as we sat on a balcony bathed in Miral's green light.

"She is interested in producing heirs with him," replied Lunette. "Why?"

"Lariella can be rather too free with her favors."

"Are you not jealous?"

"No."

"But is not Lariella your woman?"

"Definitely not."

"Do you have a lady?" asked Lunette after contemplating my reply, although not giving the slightest cue to any amourous interest in me.

"After a fashion."

"Explain?"

"She will not be born for over three thousand years."

"Ah yes, you are separated by time. How very curious. Wallas has told me a little of you. He says you have a suave way with the ladies, but seldom choose to use it. He thinks you are very silly."

"It keeps me at distance from danger."

"Danger adds such spice to lovemaking, Danolarian. Does it surprise you that I am no stranger to it?"

"All the ancient texts praise the power of restraint and virginity in the older ways of magic."

"Do they? How very much can be lost over three thousand years. Mine is a dark and sharp magic, it does not draw its power from delicate virginity or the power of frustration. Wallas says you transformed him into a glass dragon."

"I spoke some words of release that I had been told, nothing more."

It was thus that I began telling Lunette of how I had met with Wallas, and of our years together in the Wayfarers. It took quite some time, but then it was within Lunette's power to call the curfew, so there was no need for haste.

"So, Wallas started life as an obnoxious courtier who fancied himself as a bard," she said once I had finished.

"That he did," I replied.

"Then he assassinated an emperor."

"He still swears that he was innocent."

"And he became a fugitive beggar, who also fancied himself as a bard."

"His playing was not at all bad, it was his singing that let him down."

"Then a glass dragon turned his penis into a small, fire-breathing dragon that disliked women."

"Yes."

"I would love to have seen that."

"It was quite a spectacle. I only saw it once, when it burned through his trousers and bit someone."

"Why did the sorceress Wensomer turn him into an overweight cat?"

"She swore it was all his fault. Besides, he was overweight as a human."

"And he became a Wayfarer Constable? A cat?"

"Yes. He has his uses."

It was now that Halverin emerged from the stair hatch and said that Lariella and he had talked long of inventions and innovations of the future, and that he was going to his own chamber to write down as much as he could remember before retiring for what was left of the night.

"For Lariella that seemed surprisingly innocent," I said once Halverin was gone.

"A man and a woman can do a lot more than talk while they are talking," Lunette suggested.

She got up, gestured for me to follow, and led me to a chamber on the other side of the tower. Here the time engine stood, illuminated by a single oil lamp.

"I am always anxious to learn, and this vessel is like nothing in all of our world," she said as she paced around it. "It has the look of a horse, yet Lariella speaks of it as if it were a ship. I see neither reins nor oars, so how is it really guided?"

"One rides it like a horse, and it is guided by levers."

"Levers? Levers such as masons used to lift heavy blocks of stone?"

"Not those sorts of levers. They are levers that are more like steering oars on a ship."

"I see no steering levers."

"They appear to have been removed."

"Oh. Who would have done that?"

"Pelmore would not have known the technique, neither would the governor. Lariella detached them, most likely. We can ask her in the morning."

"And these levers, they are all that one needs to ride the time engine?"

"Oh yes, even one as thick as Pelmore can manage it."

"Yet it stopped working for him. Why was that?"

"It was damaged, I am not sure of the details. Best to ask Lariella in the morning."

"You seem to keep hinting about going to bed," she said coyly, her head inclined toward the stairs.

"Ladyship, in terms of my body's experience of time I have been two days awake, during which I have been in four fights of one sort or another, shipwrecked, whirled through the night sky in the claws of a glass dragon, run ten miles, ridden quite a lot more, and traveled just over three thousand years through time. Are you not amazed that I am still on my feet and able to string more than two words together?"

"Ah yes, I had forgotten. Your chamber is one floor down, and you will notice that there are heavy bars on both sides of the door. Keep the door barred from within until dawnlight, and do not leave your chamber for any reason."

"I gather that you have very dangerous guards."

"Again, just take my word upon it."

⁎　⁎　⁎

For all my exhaustion I slept little, and was awake again soon after dawn. Lunette had said that my door would be barred on the outside for my own safety during the night, but it was unbarred when I pushed at it. I emerged into a deserted corridor. The doors of empty bedchambers stood open, but all those that were closed were barred as well. Mine had not been, which was odd.

I found and inspected the time engine. Although I understood little of its operation, I could see that it had sustained no more damage than that from my own crossbow bolt and Pelmore's kicks. That was quite a relief to me.

Next I went to the tower's battlements to take in the view by daylight, and to check whether hordes of barbarians had put the tower under siege. I came upon Wallas, who was again cat-sized, furry, and more or less globular. At his feet was part of a small, grey mouse.

"Don't make a fuss, I found my own breakfast," he said sourly.

"You're a cat again," I said, feeling relieved that he was a manageable size, but alarmed that we did not have his services as a glass dragon available.

"Some archaic spell of Lunette's that I can't begin to understand. Magic is different in these olden times."

"The sparkle around your neck, it looks like an afterlife tether."

"It is. Lunette cast it upon me, it's part of some transformation spell. Only sorcerers can cast them or take them over, they are very exclusive. I notice you don't have one."

"I suppose I do not measure up," I said casually.

Only sorcerers could cast or take over afterlife tethers. Was that significant?

"Lunette said my current state will last until about now, so I am bracing myself for the next transformation. She thinks she can eventually sustain me as a cat permanently, but it will require more work."

"How did you meet her?"

"It was through her eagle. I was lost and all alone after the ship sank, you never even warned—"

"Yes, yes, yes, I apologize," I said impatiently. "Her eagle, you say?"

"Yes. Glass dragons rarely visit North Scalticar, so naturally I stood out. One moment I was in a cage, and the ship was sinking, the next I was growing, bursting out of the cage. Suddenly I was in a cage again, but the cage was the ship itself. Again I burst out. I tried to scream with fright, but flames came out of my mouth and set fire to everything. I had to paddle ashore like some damn duck."

"Then Lunette found you?"

"She saw the fire in the harbor from this tower, and sent her eagle to investigate. It spoke to me, that was quite a surprise. Lunette then rode out to meet me. Nobody saw us, because Miral was still down. Dragon eyes see in the dark, you know. Not as well as cats, of course. Did you know that?"

"No. Do go on."

"Lunette and I discussed matters, in fact we got along rather well. She was good enough to teach me some basics of dragon life, like drinking water for ballast, how to speak without breathing flame, and so on. Naturally I told her my life story, and unlike some people I could mention, she found it fascinating."

"You told her everything?"

"The important parts, yes."

"The time engine, Lariella, Pelmore—"

"Yes, yes, yes, even that disgusting business of the emperor's assassination. She was very sympathetic *and* she believed my version of events."

For some reason I felt alarmed. What did Lunette want from us? Wallas did not know enough magic to burst a pimple, so he could teach her nothing. Neither could I, for that matter. I had merely recited words of power when I transformed Wallas. As for Lariella, her skills were in the cold sciences. Again the thought returned to me, she wanted the time engine, and not just for amusing historical jaunts.

Lunette had spent time with Pelmore at the imperial court, thousands of miles to the north, and she had doubtlessly questioned him at great length. She probably knew more about the time engine than anyone else on the moonworld, aside from Lariella and myself, yet she feigned ignorance. Were she to travel into the future and bring back even a few basic books on the glamours, castings, enchantments, and spells from my time, she would become the most powerful mage alive. That worried me, yet I knew that I was the key to any plans which involved a working time engine. In all the moonworld, only I could make mercury, and without mercury the time engine would not work.

Wallas was not to be trusted. He liked to gossip, and he had little discretion when trying to impress people. Lariella was showing signs of being besotted with Halverin; some women can be so susceptible where royalty is concerned. She was definitely not to be trusted with any secret plans, because Halverin and Lunette were probably on rather physical terms as well. Were I to do anything in secret, I would have to do it alone.

"So, you could not fly at first?" I asked Wallas, unashamedly changing the subject.

"No, and it was Lunette who taught me the skill. She spends a lot of time with her eagle, so she knows more of flying than most humans. About dawn I felt so confident that I flew deep into the Ridgeback Mountains to practice by myself. As a glass dragon I draw attention and cause alarm, you know."

"And you are soon to transform back? It is dawn now, you know."

"Yes, probably."

"Probably? You do not know?"

"No. I don't really understand the how or why—oh, apart from this afterlife tether. Do look after Lunette, she and I are bound by it, so if she dies I am in trouble."

"Do you think that being bound to her is the price of being a cat again?"

"Who cares what I think?" he sighed.

"Well, I try to."

"Then I want a full and frank account of that—that *incident*," demanded Wallas, batting the remains of his breakfast over the edge of the tower. "You know the one that I mean."

"There is little to say, Wallas. A glass dragon approached me—"

"Which one?"

"Velander."

"Velander! She's the one who preys on other glass dragons."

"Only nasty ones. She told me the words of release for you. She said you would be released to your original form when the time was right."

"*My* original form was *not* that of a glass dragon."

"Strange, she was quite emphatic that you would become a man again. She said I should choose a good moment."

"Oh you certainly managed that! Bloody humiliating, in front of all those sailors, too."

"They're hardly going to make jokes about you, Wallas. You roasted them alive."

"I was trying to utter a cry of distress."

"Well *they* were distressed. For a short time, anyway."

"It was an accident!"

"So was turning you into a damn glass dragon!"

"All right, then, truce, truce."

"Just why are you so scratchy about being something as powerful and magnificent as a glass dragon?"

"It's . . . a very cattish thing. A dragon is like a bird, and for a cat to be like a bird is, well . . . dirty. Base. Perverted."

"When have you ever worried about being dirty, base or perverted?"

"Being a dirty, base, perverted cat is entirely different from merely being dirty, base, and perverted. There are issues of style involved that—"

"Enough, enough, I know when I am beaten."

✳   ✳   ✳

Returning to my bedchamber, I stretched out on my bunk and fell asleep about as soon as my eyes closed. I found myself on the dark riverbank at the edge of the Darkwalking Realm yet again.

"You have prospered through my gifts, Danolarian," said Chance, who was standing before me. "I like that. You take my opportunities, yet spurn my traps. Very clever."

"Prospered?" I replied. "I am a stranger in a weird world, with no more than boots and trews to call my own."

"Ah, but you have your background. You are no great bowman, yet you know about the tactical use of archers in your own time. Barrages of arrows from massed peasant archers can break any cavalry charge by naked horse warriors."

"True," I replied. "Were I to teach that to the mountain warlords, the Vindician colonizers and the horsemen of the southern plains might well find themselves looking for honest work. If it comes to that, no horseman uses stirrups in this age. Most of the skills of horsemanship seem to involve striking a blow from horseback without falling off. With stirrups we could have effective mounted archers."

"It is merely an idea, but it could change a world," said Temptation, gliding into view from behind me.

I saw the green glow of Revenge's eyes before the rest of her materialized out of the background darkness.

"Think of what else you might unleash!" she hissed. "Scorched earth! If an advancing army is going to capture farms and barns anyway, why not burn them? Revenge, for their invasion. Use caltrops to render enemy horses lame, you know you despise these stupid, arrogant horse nomads."

"But all sides are horse-besotted cavalrymen," I replied. "They would throw up their hands in horror if anyone suggested hurting a horse."

"But those with ideas about putting the mounted nomads and Vidicians in their place would welcome such an idea," said Temptation. "You could even change horse culture. All you have to do is remind the Dorcians and Metrians that those Vindician perverts do not include their horses in their marriage ceremony."

"Ah yes, suddenly those sinful Vindician horses would deserve everything that was coming to them," I responded.

Did I do something to change the world, I wondered? Did Lariella? I tried to recall ancient chronicles that I had read, but my tastes have always run to royal scandals and erotic poetry rather than the outcomes of battles and the fortunes of empires. I knew that in this year the Vindician Empire had suffered its first major defeat. Why? The great island of Vindic was in the tropics, but the Vindician Empire extended all the way down the east coast of the continent of Acrema, and included northeast Scalticar. South of that was too cold for naked horsemen. Sargol had become the center of the Placidian Empire, the first maritime empire in the history of the world. That had been around this time as well . . . and the calendar we used in my time was Sargolan.

"You tried to change the future's opinion of you by writing that pathetic chronicle," said Temptation silkily, "but now you can change the future *and* be master of the world. You are now the right person at the right time, Danolarian. Leave the time engine crippled. Rule this world, shape the future."

"Temptation's gifts are prettier than mine, but they are also more dangerous," warned Chance.

"My father wanted to rule the world," I said stubbornly. "He destroyed a continent instead. I have spent my life avoiding power."

"You are only nineteen," said Temptation, laughing.

There was a bright glow from behind me, and I knew who had joined us.

"He may want to give up the entire world for me!" declared Romance. "Danolarian, your new truelove, Dolvienne, is in the future. If you give up everything to return to her you will make me very happy."

"If you have me, you do not need Romance," said Revenge.

"Without me, you would have no work at all," retorted Romance, and they began arguing.

The other gods joined in, and now that I was being ignored I made a conscious attempt to fade away. To my surprise, I was successful.

I awoke as someone knocked on my chamber door, and I opened it to find Halverin standing there. For some reason I remembered what my mother had told me about fifteen years earlier: if any naked man tries to enter your bedchamber, hide under the bed and call for the guards. In this case there was no need for that. Halverin actually looked very worried, and was staring at the door rather than me.

"The door, it's open!" he exclaimed.

"Yes, they do that when you open them," I replied.

"Why was it not barred on the outside?"

"I have many talents, but barring a door from the other side is not one of them."

I already suspected that someone had forgotten to bar my door. I now suspected that someone to be the prince himself.

"You were very lucky, the daemon guards that patrol the corridors after curfew probably thought the door was barred from inside."

"But I did bar it from the inside."

"Ah, I see. Good."

"Who was supposed to bar it from the outside?"

"I was," he said in something of an embarrassed mutter. "I . . . must have barred the wrong door."

I had ventured out, but I had seen no daemons. Did they exist? Was all the talk of barred doors a trick to keep me from exploring the tower while the others slept—or worse, repairing the time engine and leaving?

"So, the daemon guards have gone now?" I asked innocently.

"Yes, and I am unbarring the doors for everyone. Tonight I'll bar your door properly."

"Can the daemons not lift the outer bars?"

"No, the bars are, are englamoured against daemons," replied Halverin, but not very convincingly.

By the time Lunette and Lariella were up and about, Wallas had reverted to the form of a glass dragon. Again I missed the transformation, but I must admit that he looked magnificent as a semi-opaque, smoky black nightmare with wings. Perched on the battlements, he was a powerful deterrent to anyone who had ideas about attacking Lunette's tower. Lariella found Lunette, Halverin, and myself with the time engine. We had already assembled a range of carpentry tools, weapons, surgical equipment, and even kitchen utensils that might be of use in repairing it. Lariella soon had Halverin and Lunette away in the tower workshops, modifying various tools to be of greater use to her.

"Lariella, you have not told me much about your time with the governor," I said genially as she began to remove the metal covers of the time engine and expose the delicate and frail-looking innards. "I thought he would torture you or some such. I thought he might even be Pelmore himself."

"Oh Pelmore was never master of anything here," she said dismissively. "The charge of the stuncast ran out in a week or so, then he was in a lot of trouble with the people he had shot."

That news gave me considerable cheer, yet it also made me suspicious.

"So, what did they do to him?" I asked, forcing a laugh.

"Who knows? He was eventually sent to Vindic, with a replica of the time engine. He is there now, apparently."

This told me a great deal. Two days earlier she would have been screaming about social justice and offender rehabilitation programs. Now she was quite detached, and strangely cool. What had happened to her while she had been in the governor's fortress? I doubted that he would have hurt her before the time engine was working again. Was it that she was now besotted with Halverin?

"I wager the governor demanded you get the time engine working again," I suggested, trying to keep her talking.

"Yes he did, he took me to it and told me to repair it immediately. I told him that I could do everything except make mercury, and that only you knew the secret of its smelting. That was when he ordered the galley to ram Prince Halverin's ship and fetch you back."

"Strange that he accepted your word so readily," I remarked. "These people despise women, except for Lunette."

"Oh but Pelmore had already told him what I had said. I just confirmed it."

"Yes, yes, Pelmore heard us discussing all that before he stole the time engine," I now recalled. "He would have told the governor everything he knew as soon as the torturer pulled the first hot iron out of the coals."

"Probably."

"So, when did the governor put his afterlife tether on you?"

"He didn't, he is no sorcerer. Some hooded, cloaked sorcerer did it while I was left chained to the time engine."

"Really? A man?"

"Yes, he had a very deep voice. He said that he would put the other instance of the tether on the governor, binding us together."

The magistrate in me suddenly had her on trial, although she did not know it. Afterlife tethers . . . they could only be cast by a sorcerer, they could not be cast on behalf of anyone else, emperor or empress. Magic could give a woman a deep voice, but in this day men went about naked, even sorcerers. Might the cloaked, hooded sorcerer have been Lunette?

The empress cast afterlife tethers upon the manhood of her royal guardsmen, or so I had been told. Thus the empress was a sorceress. The governor was no sorcerer, yet Lariella had an afterlife tether around her neck. What had Lunette done with the dying governor the day before? Nothing more than a few amusing tricks with sparkly castings, most likely. That meant Lunette had been the hooded sorcerer in the governor's fortress, and that the afterlife casting had bound Lariella to Lunette all along.

Lunette is the empress.

The thought had me more thoroughly chilled than a naked Vindician horseman caught in a blizzard. Lunette was Empress of Vindic. Lunette was pretending to be her own sorceress. It was as clear as meltwater what had happened. The governor had shipped Pelmore and a mockup of the time engine to Vindic. The empress had taken one look at the mockup and threatened Pelmore with a molten lead enema. Pelmore had confessed that the mockup was lacking the four bands of nothingness that circled the original time engine, and which the governor's carpenters, black-smiths, and jewelers had not been able to reproduce. The empress had de-cided that if she wanted to become mistress of a working time engine she was faced with a task somewhat akin to murder: if you want to do a good job, do it yourself. She had traveled here as her own sorceress, and she did indeed know a primitive but powerful sorcery. She was in league with Halverin, but I doubted that anyone else knew just who she was.

Lunette was trying to get herself into our trust and confidence, and was attacking our suspicions on multiple fronts. Halverin was bedding Lariella. While that was no surprise, I was shocked by how distant and cool she had suddenly grown. I should have been relieved, yet I felt so very alone and isolated. Lunette had made no overt play for me, yet she was intelligent enough not to be so clumsy. Isolate me, slowly become my friend, comfort me . . . learn the secret of making mercury. Perhaps she would even feign some rivalry with Halverin.

All at once I just wanted to get away.

"So, I can make mercury and you can repair the time engine," I said to Lariella. "My thought is that we should hurry back to our own times at the first opportunity."

"We can't do that without the levers," Lariella said, without sound-ing particularly concerned.

"Yes, yes, they are missing!" I exclaimed, hoping to sound dismayed. "Who took them?"

"Why, the governor. Pelmore told him that they could be detached, but did not know the method. As soon as I was taken into his fortress he demanded that I should remove them."

"But—but who has them now?" I demanded. "He is dead."

"They are with his body, but that need not be our concern. Given a few months I can develop the tools and parts to bypass those controls."

"A few months!" I exclaimed.

"This is a nice place, and Prince Halverin is like no other man I have known. At first I thought that about you too, Danolarian, but now I am not so sure. You are neither one thing nor another, you walk the path between the mindless litigation of my time and the glorious freedoms that the prince's people enjoy."

"The men of Halverin's people, you mean. You are not a man."

"Lunette has the freedoms that I speak of. Lunette is the—Lunette is the exception."

"The only exception."

"I'll be another."

People were making her promises, and she was too stupid to see them as empty promises. Stupid or not, however, she was the only person on the face of the moonworld who could repair the time engine. Suddenly another thought came to me.

"Ah, so you will gain Lunette's patronage by letting her explore the ages with your time engine?"

"That's something I can offer her."

"Well then, and as your people say, we have a victory—victory circumstance. You get Prince Halverin and a man's freedom in this age, Lunette gets the time engine, and I get a trip back to the year 3145. Wallas—"

"Wallas will stay here, as a glass dragon."

She seemed strangely emphatic. This was a surprise, but I tried not to show it.

"Does Wallas know this?" I asked.

"Wallas is new to being a shapeshifter, the minds of neophyte shapeshifters are unstable, selfish, even greedy."

"He longs to be a cat again."

"That is but a symptom of his brittle mind. The glories of being a glass dragon in the service of Lunette will win him over."

"You always seem to know best," I answered softly, sighing as if I had no fight left. "I just want to go home."

"Lunette fancies you, you must know that," Lariella now said in an unnerving purr.

"What have I that she could possibly want?" I said dismissively. "I am not as strong as the least of her guardsmen, and I know little of magic."

"You can make mercury."

"A simple trick, I just happen to know it. She can have her mercury without paying for it in my bed."

"Danolarian, you are such a boring man."

"In this age, perhaps so. My skills are suited to my time, and I wish to return to it."

At this point Lunette returned, and she dropped to her knees before the exposed interior of the time engine as if it were a chest of jewelry.

"So, so pretty," she breathed, and I did indeed agree with her.

"Precisely what is broken?" I asked Lariella..

Lariella pointed into the glittering, complex mechanism, then pulled out a broken length of curved glass tube. I could see two jagged stumps. That was where the tube had been installed, I understood as much as that.

"How did it keep working if this was broken?" I asked.

"Mercury poured out of the top pipe, here, and splashed down here, over this inlet. Most drained away and was lost, but enough fell into the tube to keep the mechanism fed for a while. See this?"

She pointed to a thing like an oddly shaped bottle. There was no cork, but by flipping up a type of key she opened an access spout.

"The mercury must be poured into here until it is full."

"But the glass pipe must be replaced first?"

"Yes."

Lariella held up the covering plate. There was a dent in it.

"Pelmore kicked this access plate, see the dent here?" she said. "It was just enough to break the glass tube behind it."

"Can you make another?"

"Glassmaking is a very young art in these times," said Lunette. "There is probably not an artisan skilled enough to duplicate that tube on this side of the equator."

"Do you know anything of glassmaking, Danolarian?" asked Lariella.

"No."

"Then you had better just make the mercury," said Lunette, sounding a little edgy. "There are glassmakers in the port of Diomeda, I shall send for a one. Wallas can make the flight there and back within a week."

"What about the dent in the plate?" I asked.

By way of reply Lariella put the plate on the floor and stepped within it. The dent popped out under her weight.

"You see, repairs just have to work, they need not be anything fancy," she said, holding up the cover plate. "How do you make mercury, anyway?"

"The ore is called bloodred, it's a red powder found in some gold mines," I explained.

"Cherrydust, it is used in hedgerow magic," said Lunette, who had been making notes on a slate. "It can be bought in the market of Bucadria. What else is needed to make mercury from it?"

"Oh, odds and ends. I can improvise what is needed from jars, beeswax, and the like. It is easier to do it than explain."

Actually you just heat bloodred in a pot with a long tube running out of the top. Cool the tube with snow or even cold water, put the end over a jar, and mercury drips out. Just a tube was needed, any tube. Perhaps the long, hollow wing bone of some reptilian gliding dragon, or even a thick artery from some giant sea creature found dead on the shore and butchered for meat. Such an artery might also replace the broken glass tube. *Repairs just have to work,* Lariella had said. *A length of artery tied to the stumps with waxed thread, would that do?* I very nearly asked the question out aloud, but I did not. I was the only person upon the moonworld who could make mercury, and now I could probably repair the time engine, too.

"We should arrange for a trip to the Bucadria market," said Lunette. "I am anxious to see this mercury that is the lifeblood of your time vessel."

* * *

Because I needed to take a pushcart, I was forced to walk the three miles across the Lakita Plain, in spite of Wallas being perched on the battlements of the tower and able to fly the distance with me in little more than a minute.

"Who do you think I am, the damn ferrygirl?" Wallas rumbled when I suggested that he give me a ride.

Halverin rode, of course. Horses were kept in undefended stables at the base of the tower, the understanding being that no enemy would be dishonorable enough to molest one's horses. Only war horses were available, and hitching a war horse to a cart was also considered to be dishonorable, however, so I became an honorary horse. A long, steep path had been cut into the cliff near Lunette's tower when the road north had been built, making the descent easy. The return trip, with the cart loaded, would be a lot harder. To the east I could see nomads making their way back from Towergate through washaways in the cliffs. They were lowering their horses by means of ropes and large teams of men. Having Wallas perched on Lunette's tower discouraged them from approaching.

It took me just over an hour to push a handcart to the Alber River, then cross to Bucadria by the narrow, rickety bridge of logs and ropes. The market turned out to be larger than I had expected for such a small port. It was, after all, at the mouth of a long and placid river, and a huge amount of trade from inland passed through its grounds. As soon as we reached the southern bank a group of men who appeared to be the tollmaster and his guards pointed back the way we had come, screamed, and fled. Wallas had leaped from the tower's battlements and was gliding over the Lakita Plain at several times the speed of the fastest horse. Amid considerable consternation, he landed beside the market.

"Nobody leaves until I give leave," he warned in a voice like a very close earthquake.

Remarkably, once Wallas had established himself as being harmless, the business of the market returned to normal very quickly. Admittedly no other patrons were a hundred feet in length and semi-transparent, but people seemed to accept that death at the hands of a drunken nomad horseman was no less final than the sort of death dispensed by an enormous dragon. Because he wanted to see precisely what I was buying, Halverin dismounted and walked with me.

I had not yet encountered my first horse tavern. Nomads and Vindicians spent most of their lives on horseback, and that included visits to the tavern. Any tavern that served them thus needed a high roof and tall doors so that the patrons could ride in for a drink, and even gather around tables that stood about six feet off the ground. Halverin and I had just entered the market when four nomads rode out of the High Horse tavern and confronted us. The problem was that we had axes, which were the weapons of free men. We were also walking, and I was pushing a cart. This made us slaves. As Halverin later explained, an armed, walking slave was considered to be an escaped slave, and thus fair game for the first mounted nomad to canter by. Worse, I was wearing trews and boots. That made me a pervert, when added to everything else.

"You! You!" the man who was the leader of the group barked at us, apparently unable to remember the word "two," and perhaps even ignorant of it. "Slaves, mine you become."

Wallas, who was behind them, had already bent over to listen. A blast of blue fire incinerated both the nomad and his horse in an inferno that singed my eyebrows and hair, and set several nearby stalls alight. The other three nomads turned around, then looked up—and up, and up. They had been indoors when Wallas had arrived, and because Wallas had decided to have a catnap while I was shopping, he had been out of sight.

"All of you, dismount," rumbled Wallas.

They dismounted.

"You, long hair. Push the cart for my friends."

The nomad actually knocked me aside in his haste to seize the cart's push bar.

"Tall one, lead the horses."

The man was only too happy to comply.

"Small gronnic, you will—"

"My gronnic is proud size—" was as far as the nomad got before Wallas reduced him to ash.

"Nobody answers back when a glass dragon gives orders," Wallas announced.

Halverin and I continued our shopping, accompanied by our two eager helpers. *Was this where the Dorcians' Order of the Dragon was founded?* I wondered. The more I found out about the past, the more trivial and accidental the great events became. I found bloodred ore almost at once, and bought the merchant's entire sack. The long, hollow wing bones of a small lizard dragon provided suitable tubing for the condensing process, and aside from that I only needed beeswax, resins, earthenware pots and jars, potting clay, and sundry items that made sense to none but me.

"What a pity that the spines are straight and brittle," said Halverin, pointing at a poisonous fish on a slab.

"They serve the fish well enough," I replied.

"But were they curved, we could use one to repair the time engine."

So, Lunette and Prince Halverin are pooling their knowledge, I realized.

"Ah yes, it could replace the broken glass tube," I said openly, calling upon all my skills at hiding my true thoughts from defendants and witnesses during trials. "I know of no fish that has curved, hollow spines, however."

"As I said, such a pity," concluded Halverin. "What else do you need?"

"I am thinking," I said as I glanced over the nearby stalls. "Wait here, I want to visit the butchery tables."

"You need meat to make mercury?"

"No, I need meat to make a nice stew." I laughed.

"A man?" Halverin exclaimed. "Cooking?"

"Why not? How do *you* get cooked meals when traveling the wilderness?"

"Have you never heard of slaves?"

"So shopping for meat is not a free man's work?"

"No, absolutely not. I shall wait near the bulletin board and check the news of the day. Will it take long, this meat shopping?"

"No, not at all."

Actually I needed meat to repair the time engine, but I did not want Halverin to know that. Before long I had several cuts of rump steak that would certainly render down into a very nice stew if Lunette's cook had some onions, flour, and spices, but I also had a length of some large animal's artery in my purse, and several flattened pigs' bladders. The grip of the knife in my belt was wound with more than enough waxed thread for my needs, and a set of duplicate lever-keys were concealed within the heel of my right boot. Nothing now stood between me and a three-thousand-year journey back to my own time.

I rejoined the prince at the bulletin board, which was a very large rectangle of slate upon which notices were chalked. Halverin took my arm and pointed out the news of the day. It was in the local language, which I could not read, even though I was curiously fluent in it after just two days. Why was the spoken word so easy to learn? I had learned languages before. It took weeks to learn enough basic words to get by without a lot of pointing and hand waving. How was I learning so fast? It was almost as if everyone was learning to speak words that I understood.

"What have they chalked on the board?" I asked Halverin. "I cannot read it."

"*Prince Halverin . . . defender of the temples . . . shield of the weak . . . hammer of the unjust . . . patron of the—*"

"Please, can we move on to the actual news?" I asked.

"*Great battle . . . army of a thousand loyal allies against the governor's half a million warriors.*"

"Whatever happened to five thousand versus forty-seven?"

"Few here can count above twenty."

"Ah."

"*Great siege fought at Towergate.*"

"A minor siege lasting a quarter hour?"

"*One thousand sorcerers loyal to the prince died in the fighting.*"

"Five died, trampled by your own nomad allies."

"Former nomad allies, if you please. *The entire army of the governor was wiped out, including his elite guard of female warriors.* There is a list of dead nobility. Shall I read the names out?"

"No thank you, I happen to know that all were killed in drunken brawls during the victory celebrations."

"Apart from those I ate," added Wallas, who was leaning down over us to listen.

"*The prince drove off a glass dragon allied to the governor.*"

"Indigestion drove me off," muttered Wallas.

"Look, can we just return to Lunette's tower?" asked Halverin, turning away from the slate with a hand to his forehead. "This is so embarrassing, I never realized such drivel was written about me. Heads will roll."

"If there is anyone you want eaten, just say the word and point, Your Highness," said Wallas. "It is so good to be in the service of a monarch again. Did I ever mention that I was once Master of the Royal Music for an emperor?"

As Halverin and I returned to the tower we were accompanied by the two nomads, who were apparently too frightened to leave us. For my own part, I was quite pleased to have them to push the cart up the steep cliff-side road to Lunette's tower. Wallas stayed behind in Bucadria, having decided to tear the roof off the High Horse tavern and have lunch there.

✦ ✦ ✦

The advantage of having the time engine in a different room to that where I had set up my mercury smelter was that Lunette could not be in the two places at once. Halverin stayed to make sketches and notes, but when I told him that once I had enough mercury for the time engine to function we would never need any more, he lost interest and hurried away to sketch the exposed innards of the time engine. I pretended to work on the process of making mercury, but spent most of my time carving an extra hollow wing bone into a whistle and practicing dance tunes.

Thus it was that I was alone when the first of the mercury began to flow, and there was nobody present to see me storing it in my pigs' bladders. These I concealed in my trews, thankful for my clothing even though it did mark me as a fashion pervert at the very least. In order to demonstrate real progress, however, I collected a tiny amount of mercury in a goblet and took this to present to Lariella. Naturally enough, everyone was delighted.

"How much will you need to make it functional?" I asked. "In terms of the volume of a pig's bladder, that is?"

"I don't know the pig's bladder standard," she said, laughing, and snaked an arm around Halverin.

"It is about the volume of my fist," explained Lunette.

"Oh, in that case three. One for the inner, ah, mechanisms, and two more for the reserve tank."

"As little as that?" I asked. "It will take only a week."

"Wonderful."

I could scarcely conceal my excitement. I already had the volume of five pigs' bladders on my person, so I did not even need to make more. All that I had to do was to tie a length of some deceased sea monster's artery to the broken stumps of glass. I could have the time engine working that very night.

"So in one week the time engine will be working," said Lunette dreamily, doubtless already having fantasies about using the time engine to rule history itself. "Wallas can fly with me to Diomeda to fetch a glassmaker, we can leave tomorrow."

"Surely the lever-keys will be needed as well?" I asked, looking to the four empty slots.

"Ah yes, the lever-keys," muttered Lunette, with a sheepish glance at Halverin. "Danolarian mentioned them to me."

"The governor had me remove them," said Lariella.

"What are they needed for?" demanded Halverin.

"They are a type of control," I explained.

"Control?" asked the prince.

"Er, a lock."

"Lock?"

This was an age without locks, and it had very little else that even a primitive like myself took for granted.

"Um, a thing like a bar on a door" was all that I could think of.

"But if they have been removed, the time vessel is unbarred!" insisted Halverin.

"Er, this bar is like speaking a truename or a word of power. It has to be there before it will work."

"Well make more of these lever-keys," said Lunette.

"I cannot," explained Lariella. "Losing them is like forgetting the words to a spell."

Lunette's eyes bulged with fury for a moment as she realized that the lack of lever-keys was a very serious problem. She put a hand to her forehead, took several deep breaths, and forced a smile. *What might she do with us once we are not standing between her and a functioning time engine,* I wondered.

"You made this thing, surely you can make it work without the lever-keys," she said.

"That will be very hard," explained Lariella. "See these boxes with the slots where they fit? They are sealed units, and I don't have the tools to take them apart."

"They must be still with the governor's body!" said Halverin.

"His body is at Towergate, or at least on the way back as some warlord's trophy."

"Where does a naked man keep such things?" I asked. "The warriors that I killed wore necklaces to carry their valuables, and belts for their knives and axes, but the governor wore nothing at all."

"The richer the Vincidian man, the less he wears," said Halverin. "One of the governor's lackeys probably had the lever-keys in a pouch on his belt."

"So by now some chieftain is sure to be wearing them around his neck as talismans," said Lunette. "That is a hopeful thought. What do they look like?"

"I can make a sketch of what to look for," said Lariella.

"Yes, yes, do so!" exclaimed Lunette urgently. "I can search—I can send my spies to search among the nomads."

"I could duplicate the keys by trial and error," said Lariella. "They are simple enough."

"How long?" asked Lunette.

"Two years, at worst."

Lunette shuddered, as if at the very edge of her self-control.

"In two years . . ." Lunette seemed to think through various unspoken consequences. "Lariella, what will you need to make new lever-keys?"

"Small rods of brass, files, er . . . I can make a list."

"I'll get a chalkboard," said Halverin. "Danolarian, we must make another trip to the market in Bucadria tomorrow."

"Take a chalk, sketch the lever-keys for me," said Lunette. "As I said, I have spies, they have ways of finding things."

In the heel of my boot were four duplicate lever-keys, but I was in no hurry to tell anyone about them. This was better than I could ever have hoped. I had a set of duplicate lever-keys, yet everyone else thought the time engine unusable. Lunette might not think a guard was necessary for it, and that would give me a lot of freedom. All that I needed to do was check that the time engine was indeed working, then wait until Wallas was in his cat form, tie Lariella into a large sack, and take us all back to a more civilized century—mine! The end of the nightmare was within sight.

✦　✦　✦

I asked the guards to tell me when Wallas returned from Bucadria, then climbed to the tower's battlements once word came that he was back. I dared not talk of escape on the time engine, not with the guards present, yet all that I needed to know was when he might revert to being a cat. A cat would fit on the time engine, a glass dragon would not fit on anything that moved, either in time or space.

"Still perched up here?" I asked.

"Where else should I perch?" he muttered, as if suspecting that there was a subtle joke in my words.

"You look like a vulture on a rock in some desert, watching for dying travelers."

"I ate a couple of plump, marinated tapmen at the High Horse today, I have no interest in dying travelers."

"You are such a wastrel, Wallas. You are a glass dragon! Were I to suddenly become a glass dragon, I would spend the whole day soaring on the winds, miles above the ground."

"Were the risk of suddenly becoming a cat again hanging over you, the thought of soaring miles above the ground would hold nothing but terror."

"Oh. So the change happens at random?"

"Let us just say that I have no say in the matter, although I am given notice. Lunette said I shall become a cat again tonight, for example, but gave no reason. In such circumstances, would you go flying?"

"Perhaps not," I said, barely able to control my excitement. "Did she say when?"

"Soon after dusk. She warned me to stay up here, however. She is going to unleash guard daemons to patrol the floors of the tower until dawn."

"Why not her guards?"

"Because men go about naked in this century and the nights are cold! Use your head, look at the evidence, are you an inspector in the Wayfarers or not? Daemons don't mind the cold."

Wallas was going to be cat-sized all night. Provided the time engine was working, there was nothing to prevent the three of us escaping. The guard daemons might be a problem, but only if they existed. Getting my bedchamber door open? That would not even be a challenge.

I had bought such a variety of items in the market that even Halverin had lost track of what things I possessed and what they might be used for. Further, in his zeal to provide us with any and all tools that might be of use in repairing the time engine, he had included an iron pry-lever. The bar mountings on my bedchamber door were of iron, and were fastened to the frame of the door with iron spikes as long as my index finger and nearly as thick. Some straining with the pry-lever had the mountings removed from the frame, and a little quick work with my knife whittled pinewood spikes to replace the iron ones. Tapped gently into place, they held the bar mountings and bar perfectly. Some brushwork with squid ink turned the yellowish wooden heads of my spikes to the same color as blackened iron.

Around sunset Halverin found me at work on the time engine.

"I thought only Lari was able to work on the time vessel," he said, a definite edge of concern in his voice.

"I am just removing the broken and jagged edges of glass from the tube stubs and smoothing them down with a sharpening stone," I said casually. "Even a primitive yokel like me can do that."

"Does Lari know?"

"Yes. It is tedious, boring work, and requires patience rather than skill. She was happy to show me what to do and leave me to it."

What I did not say was that I had finished a half hour earlier.

"Well what remains to be done can wait until morning, we all have to be locked away now."

"Because of the guard daemons?"

"Yes."

"If you bar the doors of Lunette, Lariella, myself, and the servants, and bar the hatch leading to the roof deck, who bars your door from outside?" I asked as I picked up my thumblamp and set off with him.

"Nobody. There is no bar on the outside of my door."

"So it is barred only from the inside?"

"Yes."

"Why is it different for you?"

"Because visitors have been known to be curious about the guard daemons. After losing several guests, we decided to confine people for their own good during the night. I have seen what happens to the curious, so I do not need an outer bar on my door to convince me to stay inside at night."

"Last night it was safe enough, we were out and about until well after midnight."

"Only until Lunette called up her daemons."

* * *

We reached my room. I had tried dropping the outer bar in place roughly and my pinewood spikes had held, yet I was still filled with apprehension as the door closed behind me. I heard the heavy clunk of the outer bar dropping, then the soft slap of Halverin patting it. He walked on, presumably to visit Lariella before returning to his own bedchamber.

By the light of my thumblamp I gathered together everything that I needed for my excursion into the empty corridors of the tower, removed the duplicate lever-keys from my hollowed boot heel, then blew out the flame. I waited in the darkness. While I waited I practiced attaching a length of artery to two short sticks and tying the ends tightly with waxed string. I took it all apart and repeated the procedure again—and again, and again. After about an hour and a half, by the view of the stars through the window, I heard the soft slapping of Halverin's bare feet, then the pat-pat of his hand on my door's outer bar as he passed. I did not move. With the extreme patience that those of Halverin's age had not developed, and that those of Lariella's age had forgotten, I waited, continuing to practice attaching and tying the length of artery to the two sticks in the dark. After another hour and a half Halverin came by again, softly patting the outer bar without so much as breaking stride.

Now I knew both the interval at which Halverin checked the empty corridors, and that there were no daemons out there to eat him. After waiting a short time I put my ax and newly made whistle into my belt. Why did I pack a whistle and a weapon before traveling into time? A weapon warns the bullies off, while someone playing dance tunes always looks harmless.

Thus looking dangerous yet harmless in preparation for my first solo trip through time, I pressed firmly against the door of my room. Slowly the wooden spikes came free. I put my hand through the narrow gap, took hold of the bar mount so that it would not fall, then pushed again. Once out in the corridor, I replaced the bar mounting and bar, then set off for the chamber containing the time engine. Needless to say I was not eaten alive.

There was plenty of light coming through the windows from the lordworld, so that I could actually see what I was doing as I attached the artery between the two stubs of tube in the time engine. Fortunately Lariella had left it reassembled, except for the cover over the mercury reserve. I did not know how to lock the cover back in, but I did know that the time engine would work without it. By the time I had tied off both ends of the artery, I had counted just over a hundred heartbeats. Now I began to empty the mercury from my pig-bladder vessels into the time engine's tank. After three of them I could see the faint gleam of mercury down in the nozzle, but the artery was still flaccid. No mercury was flowing. I teetered on the edge of panic, but forced myself to think through the problem. Perhaps mercury only leaked when the time engine was not just activated, but in motion through time. Perhaps there was no problem after all.

I inserted a lever-key in the ACTIVE slot. It did not fit. Again I forced myself not to panic as I tried the others. Naturally it was the last lever-key that fitted and locked into place. I repeated the harrowing process with the other lever-keys. TEMPORAL locked down at the first attempt, then LATERAL was safely in place. The remaining lever-key should have fitted into VERTICAL . . . but it did not fit! It did not go down as far as the others, neither did it turn. It certainly did not move back and forth.

This was like speaking the words of power to break the spell that kept Wallas in the shape of a cat. I had only the vaguest idea of what I was doing, so that if anything went wrong I would be very short on constructive improvisations. Teetering at the edge of the chasm of blind panic, I tried to think whether there was anything I could do apart from wave my hands about in frustration and scream hysterically. Did I really need the VERTICAL lever-key? I only wanted to travel through time, not space. A quick jaunt back through time would prove that the time engine worked, I would not need VERTICAL. On the other hand if all four lever-keys were required before the thing would work at all . . . no, that did not bear thinking about.

Very slowly and cautiously I climbed onto the time engine, my heart pounding. I drew the ACTIVE down to bring it to life—then quickly pulled the TEMPORAL lever-key back toward myself before my fears could get the better of me.

Part Four

FUTURE PAST

Immediately the flickering greyness of time travel replaced the green light of the lordworld, and one thing was absolutely apparent to me: the time engine worked! I threw my head back and shouted gleefully in triumph. In retrospect, perhaps I should have been a little more on my guard for the unexpected, but people tend to be curiously careless and euphoric when faced with a glorious triumph.

The tower vanished. I had forgotten how recently it had been built; I should have just taken the time engine a month or two into the past, stopped for a moment in the gloom of night, then returned, but I had not thought that part through. Immediately another problem manifested itself: I was now fifty or sixty feet above the clifftop where the tower was to be built. It was not great effort to lower the time engine to the hilltop by moving the VERTICAL lever-key . . . except that the lever-key did not fit! Filewright's work had clearly been a little less than accurate on this particular lever-key, and now I could not lower the time engine through space while traveling through time.

I could always stop, of course, but the sixty-foot drop to the rocks at the top of the cliff was certain to damage the time engine, and even more certain to damage me. Damage. The thought suddenly entered my mind as a paradox. I had fired a crossbow bolt and damaged the time engine. It had not killed me. Pelmore had kicked the time engine twice. Again, it had not defended itself. In my case it had been a warning shot, not intended to damage anything. Pelmore was most likely lashing out in mindless terror. When the Deathstalker guardsman had deliberately attempted to damage it, however, it had reduced him to ash from the waist up. The thought to damage it had been in his mind. Thus it could read minds, at least in a limited manner. I was currently riding it. Could it read my mind? If I decided to stop it in midair and take my chances with the long drop that would almost certainly damage the time engine, would it reduce me to ash as I reached out for the TEMPORAL lever? If so, how would it stop? Would it just travel back to the beginning of time?

Were I to stop to go back, even for an instant, I would start falling. That meant I would reappear . . . where? In the room below the chamber where I had started? I was not even sure what was in there. Would my downward motion continue while time traveling? Would I fall hundreds of feet into the cliff? Outside my bubble of personal time, the landscape flickered and flowed. At a thousand years farther into the past there was a brilliant flash of light in the sky. *The original Dragonwall, the first of the great etheric engines,* I thought, pleased that at least something in the chronicles was true.

Very, very carefully I moved the LATERAL key. The time engine drifted slightly to the left. A push in the other direction had it back to where I had started, at least as far as I could tell. I removed the VERTICAL and LATERAL keys and examined them. The teeth were different. I tried swapping them anyway. Naturally, they did not fit. I put them back. Glancing at the little glowing windows, I saw that the three windows to the left of the THOUSANDS figure had numbers in them. I was over five hundred thousand years into the past. The world turned white for fifty thousand years, and a river of ice flowed over the Lakita Plain and the future site of Alberin. Again it became green, then the ice came back. *There are seasons so long that only immortals can know them,* I realized.

I told myself that I should think laterally, as Lariella termed it, then immediately thought of moving the time engine with the LATERAL key until I had solid ground under me. Looking to my left, I saw the Placidian

Ocean. A glance to my right showed the floodplain of the Alber River, with no sufficiently high land in sight. That was wrong, there were actually low mountains there—except they were *too* low! They were sinking. Mountains actually sank and rose over time!

It may seem odd that I did not leap to the next conclusion straightaway, but in situations such as the one I was in, clear thought is not always possible. I looked straight down, and to my inexpressible relief I saw that the cliff below me was a little higher than it had been half a million years earlier. As one range of highlands was falling, another was rising. In reverse, it meant that over a span of years that my mind could not envision except as the coldest of figures, the cliff below me was rising. Perhaps the rivers of ice and their tributaries ground it down over the years; I could not tell but I did not care. In reality the cliff had started out taller and sunk. If I went sufficiently far back, I would eventually have a solid surface to stop upon.

The windows on the time engine's lectern did not go as far as millions, but by noting how many times the figure for years reset itself to all zeroes I was able to continue counting. The land in the valley below seemed to have an immense snake writhing on it, but I knew that it was just the River Alber changing course very slowly. More ages of ice flowed past in reverse, the millions reset the numerals a second time, and I noticed that while the ground was still about twenty feet below me, the mountain behind me was already above my height. By the time three million passed I was only a few feet from the ground, and the temptation to stop and thump down was almost overwhelming. I saw that the cliff had become a hillside, but the area where the time engine was actually sited was near to level. The ground continued to ease upward.

At last, three and a quarter million years into the past, I pushed the TEMPORAL key back to the neutral position. The time engine stopped, and I was again in normal time.

* * *

It took me a while to comprehend that I was in excess of three million years into the past. My normal reaction to arriving in a new place is to glance about for threats, but on this occasion I looked first to the windows. They declared me to be three and a quarter million years into the past. The windows also indicated that it was the seventeenth day of Ninemonth, but that hardly seemed to matter. My next thought was to return forward through time, but curiosity overtook me even as my muscles tightened to push the TEMPORAL lever forward.

Looking about myself, I saw that the landscape had changed from the blurred grey of time travel to a brilliant green. Some of the nearby trees seemed to be in excess of ten feet across at the base of the trunk, while the grass was uniformly about two inches in height. Bushes bore flowers of white, crimson, violet, and orange, while the scent on the air was like honeysuckle mixed with jasmine. The air was balmy, and had the suggestion of an afternoon in late spring, when all sensible people would be sitting outside the nearest tavern.

I was on the side of a gently sloping hill overlooking the sea. Castles were visible in the distance, but the River Alber was no longer to be seen. *Castles?* I was three million years into the past, yet there were castles. I was surprised that even the world beneath my feet existed as long ago as that, so it felt wrong that castles should be seen. The nearest of them had pennants fluttering from the poles on the towers. Cloth does not last long when left to itself, I have seen the pennants of deserted castles reduced to raggy shreds after just a single winter of storms. Clearly someone lived here, or there would be no pennants. People living in castles also meant threats outside the castle walls. Outside was where *I* was.

Removing the heel from one of my boots, I took out the two glasses and held them in the aspect of a farsight, training them on the nearest castle. Each of the crenellations was crowned with a flowerpot, within which were growing quite healthy flowering bushes. *Clearly these are not there to be flung down at besieging enemies*, I thought as I examined the walls. I saw windows. Not only were there windows, but they were glazed with leadlight glass. *What manner of castle has broad windows instead of narrow arrowslits?* I wondered. The conclusion was obvious: the castle belonged to a lord with no enemies. The place was a residence, built with military nostalgia as the theme. This land was at peace, and totally safe.

I was three million years into the past, I reminded myself. *Have gods been invented in these times? Does magic exist?* I looked at the castle again. It seemed solid enough, but I did not remember even ruins being on its site in my time. *Do ruins last three million years?* On the one hand I was frightened, but on the other I was fascinated. This past seemed so much newer, nicer, cleaner, fresher. I felt strangely invigorated, almost intoxicated. Stepping from the time engine, I glanced back to the lectern. Without the removable lever-keys, nobody could set it in motion. If anyone tried to damage it deliberately, the time engine could defend itself. Thus it was that I carefully removed the lever-keys, returned them to my hollowed heel, then set off to explore the world feeling confident that the time engine would be safe while I was gone.

At first I wandered the woods nearby, and I was immediately struck by the awsome ruins that they concealed. Massive blocks of stone jutted out of the grass, yet old, enormous trees had roots that curled all about the ancient masonry. Whatever this place had once been, it had also been a ruin for centuries, perhaps millennia. It was certainly far larger than the castles in the distance. The trees were of a type not at all familiar to me, but they had the look of red-heart oaks. Flowers of great complexity grew wherever the sunlight penetrated the woodland canopy. It was like a garden in the wilderness, or even a wilderness that was a garden.

On the other hand, there was nothing that resembled a berry bush or a fruit tree, and it had been some time since I had eaten. I decided to make my way over to the castle, assuming that any lord who kept flowerpots on the battlements would not be at all hostile, and might even extend hospitality to strangers. Working my way down the hill, I discovered a path. At first I was not inclined to use it, for fear of what might be waiting in ambush, but the option of spurning it was promptly taken away from me. At the sound of voices and the clopping of hoofs I had the idea of convincing the locals that I was a traveler from distant lands who did not speak the language.

The group that rode into view quite literally took my breath away. Try to imagine the most handsomely bred palfreys possible, some honey brown, some char black, and the rest as white as the windblown snow. The riders were tall, svelte, and so elegant that they might have been swans gliding on a lake in the emperor's gardens in Palion. Their eyes were large in proportion to their faces, and their faces were long without seeming ungainly. The hair of the men reached their shoulders, while that of the women trailed as far as the backs of the horses upon which they rode. Their cloaks were of a cloth that glittered slightly, as if englamoured. The colors of their robes were all pastels, and even in the distance I could see the gemstones that the women wore flashing and sparkling in the dappled sunlight.

My first thought was to flee, not because I felt threatened, but ashamed. They were as fair as gods, perhaps they really were gods, while I was mortal, brutish, and above all ugly. The party of perhaps a dozen reined in as they caught sight of me; then two men, both carrying boar spears, approached. By now it was too late to try to flee, yet I still had with me the one item of armor that deflects weapons more surely than any other. Taking the whistle from my belt, I began to play "The Bargeman's Fancy."

My hope was that I would be taken to be some harmless, itinerant musician, and the tactic seemed to work. The boar spears were not lowered to skewer me, and the others in the party rode forward. By the time I moved on to "Merrily Tread the Cobbles," the tall, beautiful people were laughing and nodding. As I ended the second tune one of the men rode up to me. I thought it wise to bow and go down on one knee.

"Affr, beythow froam?" he asked in a deep yet melodious voice that seemed to resonate through my body.

The words were at first nonsense to me, then I thought that what I was hearing might be a distant ancestor of Alberinese. "Afar, be thou from?" could well have been the meaning behind the words.

"I am indeed, my lord," I replied slowly, bowing again.

There was much discussion about my words, and I caught the words "afar" and "indeed" several times. At last the man turned back to me.

"Joyn'ss, beyarg est" were his words, and hoping that the words really meant "Join us, be our guest" rather than "Be off with you, horrid smelly peasant," I started off along the road with them as they rode on, playing "The Dashing White Lancer."

I listened to the speech of these lordly nobles of the remote past as I walked and played, and slowly I began to tease out the intonations and grammatical peculiarities of their accent. I say accent rather than language, for what they were speaking was basically Alberinese. This was impossible, because as a scholar—and by now even a passably experienced timefarer—I knew how quickly words and grammar can change even in a century. Over thirty thousand centuries separated me from these people, yet I was able to understand some of what they were saying. Were languages more stable than I could have ever dreamed? The architecture, clothing, manners, and even government of this past land were also like an idealized painting of the imperial Alberin of my time.

Strange to say, the group's grasp of my language improved from minute to minute. Stranger still was that *everyone*'s grasp of my speech improved, even those of that past world I had only just met!

* * *

We traveled on, ambling along at the pace of an easy walk. Woodland gave way to tilled fields, and the road led into a village before continuing along to the castle that I had seen in the distance. None of the clothing of my hosts was patched, torn, or ragged, or showed any signs of grime or stains. Both sexes had flowers in their hair, and from this I assumed that I had arrived in the middle of some festival.

Peasant girls fell in with us, and I was decorated with flowers as we walked a quarter mile farther through orchards and parklands to the village. This consisted of two or three dozen cottages, a little market, and a scatter of artisans' shops. Here the interest in me was so great that we were stopped by the crowd.

The village's houses were all solidly built and in perfect repair. Every window had a sill-box planted with herbs and flowers, neatly hung laundry fluttered above weed-free vegetable plots, and there was not one broken shingle or misbound thatch on any roof. I was surprised to see no temple, chapel, shrine, or indeed any place of worship. The place did not even have a meeting hall. There was the scent of cooking on the air, everything from bread baking to pies and stews. Not at any time during my stay did I see an indication that shortages or starvation had ever been known in this place.

Presently I noticed that riders were approaching from the castle. They were on white warhorses, and looked like armored kavelars. Behind each kavelar was a lady, and they were dressed gaudily, in finely tailored robes. The villagers bowed down as they arrived. I made a point of bowing graciously, while not seeming servile. They responded with nods of acknowledgment, and after a long and involved series of gestures and confusing conversations, I found myself walking with the riders toward the castle.

✳   ✳   ✳

The castle's drawbridge was not a drawbridge. There was a wide stone bridge over the moat, and beyond this there was an archway with no gates. Trumpeters on the archway played a fanfare as we entered, then I was escorted into a vast hall that was set out for the midday meal.

Presiding over the feast was a couple that seemed to be the local ruler and his consort. Some very confused gestures and questioning of those around me established that the couple was Aral and Reyvelt, and that the kingdom was called Arvelderian. I was seated between these two, and the meal was conducted with a great deal of formality. I counted thirty-seven courses, ranging from the very first platter of candied nuts that arrived at noon, to the sugar dates that were set before me when it was nearly evening. Each course was preceded by a trumpet fanfare and declaration by a herald, then a procession of servery maids would bring out the actual food. There was no alcoholic drink, and the portions were so moderate that I felt no more than merely satisfied by the time Aral stood up to indicate that the meal was at an end.

For some time there was a lot of milling about, and I was introduced to any number of individuals and couples. Two nobles named Merleand and Linsey took my attention, because unlike any of the others, there seemed friction between them. At a signal from some herald, the entire company now paraded behind King Aral and Queen Reyvelt into another hall. Here a consort of woodwinds played as the courtiers stepped, bowed, flourished, and gestured their way through a series of stately dances. It was during the dancing that I noticed Linsey being exceedingly suspicious of any other woman who approached Merleand, and the music was often punctuated by a shrill outburst from her if even a serving maid came near them.

By the end of the dancing the sun was near the horizon, and I now became an audience of one as the dancers paired off with each other in an elaborate series of courtship rituals that rivaled the dances in complexity. Again, Linsey made it plain in a loud and shrill voice that no other woman was welcome anywhere near her lord. The company gradually dispersed in pairs, but not one of them matched the pairs that had been seated together at the meal or introduced to me later. No amorous advances were made in my direction, but this was more of a relief than anything else. Very strangely, many of the company were developing a grasp of Imperial Alberinese, and even using words that I had not yet spoken.

Going out into the cloisters, I passed several couples that sat or stood fondling each other. Looking up, I saw a suitor climbing a rope to a second-floor window, then I surprised a handmaid as she opened a side gate to a man in a dark cloak. Merleand must have eluded Linsey in search of other company, because her sharp, shrill voice echoed through the castle as she searched for him. For the next few minutes any number of masked and cloaked figures hurried to and fro amid the gathering shadows on silent, slippered feet.

Linsey appeared out of the shadows as I sat watching the show, and she was grim and unsmiling as she came striding up to my bench. Sitting stiffly on the edge, she snatched up my hand, slapped it down on the velvety cloth covering her thigh, then proceeded to deliver a diatribe that involved Merleand, but which I did not understand. My hand being placed upon her thigh appeared to constitute some type of symbolic sexual encounter, which was a means of saving face because of Merleand being with someone else. With face saved and honor satisfied, Linsey now stood up and marched away. For a time I pondered my curious new status as a sex object, while other individuals and couples darted to and fro. It was only now that I realized that Linsey did not have the slightest grasp of Imperial Alberinese, unlike the others, who were continually improving their grasp of it.

As dusk faded into night the castle became still and silent. Nobody had thought to give me a place to sleep in the general rush to seduce each other, but the air was warm and the night windless, so I stretched out on one of the padded benches in the cloisters and draped the backrest cloth over myself. For no special reason I calculated how many days of my own, personal time it had been since I had been abducted. It had been seventeen days, and somewhere in the future it was the seventeenth day of the first month of 3145. It was my nineteenth birthday.

✦ ✦ ✦

Aside from Linsey, I was probably the only person in that castle who did not sleep with someone else that night. I awoke with dawn's light streaming in from the east, then set off to find breakfast in whatever form it came. I soon learned that nobody was up and about at that hour: not a servant, not a peasant, and certainly not a noble. I drank from a fountain in the gardens, then picked some fruit from the trees to break the night's fast. With nobody to bar my way, I began to explore the place.

The castle was devoid of anything military, apart from the guards, and even these only seemed to be there to chase dogs and chickens away when they wandered where they were not wanted. The coats of arms on the shields in the feasting hall mostly featured flowers, with occasional birds or animals. The shields were merely painted canvas stretched over wicker frames. Nobody seemed to own anything more offensive than boar spears and hunting bows. There were no dungeons, and the suits of armor and chain mail were all the specialized tourney variety. Even more surprising was that there were no strongboxes. Jewelry was strewn about here and there amid discarded clothing, apparently on the assumption that nobody would think of taking it. Down in the stables a dozen or so horses munched chaff, while two pairs of intertwined legs thrashed and wriggled in the hayloft. One pair of feet was grubby and bare, the other wore richly embroidered slippers.

It was no different in the village. Clearly nobody whatsoever rose with the sun. A brisk walk up the hill took me to my time engine, and I was surprised to find that it had been decorated with flowers. A hurried inspection showed that it had not been interfered with in any other way. I sat on a weathered stone bench that I found nearby, then looked out over the landscape for a long time.

My impression was that the world of the past had been tamed, then transformed into one vast estate garden. Violence had vanished into the guise of sports like hunting and tourneys, and adventure of a sexual nature was now the only other outlet for people's energies. They courted, fell in love, slept with their lovers, cheated upon their lovers, fell out of love, then moved on to new lovers—all in the space of a single night, from what I had seen.

There appeared to be no money in circulation. People merely did what required doing because it was their place to do it, or bartered what they had for what they wanted. War, commerce, and scholarship did not yet exist, while courtship, fine arts, and hospitality trades were flourishing. As lives go, those of these people seemed futile to me, yet I had to admit that it was philosophically difficult to pass judgment on them. This was indeed a beautiful and peaceful society.

Upon close inspection I found the buildings to be very old, and while the repairs to some wooden fittings appeared recent, the core structures seemed designed to survive for as long as mountains. The stones of the walls were some type of ceramic, while the roof beams seemed to be a type of wood with the properties of steel. The villagers knew enough masonry and carpentry to perform minor repairs to buildings, but no more. Who, then, had built the core structures?

I returned to the village to discover that a tournament was being organized on the green between the village and the castle. I watched as stands and a tilting race were set up by both villagers and castle servants. A fanfare signaled that the stands were ready, and they were quickly filled by courtiers and lesser nobles. The servants and villagers settled down to watch from the surrounding fields. My expectations of seeing something martial quickly came to an end. Two kavelars faced each other, both on white stallions, and wearing their courtly robes under expensive, shining plate armor. Both were armed with a shield and a lance.

After an elaborate series of salutes and declarations, they rode at each other. There was a clang and snap as a lance shattered. Everyone clapped. The kavelars wore elaborately embroidered favors on the right arm, and after each bout there was a great show of emotion from the ladies who had fashioned them. It was not the stuff that great deeds of arms are made of, and I must admit to becoming bored very quickly. I was also disappointed, for I felt that this very distant past was even worse than the world of Lariella's hedonistic Fourth Millennium. That society was at least dynamic, but this one was just a tedious historical stage drama with the plot removed.

I was soon to learn how very wrong it is possible to be.

⁕   ⁕   ⁕

For the next few days I made the castle my base while I explored everything within a half day's ride. At first I thought that borrowing a horse might be a problem, but merely presenting myself at the stables resulted in a horse being saddled for me.

The three other castles that I visited were in almost precisely the same mold. Apart from horses, there were no domestic animals larger than a sheep. Wildlife appeared to be mainly birds, although once I caught sight of a wolf-like animal about the size of a spaniel. *Where are all the large and dangerous animals?* I wondered. *Were wolves and suchlike created in what was the future of this time? If so, what created them?* Legends told that glass dragons had begun their existence a mere five thousand years before I was born, so there would be none of those here.

Linsey spent time with me whenever I returned to the castle of Aral and Reyvelt, because Merleand managed to elude her fairly often. I became depressingly familiar with her left thigh, which she kept my hand clamped firmly upon whenever we sat together, but she never invited any familiarities that went beyond this.

Because I could ride, I was invited on the hunts, which appeared to be the main diversions aside from amorous frolics, tournaments, eating, and dancing. The tiny boars of the woodlands were a popular quarry in the hunts because they provided a fine roast, but they had no tusks so there was no danger from them. My ability to play a lute while riding was the cause of much amusement, and the luthier of the village was kept busy repairing instruments damaged by others trying to copy me.

⁕   ⁕   ⁕

As the days passed I began to lose track of time. One evening I sat on what had become my bench in the cloisters, wondering whether to explore this world of the past further, or to journey back, rescue Wallas and Lariella, then return to our own respective centuries. Linsey was with me, sitting rigidly upright and unsmiling, but holding one of my hands firmly on her thigh to let passersby know that she was engaged in courtship activities, even though Merleand was not there. By now I had learned that they were count and countess.

My thoughts were interrupted when Merleand strolled through the gate arm in arm with a barefoot peasant girl. Linsey immediately bounded up from the bench and dashed for them, shrieking what was probably abuse and waving her hands in the air. The peasant girl ran back the way she had come, while Merleand dashed for his apartment tower. Even though she was the most disagreeable of these people of the past, I could not help but like the countess. She at least had some spirit about her, and I fancied that her descendants would one day liberate the world from this living tapestry of futile romance and dalliance. Perhaps I would be one of them.

During the dancing of that evening I was called upon to perform various feats of strength, such as taking two of the women around the waist and lifting them from the ground. I was also developing a role for myself akin to that of a jester or juggler. While this was hardly my idea of a career, it did at least give me a place and identity. All the while I was struck by the lack of originality among these people. Virtually everything that I did was fantastically clever or hysterically funny as far as they were concerned. Jokes that would barely raise a smile from the drinkers in a tavern of my time would have many of these people quite literally rolling about on the floor, helpless with mirth.

That night I retired to my bench early, and spent some time thinking about when I might climb the hill to the time engine and travel home. I awoke with the lordworld high. The castle was in absolute silence, and I was not at all sure what had roused me. I fancied that I dreamed of a shriek of terror echoing through the corridors and cloisters of the palace, something absolutely out of place in this perfect world. Could it have been something else? Some woman having an orgasm, perhaps? With the amount of copulation that was going on, I thought it a wonder that I had not heard more of that sort of thing. I was settling down to get back to sleep when I caught sight of half a dozen shadows hurrying past in the distance, carrying something between them. *All going to the same orgy,* I thought, and soon I began to doze again.

✳ ✳ ✳

The following morning I set off into the woods, thinking to explore some ruins that I had seen from the castle's towers. After following a well-worn path for a mile or so, I came to a clearing that was scattered with bones. They were of humans, by their look and size. They had been gnawed thoroughly, and many had been cracked open for the marrow. All were very old, and some crumbled as I touched them. Here and there I saw the pad prints of what might have been the spaniel-sized wolves. This immediately explained the lack of graveyards. When people died, they were carried out into the forest and literally thrown to the wolves. I had learned that religion and ideas of an afterlife were in the distant future, along with war, taxation, and verbally incorrect jokes, so the unceremonious disposal of the dead came as no surprise. A few scraps of fine cloth confirmed my theory, and I was about to walk on when a whimper from above drew my attention. Ten feet from the ground, clinging to a tree trunk and sitting on a branch, was Countess Linsey.

It was the work of moments to climb up beside her, but it took a lot longer to persuade her to release the tree trunk and allow me to help her down. Her left temple featured a large and ugly wound, and there was blood matted in her hair and on her bed robe. Her feet were bare, but did not show the dirt and scratches that walking such a distance would have caused.

It was no effort to carry Linsey out of the woods, because she was quite lightly built. I stopped at a fountain in the village so that she could drink, and I washed the blood from her hair and cleaned her up as best as I could. At the castle we were greeted with both joy and shock, and even as I laid her in her own bedchamber the place began to fill up with maidservants and well-wishers. The countess displayed not a trace of the sharp-tongued antagonism that I had seen ever since my arrival.

By now I had realized that these people had virtually no medical skills beyond bandaging up cuts and scratches, and I suspected that the killer diseases of my time were also in the future. Victims of serious accidents were just left to die, however. As far as I could tell from her single injury, Linsey had fallen and hit her head, probably during some late-night pursuit of the count or one of his lovers. Because she seemed dead, she had been carried out into the woods for disposal by the wolves, but there she had revived. I now felt particularly sorry for her, because it was certain that the count would spend little, if any, time by her bedside. As always, that duty would be mine, and for the whole of that day I kept Linsey company, bringing her food, playing tunes on a lute, and even holding her hand. From time to time she smiled at me, and these were the only smiles I had seen her favor anyone with in all of the time that I knew her.

* * *

The sun was some minutes below the horizon as I left the kitchens, carrying with me a selection of leftovers from the courses of the afternoon's banquet for Linsey. I looked to her tower as I walked across the courtyard, and noticed that the leadlight windows were wide open. Quite without warning, a figure dressed in white toppled straight out of the window and plunged at least a hundred feet to the cobbled courtyard below. I dropped the tray that I had been carrying and ran across the body. Most eerily, there had been no cry or scream, just the final, heavy thud.

By the time I reached Linsey she was not breathing, nor did she have a pulse. Several pale faces appeared at the window and looked down. They did not seem at all concerned that I could see them. A crowd quickly gathered, but the concept of death did not sit easily with the nobles and servants of the palace, and they soon dispersed. It was not that they feared death, it was more that it was a blank spot in their lives. People suddenly vanished, and there was an end to it. I carried Linsey's body to a nearby bench, where I laid her out and satisfied myself that she was indeed dead.

Now I dashed up to her chamber, but those who had looked down from her window were no longer there. Boiling with anger, I stormed down the stairs and across to the feasting hall, and in front of the revelers I tore down a hanging. This I draped over Linsey's body, but there was nobody about to see the gesture. Finally I sat down to keep a vigil peculiar to my home kingdom, that of sitting with the recently dead until the warmth had gone out of the body.

I decided that Linsey had probably attempted suicide the night before.

The undertakers of this future must have carried her away for disposal by the wolves, thinking that she was dead rather than stunned. Perhaps later she had revived and climbed into the tree. Perhaps she found a quick, clean death from a fall more bearable than the terror of being torn apart by wolves. *What drove her to such despair?* I wondered. She did have serious problems with the behavior of the count, but she did not seem to love him and could have easily found any number of other partners. Was it merely jealousy? I understood jealousy. Was jealousy a disease here? Was I in danger?

I cannot say low long I sat by the body of my only real companion in that world, holding her hand as it grew cold. The air became chilly, and the lordworld shone down, illuminating the cloisters and garden. I remember thinking how quiet the castle had become. All the secretive scurryings of lovers going to assignations had ceased. Silence can be more profoundly unsettling than even battle cries, and that was certainly the case now.

✳ ✳ ✳

When I first caught sight of the cluster of pale figures that kept to the shadows, I assumed them to be the undertakers. I looked down at Linsey, and thought that she looked more relaxed and attractive than I had known her to be in life. Still, it was quite a relief to let go of her dead hand. I had felt sorry for Linsey in life, yet she had brought neglect and isolation down upon herself. If she had behaved like everyone else . . . she would have been just like everyone else. There was no real love in this time, even though recreational dalliance was the preferred pastime over hunting, jousting, and even feasting. Linsey's jealousy was the closest approximation to love that I had encountered, it was at least some sort of constancy, however disruptive it might have been. As I stood up I pulled the tapestry away to signify to the undertakers that she was indeed dead.

The act of standing was what saved my life, for someone else had stolen up behind me. The blow from a club that struck my left biceps had been aimed at my head, and had it landed upon its intended target, I certainly would have been stunned.

I seized the end of the club with my right hand. My left arm was barely usable from the blow, but by raising my right arm and twisting my body right around I drew the club back over my attacker's shoulder and out of his grip, then rammed the butt into his diaphragm. He doubled over and collapsed. The other undertakers spread out to encircle the bench, but no more than a dozen blows from myself had six tall, thin bodies laid out on the flagstones of the cloisters. By Miral's light I saw that all of my attackers were dressed in white, and were armed with the tools of village artisans.

It was at that very moment that I resolved to leave. I was in no doubt at all that these undertaker folk had killed Linsey. She had been culled for being different, and as a field magistrate I would have been quite happy to convict pretty well any villager for playing a part in her death. The villagers not only maintained the castle, they managed the behavior of the nobles as if they were cattle, I was quite convinced of that. I was again about as wrong as it is possible to be, of course, but then I was a very young and inexperienced field magistrate in very strange circumstances.

The danger seemed to arise once the sun was down, but all my other nights in this past had been free of such incidents. Perhaps certain nights of the month were bad ones for nonconformists, and Linsey and I had been just that. I had put the undertaker folk to flight, but they would be back. Like peasants everywhere, they were brawlers rather than skilled opponents, but they had the advantage of numbers. I went to the feasting hall to arm myself, and found it entirely deserted. Deep within my mind I felt that the situation was probably worse than it seemed, but at that point I was more interested in selecting a suitable ax from the many mounted on the wall. Armed with a well-balanced short-ax, plus a shield whose coat of arms featured three fanged birds in saltire, I appropriated a burning torch from a rack and set off for the time engine.

As I walked, I thought about what was really happening in that remote and distant time. There were no constables, so what happened when someone transgressed the protocols? Countess Linsey had clearly been such a transgressor, and her fate had been harsh and swift. Her first bruise had not been from a suicide attempt, but from a club in the hand of some servant. The second time a group of servants had probably flung her through the window.

Something was farming these folk. Even I knew that the more

aggressive and domineering people tended to be more successful in life, and so have more children. Dominance and competition were thus common in my time, so war was common. The farmer of this past was removing such people very cleverly. To preserve the line into the future he had bred his people to act as a culling militia, possibly on nights when the lordworld was near full in the sky.

I did not understand it. The act of culling is an act of power, but how can there be an act of power in a world without power? The solution had been to enshrine the role of executioner in everyone. The imperfect were identified and weeded out by everyone . . . Everyone? I suddenly realized that there was no reason for only the peasants from the village to participate in the culling. Those of the castle practiced hunting and tourney fighting. True, they were not very effective, but they were good enough to be dangerous in a group. I quickened my pace. Monsters of the night had been all around me in the daylight, laughing, singing, feasting, and playing. By day and most nights these tranquil, hedonistic folk indulged in their facile adulteries and other pleasures, but from time to time those who were most normal—in terms of what passed for normal—hunted down and killed those of their number who did not conform.

As I made for the wooded hillside beyond the village, the fleeting shapes of white stalkers in the lordworld's light warned that the militia of the night had not given up on me. *Why do they dress in white,* I wondered. Perhaps it signified stepping outside everyday behavior. From somewhere in the darkness came the thin howl of a little wolf, but this enemy from my past now held no terrors for me.

The white shapes were becoming more numerous and bold, and I knew that an attack would not be long in coming. The first rock very nearly knocked me senseless, but although I staggered, I did not go down. Without stopping, I raised my jacket over my head to blunt the force of any further missiles. Leaving the road, I dodged into the woods, steadily moving in the direction of the time engine and navigating by glimpses of the lordworld through the trees. Every so often a shower of rocks would come out of the shadows, but I was able to elude the hunters, or so I thought.

I did not realize that I was being shepherded until I emerged into a clearing and was confronted by a kavelar sitting astride a white stallion.

He was holding a long, white lance high, and I saw more riders appearing from amid the trees.

"Who wishes to die?" I called loudly. "Hurry now, I am a busy man."

The first rider lowered his lance and charged, bearing down on me as if this were a hunt and I a boar. The tip of his lance was absolutely steady; it was as if he expected no resistance from me. I took the ax from my belt and flung it more to distract him than with the intention of causing harm. The head buried itself in his chest, and he tumbled from the stallion and lay still.

I snatched up the fallen lance as a second rider charged, but this time I parried his lance as he closed with me. He rode harmlessly past. Two riders now charged together, and I suddenly realized that the military personas of these people were more intelligent than those of their dalliance selves. The metal tips of the approaching lances glinted in the lordworld's light as I looked one way, then the other. This time I flung my torch into the face of one, then parried the lance of the other. They rode away, one with his hair on fire. I looked about the clearing and found myself suddenly alone, apart from the dead kavelar lying nearby. Tossing the lance away, I removed my ax from his chest.

I was wiping the blood from the blade on the grass when the first arrow hit me in the left shoulder. Two more followed, almost together, hitting me in the leg and upper chest. *Two, maybe three archers,* I thought as I dropped to my knees. I knew this was the end. There is no answer to accurate, concealed archers, except to have one's own archers. I waited. No more arrows came, but two riders emerged from amid the trees and charged me as a pair.

A third rider cut across the path of my attackers, and to my astonishment, the two kavelars broke off and rode away into the woods. The newcomer was a woman, riding sidesaddle. As she drew near I recognized Queen Reyvelt.

Under such circumstances, it is never obvious whether one is to be rescued, or merely saved for some member of the nobility to enjoy the actual kill. Although I had an arrow in one leg, I forced myself to my feet and brandished my ax. Abruptly the ax burst into flame along its entire length, turned to ash, and dispersed into the air. The fact that my hand had not been burned caused me quite a lot of surprise, but what really caught my attention was the way that the iron ax head had burned along with the wood. The queen reined her horse in . . . and I do believe that I collapsed.

✳   ✳   ✳

I was not surprised to find myself in darkness, but I was not beside the river at the edge of life. This time I was floating, and there were dim, glowing shapes and sparkles in the distance. They drifted slowly, and some seemed to be avoiding others. For some reason none of them came anywhere near me. Something that seemed composed of millions of bright points of light floated beside me. It was in the shape of a robed woman with enormous wings growing out of her back.

"I have taken you back to the castle," said the voice of Queen Reyvelt in flawless Imperial Alberinese. "Your time engine is perfectly safe."

"This is not the castle," I said, even though I spoke meaning rather than words.

"Of course, this is the Darkwalking Realm. Sorcerers know how to visit this plane in your century, there is nothing mysterious about it."

"Your people were trying to kill me," I replied.

"The danger is past. Look."

A circle of the real world appeared before me, and I found myself looking at myself lying naked on a bed in the castle. The queen was sitting on the edge of the bed, and I watched in astonishment as one of her hands sank into my chest. One by one she withdrew the arrows that had hit me. They were snaggleheads, they should have snared themselves on my flesh and ripped me apart from the inside as they were withdrawn, yet I did not even bleed.

"You have other damage to your body," she said. "Blades of metal, falls, spells, castings, burns, glamours, and floggings. There are spots of rot within your teeth, and five of your hairs are grey. You are definitely not of this age."

"That sort of thing happened in my time," I replied, prudently preferring few words to many.

"Time," she said, then seemed to give the matter some thought. "A timefarer," she finally concluded. "Are you from the future?"

"Well, yes."

"In that case I do not exist, but that is not a problem."

"You do not exist?"

"Yes and no, definitions are such imprecise things when put into words. Watch now, as I heal you more completely. My . . . methods will convince you that I am someone rather special. There is no point in telling you not to panic, Timefarer, for panic you most certainly will. Just cling to my word that you will come to no harm."

Within our view into reality I saw Queen Reyvelt stand up beside the bed and disrobe. When she climbed onto the bed and straddled me, I expected to see some tasteless act of dalliance performed with my unconscious body. Instead she leaned forward and merged with me completely. Everything suddenly reeled before me as my mind declared itself unable to cope.

"Well, perhaps that might not be very good for your sanity," said Reyvelt as she caused the window on reality to wink out.

✳ ✳ ✳

I opened my eyes, and found myself staring at the rafters of a circular tower room in the castle. It was daylight, and Queen Reyvelt was sitting by one of the windows, gazing out over the ocean.

"Sit up, Timefarer," she said without turning. "Look beneath you."

Trying very had to keep a grip on my sanity, I sat up and looked at the place where I had been lying. Upon the sheet were three small chunks of metal, some splinters, lengths of wax thread, and various dark stains.

"I swept those from your body as I was healing the other damage," she said as I picked up what looked like a piece of broken arrowhead. "The stains are toxins, tooth rot, and the like. I left all your scars. Deep within your mind you are proud of them."

I dropped the piece of metal and began to examine myself. The scars from the past were all there, but those from the three arrows of the night before had ceased to exist.

"I have never seen a body so limited as yours," Reyvelt said as she turned to gaze at me. "I have made you whole, but in my host-image."

"What does that mean?" I asked, not liking what I was hearing.

"I made you as I am, in body."

I experienced a moment of unimaginably intense panic. Suddenly I was Pelmore, lying upon the workshop table of Horvis the Chop. Fighting an almost overwhelming fear of what I might not find, I reached down to check the status of my genitals. They were present and intact. The wave of sheer relief that swept over me had the room spinning before my eyes.

"Your mind is still yours," the queen continued.

"But who are you? What are you?"

"Who is Reyvelt? What is Arvelderian?"

"Arvelderian is the name of this kingdom."

"I am this kingdom."

I did not reply because I could not think what to say. I had no grasp whatever of what she was talking about.

"Come with me," she said, standing up, then added, "but dress yourself first, if you feel inclined."

The Wayfarers' boots and trews from the Alberin of 3144 lay beside sundry other clothing from the queen's time. My own clothing had an indescribably reassuring effect upon me, probably because it allowed me to cling to what I am. After I had dressed, Queen Reyvelt led me into another chamber, where the king was dressing. On the bed lay a naked courtesan, still asleep. My instinct was to cower behind the queen, but both of them seemed quite oblivious of us. Reyvelt waved her hand before the monarch's face. He did not react at all. Slowly and deliberately she made a fist, held it up for me to see, smiled reassuringly to let me know that all was well, then punched the king's stomach as hard as she could. He doubled over, then collapsed to the floor, where he lay gasping.

"Am I allowed to ask questions?" I asked.

"Better to watch," replied the queen.

After some moments the king managed to recover his breath and wheeze for the attention of the woman on the bed. She awoke, looked about, saw him on the floor, then screamed. Chambermaids and guardsmen came running.

"Had a fit, like a blow to the stomach," gasped the king as he was lifted from the floor and seated on the edge of the bed.

"They cannot see us?" I asked.

"We are not part of their reality," replied Reyvelt.

"I don't understand. Did you hit him because you are jealous?"

"Timefarer, I am not the queen, she is not conscious. Try to understand, I am all the millions of subjects of this kingdom as well as the rulers. Just now I am manifesting through the queen. Had I reached into your body as the king, it would have been distressing for your sensibilities, would it not?"

"Oh, yes," I mumbled. "Considerate of you."

"Come, we shall talk as we ride to your time engine. Breakfast awaits us there."

✳   ✳   ✳

A groom was waiting with two palfreys when we reached the castle's courtyard. He did not seem to know why he was there, and he wandered back into the stables as we took the reins. The guards ignored us as we rode out through the castle gate and across the green.

"Here is a thought for you to ponder," said the queen as we made for the village. "This is the year 3145, in Twomonth."

"But, but the castle, this kingdom, the whole moonworld . . ." I began, not sure how to even frame my next question.

"This is only a pretty image, Timefarer. It does not exist."

"But you are part of it."

"Three million years ago I existed. You are seeing a memory of what I was."

"But what are you? Do not say human, I know you are not."

"Very good, I am impressed. Think of a kingdom from your own time as you would a person. Both have to eat, clothe themselves, have shelter, earn a living, and sometimes even fight. A person has arms, legs, and a head, just as a kingdom is a collection of artisans, sailors, rulers, and all else. In this past, however, kingdoms were more than just collections of people following the rules."

"Were you a god?" I asked.

"No, just the merged minds of millions of people."

"But, but . . . were they slaves?"

"No, they lived in comfortable, pleasant places such as the castle behind us and the village ahead. Their lives were free from the risk of war, disease, and all other things horrible."

"So if my hands, arms, and legs could think for themselves, I would be like you?" I ventured.

"Excellent, Timefarer. The millions of people in this kingdom are my body. To me, you are like an intelligent hand, crawling about by itself."

I did not like that analogy, and felt flushed with anger.

"I know what is in your mind, Timefarer," said Reyvelt. "I offend you."

The thought had been there, and for a moment I was both shocked and ashamed.

"I had expected something better from creation gods," I admitted.

"I know. I am neither human, nor a person, nor even real. I am the king, getting dressed in the castle, the cooks in his kitchen, the maidservant tending his bedroom, the laundress boiling vats of water, the guards at the castle gate, the fletcher preparing arrows for this afternoon's hunt, the swineherd scratching his ear, the baker's wife preparing the dough, the blacksmith stoking his fire, and even the baker stoking the fire of the blacksmith's wife—to use a euphemism from your future."

"But that woman who died, Linsey, she was part of you too."

"Countess Linsey was a flawed and twisted part of me."

"So . . . everyone exists to be you?" I managed.

"Yes. In a past even older than this one, humans roamed in small tribes, hunting beasts and gathering anything they could eat. Slowly they learned skills and began to organize themselves. They built villages, then kingdoms. The kings of those kingdoms sponsored sorcerers, who then studied the very nature of wisdom itself. They learned to merge minds together, to deal with difficult problems of scholarship. Once enough minds had been merged, beings like me began to exist."

"But, but in my century nothing remains of you."

"That is true, but I have looked into your mind, and seen what you saw from the time engine. You did not know what to look for, and I cannot simplify it enough to explain. Through your eyes, in reverse, I see myself and my kind develop beyond the need for host bodies, then vanish to attend matters that even I do not understand. The host people were left behind."

"So my ancestors are the rubbish remaining from your great age?" I concluded. "What a depressing thought."

"Look around you, Timefarer. Is this world a better place than yours?"

"It is not my world, Your Highness, I cannot tell. Folk live in tranquillity, yet they are not folk. Most are happy, yet ladies of free thought are killed and fed to wild beasts. None of that seems just."

"Tell me, Timefarer, were Linsey that enemy of yours, Pelmore, would you feel she was treated unjustly?"

"Pelmore?" I exclaimed angrily. "That bastard deserves death! Decent folk need protecting from the like of him, I . . ."

I caught myself, then felt mightily foolish.

"I think you begin to understand. I need protection from the malignant components within my own body, and Linsey was one of them. Your hatred for Pelmore is like a disease to me, do you realize that?"

"Could you not have healed her?"

"If you tear a fingernail would you pare it off, or go to the effort of repairing it with resin?"

That analogy left me severely shaken. Linsey was the single person that I had felt any empathy for in that time, yet she was just a minor, ragged edge of Reyvelt's body.

"She was no more than a torn fingernail?" I exclaimed.

"Yes. A woman in the village is pregnant with a child that will replace Linsey."

"Does this happen often?"

"Occasionally. I allowed Linsey to live because she provided a certain spontaneity. Your arrival sent her into . . . think of a pebble tossed down a mountainside that causes an avalanche. It was like that."

✴ ✴ ✴

Nobody was aware of us as we rode through the village, and the fields of barley beyond it were tended only by children chasing the birds away. The woodlands swallowed us up in cool shade. Overgrown stonework loomed amid the trees, and a kavelar errant and his squire rode past without seeing us, even though we were in plain sight.

"Why this parody of olden times?" I asked. "Why all the lords and ladies, hey nonny no, morris dancers and jousting? Why not great cities and glass towers, like they have in 4150?"

"Look amid the trees. What do you see?"

"Ruins."

"Indeed. Ruins that include those of civilizations such as you describe. I change civilizations like you change the fashions of your clothing. It gives me delight, and it is important to feel delight. That little we do have in common."

I thought about her words, but was barely able to piece together any sense from what she had told me. She probably saw all that in my mind, but was too polite to comment on it.

"Many, many confusing and meaningless words ago, Your Highness, you said that you—that you were a memory. What did you mean?"

"Just that, Timefarer. Were you to find the drawings for an ancient Vindician war galley in a book, then commission a shipyard to build one, what would you have?"

"An ancient Vindician war galley."

"No you would not, it would be a dead thing. To bring it to life you must train a crew in its use, teach them to speak ancient Vindician, then dress them, feed them, and even discipline them like ancient Vindician sailors. Only then would you have a warship that looks, sails, and fights very much like the original. I too have been constructed from memories, Timefarer, as has this entire past. All this world is illusion. You are still in 3145."

"No!" I exclaimed. "Not possible! I am here, this is real."

She apparently decided to let me think upon what I had already learned, so we rode on in silence until we came to the glade where the time engine stood. We dismounted and let the horses free to graze unhobbled. I watched as the queen put her hands into the structure of the time engine as easily as if it were made of smoke. When *I* reached out to touch it, the surface was still as hard as metal and crystal ought to be. The bands of nothingness remained just that: visible, but intangible.

The queen withdrew her hand holding . . . distortion. Just distortion. Nothing else. Her hand was distorted by something that was clearly in it, and which affected light, but which could be seen into.

"What is it?" I asked.

"A focus."

"Like the lens of my farsight?"

"The lens is not the focus, the focus is a property of the lens. It does not exist as matter, yet it is there. It endures through time more surely than the lens, it existed as a property of that lens before the lens was ground. The lens was ground around the focus, and it will endure if the lens is crushed to powder."

"You have lost me quite completely."

"I know, I can see your mind," she said, sighing. "Trust my word upon it, this focus in my hand can flick back and forth through history like a scholar glancing up and down a scroll."

"Please, please, you keep leaving loose threads untied in this tapestry that you weave. You said this is time engine is built from, er, focus?"

"More than that. The time engine is built from memories. All the memories of this world."

This time I understood enough to disagree. I reached up and broke a twig from an overhanging branch.

"This is not a memory," I said flatly. "This is a piece of tree."

The queen waved her hand at me.

"Is this a tree?" she asked.

"No."

"How do you know?"

"I was taught it."

"So you remember the lesson?"

"Of course, I remember . . . damn!"

I should have known better than to argue further with her. She was not like the gods of the riverbank, she was far more daunting.

"You dislike me, Timefarer. You think I used humans as hosts, then abandoned them."

"Yes! How could you do that to—to my ancestors?"

"I have no answer. The memories of even countless generations of your ancestors cannot encompass the thoughts of what was once me and my kind. I am but a poor reconstruction, Timefarer. I feel compassion for you and all the other people of the moonworld. My original self would not. Gradually humans learned to think for themselves again, and began to build new kingdoms and civilizations."

I looked out over the lush, rolling landscape of green woodlands and fields, castles of gleaming white stone, and terra-cotta roofs as red as the lips of a lamplight girl. It was indeed a paradise, but one maintained and tended meticulously by the thing speaking to me. I had no place here, and anyway this place did not exist. There was no time travel. The time engine merely built an illusion of the past or future from memories.

"If this is all illusion, and I really am in 3145 . . . how do I return to 3145?" I asked.

"You play by their rules," replied the queen holding out the handful of nothingness.

"*Their* rules? Are there once more gods like you?"

"No, but there is a vast, vast field of memories for the use of whoever cares to focus them. When your sorcerers go darkwalking they see this field. The Darkwalking Realm is filled with the memories of the dead, Timefarer."

"But I saw Lariella's future."

"An image, based on the fancies of those that you know as gods of the riverbank. The future may be like what you saw, but then it may not."

"So my time is an image too?"

"Oh no, it is actual, and we are living in it."

The queen reached back into the time engine and replaced the nothingness of the focus.

"May I have the ill-fitting lever?" she asked.

I pressed the lever-key into her palm. Her skin was soft and warm; it was the type of skin that never knows toil.

Holding the lever-key in one hand, Reyvelt reached down into the lectern of the time engine with the other. The tip of the lever-key glowed like a star for a moment, and a wisp of smoke curled upward.

"The key will fit now," she said, handing the lever-key back to me.

"You have the power to shape metals?"

"No. The light and smoke was just to give *you* the feeling that something happened, but by all means try the lever-key for yourself."

"Oh I believe you."

"Actually you do not. Try it."

The lever-key now fitted, and once locked in place it moved back and forth smoothly. I could leave, return to my own century, yet . . . yet the queen had said we were already in 3145.

"You are very confused," she said.

"We are here, three million years in the past. How can we be otherwise?"

"Because we are not, this is all illusion. When you set off into the future, all this will vanish."

That gave me cause for thought. My memories of Torea were all that I had of the place. Take someone else and give them my memories, and they might as well have lived my life on the dead continent.

"Splendid progress, Timefarer, that was a clever analogy," said the queen, looping her arm through mine. "Come, let us walk."

We ambled across the grass, following the gentle slope of the hill. Try as I might, I could not escape the feeling that the world was somehow newer and fresher than I had ever known it to be.

As she was speaking, a trestle covered with a white cloth and set out with platters of meats, fruits, and bread appeared ahead. It was not as if it had been there and I suddenly noticed it, I literally saw it materialize. As if by an afterthought, two goblets and a pitcher of wine added themselves to the spread.

"I am breaking down your faith in reality," the queen warned me.

"You are doing a good job of it, too."

For a time she left me alone to stand on the hillside, a goblet of wine in my hand, a roast lamb shank in the other. It all seemed so comfortingly real.

"Gods like you have returned," I said.

"Not gods, just powerful darkwalkers."

"Darkwalkers? They are just sorcerers who die when they step out of their bodies too long."

"Not so, Timefarer. They do not die. If they did, the moonworld would be a better place."

"What do you care for the moonworld's fate?" I asked.

"Very little," she replied after the slightest of pauses, then her head slowly turned to take in the vista of her world. "Perhaps I should have, when I was real, but I was always so busy."

"Well, an apology is more than anyone else has given me for a very long time," I said, sighing, feeling some of my anger drain away. "This may not be the sort of thing one says to a god, but I like you, Queen Reyvelt."

To my surprise she slipped her arms about me and hugged tightly—then I found myself hugging nothing at all. The queen, the trestle, the horses, all were gone. Only the time engine remained, an incongruous sculpture of meaningless shapes and impossible materials. In the distance was the Placidian Ocean, and below me the valley that would become the Lakita Plain almost glowed green with lush and fertile fields and woodlands. Studded here and there were castles and villages, and it all seemed so real.

I walked across to the time engine, the three remaining lever-keys in my hand. I fitted and tested TEMPORAL and LATERAL first. I knew that all worked, of course, but I was no longer in a mood to leave anything to chance. There was a time when I would have picked up some stone or flower as a memento of my visit to this place, but not anymore. It was not real, and I was going to a time that was no more real to rescue a real overweight black cat and someone called Lariella who did not exist. After that I would return to the reality of my time, if that existed at all.

I pushed the ACTIVE lever-key. The counter windows glowed from within. I moved TEMPORAL forward, and with a lurch the flickering greyness of time travel replaced the illusion of the younger and fresher world where I had been a guest.

✳ ✳ ✳

Lunette's tower was still echoing with the thunderclap of the time engine materializing as I came to a stop. The sound was a product of the thing not existing in our time as it traveled. When I had set off, the air had rushed in to fill the nothingness left by myself and the time engine as we collapsed to a point. When I stopped, it expanded out from a point, pushing the air aside with an identical thunderclap of sound. Lariella had once told me that the time engine could push things like air, smoke, and even flying insects out of the way, but solid things were to be avoided.

It was only now that I realized one did not just quietly slip away on the time engine, one arrived and departed with a thunderclap. Everyone would have heard me go, and now they would know that I was back.

I removed the lever-keys, noting from the beams of light that the lordworld cast through the windows and onto the floor that it was a full hour since I had left. I had hoped to be gone for mere minutes, but over very short intervals the time engine was clumsy and difficult to control with any precision. Queen Reyvelt had said that all this was also illusion, but everything seemed annoyingly real as I set off into the gloom in search of Wallas.

Occasional wall lamps showed me the way ahead, but their wicks were untended, and some were so low on oil that they were guttering. *Nobody to attend the lamps,* I realized. That meant no Halverin, and *that* had me both puzzled and suspicious. The tower was sealed and secure, the crane at the summit being the only way in or out. Any attack would be bound to take days to breach the place, and I had only been gone an hour—in a curious sort of way.

First I went to the battlements. Wallas was not there. That was possibly good, because he might be a cat again, and thus fit on the time engine. It might also be bad were he still a glass dragon, and merely away to stretch his wings.

There was a soft meow from behind the crane.

"Wallas?" I called softly.

"Sir, you're safe, thank the World Mother and all the gods of the lordworld!" he babbled as he scrambled out and bounded into my arms.

"There is a problem?" I now asked.

"A problem! Sir you don't know the tenth of it."

"Well, try telling me."

"Lariella and Halverin, sir. They've been splattered all over her bedchamber."

It took my mind a moment to catch up with the words. Suddenly all the queen's talk of illusion was smothered by the reality of danger. I tried telling myself that Lariella and Halverin were mere colored images, that all of this was illusion. I was not convinced.

"Is that a dramatic way of saying that they are dead?" I asked Wallas.

"Nothing looking as they do could possibly be alive, sir."

"But Halverin was a big, strong man."

"There were screams, perhaps an hour ago. You have never heard the like. I had become a cat again by then, so I fear that I just hid. I'm sorry, I'm sorry—"

"You're a cat, you could have done nothing. What of Lunette?"

"Oh she's away. Halverin lowered her to the ground with the crane, then went back down into the tower and locked the hatch. Shortly after that I became as you see me."

"So Lunette was gone before the guard-fiend was let out to keep an eye on things. Perhaps Halverin let it out. Tell me, what did you see?"

"Well, being a cat I was able to climb down the wall to a window. Oh sir, and the time engine is gone—"

"The time engine is back, Wallas. Continue."

"There was something very large."

"You mean a glass dragon."

"No, family. A cat. Huge, as big as Lunette—that is, you."

I had not expected to catch him out so easily. Wallas was aware that he had been ensnared, so he just waited for me to ask the obvious question.

"Wallas, how long have you known that Lunette is a shapeshifter?"

"The very first night, sir, when she put an afterlife tether on me. They do more than just make sure that people die together. When Lunette changes into a panther or some such, I transform from glass dragon to cat."

"None of this follows the rules of magic as I know them."

"These are ancient times, sir. Lunette's magic may be different."

Or some overmind might be changing the rules for fun and amusement. Were this all an illusion, that might be possible. Can these new overminds read thoughts? I suspected not.

"You should have told me about Lunette!" I muttered.

"She swore me to silence, sir."

"And now you know why! She must have been holding herself back, knowing that the time engine would be lost to her if she killed any of us before it was repaired. Wallas, we have to leave."

"Oh splendid idea, sir."

"As a panther she could go straight over the mountains to Towergate, then she could glide like a shadow into the camp of the warlord who has the lever-keys, or at least force someone to give honest answers about his location."

"All very plausible, sir, but could we please leave?"

Lunette might have been close by when the blast of the time engine's departure announced that it was again working. She would have returned, climbed the stone walls as a huge cat, and entered by a window.

The time engine's absence would have told her that I had lever-keys, and had refined enough mercury to complete the repairs. She did not need me. She certainly did not need Lariella and Halverin. As for Wallas, he would be one mouthful—or perhaps two, if one wanted to be realistic. Lunette needed none of us . . . yet Lunette was not supposed to be real. Still, she seemed real, and I was afraid of her. Was Lariella real? If she was, I had to check that she was indeed dead before fleeing without her.

"We are going back down into the tower, Wallas," I announced, taking an ax and shield from the armory rack. "I must look upon the bodies."

"Must you, sir?"

"I am an inspector of the Wayfarer Constables. There are murders to check upon."

"Can you not take the word of your constable, sir?"

"If you wish to become an inspector, Wallas, you must watch an inspector at work."

"I've never wished to be an inspector. Can't I hide up here and read your journal entry later?"

I used Wallas as my eyes as I descended back into the tower. The time engine was as I had left it. We went on.

"Stairs clear," Wallas reported, and I descended another floor with him.

The outer bar of my bedchamber door had been removed, and the door stood open. Someone, possibly Halverin, had discovered the time engine to be missing, and naturally came looking for me. When he had discovered that I was missing, he would have gone to check upon Lariella before going to the battlements to look for Wallas.

There was a torch in a wall rack not far from Lariella's door—which like mine stood open. Bits of well-gnawed body were scattered about directly in front of the door, yet there were no bloody scraps of clothing. Halverin wore nothing, but Lariella certainly did robe herself. There were only enough bones for one body here. A highly significant conclusion began waving for my attention.

Lariella was wearing an afterlife tether shared with Lunette; it was probably a way of making the woman from the future a prisoner. When Lunette shapeshifted into her panther form, Wallas shapeshifted from glass dragon to cat. Lariella must have shapeshifted too, but into the same species as Lunette. When Halverin had opened her bedchamber door . . .

"I say, looks like Lunette dragged Lariella away to unwrap—oh shyte!" said Wallas just a trifle too loudly as his reasoning began to follow mine, but just a little to slowly for his own good.

A deep, annoyed rumble came from within Lariella's room, where her shapeshifted form was sleeping off what she had eaten of Prince Halverin.

"Wallas, try to keep up!" I said as I turned and fled.

Wallas shot past me as I ascended the stairs, four or five at a time, and he was already in the chamber with the time engine when I slammed the door behind me and dropped the inner bar. Something smashed into the door behind me, but bar, hinges, and timbers held. There was a feline yowl of anger and frustration as I hurried over to the time engine.

"Sir, she just said some very rude and untrue words about our relationship," translated Wallas.

"How verbally incorrect of her," I said as I began to fit the lever-keys and lock them down.

"Can you get the time engine going before she smashes the door down?"

Directly above me I heard something bounding across the decking of the battlements, and now I remembered leaving the hatchway open when I had collected Wallas. If Wallas could climb down the outer wall to the chamber windows, so too could the nightmare Lariella. Proving that more haste means less speed, I lost my grip on the ACTIVE lever-key just as a large, dark shape blotted out the lordworld's light in one of the three windows.

"Wallas, fetch back that lever-key!" I shouted as I snatched up my shield and ax.

"Dogs fetch, cats cooperate if they feel—"

"Find the frigging lever-key or we're both dead!"

By now Lariella was in the chamber, a sinuous length of shadow with two gleaming eyes and long, pale dirk-fangs. She sprang. I brought my shield up, sidestepped, and spun around. Lariella went flailing past me, clawing my shoulder then smashing into the wall. With a frantic flailing of claws she turned and sprang again, but this time I struck out with my ax as I repeated the spin-dodge. The blade dug into flesh, then was wrenched out of my hand. For a third time Lariella sprang, but this time I rolled down onto my back and flipped her over me to crash into the wall again. I had just enough time to locate the ax and roll back to my feet before the gleaming eyes turned in my direction.

"I've found the lever-key, if anyone is interested," said Wallas from somewhere behind me.

"Speak to me, Wallas, what can you see of her?"

"She is bleeding at the ribs, and there is blood on her head, sir. You are bleeding at one shoulder, both arms, the chest, and have a rather well-placed gash on your cheek that a certain lady in my past would have found very alluring as scars go."

Lariella only had to wait. We were both bleeding, but I was bleeding more. What I needed was another attack from her. It would not be a spring at full strength, because she was injured. All I needed was for her to spring.

"Wallas, take the lever-key in your teeth as soon as the way is clear," I said slowly, enunciating every word with care. "Climb down the tower wall and escape."

"But sir, what about you?"

"Forget me, I am lost. Deny these lunatics the time engine, then live as best you can."

Lariella did not like the sound of that, but she did not oblige me by springing. She advanced slowly, parried my ax blow aside with a very impressive paw stroke, then surged upward, reaching around my shield and bracketing me with her paws. I staggered backward as fast as I could, struck the windowsill, then toppled out into space with the shapeshifted Lariella clinging to me.

I heard voices, familiar voices. I was gratified by the signs of sheer panic in their tone.

"His neck is broken!"

"He can never recover from that."

"Well, how do we refocus the time engine?"

"All the other humans nearby are constructs."

"The Wayfarer is a construct too."

"He is a focal construct. Without him the causative consistency collapses."

"All that work, wasted!"

"There are two other focal constructs in this illusion."

"Yes, Pelmore and Wallas."

"Pelmore cannot be brought there in minutes, that would violate spatial resolution."

"Minutes are all we have left."

"That leaves Wallas."

"Wallas is a cat!"

"He's all we have."

"Where in all hells did the Wayfarer go for that hour, anyway?"

"The extreme past. I did not even realize that memories existed from so long ago."

"How did you lose him?"

"It was like tracking a pebble flung into a waterfall . . ."

The voices faded, and I suspected that I would see stars above me when I opened my eyes again. I was not wrong.

✳ ✳ ✳

I was not aware of any pain as I awoke, but neither could I move. The stars of the night sky were above me, and at the edge of my field of view was the lordworld. It was suddenly blotted out by the outline of Wallas's head.

"Sir?" he said anxiously.

"Wallas, how is your health?"

"I have just climbed all the way down the tower's outer wall with the damn lever-key in my teeth, so my pulse is elevated. The lever-key is now in your hand."

"I can feel nothing, I suspect that my neck is broken. What of Lariella?"

"You appear to have landed on her, sir. She is dead."

"Are you sure you are all right?"

"Not a scratch, sir."

"Scratches, I have quite a few. You're . . . my constable. Never lost a constable."

"Sir, sir, I can get you onto the time engine! I can climb the tower, release a guardsman from his chamber, then have you winched back into the tower. We can go to Lariella's time, their physicians can cure all manner of injuries."

"No, Wallas, death is the only way."

"But why won't you try?"

"Trust me . . ."

"Please sir, fight back! This need not be the end."

"Not the end, Wallas. I know what I am doing."

I knew that blood was pouring from my wounds, and I had seen enough people bleed to death to know how long I had. Staying awake was becoming a big issue.

"Sir, remember your lady, your friends, your tavern, your life. Don't give up."

"I'm going to die now, best not to make a fuss."

"Sir . . ."

"Yes?"

"Spoken like a cat."

The night sky above me faded into a deeper darkness, yet I was aware of a scene underlying the gloom. I was still lying on my back, but my feeling and strength had returned. I was where I expected to be, and that was beside a river.

The ferrygirl stood over me, her hands on her hips and shaking her head. I was then treated to a most gratifying view of her cleavage as she bent over and extended a hand to me.

"Ah Danolarian, one might almost think that you are anxious to take a ride with me," she said as she helped me to my feet.

"Madame Jilli," I replied. "Delighted, as always."

"You are perilously close to a ride in my boat," she said firmly.

"Not yet."

"So many say that."

"Quite probably, but I know I am not dead."

"True, but you are dying."

"I do not think so."

"You do not?"

"No."

"I suppose you think that Lunette returns, that she bears you back into the tower, then uses the time engine to take you to Lariella's time and physicians."

"You have been listening to Wallas. He is so good at conjuring stories."

"This time the story is true."

"I wonder."

Gradually other figures began to materialize on the riverbank, and some of them were familiar. Chance, Fortune, Destiny, Fate, and Change were there, and of course Romance was glowing behind me. The ferrygirl introduced me to Vengeance, Despair, and several others that I had not met before.

"So, you chose to die, Danolarian," said Despair. "I did not think you were a devotee of mine."

"I am not," I replied. "What I chose to do was quite deliberate, and I doubt that I am dying."

This was apparently not the answer that anyone was expecting. A few glances were exchanged between various beautiful and elegant gods.

"You obviously wanted my company," said Change, a figure that began the sentence as a little girl with a rag doll and finished it as a sorcerer.

"I think I can manage a little change without your help."

Souls were not meant to be insolent in the borderlands of the afterlife. The expressions on most faces hardened, and Change forget to change.

"You spurned my gift, Inspector," said Chance. "Chance allowed you to aim the were-Lunette at one of the windows the first time you did that backwards roll-throw, but you gave yourself away."

"I actually did that to see if I could get everyone worried," I replied. "I would say that I succeeded, by the look of you all."

The hard expressions of annoyance softened into fearful apprehension. Suddenly I realized that this was not me speaking.

"Inspector, you are so bold and confident," said Romance as she pressed her breasts into my back and wrapped glowing arms about me. "You could be one of us."

"Who could he be?" asked Fate doubtfully.

"What about Control?" suggested a suddenly nervous Fortune. "We are so random in the way we influence the lives of humans."

"Speak for yourself," said Chance.

"But Control would be my enemy," said Romance. "Romantic people are never in control."

"He could be Discipline," said Destiny. "Some romantic people like a bit of that."

"I just cannot picture him in leather straps and waving a whip," responded Romance.

"You must be Control, Danolarian," Chance decided. "You could be a counter to Romance, she has given you a very bad time lately."

"But were you to die you would be just another spirit of the dead," said Romance, placing her hands on my shoulders.

"Danolarian will not die," said Fortune. "Even now Archmage Lunette is scaling the tower walls in her cat form, with him slung over her shoulder. Chance had it that she heard the blast of the time engine departing in the distance and started back for the tower while it was away. She was close by when he fell from the window with Lariella."

"I have decreed that you will live," said Chance, "but don't get ideas about depending on me."

"You will be Control, the god who walks the moonworld as a man!" decreed Fortune. "But you must first—"

"Madame Jilli, ferrygirl," I interjected, ignoring Fortune, "you do not become the ferrygirl for another three thousand years. How is it that you are here?"

Madame Jilli looked uneasy rather than frightened.

"That is the will of the gods," she replied simply.

"Clever gods," I found myself saying. "Not only can you tell the future, you can also bring folk from the future into the past without a time engine . . . or can you? I strongly suspect that this is 3145."

Queen Reyvelt suddenly stepped out of me.

✳　✳　✳

Although the riverbank on the edge of the afterlife was mostly darkness anyway, the nature of the darkness lost focus and shimmered into something else. We found ourselves standing on an immense, curving field of glitter and sparkles, and after a moment I realized that we were now suspended just above the rings of Miral, the great lordworld itself. Two or three dozen quite disconcerted people were standing on nothingness nearby, but they were not the Gods of the Moonworld. They were all fairly old men and women, and they had the slightly shabby, unkempt look of elderly sorcerers about them. Their robes varied in style, and some of the styles were known to me only from the illustrations in old chronicles. While the clothing of most looked to be passably expensive, it was expensive clothing that had been neglected for a very long time, and had been allowed to go ragged, and become stained and grimy. Madame Jilli looked much the same as before, with her immaculately clean red gown covering nothing important, but I suspected that she was not responsible for our new venue by the way she kept her eyes squeezed shut.

Queen Reyvelt now stood about forty or fifty feet tall, and was looking down at the Gods of the Moonworld. She appeared to be wearing a gown of lace beaded with diamonds, and her hands and neck were smothered with ruffles. What I could see, her fingers featured rings so encrusted with diamonds that one could not see the metal. Strings of pearls bound her hair up tightly, and her black hair and eyes had the only color about her that was not white. After my initial shock, I realized that she was probably presenting herself and cold, impartial, rich, and very, very powerful. Her expression was quite stern, and I was certainly intimidated, even though I was fairly sure that I was her ally.

"Should I make introductions?" I asked.

"You know what a reading glass is, Danolarian," she said, ignoring my question.

"The short of sight use them to bring the writing in books into focus for their weak eyes," I replied.

"Quite right. The time engine is like a reading glass. It can be used to look into areas of the Darkwalking Realm, where the memories of those who were once alive may be found. It can focus those memories into time, landscape, and characters from the past. With a little creative tuning, it can even produce possible futures."

"So we are still in 3145?" I asked.

"Oh yes. You never left it."

"But—but then where did you come from? What are you?"

"That is very hard to put into words that you could comprehend. Imagine that some elderly sorcerer devises a powerful new spell to make geese lay golden eggs. He writes it down, but dies soon after. His journal of spells molders in a library for a thousand years, then some scholar reads the spell. Where has the spell come from?"

"The book?" seemed like the right answer.

"Quite so. You are the scholar, the time engine is the reading glass, and the memories of me in the Darkwalking Realm are the chronicle. You have brought me back to life, and I do not like what I see."

She looked down on the collection of aged sorcerers with her hands on her hips. Suddenly I made the connection with the riverbank and what I was now seeing.

"What happened to the Gods of the Moonworld?" I exclaimed.

"These are not gods," replied Reyvelt. "They are the twisted, petty little spirits of long-dead sorcerers who have been lingering in the Darkwalking Realm and playing with the moonworld of Verral."

One of the elderly men tried to throw a fireball of gleaming stars at the queen, but the weapon faded into blackness after it had barely left his hand.

"You pathetic little rabble," said Reyvelt. "You were so busy playing with *my* world and *my* people that you took no trouble to learn its workings. *I* know its workings."

"This is not your world anymore!" protested someone.

"Fight me for it," said the queen.

This time they tried to make a united stand, and a flurry of fire castings that I knew to be quite deadly burst from the group of sorcerers. None of them traveled more than ten feet. One of them made quite an impressive attempt to transform into a dragon, but the shapeshift somehow resolved into a chicken about the size of a warhorse. Reyvelt became a huge, white fox, but maintained her height of nine or so yards. The chicken hurriedly shrank and formed back into the original sorcerer. Reyvelt transformed back too.

"You have no authority here!" whined a thin wheeze of a voice.

"The creation gods abandoned this world!" called someone else. "All the holy books tell of it."

"We did nothing wrong, we stepped into the void that you left behind!" shouted a third.

Now I found myself floating upward, which was quite a surprise in itself, but suddenly I realized that I was growing to match Reyvelt's size. A field magistrate's folding table and cross-bench stood on nothingness beside me.

"We just happen to have a field magistrate here," said Reyvelt. "Will you preside, Inspector?"

I bowed to her and seated myself.

"Proceedings are declared open in the case of the creation god sometimes known as Queen Reyvelt versus the Gods of the Moonworld," I improvised. "Charges appear to include trespass, burglary, and petty theft. Anything else, Your Majesty?"

"The destruction of the continent of Torea at the cost of several million lives using the ether machine Silverdeath."

"Ah yes."

"The construction of the ether machine Dragonwall, which resulted in the loss of nine hundred thousand lives and several dozen cities melted."

"How could I have forgotten?"

"The abduction of an inspector of the Wayfarer Constables of Greater Alberin."

"I cannot preside in a trial involving myself as a witness, defendant, or felon, but I think we have enough to go on with. First witness?"

"I have access to the memories of seven hundred million lives, and they include all those relevant to this case."

"Very well, do you swear to tell the truth by the World Mother . . . er, *are* you the World Mother?"

"After a fashion."

"That makes the oath a bit of an issue."

"But I am not capable of telling lies."

"I suppose that will have to do. Please proceed."

A bubble of shimmering, translucent violet formed around the crowd of sorcerers. Reyvelt reached into it and selected a thin, tall sorcerer with piercing blue eyes. She held him out before me on the palm of her hand. A smaller violet bubble enclosed him.

"Archmage Porial Basintye, also known as the beautiful God of the

Moonworld, Fortune," declared Reyvelt. "Born 2117, Acrema, vanished into the plane of etheric energies known as the Darkwalking Realm 2188. Is it not a fact that you consumed the memories of seven hundred dead sorcerers, then used their scholarship to devise Silverdeath?"

"That is a lie—"

There was a bright flash from within the bubble, and traceries of purple fire lashed across the body of the sorcerer. He collapsed to the palm of Reyvelt's hand.

"The bubble that imprisons you is also a verity casting," Reyvelt announced. "Best not to stray from the truth."

"It's true, I fashioned Silverdeath with energies of the Darkwalking Realm," he panted.

"Why?"

"To see the peoples of the world cower before its terrible might, to humble kings, to prove to all other sorcerers that I am the most powerful—"

"Guilty of murder in the first degree!" I interrupted, banging my fist on the table. "Next."

Reyvelt returned Basintye to the others and selected another spirit.

"Ladymage Der'Vel of Lensiar, also known as Fate. Born in the year 21 of the reign of King Kovor the Plunderer, vanished into the Darkwalking Realm in year 5 of King Distrel the Invader. Did you or did you not devise the principle for the ether machine Dragonwall, and communicate it to the mortal sorcerer T'ammeral in a dream?"

"I did that!" she cried defiantly. "They were all fools, those petty casters of charms. I tempted them to die through their own stupidity by giving them something that only the wise could use."

"What about the seventy thousand others who died?"

"They were fools too."

"Five thousand four hundred years later you gave the secret of the Dragonwall etheric engine to the glass dragon Astential."

"That was to prove that glass dragons can be fools."

"And the nine hundred thousand who died when the second Dragonwall was built?"

"There were too many fools in the world, I was just culling them."

"Guilty of murder," I said, thumping the table again. "Next?"

"Helgres laf Estillian, also known as Romance. Born in 171 of the Sargolan calendar, vanished into the Darkwalking Realm thirty years later after being jilted by six suitors in succession due to her liking for cruel and malicious games."

"At last, someone the same sex as their god persona," I said. "Charges?"

"Driving twenty-one thousand lovers to suicide, devising the constancy glamour and communicating it to a mortal in a dream, causing—"

"Guilty. Next?"

All thirty-eight of those on trial were found guilty of at least one charge involving thousands of deaths and an unimaginable amount of suffering. Two-thirds were a different sex from the sex of their identities as Gods of the Moonworld, and those that I questioned on this matter replied that they were liberating their inner souls. At last we came to Madame Jilli.

"Madame Jilli, also known as the ferrygirl, born 3111, died 3141 . . . and you have caused the deaths of nobody!" said Reyvelt. "Explain to the magistrate what you are doing in the company of the undead overminds also known as the Gods of the Moonworld."

"Well, Your Majesty, I died."

"Please address your replies to the field magistrate," said Reyvelt.

"Er, sir, I died."

"As one does," I said, folding my arms and leaning forward on the table. "Go on."

"Well, the previous ferrygirl had moved on, so I was offered the job. I like meeting people, and it's not as if I was doing anything else, so I took it."

"If I may explain, Your Honor," interjected Reyvelt. "The institution of ferrygirl goes all the way back to my time, three million years into the past. Many spirits of the dead need assistance into the Darkwalking Realm, otherwise they manifest to the living as ghosts and do not add their memories to the greater whole. Ferrygirls can be dead or living, or even from other worlds."

"But is this ferrygirl charged with murder or atrocity?"

"No, but she struck the spirits of certain dead people that she did not like."

"Struck them?"

"Yes, with her ferry pole."

"Madame Jilli, did you strike these spirits under provocation?" I asked.

"Er, yes!" she said, anger blazing up in her expression as she recalled whoever those people were. "They were real beasts when alive."

"She acted under provocation, case dismissed," I decreed. "Next?"

"Myself, Your Honor," said Reyvelt.

"You are charging yourself?"

"Yes. A long time ago, perhaps two and a half million years, I abandoned this world. I had lived in the collective minds of this moonworld's people, they were my hosts. I left them because . . . probably because I developed such vast powers that I no longer needed living hosts."

"Oh, and, ah, what is the charge that you bring against yourself?"

"That I did abdicate my place in the moonworld of Verral without making provision for the welfare of my hosts."

"Your hosts. You mean we humans of this moonworld."

"Yes."

"But you are not your original self?"

"Yes and no. I was . . . focused into existence by the time engine, and I rode within your body to enter this reality. I am actually only a tiny part of my original self, built of the memories of my ancient hosts in the Darkwalking Realm."

"So you are not . . . er, the original you?" I asked, struggling with some very difficult concepts that involved being alive and existing.

"I am not the original Arvelderian, but you can think of me as Queen Reyvelt. I no longer use the minds of the people of the moonworld Verral as my hosts. I have become like those sorcerers trapped in the bubble of ether, just an overmind of the Darkwalking Realm."

"But a very powerful overmind."

"True."

This was not an easy judgment. I was nineteen, with only a year's experience in the most junior of magistrate positions. The guilt of the fallen Gods of the Moonworld was as obvious as the intentions of a lamplight girl on a wharf where a large battle galley was in the process of docking. Was someone guilty who was made from the memories of someone who had committed a crime?

"I find you guilty, Queen Reyvelt, image of Arvelderian," I concluded. "How long did you say the Darkwalking Realm has been without . . . without being patrolled by an overmind constable?"

"Two and one half million years."

"Then I sentence you to patrol the Darkwalking Realm for the same period. After that, you must make provision for Verral's safety if you wish to leave."

"I shall consider the sentence commenced," said Reyvelt with a low bow.

I looked to the bubble containing the sorcerers, clasped my hands, and shook my head. How was I to sentence spirits whose bodies had died long ago? I could not really pass the death sentence. Exile? How did one exile someone who existed on another plane from one's own world? Imprisonment? Immortals left confined might well survive until their dungeon crumbled, or until someone liberated them in return for their services.

"Queen Reyvelt, is the time engine an ether machine?" I asked.

"It is."

"Why did they build it?"

"Through fear of power and lust for power. Verral has nearly been destroyed four times: twice by Silverdeath and twice by Dragonwall. With the time engine, they can make an image of the moonworld, then put a few players into it and cause as much mayhem as they like. They played both mortals and gods. Fate was also Lunette, and Fortune played Lariella. Others were real. Danolarian, you are the secret prince of a dead empire, you had fabulous scope for drama. Wallas the enchanted cat was peerless for comic relief. Pelmore was the rogue, but there can be no proper story without a rogue. Andry was the poor boy who wanted to better himself. Had you returned to ten years after you marooned him, you would have seen him crowned king of Greater Alberin."

"Really?" I gasped.

"Some other Gods of the Moonworld were participating in a separate story involving him."

I very nearly said something unbecoming to a magistrate, then I had a horrible thought.

"Can I stand to know who played the part of Lady Dolvienne with, ah . . . myself?"

"Romance."

Relief flooded through me, but my mood was not improved particularly.

"Tell me, Your Majesty, can a real time engine be built?"

"Only to go forwards. The past is done and fixed. You cannot travel back to it, and it cannot be changed."

This was better news than I had hoped. I pointed to the time engine.

"Can you modify that time engine to be real?"

"I am doing it now," said Reyvelt as a second, smaller image of her materialized and began tinkering with the innards of the time engine. "What else?"

"Shrink the sphere with the sorcerers to perhaps a half yard across."

The violet bubble shrank even as I looked at it.

"All done," said Reyvelt, becoming one image again.

"Now shrink me to human size."

All the while I had been wearing a pack, and I now took it from my back and shook it empty. The ghosts of my few possessions floated down past my feet, bound for the glittering rings of the lordworld. As I reached for the bubble that enclosed the sorcerers they chittered and squealed in desperation with tiny, rat-like voices. It was a neat fit in my pack, and I strapped the cover flap down. Violet light leaked out here and there through small holes. *At least they will have a view where they are going,* I thought as I strapped my pack to the backrest at the rear of the time engine.

"I think you are a very clever magistrate," said Queen Reyvelt as I engaged the ACTIVE lever. I saw that the TEMPORAL lever had only two settings now: REST and FORWARD.

"Madame Jilli, if you please?" I asked, holding out my hand for her ferry pole.

This was the moment that the executioner slaps the rump of the horse, the cart is pulled forward, and the condemned prisoner is left suspended by nothing more than a rope. I cleared my throat. I hesitated. These were the Gods of the Moonworld, and I felt as if I should say something.

"By the authority invested in me as a field magistrate of Greater

Alberin, ratified to carry out executions of sentences without reference to a district magistrate, I hereby condemn you who are known as Gods of the Moonworld to eternal exile."

✳   ✳   ✳

A nudge from the tip of the ferry pole pushed the TEMPORAL lever to FORWARD. The time engine vanished into the future, along with the last yard of Madame Jilli's ferry pole. A very long silence followed, but it was probably no more than a few heartbeats.

"Now what?" asked Madame Jilli.

"You are the ferrygirl," said the queen. "You must return to welcoming spirits of the dead into the afterlife."

"You mean nothing will happen to me?"

"Why should it? You are guilty of nothing. Now return to work, there are dead people queuing up at the riverbank."

"But—but I was appointed as a joke, by the Gods of the Moonworld."

"I want you to stay on."

"But I'm a lamplight girl. People despise me. Some of the dead have even been my ex-customers."

"Nothing unsettles people so much as seeing someone they despise in a position of power, yet at the same time lamplight girls are neither threatening nor frightening."

"But why is this good?"

"Too many people die with firm ideas of what the afterlife holds for them. There is nothing worse than someone who is confident about death. They have ideas about what they deserve in the afterlife."

"But why not someone dignified, like a priest?"

"No style. Besides, they believe in gods that do not exist. Not any-more, anyway." "

"A constable?"

"The self-righteous would love it."

"What about a magistrate? I was always unsettled when I was hauled up in front of the magistrates."

"Women will not become magistrates for several centuries more, so people would not be convinced. Now be off with you."

✳ ✳ ✳

Madame Jilli faded so quickly that I did not even have a chance to say goodbye. The queen now shrank to a figure no taller than myself.

"So, the Gods of the Moonworld are exiled into eternity," she said as we stood in dark nothingness, looking out over the rings of the lordworld to the bright crescent that was Verral. "Your world might be a quieter place now. It might even become boring."

"Good, I want to be bored."

"What else do you want?"

"I want to go home!" I said slowly, and with every word clearly enunciated.

"Is that your only wish?"

"Yes!" I insisted, surprised that my wishes were not absolutely obvious to the omnipotent overmind. "I wish to return to my world and time."

"You do not understand. Two months have passed in your time frame. Your sorceress beloved, Lavenci, has returned to her old lover Laron."

"I thought you said that future was conjured by the time engine."

"The image-future was based on projections of trends already in motion. Lavenci had longings for Laron that were kept secret from you."

"I see. So I never had a chance?"

"No."

"I became somewhat special to the image Dolvienne," I said hesitantly. "Do I have a chance with the real one?"

"The two are not at all similar, Timefarer. The one you slept with was a construct, based on your limited knowledge of the real Dolvienne, made ideal for you, and played out by the spirit of a sorceress. The Dolvienne who walks, breathes, and lives a life is not this Dolvienne."

"Still, I should like to try."

"Then do so. Is there anything else before I send you back to your world and realm of reality?"

"Just some trivia," I said at once, because I had been hoping for such an offer. "Why did the Gods of the Moonworld cause the Lupanians to fly to Verral in their voidships and invade us?"

"They did not. The Lupanians did that by themselves."

"They did?"

"Yes. Silverdeath drew their attention when it destroyed Torea, even across the gulf between moonworlds it was easy to see. Dragonwall was rather hard to miss as well. A faction of Lupanians thought to conquer this world, learn the secrets of your ether machines, then return and conquer Lupan. The Gods of the Moonworld were as surprised by the invasion as everyone else."

That was the last panel of the tapestry complete. I only had a few requests now.

"Can you blot out Wallas's memories of all that happened after we were first put aboard the time engine?" I asked next.

"Easily."

"Can you do the same for Andry and Pelmore? No memories after they are put aboard the time engine?"

"Yes, but there will be a lot of time missing. Several weeks will be missing for Wallas, while Andry and Pelmore will be unable to account for the past year."

"Good. Pelmore, is he, ah . . ."

"Gelded? No. That all happened in the image world."

Relief closed over me like the water of a warm bath.

"It is rare that someone gets a chance to undo mistakes of the past, and I shall concede that the visit to Horvis was a mistake," I confessed.

"As someone else who has been given the chance to set the past right, I must agree," replied Reyvelt. "What memories would you like Pelmore to have?"

"Your pardon?"

"He had contact with image-world people in the real world. He cannot be allowed to keep too many of those memories or else he will remember what was not meant to happen."

"Then let him remember being abducted from the palace dungeon by Lariella and me. He can have spent the remaining days in the room in Wall Tower, tied up and gagged. I visit him every day with food and drink, and give him an occasional kick. His last memory can be being struck over the head on the way to the time engine."

"Done. One word of warning about Wallas, Timefarer. The words of release that Velander taught you in the image world really will transform him, so speak them with care. Wallas is a glass dragon who manifests as a cat. He is as close to immortal as a glass dragon might be, but best not to tell him that yet. He has a rare and precious gift: he enjoys being what he is."

"A cat?"

"A special cat. As a human he was never special, and as a dragon he was rather substandard. Do not speak the words of release lightly. My advice would be not to speak them at all. Ever."

"He still needs to be moved out of his comfort province," I insisted.

"Would you like me to visit him in nightmares?"

"No, I think I can provide him with some very nice nightmares by myself, thank you."

"Good, you will be close companions in the centuries to come."

"Wait! What do you mean, centuries?"

"Timefarer, when I merged with you I changed your body to be as my hosts once were. You are immortal now."

"What?" I cried. "No! Change me back."

"Oh no. You have judged immortals, so you must fill some of the space they left behind."

"But I had plans to be an ordinary person."

"You can be an ordinary immortal."

"Stop that!! You cannot do this to me. I am the son of Emperor Warsovran, the idiot who used Silverdeath to destroy the entire continent of Torea. I have spent my life fleeing power, lest I do even worse. Please! Do not make me immortal, evil will come of it."

"You live your life in fear of yourself, yet you are not your father. Do not let your fear of doing evil smother your talent for doing good. You have just removed a blight of unimaginable power from this world, Timefarer. You may need to do it again."

"You could have done everything I did."

"But you know this world and time, and I am new to it. I need an ambassador and advisor in this reality, Timefarer. There is a vast field of power and memory in the Darkwalking Realm, a plane very close to this world. If it is left untended, interlopers will move into odd corners of it and cause trouble again. I shall be very busy, and I need help in your reality."

"But why me?"

"Because there is nobody better. Name someone better suited than yourself to be my immortal ambassador and I shall end your immortality."

It was not pride that kept me silent, so much as fear. No, I was not worthy to wield the influence that was being thrust into my hands, but then who else could do better? I merely had to name someone. Anyone. I did not have the courage.

"Whenever you wish to die, Danolarian, just name a successor," she said softly.

"Send me back, please," I said hurriedly, before my resolution wavered. "Send me now."

"But Timefarer, you have asked for nothing substantial yet. What about a title?"

"I have one: Inspector."

"Riches?"

"The pay is adequate in the Wayfarers."

"Knowledge?"

"If it is not in my almanac, law book, or copy of *What Predator is That?*, then I do not need to know it."

"Power?"

"I have tried, judged, and condemned the Gods of the Moonworld. How much more power do I need than that?"

I cannot deny that the temptation to at least ask for a purse full of gold, a good pair of boots, and working knowledge of scandals involving my superiors in the Wayfarers was very strong, but I resisted. Returning to my real life with all those advantages would be returning to a different life. Being immortal was going to make that hard enough as it was.

"Well, can I go now?" I asked when the silence between us began to lengthen.

"It seems I have a lot to learn about hosts that have independent minds," the queen conceded.

"And I need to learn about everyday life as an immortal. Perhaps we can talk from time to time, but for now can I be returned to whatever the actual time and date is in the city of Alberin, preferably in Lordworld Plaza."

"Until our next meeting, Timefarer, farewell."

My view of the lordworld and its rings began to soften into a blur, then something began to solidify before me. It was a view of four bodies lying in a city square. One was that of a cat, the others were humans, and one was mine.

I began to fall into myself.

⋆   ⋆   ⋆

I have related the story of myself and the time engine as best as I understood it, but many of my impressions are confused and fragmented. Most of the time I was under a barrage of strange and unfamiliar sights, sounds, people, and things for which I have no words, so I have written down what I remembered of it with whatever words are to hand. One memory was absolutely clear at the end of the nightmare, however: I might have been made an immortal, I might be the advisor of a god, but I was at least going back to a normal life.

⋆   ⋆   ⋆

At first I felt just cold cobblestones beneath me. I opened my eyes, to find myself in Lordworld Plaza. Andry, Wallas, and Pelmore lay sprawled nearby. A notice on a public chalkboard declared it to be the twentieth day of Twomonth, 3145.

It was six weeks from when Varria, the image-girl, abducted me. They were the six weeks that I lived in illusion worlds, but real time had passed.

Wallas would have no illusion memories at all, Andry would remember bursting into a room in Wall Tower one year ago, and Pelmore . . . what to do about Pelmore?

My three companions began to stir. I was immortal! Somehow I did not feel very different. *Perhaps nobody will notice for a while,* I thought hopefully. Meantime, I was still an inspector in the Wayfarers.

I strode across to Pelmore and placed a boot upon his neck.

"Pelmore Haftbrace, you are under arrest!" I declared. "Do not try to stand until I tell you to."

"Sir, I just saw you shot with something that didn't use arrows!" exclaimed Wallas.

"I am feeling better now."

"And this is Alberin! This is Lordworld Plaza. A strange little wench carried us to Wall Tower . . . but now we are back here."

"What happened?" asked Andry. "Something hit me. Was it a Lupanian weapon?"

"For you, a year has passed," I explained, choosing my words with care. "You were flung through time, Andry, it will take a while to explain."

"The Lupanians were defeated, it was a splendid battle," said Wallas. "I am proud to say that I played an important part—"

"And so you did, Wallas. Come along, everyone, I do believe that we all have business at the palace."

"But—a year!" gasped Andry. "I must see my family first."

"You wife . . . she died in the Lupanian Invasion," I said bluntly.

"Died?" he gasped.

"But your children are alive, and being raised in the palace. Best to stay with us for a while, everything is going to be a shock for all of us in the days to come."

Our arrival at the Palace of Electocracy was the cause of considerable embarrassment, discomfort, and general inconvenience for pretty well everyone who was at all important. As we walked across Riellen Square I noticed a memorial to me, upon whose head a pigeon was asleep. The square was littered with trampled leaves, flowers, and reedpaper pennants from some recent celebration, and above the palace gateway was a huge banner portrait of Presidian Laron and the sorceress Lavenci within a heart.

"Did anyone think to bring a wedding present?" asked Wallas.

"I did," I replied, twisting Pelmore's arm a little tighter behind his back.

We approached the guards, who were still garlanded with flowers from the festivities of the day just past.

"Night's compliments, good citizens!" called the officer of the shift. "Halt, who goes there, and all those sorts of words on this happy night."

"Do I remind you of any recently erected statues?" I asked, pointing across to my memorial.

The man looked to me, then to the statue, then snapped his fingers for a light. One of his guards brought over a length of burning reed that he had lit in their brazier and held it up to my face

"Oh shyte!" exclaimed all the guards together.

Laron and Lavenci were roused from the matrimonial bed, but I knew them to have consummated their relationship over four years earlier, so this did not trouble my conscience. At the sight of Pelmore, Lavenci began shouting for a chopping block and a sharp ax, and she had to be restrained by Laron and myself until my prisoner was put into the care of two guards and taken away. Andry hurried off to meet with his children, and Wallas kept hinting that he had not had access to a nice white wine for quite some time. Once Wallas was sitting comfortably on a table with a bowl, a jar, and a servant, Laron, Lavenci, and I went into the old throne room and sat at the circular Table of Electocratic Senators. With meticulous care I began telling what I thought was a very plausible story.

"The four of us were abducted by glass dragons," I began. "Pelmore and Andry went first, that was a year and one week ago today. They were held in an enchantment, some magical casting that made them neither alive nor dead. In Pelmore's case it broke the constancy glamour between himself and yourself, Madame Presidian Consort. Andry was merely being held in safety until the danger from the insane dragon, Terikel, was past."

"But you and Wallas vanished as well," said Laron. "A witness saw you fighting Terikel in Lordworld Plaza, and when the city militia arrived only a pile of ashes and your Lupanian glass sword remained—"

"I would like it back, please."

"It will be in your belt before you leave the palace," said Laron. "Pray continue."

"Terikel . . . the ashes were hers, I killed her. Wallas and I were taken away for trial. The death of even a young glass dragon is no trifling matter, so there had to be explanations and inquiries."

"I was not told," whispered Lavenci, holding strands of her gleaming white hair across her lips as she spoke.

"Glass dragons are no longer human, they care nothing for our laws or feelings," I explained. "For a month and a half I might as well have been dead. Had the ruling gone against me, I would have been truly dead. Now here I am."

"Of course our marriage must be annulled," mumbled Laron, and Lavenci nodded, a hand over her eyes.

"Why?" I asked. "Lavenci and I have never been married. Think of it as a love triangle that was conveniently broken."

Lavenci and I locked eyes for a moment, then she looked away.

"You must think me so shallow, marrying Laron in such haste after you died—er, seemed dead," she said. "How can I ever, ever earn your forgiveness?"

"There is nothing to—" I began.

"I spent a month in mourning, I really did. Then there was the first anniversary of the Lupanian Invasion, and that of the electocratic revolution. Everything was so joyful, people wanted to celebrate things. After your—that is, after you vanished, Laron and I became close again. I had grown up a lot, I understood him so much better. It was so easy, it was almost as if Fate were guiding my every step."

The bastard, I am sure he was, I thought.

"Was your time with me happy?" I asked.

"Yes, but—"

"Splendid, and now I want you to remain happy. For that, I must go."

"I did care for you, I—I still care for you," said Lavenci, reaching out and squeezing my hand.

I squeezed back, but then very slowly and pointedly drew back and folded my arms.

"What can I do for you?" Laron now asked. "This is a truly unfortunate circumstance."

"I have some suggestions that might ease our situation, sir. Speak with the directant of Wayfarers, you are his supreme commander. Have him transfer me to Palion, in the new East Sargol Empire. The emperor is trying to establish a new Wayfarer service there, and was about to send some constables here for training when I vanished. Send me there on an exchange."

"But you are under sentence of death there," said Lavenci.

"Only in West Sargol, which is currently at war with East Sargol. If anything, I shall be treated as a hero in Palion."

"Done," said Laron. "What else?"

"Pelmore. He was under sentence of death or exile for murder, but he evaded the executioner's noose thanks to, ah, people of influence in the old imperial court. Deal with him in whatever way satisfies our laws, I wish to have no more to do with him."

"I would have done all that anyway," said Laron. "Anything else?"

"Have a sculptor change the face on my memorial in Riellen Square to that of some Wayfarer who died on duty, and rededicate it to all Wayfarer Constables."

✳   ✳   ✳

It was already past midnight when I left the palace with Pelmore, Andry, and Laron. In spite of Lavenci's protests, Laron and I agreed that in a legal sense Pelmore should be exiled. Someone else had been executed in his place. That meant he was now under sentence of exile, according to some precedent in the books.

We entered the Mermaid's Slipper, selected a table, ordered the patrons seated there to leave, and threatened them with arrest if they did not. Because all patrons of the Mermaid's Slipper were guilty of something or other, we got our table after little more than muttered curses.

"Pelmore, you will be put aboard a deepwater trader to await the tide's turn," explained Laron. "Your passage to Vindic will be paid, but nothing more."

I flipped a florin to Pelmore.

"Have yourself gelded, it will open up opportunities for new and exotic careers" was my advice.

Pelmore was one of those people clever enough to recognize tactical advantage, but too stupid to recognize strategic danger. He sat up and smiled complacently.

"Oh no, I think I would like a very large and full purse to take with me, and after that I'd like an annual pension of ten thousand florins."

"You'd have a better chance of a kick up the arse to see you on your way," said Andry.

"Oh but I'm thinking of my career," said Pelmore. "I'm thinking of a career telling the Vindician noblity about how I sampled the delights of the presidian of Greater Alberin's wife."

Having played his best card, Pelmore sat back and folded his arms. Andry picked up his tankard and flung the contents in Pelmore's face.

"Twenty thousand florins per annum," spluttered Pelmore as he rubbed his eyes.

Laron began to unwrap the headband that he always wore. He was slow and methodical about it, and as the cloth came away I saw that he wore a type of circlet with a large stone at the center. He reached up and began disengaging the clips that held the stone in place. In a curious way, it reminded me of the sphere that Reyvelt had created for the overminds on the time engine.

"Look after this for some moments," he said, holding it out to me, "and do be sure to give it back when I ask."

"As you wish, sir," I replied. "What is in it?"

"My life force."

Laron dropped the stone into my hand, and I found that it weighed so very little that it might have been hollow. Stranger still was its size. It should have extended back into his forehead, yet the skin behind the space in the circlet was smooth and flat.

As I watched, Laron's pupils shrank to slits, and his mouth dropped open to reveal twin cones of sparkles condensing into quite impressive fangs. The claws expanding from his fingertips were already raising splinters in the tabletop.

"Get him away from—" was as far as Pelmore got before Laron lunged across the table, dragged Pelmore back over as easily as if his body had been a pillow stuffed with down feathers, then bit into his neck with a stomach-turning crunch of gristle. Andry and I scrambled back against the wall, only to find that every other patron of the Mermaid's Slipper was already backed against all the wall space available. Strangely, nobody tried to leave, in fact all seemed oddly intrigued by the sight of the presidian of Greater Alberin tearing out the throat of a fellow drinker and gulping down his blood.

"Gives a whole new meaning ter poppin' in for a quick one," said whoever was beside me.

There was more crunching and crackling as Laron began chewing and tearing through all that still connected Pelmore's head to his body. The lifeless head rolled free and thudded to the floor.

"Did you see that, Inspector?" whispered Andry.

"See what, Constable?" I responded.

"Assault upon a citizen."

"I'll fine him one florin if you are willing to collect it."

Laron now looked to me as he straightened. I held out my hand with the sphere on my palm as he approached, but to my relief he merely snatched it up and pressed it back into his circlet.

"I'm feeling better now," he said as he snapped the clips back into place.

Very tentatively the drinkers returned to their tables, corners, and stools by the fireplace. It was hard to ignore the fact of a messily decapitated corpse lying across one of the tables, but nobody seemed to want to be the first to mention it. While Andry got a cloak around Laron and helped him bind the headband back over his circlet, I strode over to Craglin, the tapman.

"About what just happened," I began.

"Nothin' ter do wi' us, we's not licensed ter serve meals, 'specially when they's patrons," he babbled.

"Public execution," I explained, slapping half a dozen florins into his hand.

"In 'ere?" he quavered.

"The new electocratic government of Greater Alberin has decided that some death sentences will be carried out in the presence of the miscreant's peers."

"Yer mean put the wind up those what's like 'em?"

"Yes. Do be sure to tell people."

Some days later I watched as the newest squad of Wayfarers in Greater Alberin was assembled before the steps of Wayfarer Headquarters. Those present were known to me, and all had served with me in the past. Wallas sat on the pile of backpacks, grooming his whiskers. Gnomes were being used increasingly as infiltration agents, yet a cat always seems less suspicious than a gnome, so Wallas had unique value. Roval was still just a constable, but I knew him to be more than he seemed. The squad would be touring the border with the kingdom of Hadraly, and there was a strong electocratic underground movement there. Roval would be doing secret work for someone, there was nothing more certain.

My old commander, Essen, was back in the Wayfarers, but that was no surprise. His recent marriage to a rather eccentric sorceress had turned out to be a little more intense than he had expected, and he was in search of some peace and quiet on the road, on patrol. I wondered if his wife knew that he had come out of retirement, but that was none of my business. Andry was a surprise. At first his inclination had been to stay with his children in the palace, but then he decided that they should be brought up seeing him earning an honest living in a real job.

I strode forward, waving a scroll in the air.

"Stand ready, secure your packs," I said as I unrolled the scroll. "Constable Wallas?"

"Present, in all my glory, sir."

"Constable Roval?"

"Present, sir."

"Constable Essen?"

"Please keep your voice down, sir."

"Constable Gelderine?" I asked.

Everyone glanced about.

"Not present," suggested Wallas.

"Constable Andry?"

"Present, sir."

I unrolled the scroll further and began to read by way of introducing the absent Constable Gelderine to the squad.

"Regarding Gelderine Demallien of Palion, I have a decree from Emperor Malsor of the East Sargol Empire, vanquisher of pretenders, annihilator of rebellions . . . lots of other boring things . . . anyway, he hereby sends the finest student of the new East Sargol Imperial Academy of Constabulary to study the workings of the Wayfarer Constables of Greater Alberin." I lowered the note and looked about, but there was still no Gelderine to be seen. "The emperor recently established a similar service to the Wayfarers, and he wants to draw upon our experience. I am to be transferred to Palion to help get the new service established."

"Er, Gelderine's, like, a lady's name," Andry pointed out.

"Correct. She will be replacing Constable Lavenci as your investigative magic specialist."

"The wench will have trouble filling Lavenci's bodice where investigative magic is concerned," Essen said as he heaved his backpack up.

It was about now he noticed that Roval and Andry were standing with their mouths open, staring past him.

"I doubt that Constable Gelderine would have trouble filling any bodice on the face of the moonworld," said Wallas as Essen turned.

Constable Gelderine was wearing knee-high boots with tower heels, riding trews, and a tunic that clung very flatteringly to her figure. Some green lacings were making a vague attempt to hold the ruffles of her upper tunic over her breasts, and a blue trail cloak of crushed velvet billowed out behind her as she walked. Behind her the directant of Wayfarers was carrying her pack, the deputy directant had her fencing ax, and the diminutive registrar was bringing up the rear with a cup of tea on a tray.

I knew that face. It was not precisely the face of Dolvienne, and this woman's hair was dark, wavy, and down past her shoulders, but there was definitely something of the lover who had never been my lover within the newest addition to the Wayfarers. My mind reached back five years, to a rather gangly, spotty girl of about sixteen who was reading some sorcery text in the laundry of the imperial palace in Palion, determined to better herself by study. Five years had left the face identifiably the same, yet had worked wonders upon it—along with pretty well every other aspect of her body and dress sense.

"Danolarian, it is such an honor to be in your famous squad," declared the exchange constable. "Congratulations on your promotion."

She spoke in a deep purr. Essen shrank back, severely disconcerted to discover that anything larger than Wallas could purr.

"Promotion?" asked Wallas.

"I am Commissioner Danolarian now," I explained. "The rank allows me to make promotions and appointments in the academy in Palion."

"Oh, but I think *all* officers are just so dashing," said Gelderine. "Their actual rank is not important."

"Men, cat, this is *Constable* Gelderine Demallien," I said, gesturing to Gelderine.

"She has a special interest in the new cold sciences field of forensics that is being pioneered in the East Sargolan Empire," added the directant.

Gelderine allowed the deputy directant to show her how to put the ax into her belt, then allowed the directant to pin her Wayfarer's badge onto her tunic. She must have been as brave as she was beautiful, judging by the way his hands were shaking. Meantime Roval had beaten Essen and Andry in the scramble to pick up her backpack.

"Your tea, Constable?" asked the registrar.

Gelderine took the cup from him, drained whatever was left, then kissed him on the top of his bald head and told him that he was very sweet.

"A lingering kiss would have had him suffocated," muttered Wallas softly.

Gelderine handed me her credential scroll.

"Proficient in sorcery, mathematics, languages, herb lore, ax fencing, archery, brawl combat, lacemaking, embroidery, leatherwork, autopsy forensics, and inquisition techniques," I read.

"Oh but I've never needed to use those horrible inquisition tortures," said Gelderine earnestly. "Men just seem to want to tell me *everything* about themselves."

"Very impressive," I said before I realized that I was staring at her breasts and forced myself to look back at her qualifications. "Experience . . . two patrols in Palion, both in excess of a hundred miles." I glanced at her boots. "In tower heels?"

"Oh yes. Someone always seems willing to lend me a horse."

"Constable Gelderine, welcome to the squad. Allow me to introduce Constable Roval, Constable Andry, and you already know Constable Essen, formerly of the Royal Sargolan Journey Guard."

"I—I know you?" stammered the incredulous Essen.

"I never forget a name," said Wallas, frowning his cat-frown. "Gelderine Demallien . . ."

"And this is Wallas," I said. "He's a cat, you may have heard of him."

"Oh yes, naughty Wallas," she laughed impishly. "You were once Milvarios of the old imperial court, and Master of the Royal Music, but then you assassinated the emperor. As a Sargolan constable I should smack your bottom for that."

"Oh any time, ladyship, any time!" babbled Wallas eagerly as he sat up at attention.

"Now then, I think you all should prepare to get moving before

Essen's wife comes looking for him," I decided, gesturing along the road to the riverbank.

"Constable Roval, your electocracy laws say all of us should be treated equally, so I really should carry my own pack," said Gelderine. "Still, that is very sweet of you."

Gelderine kissed Roval on the cheek as she took her pack from him. His knees began to wobble.

"About to be brought low by another woman," said Wallas, laughing, leaping onto Essen's shoulder as the squad began to move off.

"Wait, wait, I nearly forgot," I called. "There is still the matter of the new inspector."

"So, where is the lucky man?" asked Wallas.

I allowed a moment of very theatrical silence.

"Wallas old tomcat, how are you doing?"

My hand shot out to seize Wallas by the neck even as he gathered himself to spring to the ground and flee.

"Murder! Fire! Rape! Treason!" shouted Wallas, flailing about for something to slash, but I was ready for all that.

Essen held a sack open, and after an extended struggle with flailing claws and snapping fangs we managed to get the Wayfarer Constables' newest inspector tied inside with just his head protruding. I unfolded another paper.

"Be it known that Constable Wallas of the Greater Alberin Wayfarer Constables is hereby promoted to field inspector, second class, with a ratification of interim magistrate, and is assigned the West Quadrant squad formerly under the command of Inspector Danolarian Scryverin."

"You can't make me do this!" shouted Wallas.

"An additional five florins per—"

"I resign!"

"You can't, read your contract. What else? All sorts of interesting restrictions on your conduct now, Inspector Wallas. The taking of bribes above the value of ten florins, death. Drunk while sitting in judgment, death. The soliciting of sexual favors . . . I don't suppose that one really applies to you, does it?"

"I have no experience of leadership!" he protested.

"You were seneschal of the royal palace at Palion."

"For ten minutes, damn you."

"You have led small squads of men—"

"Those men were in *chamber orchestras!*" yowled Wallas, trying to scratch me through the sack.

"You will make a fine inspector, nobody is better at sniffing out scandals than you."

"You will never again be able to draw on a pair of boots without checking for cat turds," warned Wallas.

"I do already. Well, that seems to be it. Three cheers for Inspector Wallas."

I patted Wallas on the head as the squad cheered. He made quite a credible attempt to bite me, but I was too fast.

"Constable Gelderine, would you be so kind as to carry Inspector Wallas until he is a little less emotional?" I said as I handed Greater Alberin's newest inspector to its newest constable. "He seems to have forgotten that the penalty for an inspector deserting his squad while on patrol is death, and you will be officially on patrol as soon as you clear the city walls."

"There, there, Inspector Wallas, your new constable will look after you," she said, hugging his head into her very impressive cleavage. "Ah, but I do like the touch of fur."

"Oh goodness, do you really, my dear?" babbled Wallas, his outrage and fears instantly forgotten.

"I shall write your journals and reports for you, and you can ride on my shoulder so that men will look up at you."

"I don't think men will look up as far as Wallas," Andry suggested.

By now Wallas had ceased to struggle, and was actually purring.

"You see, I have a way of putting everyone at their ease," Gelderine declared proudly in her silky Sargolan accent.

With no more ceremony than that, the members of my old squad moved off to the nearby riverbank, where they took passage on a barge being towed inland. A talking cat in a sack leading the runaway husband of a sorceress, a single father, a suspiciously overqualified war hero, and a mind-blindingly alluring young exchange constable: for sheer diversity the squad had no peer.

The directant of Wayfarers joined me as I stood watching them depart. The horses strained at the tow ropes, and as the barge pulled out into the river Gelderine struck a pose as the barge figurehead. A wharfer carrying a barrel walked straight off the end of a landing; then a ferry rammed a barge on the other side of the river.

"Are you sure that was a wise choice?" the directant asked.

"Roval would be too conspicuous as an inspector, Essen is a fine leader but does not have much education, Andry has even less education, and Gelderine has no experience as a leader. Wallas really was the only choice."

"According to a very confidential report in my office, Gelderine is still a virgin," he remarked.

"What the men of the squad do not know will not hurt them" was my opinion.

"Well, all the best for Palion, Commissioner Danolarian. When do you leave?"

"On the *Green Star,* at the turning of the tide."

✳　✳　✳

As I stood at the railing of the *Green Star,* watching Alberin diminish in the distance, I pondered my weeks in a past that had never happened, and a future that would never be. All the world's rogue overminds were hurtling into the real future, bound into the structure of the time engine and never able to return. Never again would there be any bored, omnipotent idiots complicating my life for the sake of some light entertainment.

At that thought a shiver passed through me. *Have I not just done precisely that to Wallas?* For some moments I guiltily pondered nearly four years of commanding the only cat constable in the Wayfarers. He had been loyal from time to time, brave when there had been no alternative, and even my friend on occasion, but there had also been fur balls on my bedding, cat pee in my pack, marinated vomit just about everywhere, pieces of mice in my boots, interminable whining about his being in a cat situation, and sarcastic comments from under the bed nearly every time I was lucky enough to secure female company for the night. *No, I did not appoint Wallas as inspector out of boredom, and for entertainment,* I assured myself. *It was his sentence for crimes against an inspector of the Wayfarers.*

EPILOGUE
PRESENT PERFECT

I had fled the Sargolan Empire four years earlier, reviled and in disgrace, but I returned to the new empire of East Sargol as the visiting commissioner of Wayfarers. My arrival was an unexpectedly important occasion. It started with a band and an official welcome on the wharf, a parade to the partly built Sargolan Imperial Wayfarer Headquarters, and afternoon tea with the directant and other senior staff. Tailors followed me about continually, measuring and sketching as I went about my business; then I was taken away to the palace. All the while I was looking out for Dolvienne, but she was nowhere to be seen. *Does she not care enough to greet me?* I wondered. *Does she remember me at all?*

I entered under the escort of an honor guard of a dozen Sargolan Imperial Wayfarers, and was hurried into the bath chambers. I emerged at about sunset wearing the uniform of the new service, and was taken straight to court. There I was presented to the young emperor before his entire court, and subjected to predictable jokes about being the former commander of the cat who had assassinated his father. All the while I was scanning the tapestry of faces watching us, wondering how much of a difference a year might make to the face a young widow named

Dolvienne. A few of the female courtiers were wearing the black of mourning, but I recognized none of them.

Court was followed by a formal dinner in my honor, for the emperor wanted to emphasize the importance of the Sargolan Imperial Wayfarers in his plans for the empire's future. I was favored with a seat next to the emperor himself, and subjected to a couple of hours of his theories about the role of justice and order in convincing people that they got something back in return for their taxes and forced military service. He also had a hidden agenda, which he made no attempt to hide from me. Apparently the local electocratic revolutionaries wanted the emperor to abdicate and stand for election as presidian. The emperor was unenthusiastic about the plan.

"My feeling is that the Wayfarers should report back upon any injustices that those revolutionaries could use against my rule," he concluded, waving a chicken leg in the air like a sceptre.

"Wayfarers can certainly keep the capital well informed about the provinces," I agreed diplomatically.

"Yes, yes, I want to be well informed. Names and issues, I want names and issues. Unless I have names, I cannot address the issues."

By assassinating the names, I thought, but did not say as much. Whatever his motivations for setting up his Wayfarers, the institution was a good one in principle. With care, I could build something that was at least no worse than the Wayfarers of Greater Alberin—who were actually being used to spread electocracy across its borders while dispensing justice, so was there ultimately any real difference?

"My thought was to command a patrol squad and use it as something of a template for developing other squads," I suggested.

"Oh yes, so I have been told, and I agree. Do you know how to tell that I agree?"

"I am new to your court, Your Majesty."

"I am a believer in ceremony, Commissioner Danolarian, I believe that people can be best shown who I support if I honor them in public. I believe in you, and I believe in Wayfarers. That is why I have decided to introduce you to your new squad here, tonight, before the entire court."

The meal ended soon after that, and we made our way into the throne hall, which had by now been cleared for dancing. I had fancied that

Dolvienne might meet with me during a dance, that we might have some days together in the palace, letting fondness grow into love before I settled down to the serious work of leading a Wayfarer patrol out into the countryside. I scanned the faces in the court continually, but she was not there. *Again, disappointed in love,* I thought. Still, this time it was a real woman doing it, not some long-dead sorcerer playing games with me.

A fanfare announced the honoring of my new squad by the emperor himself. I was directed to the right hand of the emperor, then a herald began to call out names.

"Constable Anserran!"

The tall, cadaverous man who came forward looked like an accountant who had been subjected to a few weeks on the rack. He wore a trail cloak over a tunic emblazoned with a pair of scales, and beneath this was chain mail.

"Your background?" I asked as he bowed.

"Property law and imperial collections, Commissioner," he replied, his every word precisely enunciated and ruthlessly clear.

"Constable Valarac!" barked the herald.

Constable Valarac had the look of a rat who had formal qualifications in cunning. He also seemed to be trying to blend into the background even as he stood before the entire court.

"And what is your specialty, Constable?" I asked.

"Imperial law, sir," he mumbled softly.

"Constable Jergorat!"

"I believe we have met," I said as the slab of muscle bowed in my direction.

"No future in executions, like, sir," Jergorat explained. "Thought I'd better meself."

"Constable Dolvienne!"

Now I realized why I had not recognized Dolvienne earlier that evening. Her hair was tied back very tightly, she was dressed as a Wayfarer, and she had grown lean, focused, and somehow . . . heightened. She was nothing like the sad, grieving Dolvienne of my memory, and definitely not the soft, seductive Dolvienne that the time engine's illusion world had conjured for me.

"For the sake of the court, please declare your specialty, Constable," I said.

"Documentation and evidence, sir," she cried smartly.

This was the end of my formal role in the evening's events, but the emperor insisted that the members of my squad stay for the first of the dances. At long last, I was together with the real Dolvienne. The only actual romance between us was a kiss or two dating back over four years, but I already knew how romance between us might flower, at least if she was anything like the time engine's image of her. Both of us had loved and lost in actual time, but the death of her husband was now over a year in the past.

She would not be in the Wayfarers were her affections bound to another, I assured myself as I led her out into the dance space. The music commenced, and we joined hands, then began to dance. It was not one of the commoners' dances that I was used to from my years in Greater Alberin, but I had once been a guardsman in the old imperial court, so the steps, bows, sweeps, and gestures of the courtly dance were familiar to me.

What should I say? I wondered. *Should I lead with romantic words, or should I try circumlocutions to learn whether she is ready for a new romance?*

The matter was taken out of my hands in a manner that I had definitely not anticipated.

"Revolutionary Brother Danolarian, I never dreamed that Greater Alberin could have got both of us here to spread the message of electocracy," Dolvienne whispered, her eyes bright, her smile subtle, and the edge on her voice so manic that it reminded me of Riellen's.

I forget what I replied, but it would have been something very diplomatic and noncommittal. To my immense relief, a herald disengaged us, explaining that the emperor wished me to dance with his wife. The empress was in her early twenties, and had a sultry, bored look about her.

"My husband has very high expectations for your Wayfarers," she said as we joined hands and led the court into the next set.

"I already see intriguing strengths and possibilities amongst them," I replied.

What am I to do with a tax collector, an imperial spy, an executioner, and an international electocratic revolutionary who thinks I am a co-conspirator? I wondered. Suddenly I envied Wallas and longed to trade places with him, yet a single thought gave me cheer. This was random, there was no longer a gaggle of overminds in the Darkwalking Realm with their hands on the reins of my life, putting me into impossible situations for their own amusement. The real Dolvienne was not the idealized, sentimentally loving bedmate of illusion; she somehow combined Riellen's dedication with Lavenci's allure. Perhaps she was better.

The dance set ended, and the empress gave my hand the suggestion of a squeeze with her fore and index fingers as I bowed to her. I knew the code. Just as my hand was squeezed between her two fingers, so would my body soon be squeezed between her . . . suddenly life on the road with a tax collector, spy, executioner, and revolutionary looked very attractive indeed. I feigned ignorance of that particular courtship code, and was rewarded by a slight sniff of impatience from the empress. Very soon some courtier would approach me, and would strike up a casual conversation about seduction signals in the imperial court, in particular what a squeeze from a lady's fore and index fingers meant. I would be forced to either incur the wrath of the empress by spurning her invitation to adultery, or cuckold the emperor by accepting it.

I assembled my squad near the doors as the next dance set began.

"We leave on patrol *tonight*?" exclaimed Constable Valarac as I led the way out of the hall as fast as was seemly.

"Yes, a good Wayfarer constable must always be ready for duty."

"But it's a half hour to midnight!" protested Anserran.

"Good practice. You are dressed in your trail gear, and have your packs."

"But only for parade duty!"

"What else do you need?"

Nobody wanted to answer that question, but I had a good idea of why they all looked so dismayed. Anserran would want to collect lists of properties to assess, Valarac would be without his secret codes, Jergorat had probably not memorized the names of those he needed to assassinate, and Dolvienne would be without her disguised store of revolutionary pamphlets, but then why should I be the only person in the squad to be annoyed and inconvenienced by our sudden departure? With luck the empress would have been caught in bed with some other poor fool and executed for treason by the time we returned. On the other hand I was now to be in the company of a manic electocratic revolutionary—Dolvienne—but at least I knew better than to suggest a romantic liaison with her. That was disappointing, for she was very attractive, but I was immortal now, and that left a lot of time to search the world for some less daunting sweetheart.

By the time the gongs of the city were ringing out midnight, we were clear of the walls and riding west by the light of the lordworld, on a mission to collect taxes, murder electocratic revolutionaries, spread the electocratic revolution, and spy on anyone spreading electocratic revolution. With luck I might also be able to uphold the rule of law and dispense justice while the rest of squad was busy, but in a way that was little different from my past four years in the Wayfarer Constables of Greater Alberin. I was again on the road, and I was home.